STORYVILLE

The Eternal Triangle of Love, Sex & Money

By Stephen Foehr

ISBN: 978-0-615-38701-7

First published in Czech Republic in 2009 by Jiri Vanek Publisher

ALSO BY STEPHEN FOEHR

WAKING UP IN NASHVILLE
DANCING WITH FIDEL
JAMAICAN WARRIORS
TAJ MAHAL, AUTOBIOGRAPHY
ONE HEART'S EDGE
ECO JOURNEYS

Chapter 1.

On the night of the fire, set perhaps to cover the murder, Ant didn't go to the Arlington for the expected reason. His jealousy, as wily and dangerous as a crazed gator, pushed him through the door.

Henry the Magnificent, doorman at the Arlington, greeted Ant with his customary nod of mean-dog menace and made Ant raise his arms for a weapons check. Henry's walnut face, scrunched in a scowl, established the tone for the sporting palace: act like a gentleman or he'd throw your crude ass in the gutter and bite you for good measure. The madam, Josie Arlington, made him wear her version of classy English: a coachman's red swallowtail coat with brass buttons, pale yellow britches, white knee socks and silver buckles on his patent leather shoes. The costume embarrassed him, which accounted for his perpetual look of anger.

If he hadn't known better, Ant might have thought that he'd made a mistake, came to the wrong address on the wrong street, when he stepped into the Arlington's front parlor. The gilt-frame paintings of bucolic English gardens, the stolid furniture with wine-red upholstery and the fake Chinese vases puffed with flowers gave the room an aura of Victorian respectability. He noticed that Josie had found some cactuses, the vogue in bourgeois London. It could be a room of prosperous merchant, except for the blonde in a low-cut gown and ringlets bouncing off her bare shoulders as she flirted with the man on the love seat. Her suggestive jasmine scent had yet to overcome the john's doubts. Nervously picking at his trouser crease, the dupe shifted from ample buttock to buttock, tapped his foot, his glance skidding off her and back to make sure she was still there. She laughed at her own witticism to tease him into a smile, some indication that he thought life could be enjoyed.

You'd think, having found his way this far, the fellow would shuck off the worry about his soldier being up for the march. She put a hand on his arm and said something. He leaned forward to better hear; she breathed directly into his ear.

To Ant's experienced eye, the john's skeptical smile marked a first-timer losing his courage. He looked around the room for MayAnn.

In the corner, a man in evening clothes tilted over a woman in a scarlet Southern Belle gown and looked down her décolleté. She turned away in mock modesty. Whatever she said over her bare shoulder made him laugh. Corrupt propriety was Josie's stroke of business genius. She played to a man's dream of illicit sex with a licit lady, his fantasy wife, the neighbor's wife, the woman in the pew. It cost twenty dollars to take her upstairs.

Ant didn't see MayAnn.

Josie's sporting ladies paid him no mind as he walked toward the back parlor. They knew he worked for Tom Anderson, the vice overlord who served as the unofficial "mayor" of Storyville. Ant wasn't jealous because MayAnn took strange men to bed every night; she was only the parlor maid, not a double-backed girl. He was sour because she had banished him from her bed.

She had explained matter-of-factly she intended to be the mistress of a rich white man in order to raise her station in life. She loved him but had to think of her future and that of her future children. Surely he'd understand, she said. After all, his own mother had done the same.

Hey, Ant protested, I'm flour. I've passed as a white man all my life. All the privileges of a white man are open to me.

But the hateful one-drop Jim Crow laws – one drop of "black" blood made a person a Negro—that Southerner legislatures passed in an attempt to get back the advantage they lost in the Civil War—made Ant an imposter. His white father, Mr. Arthur Jefferies, had sent him to the University of Wittenberg in Germany for a classical education; the custom being to school the 'other' sons of black mistresses away from New Orleans so not to be cross-grained with their white first family. Looking white and educated white, Ant expected to go into white business, attend white society balls and share the prosperity and privilege enjoyed by white men, despite the fact that his mother was an octoroon. A lady of exotic Spanish/ French/Haitian beauty, which is why his father made her his mistress, she raised Ant to take his place in society, not to ride in a segregation trolley or train. The conductor could challenge him, throw him off, even have him jailed for not being white, in the white conductor's opinion.

But MayAnn was more of a hard-eyed realist than Ant. You think you can always pass, Antoine? she challenged. Do you really believe people won't know? You can't live as a white man and be a black man, not anymore. It's not allowed. I love you with all my heart, she had whispered, but with our bloodlines, our children might throw back, come out darker than either one of us. I won't risk that. I want my children to have a better start in life and a white daddy is a step in that direction. We'll always love each other, only we can't be lovers after tonight.

Ant knew mere words wouldn't persuaded her otherwise. MayAnn was a woman of conviction and action, stubborn as a deaf mule. With a woman like that, he had to be in two places at the same time—where she thinks he is and where he needs to be. If MayAnn was hunting a rich white sucker, then he'll be her faithful gun bearer—to keep the sucker in his sights.

The rustle of her skirt alerted him as she emerged from the kitchen behind the back parlor. If she saw him off to the side

7

by the piano where Tony Jackson played vigorous ragtime, she gave no indication. She balanced a sterling silver tray with two flutes of chilled champagne on her fingertips. He trailed after her into the front parlor, waiting for the moment to take her aside.

A young man wearing a long great coat with a high upturned collar entered from the foyer with the door guardian Henry at his shoulder. The first thing Ant noticed was the stranger's attitude of entitlement, and then his limp. Dark tight curls swirled about his head. His eyes, an arresting pale green seen in the shallows around Caribbean islands, picked the room apart while his nose, thin and sharp, twitched for the scent he sought. The tip of his tongue moistened his prissy rosebud lips, anticipating the taste of a sweet tart.

MayAnn walked towards him as if to offer him the champagne but veered away to serve a couple on a settee.

The newcomer posed on the step overlooking the parlor with a hand in his coat pocket, chin in an imperious tilted, shoulders back as if about to deliver a speech. Instead of withdrawing a piece of paper from his pocket, he took out a long-barreled flintlock dueling pistol. New Orleans was a gun city. Every man, every prudent man, carried a gun when going out, especially at night. So the sight of the gun in itself wasn't alarming. But when he turned sideways to a proper dueling stance—left leg forward and pistol arm cocked—Ant ducked behind a sofa. On the way down, he caught sight of MayAnn standing straight, a willing target.

Henry the Magnificent snatched the pistol as easily as plucking a ripe peach from its branch. A smile of self-amusement twitched at the corner of mouth the disarmed man. Henry tucked the gun in his coat and stood patiently with his hand out, waiting with a crinkle of faint contempt on his face. With a theatrical sigh, the poseur pulled a knife from the back of his belt and laid it in Henry's hand.

House rules: No firearms, clubs, knives, brass knuckles or saps. Only one weapon allowed and you had to be man enough to pull the trigger.

Beneath the great coat, which he handed to Henry, the newcomer wore a fitted suit that flared at the hips, a vest richly embroidered with swirls of blues and yellow, and a white silk shirt with a floppy collar. Despite the ostentation, the cut and quality of his clothes spoke of wealth and class.

(Ant tried for the same effect by buying suits at Isadro's Fine Clothes; Izzy got his suits from dead men's closets and sold them at discount.)

The stranger's unsettling green eyes looked over the eight working ladies in the parlor. MayAnn approached him hip shifting and shoulder rolling and with a smoldering look, her empty tray an invitation for a drink. If Josie or one of the workingwomen caught her poaching, Henry's belt would flay her back. She'd be tossed into the street. But she took the risk for the same reason she had purged Ant: she was ambitious for herself.

He impatiently waved her away while looking over her head to search the room.

So there's the sucker, Ant thought. He knew at a glance that the dandy was untested because a more experienced man would have been aware of his presence the way a once-wounded animal senses a hunter.

Ant stood up from behind the sofa and helped one of Josie's girls, who had sheltered with him, to her feet. "You know him?" he asked the woman. She smoothed out her skirt with abrupt hand sweeps. "That's Young Jack, a scion of one of the city's most esteemed families."

Ant stepped around the sofa with the intent to ease up alongside the mark and say in a confidant's voice, 'Beware the parlor maid. Don't let her near you for she means to ensnare you. She'll make a fool of you and bleed you dry.'

When he stepped close enough to smell his rival, MayAnn, puffed up like a mother swan, jumped forward to scare him away. "Don't bother the guest, Antoine. Don't interfere where you're not wanted." He circled to move past her but she gripped him arm. "I'll hate you to your grave, Antoine, if you spoil this for me."

"I'm saving you from yourself."

"You're condemning me." Her violent attitude slapped him up against the head solid as a plank. Still, he refused to accept that she had turned so completely against him, not after their last night together only a week before.

On that night, he had smeared her with fierce kisses and mashed her breasts against his, nipple to nipple. When he moved, she moved with him. He rolled her over and under and back up and her knees gripped his hips as if hanging onto a runaway horse for dear life and they hollered with pleasure and got slick and wet as if they'd been swimming in the Mississippi. Her black Egyptian eyes, upturned at the corners, made erotic promises she intended to keep. What man wouldn't do a one-leg jig for MayAnn? He had slid around her skin smooth as Chinese silk, creamy as butter chocolate, riding the curves and mounds. "Damn right I'll make myself a fool over you," he had shouted and twisted her fine black hair into a love tangle. She crouched on top, her hands pinning his shoulders, and sat up to still him. Then reached to his face and gently closed his eyelids and, as if lying on pennies, kissed each one. She collapsed on him, her arms wrapped around his head, her breath on his neck soft as a sob. Ant locked his arms locked around her. They lay calm and peaceful, just like the preacher promises in eternal life.

That's why Ant didn't believe her when she banned him from her bed and, in that, from the refuge of her heart. But, she had been steadfast ever since making the business decision to lie under a rich white guy. Ant could agree that taking on a white patron was smart strategy, a life plan with a long and honorable New Orleans' tradition for beautiful girls of color, but the choice didn't necessitate discarding him.

"That falderal of a man," Ant gestured toward Young Jack still surveying the parlor, "will never give you a pretty cottage with a white picket fence. He'll only cheat you out of yourself."

"I'll win," MayAnn said with fierce determination.

To avoid the immediate battle with her that he'd surely lose, Ant retreat to the back parlor where Tony Jackson, the original honky-tonk piano player, tinkered on the piano. They knew each other from the backstreet jass joints where, as a trombone man, Ant sometimes joined other musicians in after hour jam sessions.

Tony glanced at Ant and dropped the light-hearted ditty into a leaking-heart blues. "My woman, my woman/Is my condition," he sang in a gutbucket growl. His eyes were so sad he must have been at the crucifixion. The blues bathed Ant's heart in self-pity, which he mistook for love's anguish.

Tony paused, "You smell something?"

Ant raised his head.

"You smell something burning?" Tony asked, hands poised above the keyboard, and wrinkled his nose as he sniffed the air. "Somebody must have left a pot roast in the oven too long."

But the smell was too harsh for burnt food.

Ant walked down the short hall to the kitchen and pushed open the door. A scrim of smoke and the sharp tangy smell of kerosene caused him to step back. Out of the corner of his eye, Ant thought he saw motion at the back door but his attention focused on the soft whoosh of flames that ran along the skim of fuel and puddled at the base of the wall. Grabbing a towel by the sink, he doused it with water from the faucet and slapped at the flames. Paint on the wall blistered and popped. The crackle of wood splitting apart sounded like a string of firecrackers. Soon this will be a roar, a real humdinger, a conflagration equal to the Great Chicago Fire, he thought and backed out of the kitchen.

"FIRE!" he yelled at Tony, who didn't seem to hear; face up, eyes closed, he was far away in the cakewalk-boogie-woogie he paraded up and down the keyboard. "FIRE! TONY!" Storyville's premier piano professor's eyes popped open. He leapt to his feet but his hands didn't leave the ivories. He played louder and faster, as if cueing a silent movie audience to danger creeping onto the screen.

Ant walked, not ran, into the front parlor so not to alarm the men and women engaged in delicate negotiations. Several men already sniffed at the faint acid wood-burning odor and the women nervously pretended nothing was amiss. He went to MayAnn and whispered in her ear. She shrugged him off but he stayed closed to her shoulder, talking urgently. Her eyebrows arced with the question, Is that true? When Ant nodded, she rushed over to the settee where, Young Jack, the faux gunman, leaned eagerly toward a woman, a girl really, and held her hand in both of his. She peeked at him from behind a curtain of shimmering raven hair that fell across her face. MayAnn wedged herself between them. "The house is on fire. Quick!" She grabbed the girl's elbow and yanked her to her feet. "Up to your room and gather what you can, I'll warn the others," and forcibly propelled her up the stairs. As Ant quick-stepped to Henry the Magnificent by the front door, he saw Young Jack dash up the stairs after them with a hitched gait caused by his turned-in foot.

Henry had his nose up trying to find the source of the burning. "The kitchen," Ant said in a confidential whisper. Henry blinked once and then purposefully strode toward the blooming catastrophe. The flames had climbed the wall and were burning through the ceiling. As he backed out, forearm shielding his face, he nearly ran over Ant.

"Tony! Come help us!" Henry shouted. Tony danced in place at the piano while pounding out a gay upbeat ragtime, parodying a man running for his life while standing in place. Then he abruptly stopped, turned to Henry, threw out his arms and belted, "Save me! Save me!" in a booming operatic baritone.

"Come on, you goddamn fairy!" Henry rushed to grab him. Tony held his hands in front of his chest, "What do you care, Henry the Fool? Why should you care to save the white trash ass? This is the only thing you should care about." He hit the chords of a familiar blues song.

Ant ran to the front parlor to raise the alarm. A scrum of men, already recognizing the danger, massed at the door pushing and elbowing to get out. More men came down the stairs pulling suspenders over their shoulders, hopping to put on a shoe, hobbling with trousers half raised. One man calmly descended knotting his tie but without pants. Josie's ladies, clutching their best gowns and wads of cash, charged the heap of men and leapt on backs, clawed up shoulders in their desperation to escape. MayAnn appeared at the head of the stairs.

"Is anyone up there?" Ant called out.

"No." She felt her way along the wall as she descended, wobbly and unsteady on her feet. The thick pall of smoke made her appear ghostly as she moved in the languid daze of a sleepwalker unsure of the next step.

"Are you all right?"

"We must escape. Must get away." She stared past him, her arm held stiffly out in front. He guided her to the door where Henry tossed men aside to clear the logjam. Fire wagons' clanging bells sounded in the far distance. Suddenly Tom Anderson came plowing through the door, his heavyweight shoulders putting authority behind his elbow jabs.

"Where's Josie?" he panted. An arm of his suit jacket had been nearly ripped off.

"I haven't seen her all night," Ant replied.

"Help me search."

"You stay with Henry," Ant told MayAnn. Henry stood six feet six inches and could effortlessly carry a hundred-pound bale of cotton on each shoulder, which he had been doing, loading and unloading steamships on the Mississippi, when Josie hired him off the dock. If necessary, he'd hoist MayAnn on his shoulder and trample over everyone to carry her to safety.

Ant dashed after Tom down the hallway to Josie's office, where fire had nearly burned through the common wall with the kitchen. They plunged into swirls of gray-black smoke, unable to see more than six inches ahead. Tom clapped his handkerchief over his mouth and nose and cried out, "Josie! Josie!" Ant dropped down to the floor where it was possible to take shallow sips of seared air without suffocating. Arms and legs making a sweeping search, he swam along like a frog until his hand hit Josie's shoe. "Here!" Tom crawled over, following Ant's choked voice. Josie lay in front of her safe feebly trying to get the combination right by touch.

"Get the money, Tom," she said faintly.

"Money be damned. You've got money to burn."

"Fuck you, Tommy," and she passed out.

They hauled her into the front parlor as Henry cleared the door and exited, MayAnn clinging to his coat. Tom followed with Josie in his arms. As they stumbled down the front steps, Billy Struve, Tom's business partner, cleared a path through the gawkers to Tom's saloon, Anderson's Arlington Café, one door down from Josie's Arlington whorehouse.

"Get a doctor, Billy," Tom commanded, and bent over in a fit of coughing. When he regained his breath, he straightened and shouted to the crowd, "Form up a bucket brigade. Get on the rooftops and water them down. Use beer from the saloon if you have to."

When the boss man of Storyville—The Mayor, people called him—gave an order, people jumped. If you wanted to do business in Storyville, New Orleans' vice district adjacent to the French Quarter, you did everything you could to stay on Tom's good side. He settled disputes, dispensed patronage, fixed deals, brokered business contracts and gave advice. He bargained with the local police captain on the percentage of graft paid per whorehouse. If you wanted to open a gambling den, sporting mansion, saloon, dance hall, any entertainment place, buy or sell property, or get a city permit for anything in Storyville, you came to Tom Anderson. His "fees" were worth it to avoid the city taxes and paperwork. He was the godfather, the facilitator between Storyville and the city government. In the district, Tom Anderson's word had the authority of law.

So when Tom gave the order, men scrambled to form a bucket line from the saloon to the burning building, even if there weren't any buckets. Some ran with mugs of beer to throw into the flames, if for no other reason than an enthusiastic show of following Tom's orders. When the two horse-drawn fire wagons clattered to a stop, men swarmed to pull off the hoses and posed heroically, waiting for the firemen to connect them to the water tank. Volunteers dashed to and fro, shouting, waving their arms just to be seen doing something.

Two hours later, the dripping, blackened hulk of the Arlington still sizzled and steamed. Josie, sedated by the doctor, rested comfortably on Tom's office sofa. Slumped in the chair behind his desk, clothes smoke-stink, red-rimmed eyes staring from smears of black, Tom chewed on his full ginger-colored mustache that drooped around the corners of his mouth, cultivated in homage to his hero Teddy Roosevelt. Billy, Tom's business partner who enforced the "code" that kept Storyville orderly, sprawled in the wingback chair next to Ant's. After fetching the doctor for Josie, he had done double duty; fighting the fire and making sure no one stole Tom's liquor.

"What are we going to do about those guys, Billy?" Tom asked.

"What guys?"

"The Matranga brothers." Tom's smacked the desk hard enough to split the wood. "The goddamn Mafia trying to horn in on my Storyville by burning down Josie's whorehouse so they can move in their own. The fire was a shot across the bow, a declaration of war. Ever since they had Labruzzo killed, fucking Tony and Charlie Matranga act like they're Kings of the Underground."

Still on half breaths from the smoke, Ant didn't flinched at the sharp slap on wood. But his nerves went on alert at the Matrangas' name. He had no reason to believe Tom knew of his sideline with them, but if Tom suspected the double-dealing, then MayAnn would be the least of his worries.

Ant's job was to keep Tom informed of ambitious pretenders plotting against him, of pikers skimming his cut of their operations, of criminals and killers who posed a threat to Storyville's peace. Tom's profits depended on the appearance of safety and order in the red-light district. If innocent people were caught in crossfire of mayhem, then Tom's fiefdom could be fatally damaged.

As an insurance policy, Ant stayed on useful terms with the Matrangas. Tony and Charles had three hundred men under their orders, the largest Mafia family in the country at the time. Ant's motto: if you live next to a big mean dog, best throw it a choice bone every now and then. He passed on City Hall scuttlebutt, warnings of police raids, news of promising business opportunities and anything else useful he picked up, mostly in Tom's office.

"Yeah, well..." Billy's hanging silence told the history: Labruzzo had been gunned down in front of his saloon on Bienville, in the heart of Storyville. In broad daylight. In front of six witnesses. And nobody saw a thing. "Yeah, well..." Billy didn't need to state the obvious: the Matrangas had left Labruzzo's corpse on Tom's doorstep as their calling card. "They might have a hand in this. But there are plenty of hands trying to snatch your pot of gold, Tom. People see barge loads of money floating through Storyville. So some people start dreaming about becoming pirates, and not all of'em are on the wrong side of the law. Police Chief Hennessy, for example. You've got to outsmart 'em or kill 'em."

Tom had reason to worry about the Matrangas. They had recently become a serious threat after seizing control of the docks from the three Provenzanos brothers, hard-working businessmen, pillars of the Society of St. Anthony and well respected in New Orleans for their generous charitable work. When the Provenzanos refused to give the Matrangas a share in the off loading of cargo ships, including the fruit coming from South America for the Treme and Poydras and Kellers street markets, the Matrangas declared war. The final battle came when three of Provenzanos' men were hacked to death in bed next to their hysterical wives. The message was clear: your women and children are not safe. The rest of Provenzanos' workforce prudently stayed away from the docks.

With control of the docks, a potential chokehold on a key commercial point, the Mafia bosses had a powerful base from which to move into other parts of the city -- and Storyville was a natural place to expand their business.

Storyville was a scum pit of iniquity, prostitution, gambling, opium dens, greed, inequality, exploitation and a playground for thieves and murderers. There wasn't a single residence in the sixteen blocks, not a grocery, a school, a hardware store or a patch of grass, a tree, a splash of flowers. But men like Tom and the Matranga brothers could make their opportunities and successes in Storyville, where they put their finger up the establishment's nose and said, 'Out of our way. We're coming to sit at your table.' Tom had no education to speak of, no helping hand, no advantage of birth. The Matrangas, as Italian immigrants and criminals to boot, were below the bottom rung of the ladder. Negroes got more respect.

Storyville was the land of opportunity for the poor, the downtrodden, the immigrants and the Negroes, the place where they had a fighting chance to become part of the American mainstream.

Chapter 2.

The morning after the fire, Ant accompanied the fire inspector as his men picked through the charred Arlington. The walls of the front parlor looked as substantial as crusty charcoal, but the stairs to the upper rooms still stood. Love seats and settees blackened by fire and swollen with water, flipped over, legs up, looked like dead animals. Ant steered the inspector into the burned out kitchen and explained how he had discovered the fire.

"I was overcome by smoke while attempting to beat out the flames," he said, pinching his nose to keep out the sharp scratchy fire smell. The inspector poked at the debris with a long pole. Broken pieces of grayish porcelain showed through the soot. "There," Ant pointed. "The arsonist must have thrown the lamp against the wall."

A fireman popped his head in. "We've found something upstairs, sir." The fireman led the party to the upper story, which had remained largely intact although badly smoke damaged. "In here," he pointed into the room above the kitchen, where the fire had partially burned through the floor. "Careful, sir. The boards are shaky." Next to the scorched double bed laid a body. "Must be one of the girls."

Most of her hair had been burned off; half her face puckered and blistered, the eye socket a snake hole into the skull. The skin on one side of her mouth had been burned away to reveal the teeth and gum: the other half of her face was pristine, the remaining lovely brown eye wide open.

The inspector knelt and examined the dead girl's throat. "Looks like she was strangled." He pointed to a necklace of bruises.

Ant backed out of the room and retched in the hallway. Then he made his way on wobbly legs out of the whorehouse and to Tom's saloon, where he found the Mayor in his office shooting the breeze with Billy. Although Tom was a saloonkeeper, his private room wasn't a growley, a clubhouse of sorts where men, free of the constraints of female influence, put their feet on the furniture and dropped cigar ashes on the floor and grouched about women, politics and life in general. Befitting his ambitions, Tom's office had the atmosphere of a men's club with its red-tufted leather sofa and big polished desk and English hunting prints on the walls.

"Well, Ant, what did the inspector find?" Tom asked.

"Evidence of arson. And a dead girl. Murdered. Crushed windpipe."

Tom blinked in disbelief. "You sure?"

"I was there when the inspector stated his opinion."

Tom sat still, fingers lightly drumming the edge of his desk. "Christ." Then a long silence before he said, "Billy, make sure the inspector doesn't tell Chief Hennessy. He'll use it as an excuse to put his sticky fingers in our pocket."

Tom pulled open a desk drawer.

"Wrong drawer. Lower left. That's where you keep the good ones," Billy said.

Tom took out a box of expensive Cubans. "The inspector likes these cigars. He also likes dark girls. Offer the cigars first, then sweeten the pot if he balks. And if you're still unsure about his discretion, tell him I'll personally cut off his balls if a whisper of this gets out—and send his eunuch portrait to his favorite whore."

That evening, Tom and Billy took a hack into the French Quarter, where Josie was staying with her cousin on St. Claude

Street. Tom sat lost in thought. Billy gave his partner a sideways glance and knew that he was scheming because his eyes had the flat opaque look Billy recognized as Tom at work.

It's said that the eyes are windows into a person's thoughts and feelings, but Billy knew Tom never gave anything away so easily as a look into his bright blue eyes. Those eyes were actors that could spin moods from friendly and inviting to mean and threatening. Many a time Billy watched as Tom listened to a minion explain away a mistake or a disappointment and he'd appear not to be paying attention, fiddling with one of his cigars or picking lint off his sleeve. Then he'd raise his head a fraction and his eyes would lash the poor fellow before him causing the man to fall from talking to stammering then to silence, head hanging, knowing that his fate had been decided. Tom would deliver his sentence in a quiet voice. He rarely shouted, although when amused he had a high-pitched laugh completely at odds with his bulky maleness.

But Billy knew Tom wouldn't crack his whip with Josie. Their relationship had always been a bit of a mystery to Billy, who didn't like Josie. More likely, Tom would use his "warm" look used to make a person feel special and willing to pledge undying fealty. A natural politician, he'd firmly shake the person's hand while embracing them with his good will. Like any good politician, he showed real love for people. He'd tease and joke, throw a wink, bestow a nickname so his target felt a fraternal bond. When talking about a private manner, he'd lean in close, hold the person in place with a soft grip on the elbow, his head nearly touching theirs in an act of intimacy. He was the best friend, someone to confide in about an unhappy marriage, an affair, money problems or thwarted ambitions. Don't worry, he'd say. I'll take care of it. You need some bail money for your husband? Here, pay me back when you can. You need to buy medicine for your sick child? Here, no need to pay me back.

And, like any good politician, he kept score. He knew who owed him a favor and, with precise calibration, what to exact as payback.

But Josie wouldn't fall for such a sappy ploy. Billy was certain of that, given her history.

The hack jostled over narrow cobblestone streets lighted by gas lamps and past grocers and druggists scattered among the bars and saloons and dancehalls of the French Quarter. Graceful wrought-iron balconies lent a romantic touch, which was lacking in the blunt aggressiveness of Storyville. Billy slouched in the corner brooding, staring out the window and then said, apropos of nothing, "Mellow old wine doesn't announce itself whereas *nouveau vin* has a tart bite that calls attention to itself. That's the difference between the Quarter and Storyville."

Billy, who had been reading *The Hounds of the Baskervilles*, considered himself a writer of high literary aspiration, although his only experience had been as a crime reporter for the *Daily Item*. Among his duties, he served as the editor of Tom's *Blue Book*, a must-have guide to Storyville. The *Blue Book*'s preface stated, "It puts the stranger on a proper grade and path as to where to go and be secure from holdups, brace games and other illegal practices usually worked on the unwise in the Red Light District."

The blue-colored pages advertised the bagnios, the refinements of the madams, and the skills of their girls. Tom earned a tidy profit from the advertisements for restaurants, bars, saloons, cabarets, liquor dealers, breweries, cigar and tobacco stores, lawyers and quack cures.

Tom came back from whatever plan he had been mulling and looked at Billy. He thought, not for the first time, A cougar half asleep, that's Billy. Appearing docile but always ready to pounce. A harmless looking clerk with his plain brown hair neatly parted on the right side. Who would think that someone with such a slight frame could whip a men twice his size.

Billy's face was entirely forgettable, except for the soft eyes that, when he became intense or intrigued, took on a luster sometimes mistaken for seduction. Then Billy was at his most dangerous.

"You being scholarly again, Billy? Thinking philosophical thoughts? Working up another poem?"

"Just making an observation."

"What do you think we should do about this, Billy?" Tom valued his trustworthy partner: whenever he needed a mess cleaned up, or a rough message delivered, or a situation discouraged, Billy took it on as a personal mission. He didn't have any private personal relationship, no lady friend or special whore or even a dog. He had Tom.

"Don't start a fight with the wrong enemy," Billy answered.

They turned onto St. Claude, a side street barely wide enough for the one-horse hackney to squeeze down and stopped at a wall covered with ochre-colored plaster with a solid oak door. Tom banged with the door's heavy iron knocker and waited. Then banged again. Moments later, an elderly black manservant cracked open the door.

"Tom Anderson to see Josie Arlington."

The servant stood aside and they entered the interior courtyard with a three-tiered fountain, the water falling as quietly as moss. The servant showed them into a corner room under the wrap-around upper balcony. Josie sat propped up on a sofa, wrapped in a voluminous dressing robe with only her head poking out of the yellow collar.

"I'm surprised to find you up so late," Tom said.

"Not so surprised as to wait for a decent hour," she replied. Her hair smelled of smoke.

"I thought you'd want to know right away what I have to tell." Tom pulled a chair close to her. Billy hung back. He'd known Josie when she launched her career, before Tom met her. "A flesh eater," he once told Ant, with a mixture of awe and contempt. "You don't want to get in a fight with that scag if you can help it."

Bundled up on the sofa, she seemed like a wounded bird backed into a corner wishing to be left alone. "Did everyone get out all right?" her voice thin, fragile, as if she couldn't get enough air into her lungs.

Tom held her hand, fidgeted, searching for a nice way to put it, then said bluntly, "No. They found one girl upstairs. We don't know her name."

"Oh? What did she look like?"

"Very pretty, much as you could tell. Dark hair, what wasn't burned off. Young. Almost too young. In the room right above the kitchen. She wore a green dress with a cream collar and cuffs. And red high-button shoes with tall heels, according to Ant, who was there."

Josie stared in the middle distance, calling up the face of each of her girls. "Might be Laura, Laura Smith. Sounded like a runaway name to me, but I don't ask probing questions. Came to me a month or so ago. Didn't reveal much about herself or where she was from, but that's not unusual in my business. Said she needed a job and had the skills. A nice girl. Good worker. A pleasant girl."

"Do you know any family we should contact?"

Josie shook her head and clutched Tom's hand. "Do proper by her, Tom—don't put her in a wet grave. She doesn't deserve the disrespect no matter how she made a living."

"We'll make arrangements to send her home, as soon as we know where home is." Tom paused, eyes downcast. "Laura Smith was murdered, in the opinion of the fire inspector. Bruises were found around her neck."

"No!" Josie snatched her hand back and clapped it over her mouth.

A lot had been said against Josie, and by more people than Billy; that she was an unsentimental hard-heart, a shrew, a gutter-mouth street fighter who took on the pretensions of a bishop's wife – and all of it true. But her tears flowed for Laura.

"Someone choked her to death. The same person may have set the fire to cover the crime," Tom said. "Or maybe he used the fire as an opportunity to commit the crime. Or, maybe the Matrangas set the whole thing up, the murder being a red herring."

Josie sank back into the cushions, head bowed. However, her piety didn't last more than thirty seconds before she sat bolt upright and demanded, "What are you going to do about this, Tom?"

"Well, I'll have Billy and Ant investigate. We'll find who did it and serve justice our own way."

"That's good and right," Josie balled her fist on her knees, "but that's not my real concern."

"Or, we could let it drop. Won't help us to raise a fuss. Won't help having a murdered girl associated with the Arlington."

Josie reared back, jaw working to spit nails. "She was a good and decent girl, Tom, trying to make her way the best she could." Then came the nail. "If she was your daughter, would you sweep her death under the rug just to make a buck?"

Tom flinched, his head turning slightly as if slapped. His daughter was nearing womanhood. He hadn't seen her in years, ever since her mother, Tom's common law wife, had moved out on bad terms.

"We'll do what we can," his tone resentful of her low blow.

"Let justice be served in her memory but the living must go on with the business of living." Josie leaned forward to get right in Tom's face. "Mardi Gras's coming up. That's our Christmas season! We've got to be back in business by then."

Tom nodded in understanding. "The six rooms above my saloon can be your temporary *maison de joie* until we rebuild."

Josie gave a sharp nod of dismissal. "I'll send Henry to look them over."

In the carriage on the way back to his Arlington Cafe, Tom sat ramrod straight, fingers drumming on his knee. "Billy, get the boys to clean up the rooms." Billy wanted to say something but held back. "And have a sign painted that reads JOSIE'S ARLINGTON." Tom framed the words in the air with his hands. "Hang it right under my sign so everybody can see it plain as day, even the Matrangas."

When they arrived at the saloon, Tom sent for Ant. "I want you to put your ear to the street. If the Matrangas are planning another attack, I want to know about it."

Tom hired Ant, in part, because the moniker was more than a shortcut for Antoine. Ant's five feet three inches made him hard to spot. He could fade into shadows and stay below shoulders in a crowd, which was definitely to his advantage when poking about in Storyville's backstreets. Although his size was a professional asset, Ant resented his diminutiveness. He thought other men found him non-consequential, a fly to be swatted simply because they could.

"I'll make a tour tonight," Ant replied, "while the topic is still hot, so to speak."

Leaving Tom's saloon, he set out to probe Storyville's streets packed with saloons, cabarets, dance halls, dives known as "knife fights," gambling and opium dens, pits for dog and cock fights, whorehouses where, for a quarter, a man ran the risk of getting his pecker bit by the pus demon.

He started down Basin Street, past Josie's disaster and the other whorehouses, rundown brick tenements as worn out as the women who worked in them. Basin Street was so named because it started as a shallow basin of brackish water, a breeding ground for alligators, poisonous snakes, malaria-bearing mosquitoes and giant frogs that weighted up to ten pounds. General Andrew Jackson, after his victory over the British in the Battle of New Orleans, gave his ragtag soldiers full pay for saving the city. Camp followers, the pioneer ancestors of Storyville's sporting ladies, wanted to reward the flush heroes of New Orleans by setting up joy houses in the French Quarter. But the Creole residents said, Oh, no, not in our neighborhood. So the enterprising ladies, with the help of Jackson's civilian soldiers, dug ditches to drain the basin and, when the land was firm enough, put up rudimentary "hospitality" shacks and opened for business.

At the end of Basin, Ant came to St. Louis Cemetery No.1 and turned the corner to Franklin Street, an arcade of saloons, dancehalls and shooting galleries where hunters used pellet guns to knock over tin ducks. Touts, their voices loud and harsh, called out, "Hey, buddy, buddy, a fine time for a dime," in rhythmic cadence, giving a pace to the street as if calling a square dance. Barkers in flashy vests and tilted derbies promised five-cent beer buckets and the most beautiful girls on stage, wink-wink. Music stumbled drunk from every building, bouncing around in a mash-up of piano styles that made the entire street sound as if it had been splashed in bright dripping colors. Ant dodged out of the way of the oncoming Kruser's Sundries Store wagon advertising animal crackers, In back of the wagon a spasm band played jagged out-of-tune almost songs.

Franklin could well have been called the Street of Optimism. A man, or woman, could make his or her fortune there if they had gallons of gumption, iron balls and a jeering attitude about the law. So armed, they could rise out of poverty to become respectable middle class property owners, wear suits and dresses out of the fashion magazines and send their kids to school, even college.

Ant ducked into the 101 Ranch Dancehall, a hangout for roustabouts, pimps and gamblers, to confer with Tubby Phillips, a reliable informant when it came to street rumors. Like most joints on Franklin, the 101 had been built sturdy to withstand the hard use of its customers. Tubby never bothered to replace the big mirror behind the bar after a brawl shattered it for the third time. Instead, he had a painter do a fourteen-foot mural of New Orleans as the idealized Shining City. The inspiration was the original settlers' vision of a perfect city in the wilderness, a reflection of God's divine plan for man to conquer, tame and rule the raw natural world. Illusion had a great deal to do with the creation of New Orleans.

When Ant stepped up the bar, Tubby, a broad florid man wearing a striped shirt and red suspenders, greeted him with an enthusiastic handshake. "How 'bout a refresher, Ant? On the house."

A good friend and close ally of Tom's, Tubby was the dancehall king of New Orleans, the title earned because he was first saloonkeeper to dedicate a room adjacent to the bar for dancing when saloons featured only a piano player. Other saloon owners believed dancing distracted the customers from drinking. But Tubby realized dancing brought men and women together and men would buy the women drinks and the dancing might cause a thirst that had to be satisfied, especially the more they drank. So he hired bands to play, white bands only, and packed the house.

Ant accepted the drink and edged the chitchat around to Josie's fire.

"Don't know about the fire but Storyville needs its own fire station," Tubby said. "Perhaps Tom could bring his influence to bear. That would give us more substance. Give the patrons more confidence the house won't burn down until they have time to pull their pants up," he laughed.

"You have any theory about the blaze, seeing the fire inspector found signs of arson?"

"Maybe Josie had a dissatisfied customer," Tubby ventured.

"Maybe somebody's trying to worm into Tom's business," Ant countered. "You hear any rumors along those lines, like maybe the Matrangas are getting ambitious. Now that they control the docks, they might have dreams of making New Orleans a Mafia kingdom?"

"The Matrangas have some gambling dens in Storyville. Sometimes their soldiers come strutting through trying to put on the squeeze, but we tell them to fuck off. This is Tom's territory and he'll protect us."

After finishing his drink, Ant drifted deeper into the district's dark streets lined with buildings that were little more than broad-plank houses of cards. This was the remnant of The Swamp, the territory of thieves, murderers, predatory whores, criminals and ruffians – the birthplace of Storyville. Tom had learned his street smarts as a boy hawking newspapers in The Swamp.

The Swamp had also been the playground of the "Kaintocks," the bullies who brought flatboats down the Mississippi from Kentucky and stayed in Sin City to prove how sinful they could be. They relished their reputation for being no-holds-barred, kicking, stomping, clubbing, biting, gouging, stabbing coarse barbarians. And that was in a fair fight. The flatboats were too much trouble to tow back up the Mississippi so they were broken up and the thick rough timber sold as building material for saloons and crude whorehouses. Street whores used the cargo boxes as makeshift cribs in which to conduct business. Similar shanties were still housed crib girls in the back streets of Liberty, Marais, Villere and Robertson.

Ant walked on the balls of his feet ready to spring away from danger. Knife fights, murders, and beatings happened there so frequently as to be unremarkable. This backside of Storyville was the breeding ground for disease, desperation and madness. A high percent of the workingwomen roosting in those streets chose suicide over a life of syphilis, gonorrhea, tuberculosis, whooping cough, beatings and insanity: the very conditions that made the prostitutes susceptible to the Matrangas' helping hand.

From an alley came the *s-s-s-s-s* mating call of a crib girl. Twelve-year-old girls sold themselves along Robertson Street for twenty-five cents, turning tricks in cribs seven feet wide, room enough for a single bed, a nightstand with a pitcher of water and a chair. Two or more workingwomen might rent a crib for five dollars a day and share the cost by doing day and nights shifts. They didn't wash the sheets, or themselves, between customers. Only truly desperate, or very poor, men risked sex with a crib girl. A man could die in a crib, also known as coffins, from a knife in the back while face down on the whore.

Ant edged into the shadow to find her, a stick-thin girl of maybe fifteen. "You want fun, mister?"

He went only as close as needed because the girls were often used as bait for a mugging. "I want to know how's business."

"I'll show ya." She lifted the hem of her chippie, a knee-length shift easily pulled over the head for a quick undress.

"Any outsiders coming around making you promises?"

"What you mean?"

"Like you work for them, maybe they set you up in a house."

"If only God would answer my prayer."

"You be careful when dealing with that Trickster," Ant replied. He wanted to add, Have neither hope nor faith that God will hear your prayer. He has a tin ear. If you aspire to raise your station in life, the best thing is to learn some magic, or at least a few tricks of deception and misdirection. Learn to play the trombone and use fifty-cent words. But most of all, don't give away your heart to any of the bastards. Write'em a love poem if you have to, whisper that poem while licking their ear, but never ever trust'em – even if it breaks your heart.

"Come on, mister," the young white whore reached out to tug Ant into the alley's darkness. "I'm clean and good fun. You'll see."

"Here, buy some time for yourself." He gave her a quarter and walked a couple streets to a nearly invisible passageway, more a crack between two buildings. Two men couldn't pass without turning sideways in that walkway deliberately kept dark, and they always averted their eyes while brushing nearly button-to-button. He went on cat's feet, quickly yet cautiously, hands touching the crumbling brick walls on either side, to the black door of Chen the Chink's opium den. If anyone knew of the Matrangas prying their way into Storyville, it would be Chen

The Chinese controlled the drug trade in New Orleans. But, according to knowledgeable rumor, the Matrangas were importing cocaine from South America through their shipping connections and had Mexican suppliers for marijuana. That made Chen and the Matrangas competitors, and Chen kept a keen eye out for his enemies.

The door opened an inch at his coded rap. Seeing the familiar face, Jimmy Chen, the old man's son, let Ant slip in. He walked down the dim corridor to the front room, a reception area of sorts where Chen's crone of a wife collected weapons and shoes and money before allowing customers into the back room. Chen greeted him with a bow, hands pressed together in prayer.

"Most Honorable Ant, we have not had your pleasure in some time." Chen had the knack of being simultaneously obsequious and mocking, his sense of sly humor.

Ant returned his formal bow. "It has taken so long for the last pleasure to wear off, so potent are your highest quality goods."

Chen flashed long yellow teeth in welcome and ushered Ant into the back room. Men lay in bunks stacked four high around the large room, puffing on the long-stemmed clay opium pipes or staring blank-eyed. The dim cast of red lamps gave the den a netherworld mood of benevolent evil; the warm glow could become a crackling flame at the Devil's bidding or by Chen withholding a small sticky ball of opium, which amounted to the same thing. Chen's three assistants came and went from a low table in the room's center where they warmed the opium over Bunsen burners and, using a long needle, much like a darning needle only thinner, spread the narcotic goo around the broad shallow rim of the pipes. Shuffling in their cloth slippers, they glided from the table to bunks and held the bowl slanted to a flame as the customer drew in a deep lung full of dream smoke. Ant was struck by the tenderness of the assistants as they guided the pipe stem to the head lying on a wooden block.

In a smaller curtained off room, Chen's private lounge for preferred customers, Ant stretched out full length on large floor cushions. Rich tapestries of intricate dragons and misty mountains covered the walls. A beautiful young woman crouched in a corner. Perfume in the lamps' oil transported the room into a scented garden.

Chen gave a soft clap and the girl rose to prepare Ant's bowl.

"You've been well?" he inquired in a coo.

"Very well, Most Esteemed Friend."

The girl squatted at a table and heated a ball of opium, the high slit of her Chinese dress revealing the naked curve of her buttock.

"However, I am concerned," Ant said.

"Howso?"

The girl was lovely, so delicate, her long black hair half hiding her face, her every move, the turn of her hands, a whisper of grace.

"I've heard ugliness that our Italian friends wish to disturb your paradise."

Chen let the silence settle as they watched the girl. "She's the mist of a waterfall, is she not?" he asked. "Cool water to temper the hot spirit."

The girl rose to bring Ant his pipe.

"Our Italian friends, they have not displayed the bold spirit needed to come into Chen's paradise –or my marketplace," he added in a gruffer tone.

The girl offered Ant the pipe without looking into his eyes.

"Chen is touched by your solicitous concern. Tell Mr. Anderson the Matrangas are dogs." He waited while Ant took a long pull on the pipe. "You must be careful around dogs. They lick your hand and then bite you. That's why we Chinese eat them." Chen rocked back with a surprisingly loud laugh and then leaned forward to Ant and said in an earnest voice, "There's a pack of dogs roving the streets looking for scraps to snatch up. Tell Mr. Anderson to shoot them."

Ant let out a long stream of bluish opium smoke.

"Enjoy your stay, Most Respected Ant. Little Flower will care for your needs."

Hours later, still floating and slightly nauseous, Ant reported to Tom and Billy in Tom's office. Tom sat behind his desk fiddling with his new Kodak Hawk Eye Stereo camera with two lenses. Newfangled machines such as the camera, automobile and telephone piqued his curiosity. There weren't many autos in New Orleans at the time and nobody Tom knew had one of Edison's magic talking boxes. Electricity was another new interest of his, although like many people he was cautious about introducing it into his home. Stories circulated about the dangers of that invisible force that you couldn't smell. Some fashionable ladies forbade electric lights in their homes, believing it caused freckles, the undesirable "Irish" rash. Other ill-informed folk believed electricity would foster "foolishness" in encouraging people to stay up beyond their natural bedtime and seek adventures in god knows what. Electricity was too mysterious for many folks to trust, although it fascinated them.

"What did you find out, Ant?"

"Nothing to indict the Matrangas are actively setting up their own whorehouses in Storyville." Not a bald-face lie, Ant reasoned, as neither Tubby nor the young whore said as such. "They got some gambling dens, small time, nothing to worry about. At least not yet." He saw no reason to jeopardize his working relationship with the Mafia brothers by cranking up Tom's suspicions of them.

"Well, that's good to know," Tom said. "But those dagos are bank robbers and I'm a bank. Think we can pin the whore's murder on them, Billy? Doesn't matter who killed her any more than it matters who lynches a nigger. She was just a whore. We've got plenty of'em. Important thing to get the Matrangas arrested and hung for this gruesome crime."

"Christ, Tom, you got Matrangas on the brain. Why don't you just talk to them? It's not like you don't have the muscle to back you up. Tell them you've heard they have misplaced ambitions. They shouldn't upset the fruit cart. They understand that kind of talk. After all, they're in the fruit business."

Billy chuckled at his own joke but Tom stayed pokerfaced. "No, I don't want to tip them off before I have a plan. I want to catch them off guard with a knockout punch."

But, as Tom learned the next day, he was the target of a sneak punch.

Chapter 3.

Billy walked into Tom's office without knocking. "Tom, Chief Hennessy is trying to pluck a golden apple off your tree." Josie sprawled on the sofa playing with the Kodak camera. "Stick out your tongue and cross your eyes," trying to cajole Tom to mug for her. Billy didn't acknowledge her, not even a polite nod.

"What do you mean?"

"He's warned the madams of the best houses to boycott your costume ball. Beat coppers are confiscating your tickets from the saloons and hotels, and handing out strong hints. If anyone shows up at your ball, they'll be disturbing the peace. Hennessy has scheduled his Red Light Social Ball for the night before your Gentlemen's Ball."

Tom's Gentlemen's Ball, which unofficially kicked off the pre-Mardi Gras celebrations, was a New Orleans' tradition. People looked forward to it like racers waiting for the starting gun. Daring young ladies of respectable families attended in disguise, accompanied by a conniving brother or male escort. The woman behind a mask could be an amateur or a pro; the risk of finding out was a large part of the allure and excitement. Everyone understood that anything could happen at the Gentlemen's Ball, where Tom presided as the Grand Nabob, which was like being King of Comus only more amusing. He didn't hide behind a veil, as did the "King of Colon," as he jeeringly referred to the presiding royalty of the Madri Gras's most prestigious society ball. Rather, he openly received perfumed invitations by the dozens to revel with his comely "subjects." He also made a tidy sum from the ticket and liquor sales, no small consideration.

"Fucking Irish upstart," Tom muttered. "The Matrangas and now Hennessy. Nothing worse than filthy Italians and greedy Irish."

"That's not all. He knows about the murdered whore. Coroner told him. Hennessy's put word on the street that since you have an interest in the whorehouse where the murder happened, all of Storyville is unsafe. If you can't protect your own nest, how can you be trusted to protect others? People should rethink their allegiance to you. He harbors a personal hatred for you, Tom, because you're the law in Storyville. So what does that make him, a lawman that can't enforce the law? A buffo. He's a man with a wounded prickly pride and that makes him more dangerous than the Mafia."

Tom sat with his hands flat on his desk, thick shoulders hunched slightly forward in the bulldog stance Billy knew all too well: Tom was thinking clever or mean, or both. Billy relished the Bulldog Tom because life always became more interesting when he growled. The last time was when a preacher man stood on the corner of Basin and Bienville, a block from Tom's saloon, hurling brimstone at the sinners who were Storyville's loyal customers. At first, Tom gave the man no more regard than an annoying crow cawing from a branch. "He even looks like a crow," Tom had said, "all dressed in black and hopping from foot to foot."

But after two days, the annoying crow had become more than a nuisance; an increasing crowd stood around him instead of coming into Tom's saloon for a drink. So Tom threw a rock in the form of a spasm band. Whenever the preacher man started up, the spasm band answered on their homemade instruments to drown him out. The drummer pounded on his pots and buckets; the doghouse bass man thumped away on an instrument he had salvaged after it had been crushed under the wheels of a wagon; the horn man blew a bulge as if leading a cavalry charge; and the singer used a drainpipe to project his voice.

The preacher man countered with a megaphone of his own and directed his damnations directly at Tom. "He called me Satan's henchman," sputtered Tom, who wasn't a religious man but nevertheless was God-fearing. "I give more money to the poor than that sorry sap will see in all his life."

When the preacher man persisted, Tom called in Billy. "Gather up some members of the congregation," he instructed. "I want a prayer meeting held over that man's body."

The next night, when the preacher took to his corner pontificating about the evils of fun, Billy and four of Tom's special employees, big men who started bare-knuckle brawls for the enjoyment of pain, stood respectfully in the front row. The preacher raised his megaphone to his mouth and shouted, "Praise the Lord!" the wide funnel pointed upward. Billy threw a pitcher of piss down the funnel and the preacher choked on his next word. As he staggered sputtering and spewing, the four thugs walloped him with paper bags filled with fresh shit. The bags split open, covering the hapless man with excrement. The surrounding crowd, at first stunned by the sudden attack, chuckled at the crude humor, then broke into guffaws, like boys enjoying their first fart jokes.

The preacher man never returned to his corner.

But Tom knew he couldn't pelt the Mantrangas or Hennessy with bags of shit. Like a chess player, he had to checkmate his opponents. So far, he hadn't figure out how to turn Hennessy and the Matranga brothers against one another.

The makings were there to give Tom an endgame victory: the Matrangas harbored a bitter personal grudge against Hennessy, even going so far as trying to assassinate him. Hennessy publicly avowed to "destroy the Mafia vermin that infests our fair city," as the *Mascot*, Storyville's scandal sheet, reported. "I'll drive them into the Gulf of Mexico, drown'em like the rats they are."

The genesis of the police chief versus the Mafia animosity harkened back to when an ordinary dumbo gunned down young Hennessy's father, a beat copper, on St. Ann Street. As a way to help the family financially, fifteen-year-old David was made an office runner at police headquarters. He became a favorite and, when he turned eighteen, entered the force. Ambitious, opportunistic, liberal with the interpretation of the law when it worked to his advantage, he rose quickly through the ranks to detective.

However, he was dismissed from the police force after being acquitted of killing his boss, Chief of Detectives Thomas Devereaux, with whom he had a personal grudge. At the murder trial, Hennessy claimed a man with a gun had assaulted him and his cousin, Mike, in a dark alley.

"We thought we were about to be robbed," Hennessy stated under oath. "Mike drew his gun and the man shot him. That's when I opened fire. I don't know why Devereaux was threatening us."

After Hennessy was fired for "poor judgment," the cousins, David and Mike, opened the Hennessy Detective Agency, which is when they ran afoul of the Matrangas. They were hired to shadow the Mafia chieftain Giuseppi Esposito, wanted by the British for kidnapping an English clergyman in Sicily. Esposito had evaded the British's manhunt in Sicily, escaped to New Orleans and sought refuge with the Matrangas, as they shared family ties in that infamous Italian island. The Hennessys, disguised as priests, captured Esposito as he left Sunday Mass and turned him over to the British.

It didn't take long for the Matrangas to discover the real identity of the priests. Their bravos murdered Mike Hennessy in broad daylight and attempted to assassinate David, who escaped with three bullet holes in his hat.

In public diatribes against the Matrangas, Hennessy vowed anew to "scrub our city clean of the cowardly aliens."

New Orleans Mayor Shakespeare, who pledged to clean his own administration of corruption, appointed Hennessy as Chief of Police. "He is the brave man not afraid to boldly confront the criminal elements in our great and fair city," the mayor declared without irony.

The appointment caused jubilation and jeering within the police department. Hennessy's friends lined up with their hands out; his foes plotted and bid their time.

Ant, when tapping into his informant network to discover more about the Matrangas' intentions, heard whispers that Hennessy was planning a subterfuge against Tom Anderson.

"There's been a secret meeting," a porter at one of the city's finest hotel told Ant over a drink in a hole-in-the-wall where a man could buy cheap whiskey. "Hennessy met with Pollock and they struck a deal." Pollock was the top officer of the Red Light Social Club, whose members were the wealthiest and most prominent men in the city. "Hennessy presented Pollock with a plan for an irresistible bottom line – profitable lust." The porter paused to give Ant time to consider the value of the information. Ant handed him five dollars. The porter looked over both shoulders to check no one was close enough to overhear. "Hennessy suggested opening the Red Light Ball to public and selling tickets, and he will get a cut."

The ball always had been a private event for the sake of discretion. The *Mascot* occasionally ran articles speculating the gentlemen-only club indulged in "youth dances," where under-aged virgins were sold for the night.

"And here's the clincher," the porter leaned in close to Ant so their shoulders touched. "The club members can enjoy in their private entertainment without paying a dime. Hennessy has sent word to the best sporting houses to reserve their crème de la crème for a private affair on the same night. He included a detailed list of the personal preferences of the club members. He also expects the madams to sell twenty tickets to their clients."

"How do you know this?"

"The other night Pollock was in the hotel's bar showing off a pair of special-issue police pistols with mother-of-pearl handles. He bragged that Hennessy gave them to him to seal the deal."

The porter handed Ant a card of stiff expensive paper. "Pollock also passed these out."

Ant tilted the card to read the invitation in the dim light, then put the card in his coat pocket. "A round for my friend," he instructed the barkeep, and left to find Billy.

That's why Billy was irritated when he entered Tom's office with the news of Hennessy's sneak attack. And seeing Josie there upped his temperature. After filling Tom in, he said, "Ant dug out the information" giving credit where credit was due.

He turned to Josie. "Do you get such an invitation?"

She ignored him, focusing all her attention on the camera. "Why didn't you tell us so we could take some early preventive measures?"

Tom waited for her answer. She avoided him by fiddling with the camera. He tapped the desk with his forefinger. When she didn't respond, he tapped louder. "I don't remember," she said. "I've been preoccupied of late." She raised the camera and aimed at Billy, as if sighting a rifle.

Tom's finger kept a steady beat, sounding like an axe chopping wood, until she set the camera aside. Still, she didn't say anything. Finally he said to her, "Send word to all the madams they have nothing to fear from Hennessy. I'll protect them as I always have." Then shifting to Billy, "Get one of the boys dressed up like a fancy butler and have him hand deliver engraved invitations to businessmen, politicians, social climbers, and scions from the best families, especially the young sons. I'll make up a list. Send bundles of free tickets for the Gentleman's Ball to the best clubs, krewes, top hotels and benefit societies with my compliments. If Hennessy," he rummaged through a desk drawer, "even gives the appearance of prevailing against me," then shut the drawer, "that will endanger my position."

He gave Billy an exasperated look.

"Lower left," his partner said.

Tom leaned over and opened the drawer. "My enemies, those envious bastards, burned Josie out of business and my saloon might be next. We've got to stop'em." He fished a cigar out of the drawer and bit off the end in his agitation, spitting the plug across the room.

"Don't worry about the Red Light Ball," Josie said. Her tone was unmistakable; and don't worry about my loyalty. "I'll make it an unforgettable evening for everyone."

Tom held her eyes for a moment. His brief nod confirmed whatever private agreement existed between them. Billy, shifting on the sofa, threw her a cold shoulder. Josie had inserted her foot between Tom and Billy and he didn't like it.

"All right then." Tom brought his palms down flat on his desk, signaling the end to the meeting. "Let's get to work."

The day before the Red Light Ball, Tom stood in the middle of his office with arms extended straight out from his shoulders as a fussy little man buzzed around him making adjustments to the British admiral's dress coat. Billy sat on the sofa reading a newspaper. "Ant, you swabbie! You're next," Tom called out, puffing on a cigar. "You're coming with me and Josie to Hennessy's ball while you, Billy, get busy pulling together my Gentlemen's Ball for the next night. You like my coat?" He pirouetted like a figure on a music box. "This gentleman will fix you up, Ant, as my cabin boy or whatever you desire to be. An invisible man? Can you do that?" he asked the tailor. "Ant here makes a profession out of not being seen. At least not by the wrong people in the wrong place, isn't that right, Ant?"

Ant blinked so Tom wouldn't see the flash of worry in his eyes. Did Tom know about his sideline with the Matrangas?

But Tom's expression remained good-natured and there wasn't a trace of malice in his voice.

"Josie's got something up her sleeve for Hennessy's ball," he added. "She won't tell me but says I won't want to miss it. That's enemy territory so I need you to watch my back, Ant."

The next night, before Tom and Josie appearance at the ball, Ant scouted the location, the Oddfellows Hall on upper St. Charles, six blocks outside Storyville's boundaries. An early crowd of plebes stood at the bottom of the flight of broad steps leading up to the building posing as a Greek temple with Doric columns supporting the domed roof. A double line of liveried footmen took their positions on the stairs to form a passageway for the guests. All rather grand for a debauch ball, Ant thought, but this is New Orleans. The crowd mistook him, masked by blackface with white-rimmed eyes and extravagant red lips, as a harbinger and perked up with excitement. The irony, he thought. A highly visible invisible man. Hidden in full view. A neither here-nor-there man.

As the carriages began arriving, Ant stood at the curb and faced the dunderheads who hooted and hollered with a mixture of admiration and mockery as the turbaned sultans and harlequins and faux kings and queens of seduction– even a foot-six penguin wearing a sequined red cape – alighted. He wasn't at all certain what he'd do if he spotted a drawn gun aimed at Tom or if someone lunged from the crowd with a knife.

I'll shout a warning, Ant told himself, now a bit nervous. He didn't consider himself a man of direct action but rather a discreet observer, a spy. *Shove Tom aside, maybe. Or push Josie into the path of danger.*

He turned to watch a gleaming black brougham drawn by four prancing thoroughbreds come down the street. Positioning himself where a footman would be to open the carriage's door, he faced the jostling people, looking for any threatening person. *They're all rogues,* he thought, scanning the crowd pushing forward for a better view. *In that, they're all Tom's allies.* He let the thought give him comfort as the carriage came to a halt.

Tom emerged in full British Admiralty regalia splendid with gold fringe on his shoulder boards, a chest full of bogus medals and a gleaming dress sword. Instead of an admiral's hat with its mohawk cockscomb, he wore a pirate's tricorn. And an eye patch.

"Lafitte! Lafitte!" cried the onlookers. The pirate Laffite had helped defeat the Royal Navy in the Battle of New Orleans. The citizens of New Orleans, especially the ladies, adored him for providing goods at bargain prices from the ships he looted. Being a savvy politician at heart, Tom knew how to expropriate another's glory for his own advantage.

He offered a hand to help Madame Pompidou down from the high carriage. The towering powdered wig with a diamond tiara perched on top made Josie appear eight inches taller. The wig and the gown puffed around her in piles of royal red silk made her look like a tulip with an obscene stamen. The cheeks of her hand-held mask, smooth and shiny as porcelain, were dusted with gold. Pausing dramatically at the carriage door so all could appreciate her finery, she presented herself as the Queen of New Orleans.

The gaggle of spectators oohed and ahhed and shouted out "Her Majesty!" and men dipped in mock sweeping bows and women made rude noise with their lips. Josie gave a royal wave as she took Tom's arm. Ant trailed after them into the hall abuzz with the anticipation of a treasure hunt. On stage, John Robichaux's Creole Orchestra played grand ballroom hits to a dance floor sizzling with swirls of colors, flirtatious glances and – even at this early hour -- bold invitations. Was the man shielded behind the fanciful mask a potential sugar daddy? Was the veiled coquet peeking over her bare shoulder available for a price – or was she somebody's wife or daughter looking for adventure? There was no way to tell a Storyville lady from a respectable society darling.

Ant's primary task was to identify Chief Hennessy in all this camouflage. Once he showed up, Ant would signal Josie, not Tom, which he thought peculiar.

"You, boy!" A man dressed as a plantation owner with a bare-breasted woman on each arm appeared in front of Ant. "You niggrrrr." His fake Southern accent betrayed his identity: a Yankee playing out his fantasy of being a slave master. "Fetch me a drink. Shine my shoes. Send me your women." He laughed uproariously as his fawning companions wheeled him away. Ant rubbed the tip of his blackface nose until a spot of white skin showed through the greased charcoal.

The place filled with maybe three hundred adventurers. Acting like a bodyguard, Ant stayed close to Tom on his first circuit of the room. Then he moved away to sniff for anything suspicious. Standing on a chair for better view, he spotted four squires parting the crowd to make way for a knight in full black armor with gold trim carrying a lance upright. From the tip hung three colored ribbons – red, blue and gold. The helmet's visor hid his face. As the entourage moved through dancers, the orchestra's trumpets blared a royal processional march. Everyone came to a standstill and craned to glimpse the mysterious personage. The squires stopped in the middle of the ballroom and formed a hollow square around the knight. He pounded the butt of his lance on the floor three times and three women, each wearing a gown that corresponded to the color of ribbon on the lance, came forward.

Ant waved a large red handkerchief above his head to signal Josie that Hennessy was in the house.

Within moments a man in a plain suit strode onto the stage, raised his hand and commanded, "Stop the music!"

Immediately the place fell silent, so quite that the creak of the knight's armor was clearly heard as he turned toward the stage. Uniformed coppers, perhaps forty or fifty, unobtrusively ringed the dance floor.

"I'm Detective Edward Smidren of the New Orleans Police Department," the man on stage announced. "We have been informed that illegal prostitution is being conducted on the premises."

The woman next to Ant, a dancing girl in a revealing harem outfit, laughed out loud. "But that's the whole point. That 'detective' is part of a charade, just you wait and see."

"Ladies to one side of the room, gentlemen to the other!" Detective Smidren ordered.

The knight furiously banged his lance on the floor. Without warning, six court jesters rushed forward scattering the knight's squires and knocking him flat. Four jesters grabbed him by arms and legs, hoisted him over their heads and, with the two other parting the crowd, carried him off. The knight, weighted down by his costume, struggled and squirmed, his shouts of outrage muffled by the closed helmet.

"See, the play goes on," laughed the dancing girl. "I bet they'll take him on stage and his damsels will relieve him of his armor right down to his natural state to see if he's equal to his lance. Then the knight will announce his right to Fornication Under Consent of the King and a fuckfest will break out."

No one had obeyed the Detective Smidren's order. "Ladies to one side of the room, gentlemen to the other!" he repeated with stern authority.

"When is the black knight going to appear on stage?" Ant asked the dancing girl.

"Want to see his lance, do ya, darlin'?"

At Detective Smidren's signal, the coppers surrounding the crowd began to rudely enforce his order. Dust devils of scrimmages spun across the floor as many of the men took umbrage at the coppers grabbing them. The unlikely pair of a cowboy and a Mardi Gras Indian ambushed a couple of coppers and the four twirled about in each other's arms before collapsing in a heap. Detective Smidren calmly drew his revolver and fired a shot into the ceiling. The amazingly loud BOOM! froze the fighting men in mid-swing.

"All right, ladies, line up," he shouted. "You know the drill. Show your cards."

"Well," the dancing girl said, "that means me."

The uninitiated women, having no idea what Detective Smidren was talking about, milled around in panic. Some tried to leave but coppers at the doors barred their way.

The Storyville pros formed an orderly line. They knew the drill because the city ordinance required prostitutes to be registered.

The police brusquely shoved all the women into a single row. Society ladies frantically signaled for help by waving their arms above their heads, as if drowning. A swan fainted dead away into a heap of white plumes and was unceremoniously dragged to the side.

A policeman came down the line. "Show your cards." The Storyville ladies reached into their bodices and whipped out their cards.

"Right now, you without cards, off you go," Detective Smidren shouted. The society women laughed in relief, thinking they got the joke and were being released. Instead, the officers herded them out the door and into horse-drawn paddy wagons.

Outraged brothers, husbands and escorts fought to break out of the police restraining line as the women were roughly removed. Some of the gallant Southern gentlemen attempted to take cops' legs out from under them; other furiously began slugging as if to fight their way out of a poke. In response, the coppers took a two-handed grip their truncheons, like baseball bats, and whacked the men about the heads and shoulders and ribs and knees.

When the six waiting paddy wagons were stuffed full of respectable society women, the cops called for three more to take the overflow to the station house.

Ant spotted Tom and Josie standing next to the stage and joined them. "That'll give those highfalutin' better-than-thou bitches their comeuppance," she said. "Come slumming like we're an evening at the theater. They don't have the guts to do our work, but they come here for a titillating thrill. They're being disrespectful. And," she turned to Tom, "now Hennessy will have some tar on his reputation."

"*You're* responsible for this?" Tom raised his eyebrows in disbelief.

"I told you I had a surprise," Josie patted her tiara to be sure it was in place. "Let's go to your place for some celebratory champagne and I'll tell you all about it."

In Tom's office, she did a little waltz step in her royal costume, the hoop skirt flaring as she twirled. "Sit down, you're making me dizzy," he said, but the chide had no bite coming through his good-natured grin. Billy and Ant joined them to hear Josie's tale.

"Wasn't that grand, Tommy?" she crowed. "Me, dirt poor ugly me, now Queen Bee."

"Sit down and tell me, Josie." Tom leaned back in his chair thoroughly enjoying Josie's—and his—triumph.

Josie had arranged a secret meeting with a man she trusted, Detective Smidren, whom she had known since her street-fighting days. "Long ago we worked out an agreement between us," she explained. "He'd keep me out of jail whenever he could and I'd take care of his urges personally or arrange a special treat. He takes secret pleasure in being on both ends of the whip as much as he relished putting cuffs on a helpless naked woman—or a young girl. What I appreciate about Eddie Smidren is his streak of spite and meanness and crooked justice. He doesn't like Chief Hennessy because, as he told me, the man won't do his own dirty work. So we got a three-for-one tonight, didn't we, Tommy?

"Hennessy's got a lot of explaining to do. Those blue noses got their noses rubbed in their snobbery. And all those bitches who kicked me out on the street when I was a desperate young girl trying to survive, now they know that the poor ol' Josie they fired from whorehouse after whorehouse for being a troublemaker, now she is the Queen Bee." She rolled about on the sofa hugging her sides with glee. "Now they can kiss my ass, Tommy."

"Well, you had a different reputation back then," chimed in Billy, "so your fans saw you differently, like someone still trying to tell dirt from chocolate."

"And you can kiss my ass, too," she flared back. "If I'd let you. You've always wanted to give me a try, haven't you, Billy? Back in the 'good ol' days' when you thought you could wipe your ass with me. But you never had the balls to get in the saddle, and still don't. You don't have the interest – with women." She turned away, dismissing him.

Billy flushed more red than a spanked butt. Tom headed off trouble by shooing everyone out of the office. "Time to get some sleep so we'll be fresh for the Gentlemen's Ball tomorrow night. You got everything under control, Billy?"

"If Hennessy plans a retaliation, we'll be ready," he replied.

The next night Ant, dressed as a leprechaun—an emerald colored suit, peaked hat with a shamrock and his face smeared four-leaf clover green, a nod to Tom's Irish ancestry—scouted the site of Tom's ball for signs of Hennessy's men. The Masonic Temple, on the corner of Canal and Liberty, was within Tom's domain but Hennessy could cause mischief, perhaps by blocking the surrounding streets. But the only men Ant saw on the neighboring streets were the patrols Billy had sent out.

Soon carriages lined the streets for blocks in front of the building, a three-story brick rectangle decked out with red-white-blue bunting draped around the windows and front door, where two men dressed a satyrs scrutinized the arriving guests. The whole city knew that the police chief and the vice lord were trying to out dick each other. Since Hennessy had been forced to bend over first, expectation of his answer back ran high. No one wanted to miss the show; even more importantly, they didn't want to be seen as snubbing Tom.

The costumes worn, or not worn, as may be the case, would have made French libertines blush. Either serious talent had been recruited or the society debutantes' adventure bone had been tickled. Ant wormed his way through the crowd and brush against suspicious people, his hands doing a quick light search for hidden weapons. Hennessy might well try to infiltrate an assassin. At the sound of a commotion behind him, he turned and saw Josie dressed as Cinderella in a dazzling white satin gown festooned with sparkly jewels, as if sprinkled in fairy dust, and her entourage enter the ballroom. She surrounded herself with a royal court of chambermaids wearing only diaphanous robes suitable for the bedchamber and by beefy bare-chested men, who looked suspiciously like bodyguards.

Ant half expected to see MayAnn. What would she disguise herself as? An Ethiopian princess, perhaps the Queen of Sheba, half concealed behind beguiling sheers for that peek-a-boo who-am-I look? Or wearing fake whiskers and grubby clothes of a gold digger?

Ant was confident Young Jack would be in attendance, but as what? A riverboat gambler in a fancy vest and curling mustache? Or a condemned man with a noose around his neck?

If Young Jack did attend, Ant had a surprise for him.

The second-floor ballroom had been transformed into the harem quarters of a wealthy sultan. Panels of silk and brocade hid the painted walls. Swooping canopies formed a false ceiling. Dim light from the gas wall lamps, masked with red and golden shades, smudged the line between duplicity and fantasy. The rooms on the third floor had been made into famous bedrooms, such as Henry VIII's.

Ant circled the room as the band played hot ragtime and stomps, none of the polite European waltz stuff but sweaty music that ventured into the jubilation Buddy Bolden, an uptown musician, was making popular. The loud music and laughter and shrieks and hollers made the ballroom like being inside a whirligig; you couldn't think, didn't want to think, except to forget who you were and fling yourself with reckless abandonment into being someone other. People grabbed the opportunity with both hands and ate it as if it was a cream pie. Dove in face first. Smeared themselves.

Ant knew that Young Jack would wear an ostentatious, flamboyant, costume. But then, he saw at least fifty or sixty ostentatious flamboyant costumes. He hadn't anticipated this complication. When a man dressed as a peacock with bejeweled feathers towering over his head came into sight, Ant drew closer, hoping to find some way to identify Young Jack. Perhaps if he saw those strange sea-green eyes behind the bird mask with it long pointy beak. Or get a glimpse of black curly hair beneath the cap sequined in iridescent scales. The man walked on his toes, as if poised for flight, so it was difficult to tell, with his balletic prancing, if he had a limp. Nevertheless, the arrogance of the fancy would suit Young Jack, in Ant's opinion. He signaled his cohorts to prepare for the ambush.

The plan was for the four whores to sweep Young Jack off his feet, giggling and tickling him, distracting him with lewd promises, as they hustled him to a somewhat quiet corner where Bellocq, Storyville's unofficial official photographer of prostitutes, waited discreetly out of sight to photograph Young Jack in compromising positions.

Ant stepped in front of the peacock to slow him down while the women approached from behind. The peacock paused in mid-prance with one foot off the floor and elbows cocked as chicken wings. One whore came from behind and hugged his waist, then dropped her hands to his crotch. Two others latched onto each arm while the remaining woman attached herself to his front, rubbing his chest. The man let out a yelp, as if suddenly doused with cold water. The whores laughingly lifted him off his feet to the spot where Bellocq waited.

A clown bumped into Ant and whispered, "There's a killer here."

"What?"

"Bang bang. Your main man is in danger." The clown slipped away.

Ant twisted to find the peacock, then reversed direction, and turned back again, torn between finding Billy or watching the man he assumed to be Young Jack stripped and saddled by each of the women. He regretfully decided to find Billy and tell him of the warning.

A pyramid formed by six naked women with a thick ring of men around it blocked his way. As he squeezed through, his small size most helpful, the pyramid tumbled. The heap of shoving men, desperate as bridesmaids scrabbling for the bride's bouquet, buried Ant. He found himself lying on top of the one of the naked ladies, who hollered, "Get off! Get off! You're crushing me." Ant escaped by wriggling through the shifting crevices of entangled bodies.

He found Billy, costumed as Wild Bill Hickok, by the stage.

"Where's Tom?"

"I don't know. Getting ready for his grand entrance I suppose."

"A killer might be here waiting for him."

"How do you know?"

"A clown told me."

"You been drinking, Ant?"

"One of my informants. Take this seriously, Billy."

"All right. I'll alert the men. You find Tom and keep him out of here."

Chapter 3

Knowing that Tom had reserved an upstairs chamber as his boudoir/dressing room, Ant started for the stairs. But he found himself blocked by a leapfrog line of men and women vaulting over each other's upturned bare bottoms, or in some cases not quite clearing the temptation. He slid under the line, a pair of bare breasts brushing his head.

Upstairs, he found Tom in the Casanova room. "Don't you knock?" he shouted when Ant barged in. Tom stood naked in the middle of the room as two women prepared to wrap him in a toga.

"We have a problem."

"Then solve it."

"That's why I'm here."

As Ant explained the threat, the women fussed to hang the sheet laced with silver and gold threads on Tom. "How do you know it's not a ruse? A bluff to make me hide at my own ball?" he demanded.

"We don't but it's a big risk to ignore it."

One of the women knotted the sheet over Tom's bare shoulder. The other bent at his waist trying to keep the toga from a revealing slip.

"I won't be seen as a coward. That'd give Hennessy a cheap victory."

He held his arms out and turned about. "How do I look? Like a fun emperor?"

"Billy thinks you should lay low."

"No."

"Maybe another costume. Something more of a disguise."

"No. Where's my jewels?"

"At least give us time to take precautions."

One of the women opened a jewelry box and handed him a strand of pearls.

"You've got until midnight. Half an hour. And you can't empty of the building."

Back in the ballroom, Ant tracked down Billy. "He's coming. How are we going to find an assassin in this crowd?"

"Don't know but we'd better figure it out."

On the stroke of midnight, the music abruptly stopped. Six brawny black stevedores wearing loincloths and red turbans, accompanied by clanging cymbals, carried Tom, reclining on a palliasse, through the crowd. A laurel of bay leaves dipped in gold leaf encircled his head. Necklaces of diamonds and pearls and rubies looped around his Grand Nabob neck. Rings covered every finger, which he waved in royal benediction. Reaching into a brass spittoon, he threw out handfuls of crisp greenbacks as Mardi Gras trinkets.

Ant stood on the stairs scanning the room for any threat, although not knowing exactly what to look for. A phalanx of bodyguards, organized by Billy, escorted the procession as it made a circuit of the ballroom. Still, a sudden shot could come from the crowd. Ant's eyes flitted around the ballroom. Did the cowboy over there have six-shooters loaded with real bullets? Or was that fellow dressed as a circus performer an expert knife thrower?

Straddling a burly bodyguard's shoulders to better see the big picture, Billy placed himself directly in front of Tom. A woman in a Victorian formal gown approached from Billy's blind side and held aloft a furled umbrella with a six-inch sharply pointed steel tip. Working her way closer to Tom, she began waving gaily to him. Tom saw her and blew a kiss. She tried to leap closer but three of Billy's thugs barred her way. Bouncing up and down, she shouted her address but Tom was already out of earshot.

On the far side of the room, a Union soldier found a space for himself out of the jostling crowd. Ant, from his vantage point on the stairs, noticed the man stealthily draw a long-barreled revolver from his holster. The loud music and boisterous cheers drown out Ant's warning shout to Billy. The soldier, perhaps twenty feet from Ant, waited with the gun held down out of sight. Tom's procession wheeled about and slowly pushed through the mass of revelers, who threw their own Mardi Gras trinkets so the room drizzled flying fluff. Using their hats as buckets, men scooped dollar bills out of the air and women clambered up their backs for a better advantage. Ant shoved his way down the stairs and burrowed toward the soldier.

Tom, about thirty feet away, riding above the mass of happy people, was partly obscured by the blizzard of hats and waving hands and grasping women and confetti. Billy, trying to look everywhere at once, missed the soldier. The man shifted slightly towards the front door and stood on tiptoes for a clearer view of Tom.

Doubling over to better bore through the jam of bodies, Ant saw the grey pant legs of the Confederate uniform ten feet ahead. Someone stepped on his foot; to keep from falling, Ant grabbed a belt. The startled man looked down and saw a green-face leprechaun scrambling at his crotch. He reached down and seized Ant under the shoulders and threw him into the air. Billy saw the figure erupt from the throng, arms windmilling, bounce off a head and again thrown high.

The crowd around the action pushed and shoved, either to get away or to join the game. Ant grabbed a fistful of a woman's hair to prevent from going airborne again. She shrieked. Men turned to her rescue, which caused a boil of chaos that slammed the soldier into the wall. Ant, kicking and flailing like a drowning man, desperately tried to stay on the people's shoulders so not to be trampled. The mass of partygoers heaved to and fro, like a rugby scrum, as they caught and tossed Ant over their heads. Billy recognized Ant's voice, even distorted by the high-pitched scream of terror, and ordered four of Tom's men to his rescue. In the crush, the soldier lost his grip on the six-shooter and slipped out the front door unnoticed.

Tom completed his victory circuit and the evening soared to licentious, prurient, salacious, libidinous, rancorous, pornographic, bawdy heights. The details became repetitious; but good things are worth repeating. As dawn broke, Ant, battered and bruised, clothes torn, found Bellocq.

"Did you get good pictures?"

"You pay me now," replied the photographer in his heavily French accented English.

Ant laid an envelop in his hand. Bellocq expertly thumbed the bills. "More. I worked extra to rush the prints."

"I'm good for it, Ernest. You know that." Ant quickly fanned through the photos.

The peacock man had been plucked in every way the ingenious whores could act out.

He wasn't Young Jack.

Chapter 4.

The next day, Henry and MayAnn came to inspect the Arlington's temporary quarters above Tom's saloon. As they moved through the bare rooms swept clean, but still with the feel of a disused storage space, MayAnn acted like she didn't know Ant, who stood with Billy.

"We'll need all new furnishings," Henry said. If Ant hadn't personally known Henry, he'd have kept a barge pole distance so intimidating his angry face, even when not wearing his ridiculous doorman's costume. "Beds, wallpaper, love seats, something for MayAnn to set up for drinks."

"Tom will see to it," Billy replied.

Henry paced the rooms, measuring them with long strides. "Carpets. And a piano for Tony."

Billy stationed himself in front of Henry, forcing him to stand still. "You know about the girl being murdered?"

"Josie told me."

"Any idea who might have done it? Any of the girls jealous of her? Some man seeking a bonus thrill?"

"I saw her with Young Jack Bohomme before the fire. He was sweet on her. More than usual."

"Was Old Jack one of Josie's clients, too?" Billy asked. Old Jack was the Young's father.

"Naw, too old—now," Henry answered.

It wasn't unusual for the city's gay blades—and their fathers—to visit the whorehouses. It was damn near a tradition. Let the men blow off steam, the wives reasoned so we won't be burned by our husband's passion. And sometimes jealousy flared between father and son over a pretty young lady.

MayAnn slipped away into another room.

"The girl, Laura, had Young Jack hooked and was reeling him in," Henry said.

"Did he take her upstairs the night of the fire?"

"I can't say for sure. When Ant told me about the fire, I ran for the kitchen. MayAnn! Come here and tell Billy what you know about the night of the fire."

MayAnn edged up to the doorway but kept her distance, striking the pose of a demur servant, eyes down and hands clasped behind her back.

"Yes, sir, Miss Laura was talking with Mr. Bohomme when I gave the alarm about the fire. I ran upstairs to warn people and some of the other girls ran up, too, to save what they could. Miss Laura came upstairs. No, sir, I can't rightly say if Mr. Bohomme was with her. Everything was happening so fast. Sure is a pity about Miss Laura. She was such a pretty thing."

Her hips swayed back and forth, like a nervous tick; her right foot edged back, as if she couldn't wait to pivot and run.

"Come to think of it," Ant said, "I *did* see Young Jack go up the stairs when I was warning Henry about the fire. Didn't you see *Young Jack* upstairs with the murdered girl, MayAnn?" emphasizing the name to let her know that he had identified her sucker.

"No, sir, can't rightly say that I did." The "sir" hurt, made him feel like a stranger. "I escorted Miss Laura to her room and then went pounding on doors to warn the others. I didn't see him up there."

"We need to talk to this Young Jack, Billy," Ant said. "He might know something."

"We'll get to him. Right now, we need to get Josie back in business." Ant could tell Billy wasn't happy about Tom's helping hand. His whole posture was an expression of someone approaching a stinking outhouse.

"Tell her to give us a week," Billy told Henry.

Henry nodded and made for the door with MayAnn sheltering behind his broad back. Billy and Ant followed them down to the saloon and reported to Tom.

"Take care of what Henry needs, will you, Billy. And, Ant, I want you to organize the funeral parade for the girl, once we find out her real identity and where to send the body. Josie will want that courtesy shown."

The task made Ant double happy; there was only one musician he wanted for the funeral parade—Buddy Bolden, MayAnn's friend and neighbor and the hottest musician in New Orleans. Ant admired the man tremendously for his music—defiant and brave and out of bounds, a cornet player who broke the rules and grew stronger for it. As a musician himself, an amateur but an enthusiastic horn player, Ant dreamt of playing with Buddy, if only in a funeral parade. He didn't know Buddy, but MayAnn could arrange an introduction.

MayAnn lived uptown with her mother in an area known as the Battlefield, where Buddy also lived. Ant crossed Canal Street, the dividing line between downtown and uptown, white and black Storyville. He felt an edge of unease as he walked down South Rampart Street past stores selling furniture and clothing and secondhand goods. After all, he looked, walked and talked like a white man. He had taken up the trombone to have a calling card so to march in the uptown funeral parades and give himself some legitimacy in MayAnn's community—and his, too, he supposed. According to the wisdom preached in the Negroes' homes and barbershops, the white man was everything evil and then some. Why put your faith in that boogey man? they asked. If you couldn't eat in the same restaurant with the white man, break bread with him with common respect, then don't get close enough so he can kick you—again.

As he approached a corner grocery store, Negroes stepped off the sidewalk and crossed to the other side, not obsequiously as might have been the case in a white neighborhood but as a show of distain toward the arrogant white man who disrespected their privacy. Ant nodded politely, hoping a civil attitude would keep him safe. He didn't expect to find MayAnn in the grocery store, where a man could purchase a loaf of bread and a pail of beer, have a roll of the dice and a quick roll in the hay before heading off home. But, he might get lucky and so avoid going to her house and encountering her mother.

Inside the store, the men's hostile stares spun him on his heels and right back out the door. He continued on to Perdido Street, the center of the Battlefield, four blocks of bars and juke joints and whorehouses and dancehalls. The roofs of the one- and two-story pine board ramshackles, blanched gray by years of sun, extended over the wooden sidewalks to give an Old West flavor. The saloons were the offices and playpens of a corps of professional criminals -- Drop a Sack, Ratty Kate, Grand Jury, Hit'em Quick, Baggage Car Shorty and Whiskey Head. They preyed on the black and white workingmen who came to listen to music and drink and whore, hardened men who spent their days on the levees or on railroad gangs, in the cotton mills and cane fields, men who carried guns and knives and were willing to fight at the slightest excuse.

Being daytime, only occasional piano music came from the nearly empty saloons. Ant knew she wouldn't be in any of those places, unless Buddy Bolden was playing. MayAnn was a big fan of Buddy's. No matter how rough and tough the bar or dancehall, she went to every one of his gigs. Ant walked on to blocks of houses that echoed slave times, long and narrow like the plantations laid out in strips fronting the river where the steamboat tied up to load cotton bales. At one house, painted happy Caribbean pastels, gaudy tropical flowers crowded the small front yard. Ant knew first-hand that cisterns in the backyards captured rainwater for washing and drinking. There might be a vegetable patch away from the outhouse in the far corner. Puffs of dust rose from his footsteps as he crossed the streets. In the wet season, people set down bricks and laid planks on them to form a tenuous bridge across the mud. Poor people in need often took the planks for firewood.

A wizened Negress washing down her front stoop, the sinews of her forearms corded from fieldwork, watched him the way a hen watches a fox. Ant tipped his hat but she kept guard. A few men lounged on the street corners waiting out daytime. Most of the neighborhood men, recent European immigrants and poor Americans, black and white, would be breaking their backs at work and glad for the opportunity.

Rounding the corner onto First Street, he passed the Hebrew cemetery. At a Catholic cemetery, he'd automatically cross himself and doffed his hat and said "Howdy" in hope the gesture would mollify any lurking spirits. MayAnn's house was a block down and to the left. The shotgun house -- so called because if you fired a shotgun from the front door the pellets would travel straight down the central hall, unimpeded, and out the back door—was painted ocean blue with sunflower yellow trim.

Ant hoped she'd see him there on the sidewalk dressed up nice with hat in hand and come out. Otherwise, he'd have to endure her mother, whom he'd known all his life as Aunt Helayna.

The drapes twitched and moments later the front door swung open. "Antoine!" Aunt Helayna popped out with a welcoming smile. "Come on in! It's been so long."

"Yes, mam'." Ant kissed her on both cheeks, hat clutched against his chest. She crushed the hat with her embrace.

"Come in for some cool lemonade and catch me up on yourself and your mama. I haven't seen her for ages. We should all go for a picnic out by Lake Pontchartrain one fine Sunday to listen to the music." Aunt Helayna held him at arm's length for a good look. "My, my, what a handsome man you've become, Antoine! MayAnn will be glad to see you, I'm sure."

Ant pushed out the crown of his hat as Aunt Helayna towed him into the house. "MayAnn, you'll never guess who's come callin'!" she shouted.

Aunt Helayna wasn't really his aunt but she and Ant's mother went way back so the families had a kinship. When his mother improved her station by becoming the octoroon mistress to his father, she put a little cool between herself and Aunt Helayna, who was three shades darker than high yellow. Ant's father set her up in a nice house in the Fabourg Marigny district, Front o' Town, along the river where the Creole millionaire Bernard de Marigny had divided his family's plantation into smaller plots and sold them to aspiring Creole and mixed families. Aunt Helayna stayed in Back o' Town, the black section, and had MayAnn by a carpenter, who decided to take his trade elsewhere before he had set eyes on his daughter. Still, the two women would get together, especially as young mothers. Ant first knew MayAnn as a childhood playmate. Back then, neither of them took note of her milk chocolate color or his linen-white skin.

Aunt Helayna steered him into the front room, her "good" parlor for receiving guests. "Just make yourself comfortable, Antoine," leading him to the beaten down sofa. She always promoted him as the cat's meow, a good catch, someone with one foot in the white world of possibilities. She hoped that Ant's coattails would be MayAnn's magic carpet into a better life, if only they'd start canoodling. She had no idea of their real relationship. MayAnn was, in her mother's eyes, a church girl, despite her nocturnal hours, which MayAnn explained away by her job as a serving maid in an entertainment palace. But, she never saw MayAnn dancing to Buddy Bolden's hot music, when her sweet daughter turned a waltz into bump-n-grind with a simple shake of her hips.

When MayAnn slipped into the room, her mother stood and patted the sofa cushion next to him. "You sit here, MayAnn, and keep Antoine company while I fetch refreshments."

MayAnn eased down at the opposite end of the sofa. "What are you doing here, Antoine?" she said in an angry whisper.

"I need a favor."

"If you do me the favor to stand aside while I get on with my life."

Ant could never put into words, or song, or any expression that makes sense, what held him to MayAnn. What attracts a man to faith? A yearning for salvation, some sense of peace and balance in the world. Why is a man drawn to beauty? Because such rarity is a treasure. When MayAnn and Ant first got together, after they'd grown out of being childhood friends, they could boil water with the mere thought of each other. One day they'd been kids playing in the sandbox and the next day, so it seemed, Ant looked up and saw an entirely new MayAnn. The skinny girl had acquired womanly curves. He did a double take of disbelief, as if a magician had turned a weed into a rose right before his eyes. Where did she come from? Not only was her body different, but her smile, the way she cocked her head and how she stood with her shoulders held high, not high and back so to thrust herself, not that kind of proud but a pride still veiled in shyness. That was the MayAnn who jumped out from behind a tree and ambushed him.

Ant, a few years older, already had the weasel of desire in his pants. But he had no opportunities until her smile broke into a laugh and she dipped her head, chin down so to peek up with coy eyes and her arms squeezed her sides to bolster her titties into a swell at the scoop of her dress and she waggled her shoulders back and forth. That began nearly three years of heated *heated* exchange, to put a delicate point on it.

Youthful hubba-hubba had a lot to do with their sneaking around and grabbing each other in dark corners, in stolen beds, down by the big mossy cypress, wherever and whenever they

61

could. But that was just the surface roil. Down deep, down where the really big love catfish lives, they swam with each other there, too. They'd slip under the forth of passion and sink down holding hands into the cool calmness of knowing they'd always breath life into the other, always rescue the other no matter how murky life became.

Were they in love? Ant certainly thought so. But his later experience with MayAnn confirmed that love, like magic, depends on sleight of hand and mystery for its excitement. Lovers, like magicians, use deception to create the illusion that the improbable is possible.

Now, sitting on the sofa with MayAnn, Ant again posed to himself the question, Which of us is the better magician?

MayAnn's womanly instinct knew that Ant mistook salvation for love. He was neither black nor white, according to both camps, no matter which side the law put him on. Not being Irish or French or Spanish or American or African or any of that, he had no place, or people. The stark truth without roses about Ant: he claimed her so he wouldn't be a speck of nothing. His love for her was fueled by fear that he didn't otherwise exist, at least if any meaningful way. She knew that. Behind his placid good-friend facade, she saw a twitch of what? Sadness that could decay into hatred? But Ant's feelings weren't her first concern, not now. When he leaned toward her like a girlfriend about to share an intimate secret, she was already thinking how to slap him down again.

Ant tapped her on the knee. "I need to find out the dead girl's real identity. She was murdered, you know. Someone strangled her and hoped that the fire would cover his crime. We need her real family name so she can be sent home. Tom Anderson asked me to organize a proper celebration for her, as soon as we know her name and where to send the body. I want Buddy Bolden to get a band together and I need you to introduce me."

Aunt Helayna bustled into the room with a tray of lemonade and corncakes. "Isn't it nice to see Antoine again," she chirped. "I was just telling him that we should all go for a picnic out by the lake. Wouldn't that be nice, MayAnn?" They got through a glass of lemonade talking about the weather and how the Social Aid Society was starting a funeral fund so poor families could send loved ones off in style and did Ant have a young lady? asked Aunt Helayna.

"No, no." He set down his empty glass without looking at MayAnn.

"Well, sometimes the best filly is found in the nearest pasture," Aunt Helayna said and rapidly blinked her eyelashes.

MayAnn suddenly stood.

"What about the introduction to Buddy?" Ant asked before she got away.

"He lives around the corner. Just knock on his door." She was already moving across the room. "Tell him you're a friend of mine. That's all you'll need." And she was gone.

After stumbling through some more small talk so not to offend Aunt Helayna, Ant excused himself.

"You give my regards to your mother," she called after him. "I'd sure like to see her again. You come visit anytime, Antoine. You're always welcome."

He walked the half block to First Street and turned left and damn near ran into a man smelling of sweet van-van water as he came out his door with a cornet tucked under his right arm. Ant recognized Buddy Bolden from all the times he'd seen him on the bandstand.

"Mr. Bolden." He started to stammer out an apology but turned it into an introduction. "My name's Antoine, known as Ant on the street, and I'm a huge admirer of yours. Can't say I completely understand your music but I like it." Buddy nodded and smiled but his face said, How can this white man understand the first thing about my music? That's like a fish saying it understands what it's like being a bird.

"I play the trombone myself, funeral parade quality, you know, just an amateur but with a love for it," Ant rushed on. "I don't hold myself out to be in the same league as you but I love to play."

"Always glad to meet another musician," Buddy said, his attitude softening enough to give the nervous little man in front of him the benefit of doubt. The brown derby at a jaunty angle over his forehead gave the impression that he'd break out a joke right there on the spot. The top buttons of his starched yellow shirt were undone to better show the red undershirt. Having a quality red undershirt was an important style point. Buddy knew that women liked to see a spot of red, the heart's flag; told them where to aim. A lime green suspender drooped off his right shoulder as if to say to his female admirers, Damn, we ain't even met yet and already I'm droppin' drawers for you. His shiny blue pants were sausage tight, so tight he couldn't fasten the top button.

"I'm a friend of your neighbor," Ant gestured back up the street. "MayAnn. Maybe you know her? She comes to hear you play whenever you pick up the horn."

"MayAnn." Buddy's face brightened. "She can dance as if raising the dead." The promise of laughter riding the words had Ant standing nearly on tiptoes waiting to be carried away by Buddy's good spirit. "Yessiree, MayAnn's a good friend of mine." He must have seen Ant's surprise because he quickly added, "In a neighborly way, you understand. I'm playing at Lincoln Park on Monday nights. You and MayAnn come on down. It'll be a hot time."

Then he did an about face and moseyed down the banquette shooting the agate, shoulders doing a roll and a wave, hips skipping without throwing the feet out of rhythm. The strut moved from top to bottom and bottom to top, passing itself right at the manhood, the switching yard, in a continuous flow. He held his left hand down at his side, index finger jutting out as if to better snag any pretty trout coming by. The agate done right was like water rippling over a small rapid, fluid and sparkly. Ant felt a tweak of envy as he watched Buddy move down the street, pushing a wave of attitude in front of him. A man could get close to a woman if she liked the way he shot the agate. No wonder Buddy had a reputation as a ladies' man, Ant marveled and followed just see what might happen.

People called out, "Hey, Buddy!" and he'd wave back with a flash of pearlies. On every block young women leaned out of windows and called out, "You play for me, Buddy? You come by and give me your song?" and laughed as if already being tickled, and he'd respond with a few notes on his cornet.

A ragman made his way down the street, pushing his cart and chanting, "Any rags/ any rags/ain't you got/ any rags!" and followed the verse up with a riff on his penny whistle. Buddy halted in his tracks and Ant damn near ran into him. "Listen to that." He raised his horn to his lips and mimicked the tune. The ragman heard him and answered with a bit of an Irish jig. Buddy laughed and blew back some Scott Joplin ragtime.

"Here, my man," Buddy pulled a folded, pressed handkerchief from his pocket. "My rag for your song," and handed it to the man.

Further on, at a street market, Buddy stopped dead in his tracks. "Now listen to this orchestra." He stood attentively as if in church. One fellow called out WA-TER-MEL-ONS in a long baritone trombone glide. APA-APPLES/APA-APPLES/EAT MY APPLES came a raucous scat, the apple man hitting hard bright notes as if playing a horn. "Listen to that! Listen to that!" Buddy cried. From another wagon came OKRABEANSONIONSPOTATOES in a fast run-on, the sound more important than understanding the words. He raised his horn straight up and his derby toppled off as he played the rhythm back to the okra peddler, to the watermelon vendor and to the apple man. He mixed their jingles up, chopping them to pieces and putting them back together again as

APA-ME-LONS-APA-APA-OKRABEANSONIONS-PO-TA-TO-WA-TER. The men laughed and everyone on the street laughed and Buddy waved his horn and shouted out, "Callin' all my children!"

He picked up his derby and brushed it off. "Where you going, wha's your name again…Ant?"

"Where *you're* going?" Ant answered. "That's where the show is"

"Yeah, well, I'm going down to the Red Onion but I'm not sure you'd enjoy that show."

Ant had once seen a man killed in the Red Onion. A big man minding his own business, tired after a day on the docks, was standing next a small man, inconsequential, not a person you'd notice. The bar was crowded and the big man needed some room. He moved to the right, accidentally stepping on the small man's foot. Without a word, the small man set down his beer mug, pulled out his pistol and shot his neighbor through the lung.

When he followed Buddy through the front door, the stench in the Red Onion nearly sent Ant reeling back into the street: beer and rot-gut rye, the acid odor of fear, bodies reeking from weeks, if not months, of sweat and grime, the musk of women who hadn't bothered to wash off the rut of the last two, three, four men. In the twilight interior, he made out the dusky hags who, too old and ugly to work the beds, caught clients up in rounds of Cotch, three-handed Spanish poker, Faro, Blackjack, Chuck-a-luck and Brag at the gaming tables. Ant nodded to the woman running the poker table, a pale scar the length of her cheek. He had been there when she fumbled a card coming off the bottom of the deck. The razor-carrying player was offended not because she tried to cheat him but because he had caught her.

He edged between two men bent over their drinks at the bar. One man's shirt was worn to ribbons; the other had a big gun strapped across his chest Mexican bandit style. Along the bar, heavy-muscled men with cotton dust in their hair from unloading bales threw back shots without talking. The place was serious as a pine coffin, stripped down, sullen as every poor-paying working day.

Buddy threaded the room to a corner table where men sat playing cards. He stopped next to a big man with three days' worth of grizzle and an unkempt nest of hair.

"Mr. Harris." Buddy stood like a respectful servant, hat in hand.

Aaron Harris looked like a wild pig rooting in a field on a dark and stormy night. His head was buried in his card hand and his shoulders hunched up in a mound of muscle and sheaves of his coarse thick hair stuck up every which way. His very presence brewed up menace and danger. Harris was New Orleans' most notorious killer, with thirteen notches on his gun, including one each for his brother and sister. The police were afraid to touch him because he vowed never to be taken alive. Coppers didn't want to die trying: every time Harris set out to kill someone, he succeeded.

Ant was surprised to see Buddy trying to strike up a conversation with Harris. He knew the criminal and his card partners: Chicken Dick, with the shoulders and arms of a heavyweight; Sheep Eye, who murdered people to impress Harris; Raw Head, a chain gang veteran; Rough Nuts, who specialized in women; and Toodlum and Toodloo, brothers who had mastered the art of dirty fighting and invented some moves of their own. Part of Ant's job was to keep track of those hogs in case Tom ever needed their talent.

Three more hands were dealt. Buddy cleared his throat but they went on throwing down cards and pushing money back and forth. To get their attention, he cleared his throat again and launched into a funny story.

"You been on those balloon rides, the hot air one down at Lincoln Park? Don't, I'm tellin' you. Savin' your life with advice and no payback for my pocket. Free on me." None of the hogs looked up from their cards. "MayAnn boarded one of those balloons and got lost in the sky. You know MayAnn, don't you? Always at the dances and concerts in Lincoln Park."

On hearing MayAnn's name, Ant edged closer down the bar. How did Buddy know that? MayAnn had never mentioned anything about a balloon ride.

"She sat down on one of those things. You know the Frenchman doesn't have a proper standup basket like the ones in the white man's park. On the Frenchman's balloon, you gotta sit down, like on a kiddies' swing seat. A wooden board not much wider'n a kid's ass." Buddy paused but still Harris and his men paid him no mind.

"They fill this big rubber thing with smoke, you see. Rubber like you make raincoats out of. I never understood why it didn't melt with all that hot smoke pumpin' it up. Black smoke, too, not clean hot air like those white folks have. That's what makes the balloon puff up and lift off. Only 'bout twenty feet tall, maybe half that wide. Doesn't look like much but it does the job. So this balloon gets erect, so to speak, and MayAnn is strapped into the seat by this harness, and the Frenchman and his boys let go of the rope and up goes MayAnn."

Buddy pulled the cornet from under his arm and let off some going up notes. Still not a glance from the card players.

"Now, when MayAnn wanted to come down, she's supposed to pull this rope to open a flap in the top of the balloon and let out smoke. The Frenchmen and his boys followed in a wagon to gather her up. Only she didn't come down."

Buddy played some getaway music in a skipping-on-clouds tempo. He let the notes drift off, fade like a balloon coming down; then he heard a new idea and set off a shattering blast, as if a big gust of wind had come through him. This time the hogs looked up.

Now he had their attention, Buddy switched into a popular honky-tonk. But somewhere in the song he forgot what he was playing, or just let it slip away. Unexpected pauses followed by sharp up-tempo beats faded into a mournful slide. Then notes of a hymn, something for the soul, linked itself to a sad blues, like a hen complaining to the rooster he wasn't coming round to her backdoor anymore and the music grew sassy and perky like a woman talking back. Then Buddy was inside a steam engine, his horn telling how the steam sounds and feels. A man at the bar turned, recognizing the chug-a-chug rhythm of long hours feeding coal into a steamship's boiler.

At the bar, Ant slipped sideways to give room for his neighbor's shoulders as the man twitched faster and faster in the rhythmic swing. Just as the man broke into a shuffle to go with his shoulders, Buddy left him for the sound of a wagon rumbling by on cobblestones. The bumble-rumble gaining speed set the card dealers' heads bobbing to the faint echo of African drums pounding. Without warning, Buddy paused and slid the notes into the sorrow of a mother remembering the death of her child. Men at the bar who had started snapping their fingers looked confused, then embarrassed and their grins slid down with Buddy's music. Man, he put a black cloth over the whole place. Even Aaron Harris, the hand of death himself, seemed subdued by those soulful blues.

Just as he was about to wring out tears, Buddy hit bright notes, the trilling of a bird, brilliant sunshine that set everyone to smiling again and when he added the funky smell of Mississippi mud it brought on clapping and knee slapping. Ant smiled at the sound of happy children splashing in water. Happy children reminded Buddy of the death of his little sister and he collapsed the music into a dirge, long notes stretched out as a sob. But, this being New Orleans, sadness and happiness hold hands and dance to the same music. People got on their feet and started a second line snaking between the tables and dipping and bowing and clapping and singing a few "Praise Be's."

Buddy opened his eyes and seemed surprised to find himself in the Red Onion.

"That wasn't honky-tonk or ragtime or a stomp," Aaron Harris said. "What the hell was that?"

"Buddy Bolden," the cornet player answered.

"What happened to MayAnn?" Rough Nuts, a woman hater, wanted to know.

"She got so scared up there with all of New Orleans under her feet that she forgot to pull the vent rope. The Frenchman lost track of her in the dark. She was last seen floating out towards the Gulf. The Frenchman was sure someone would see the balloon in a day or two, but a week went by and not a word. Everybody thought she was dead for sure."

Buddy paused, milking the drama. "Then," he launched into jubilation church music, "then I see her come flouncing down the street. 'MayAnn, where you been?' I was so happy I cried, right there in full daylight where anybody could see. I didn't care. Seems she came down near a fisherman's camp out in the bayou. He had to tend to his lines and couldn't bring her in till he had his catch. She stayed out in the camp and cooked and fished and did all I know not."

She never told Ant about any fisherman's camp. She spent a week in the bayou alone with a man in his camp! he thought with alarm. Where did she sleep? Did she do him any favors? How many men were in that camp? How big a fool am I willing to be?

Aaron Harris folded his hand and, not looking at Buddy, said, "'Sweet Lovin'' cut you pretty bad. You ought to get yourself some players to go along with your horn."

Harris and his boys went back to playing cards. Buddy bobbed his head and backed away.

Outside, Ant asked, "What the hell were you doing in there?"

"Me and the band got in a cuttin' war with Charlie 'Sweet Lovin'' Galloway's band last night. I came to hear the verdict. You see, Harris and his pals prided themselves as music critics. They can make or break an uptown musician's career, even though they don't know anything about music. They know what they like and if they don't like you or your attitude or your music, they put the word out and you can't find work uptown, the only place us Negro musicians can find a gig in all of New Orleans.

"I got my fans. Charlie has his. Sassy Willie and Boom Bang, all these bands are battlin' to survive by stealing fans from each other. Whoever can pull the most people into a place gets the gig. So we go up against each other in cuttin' wars to prove who is the hottest, baddest, blastinest band that can outblow, outplay, out-invent and rip out the guts of the competition. It's a sporting event, you know. Each neighborhood 'round here has its homegrown favorite band. It's a matter of pride, like the Lincoln Park Giants beating all the other teams. If you get cut by a rival, outplayed, then you lose prestige and fans and paydays. So this here," he jerked his thumb back at the Red Onion, "was a career consultation. Either I get a better band or the hogs will cut me out."

Taking all this in, still reeling from the Red Onion, Ant forgot to tell Buddy about the funeral parade.

Chapter 5.

The next day, Chief of Police Hennessy entered Tom's saloon wearing his uniform of full authority, trousers with razor-sharp creases, the blue serge coat a stiff shield against mockery. His appearance caused heads to turn at the unexpected sight; coppers never came into Storyville after dark. In fact, they ventured into Tom's territory only to collect the graft, bags of cash left on the whorehouse doorsteps every Monday morning after the weekend rush. The individual bags were collectively dumped into U.S. mailbags to better haul back to the station. The coppers came in pairs, for safety and also because it took two men to carry the canvas mailbags heavy with coins and bills.

But here was Hennessy, alone, striding imperiously to the back corner where Tom sat at the "Town Hall" table, where he conducted the mayoral duties of running Storyville: settling disputes, dispensing favors and retributions, setting fees and bribes.

"You're under investigation," Hennessy boomed so everyone heard that the New Orleans chief of police lorded over Storyville's mayor.

Tom didn't to stand or even look at the chief, but rather continued talking to the man next to him. The fellow, a laborer judging by his worn and dirty clothes, sat with head down and shoulders bowed. Tom patted him on the back and spoke quietly so no one could overhear. The man nodded several times, then looked at Tom with a shine of hope on his face.

"Mr. Anderson..." Hennessy stood at the table, chest swelled, hands clasped behind his back, rocking from heel to toe.

Without looking at the interruption, Tom held up his hand for silence. Turning his back on Hennessy, Tom slipped the dejected man at the table folded bills and then helped him to his feet. Impulsively, the man tried to kiss Tom's hand but Tom turned the gesture into a handshake.

"Now then." Tom sat down. "What do we owe this visit from our esteemed chief of police?" He beamed at Hennessy the way one imagines a cat regards a bowl of cream. Many men would cower before a figure of authority looming over them, but Tom sat at ease, a teacher with a wayward student before his desk.

"This is an official police inquiry into your responsibility, if not direct involvement, in the murder of a woman in one of your establishments."

"If you are referring to unfortunate death of the woman in Josie's Arlington, then you must speak with Josie. It's my understanding that she died in the fire. You should be looking for the arsonist murderer who set the blaze. We, the citizens of New Orleans, pay your salary. That makes you *our* public servant. In return for your princely monthly stipend, we expect, indeed demand, protection and guaranteed safety from the criminals who violate the innocent and hardworking people of this city." Tom's good-natured smile never hinted at satire or ridicule.

Hennessy placed his knuckles on the table and leaned forward in what he hoped to be a show of intimidation. "I'm the law, Anderson, whatever you think. Believe me, I'll run your smug ass out of town."

"Our shining knight, or should I say black knight." Tom rose to his feet, his cordiality replaced by the hard glare of a boxer entering the ring. "Give it your best shot, you fucking potato eater." Still, his voice carried no heat, no growl, which made his calm confidence all the more freighted with menace. "My men," he nodded to the room in general, "will escort you safely out of district, being that the streets are fraught with danger."

Tom walked away and disappeared down the corridor leading to his office.

Hennessy straightened and turned to face the room. Forty men stared back with hostility. Looking straight ahead, he marched out of the saloon. As he left, Billy, standing at the end of the bar, signaled for two men to follow the chief as protectors against assault or insults. Then he joined Tom in his office.

"I warned you about Hennessy," Billy said.

"He's a dog with no bite," Tom replied from behind his desk.

"Maybe. But he'll use the murder to harass you. It'll be his legitimate excuse to come poking around in your business."

"Then we need to find the killer and offer him up, in one form or another. Maybe a copper was one of Josie's customers that night. Maybe this cop, a man accustom to violence and to treating prostitutes as worthless low life, maybe he over exercised his privilege of the badge. We should ask Henry if he recognized any law enforcement officers, on or off duty, at the Arlington that night. Even if he didn't, who's to dispute the possibility."

A loud banging on the office door caused Billy to spin around.

"What!" Tom called out.

"Come quick," came the answer.

Billy opened the door and a waiter from the 101 Ranch Dance Hall barged in.

"They're aimin' to kill Tubby Phillips!"

"Who is?" Tom demanded.

"The Parker brothers. Tubby's walked right into an ambush. It's goin' down right now."

Weeks before, members of Lefty Louie's New York gang had arrived in New Orleans. Apparently Lefty Louie, a Mafia chieftain, had gotten the worst of a murderous turf war in the Tenderloin. A rival criminal gang, Irish according to reports, went on a rampage to consolidate their territory, with the silent assistance of their brothers in the police force. Like the Matrangas, Lefty Louie had ties to the Sicilian Mafia, so, in family solidarity, Charles and Tony gave the survivors refuge while they regrouped. That didn't seem a direct threat to Tom. But the suspicious sale of the Tuxedo saloon on Franklin Street, a block behind Tom's Arlington, should have been a red flag.

All property sales the in Storyville filtered through Tom. If he didn't approve, it didn't happen. But the Tuxedo changed hands on the sly to the unknown Parker brothers. Soon afterward, when workmen started taking the place apart, Tom had sent Ant around to ask questions.

"Tearing it down or building it up?" Ant queried the barkeep, covering his beer to keep the dust out.

"New owners are adding a dance hall," the bartender replied. "Foreigners." He kept busy wiping dust-covered glasses. "New Yorkers. Call themselves Harry and Charlie Parker."

The next day Ant returned to get more information. A new man with a well-waxed mustache and shaven head stitched by a fresh scar over the right ear stood behind the bar, wiping down beer mugs the way some men pull a gun—a warning to keep your distance.

"What happened to the other barkeep?"

"Wyaskn?" he replied in a thick New York accent.

"So I can understand what he's saying."

The new bartender studiously polished a mug, holding the handle to easily swing the sturdy glass like a mallet. A second man entered from the dance hall under construction adjacent to the bar. At the slight nod from the barkeep toward Ant, the man, wearing a black suit jacket streaked with white dust and a fedora squashed down on his head, came over. "He's askn questions," the bartender muttered.

"I'm Charlie Parker. I own this place with my brother." He didn't offer to shake hands. "You the welcoming committee or just nosey?"

Being a Southerner, Ant wasn't accustom to blunt confrontation. And, being a Southerner, he took a long moment to assess the rude man before him. Charlie Parker was a good four inches taller than Ant, which didn't make him a tall man. But his wiry frame made him seem bigger, the way a buggy whip possesses danger greater than its size. His thin face covered with a dark three-day stubble was a taunt at Ant, the sneer curling his lips, the chin jutted forward in a challenge. Ant felt the familiar flutter in his gut whenever he faced a physical threat. He wasn't a weakling but he was realistic about his physical prowess; a slight man who never did a day of hard work, or a pushup, Ant considered prudence as an act of courage. Yet, he wasn't a coward.

"In the South, when we welcome someone, we do so graciously," Ant replied. Then he pointedly took a step back. "Being new in town, I thought you might need tips on hospitality, the way a cur needs the burs brushed out of its coat." He said this in an extra syrupy melodious drawl, a Southern art form of appearing benign while slipping poison into the mint julep.

Charlie Parker, not sure if he had been insulted or not, edged closer to Ant to get right in his face. "Whatda want?"

Ant stood his ground, even move his right foot forward so it was toe-to-toe with Parker's scruffy boot. "Yesterday I came in and had a beer with a friendly barkeep. But he isn't here today."

"We fired everybody and hired our friends." Charlie Parker, feeling the nudge of Ant's foot, gave a hard push back, knocking Ant's foot to the side.

Ant, recognizing the declaration of war for what it was, nodded and left. Back in Tom's office, he reported, "The Parkers are not friendly competition."

Within days, the Parkers were offering jobs back to certain employees and aggressively raiding other establishments for their best men. Being a waiter in New Orleans was an honorable well-paying job, a guaranteed a dollar-a-day plus tips, earning eight to ten dollars a shift, enough to raise a family. The Parker brothers were offering a different deal: tips only and no daily guarantee but opportunities for double pay if the "waiter" was willing to take on "extra duties."

"They're recruiting a gang," Ant warned Tom.

The offer was too good for some to turn down but most of the seasoned waiters stuck with their employers. So the Parkers took the New York approach: their tips-waiters made extra tips by beating up the wage-waiters who refused to join the "union." The two camps engaged in bloody after-hours battles, one gang or the other armed with clubs and baseball bats waiting in alleys to ambush their rivals. The Parkers' gang, better trained in ruthlessness by the New York thugs, inflicted so much damage Storyville establishments were chronically shorthanded, their waiters laid up with busted arms and heads.

As Tom and Billy ran to the Tuxedo, the 101 waiter filled them in: earlier in the evening, Tubby's headwaiter's arm was broken by Gyp the Blood, the New Yorkers' "headwaiter." Tubby, the owner of the 101 Ranch and Tom's good friend, had stormed into the Tuxedo to demand retribution.

When Tom and Billy charged into the saloon, Tubby was whacking the bar top with a three-foot stave as he shouted, "Come outside, you spineless weasel! I'll kick your ass from bayou to gulf and back."

Harry Parker stood with his hands out of sight below the bar. He flinched, but didn't back away with each WHACK.

The half a dozen or so men in the bar fanned out of the line of fire. Tom and Billy separated so not to be an easy two-in-one shot. On the fifth WHACK, the stave nearly taking off Parker's shirt buttons, Tom called for Tubby to stop.

"These guys are hurting my people and costing me money, Tom." Tubby didn't take his murderous stare off Parker. "I don't see you doing anything about it."

"Tubby, come on outside." Tom spoke casually as if asking his friend to join him for a drink. Instead of a thudding whack with his stave, Tubby tapped the bar to show he had heard.

"Yeah, *Tubby*," Harry Parker put a disdainful jeer in his voice, "why don't you lay down and get your belly scratched. You're nothing but a cowardly dog."

Tubby lunged as if jabbed in the ass by a white-hot spike, grabbed Harry Parker by the shirtfront and started to haul him over the zinc-topped bar. Parker fought back, punching Tubby on the head, but Tubby lifted him like a man unloading a bag of grain from a wagon.

Gyp the Blood, one of the men who fanned out from the bar, stepped behind Tubby, drew his gun and, before anyone could react, fired a bullet into Tubby's back. The force spun Tubby around to face his assailant. He reached for Gyp, his eyes blank from surprise, the front of his shirt dark with blood. Gyp sidestepped and aimed a headshot.

It seemed simultaneous, the blood spraying from Tubby's head and the side of Gyp's head being blown away.

Harry Parker raised a shotgun from under the bar but Billy, with his gun already in hand, the barrel smoking from the bullet that killed Gyp, had the advantage. His second shot sent Parker flying into the double row of liquor bottles lining the bar mirror. Hearing the gunfire, Charlie Parker ran in from the dance hall, gun drawn. Billy drilled him with a clean headshot.

Expecting other New York thugs to start a gunfight, Billy hit the floor. But the only sound was men running for the exit. Billy pushed up and saw Tom kneeling beside dead Tubby, head bowed as if in prayer. From the dancehall came the trampling sound of men rushing towards the bar.

"Let's go, Tom. We don't want Hennessy to find you here—dead or alive."

Back in his office, Tom paced from desk to sofa, where Billy sat. "The Matrangas are behind this, Billy, as sure as the devil lives in Hell. Now this is personal, killing Tubby and bringing a shooting war into Storyville."

"That's what I'm afraid of," Billy replied, "that they will take it very personally we killed a couple of their allies. They might feel obliged to come after you with all guns blazing. Honor and family and Sicilian pride and all that. If Storyville becomes a shooting gallery, Hennessy will seize the opportunity to restore order under his law. Then we'll see how much of a toothless dog he is."

Tom slumped in his chair behind his desk, chin resting on his chest.

Finally he said, "Is Ant around?"

"I saw him out there earlier." Billy gestured towards the bar. "Go fetch him."

A few minutes later Billy returned with Ant.

"Billy told you about the sudden problem," Tom asked.

Ant nodded.

"I want you to talk to the Matrangas. Caution them to keep their guns in their pockets. Neither of us want to hand Hennessy a victory by starting blazing conflict."

Alarm bells went off went off in Ant's head. Why did Tom assume that he could walk in and talk to the Matrangas? But he calmly replied, "I'll see about how to make contact."

Tom turned to Billy. "Why don't you take a vacation down on the Gulf for a few days? When this cools down, we'll make plans to resolve this whole mess."

Later that night, as Ant walked down the dock to the Matrangas' office, he seriously considered waving a white flag. Even had his handkerchief in hand in case he was challenged.

When he poked his head in the office door, cautiously, Charles and Tony glowered back at him. They were wearing black armbands of mourning.

"Why'd you go start this war?" Tony demanded. "Why'd you kill the Parker brothers? They were family, *donnicciola*." By his tone, Ant knew the word wasn't an endearment. "Lefty Louie's lieutenants. How are we going to explain? You've put us in a very bad situation, made us look bad to the family, *faccia di merda*," which Ant understood to loosely mean "shit of death." "We're sorry you did this to us, Ant." Tony hung his head, shaking it slowly back and forth.

"The ant ran up the elephant's back leg and now you're about to be buried in shit." Charles's voice wasn't heavy with threat but rather indifferent to whether Ant lived or died.

Ant started to make amends but Charles held up a weary hand. "It won't do any good, *leccaculo*." Ant knew enough Italian street slang to understand "bootlicker."

They all fell silent, eyes downcast, Charles leaning forward with elbows on knees; Tony propped against a wall, hands jammed in his pockets as he studied his brogans; Ant sneaking nervous glances at Charles, then Tony, back to Charles. The brothers were somber, as if in a morgue waiting for the body of a loved one to be brought in for identification.

At last Charles sat up with a sorrowful sigh. "New York Sicilians, they're mutations. The cross breeding, it's like … what's it like, Tony?"

"A bull and a crocodile." Tony didn't raise his head from looking at his feet. "A creature that neither God nor the Devil can reason with."

"So you see what we're faced with, Ant?" Charles asked softly. "Lefty Louie entrusted us with the lives of his people, his brothers. And we failed him. When he hears about this, well…" He shrugged in resignation, as if his death warrant had been signed without appeal.

Tony pushed away from the wall, hands in his pockets, and bent down to Ant's ear. "Mr. Tom Anderson, how's he going to fix this? Or how're we going to fix him, eh?"

Ant shrank back, catching a whiff of the garlic Tony had eaten recently. "Mr. Anderson sincerely regrets your lost. Although he had nothing to do with the unfortunate event, he's willing to contribute to the widows' welfare – and whatever cause you deem suitable. Mr. Anderson points out that if you and he start attacking each other, weakening each other, then Chief of Police Hennessy might be emboldened to seize Storyville and the docks."

Charles snorted. "He doesn't have the balls or the guns to chase us off the docks."

"But he can get big political guns aimed at you." Ant spoke boldly to show that he wasn't a mere dumb messenger. "He and the city's mayor can get the good citizens in a snit about criminal gangs endangering the city and the virtue of the decent women. They can make it so you won't win, even if you do beat Mr. Anderson."

"Lefty Louie, he'll need revenge," Tony said, still at Ant's side.

But Ant knew Lefty Louie was only a playing chip. The Matrangas had the largest Mafia gang in the country. Lefty Louie had gotten his butt kicked in New York. What was he going to do? Come to New Orleans and stomp around in the Matrangas' territory? Step on their toes?

"What shall I tell Mr. Anderson?"

"Tell him we're considering our options, like any prudent businessmen."

As Ant stood to leave, Tony put his arm around his shoulder. "You're a fine *magnaccia*," a despicable term for a pimp, he said and reached down and squeezed Ant's balls, not hard enough to double him over but enough to stop him in his tracks. Tony laughed and let go. "You be careful around elephants, Ant."

For a couple days after the Parker brothers killing, the very air in Storyville seemed permeated with highly explosive vapors that one spark would ignite. Everyone, all of New Orleans, knew, told by screaming headlines, of the sensational killings at the Tuxedo. The entire city gathered, at least figuratively, at Storyville's boundaries, a crowd at the ropes of a boxing ring, waiting for the two contenders to bloody each other. Billy left town on his enforced vacation, so it fell to Ant, temporarily promoted to Tom's right-hand man, to spread the word among the cadres of Tom's "men-in-waiting" to arm themselves and patrol the streets.

Chief Hennessy doubled the foot patrols in Storyville and threatened to fire any copper who backed down to Tom's men. Accompanied by twenty patrolmen, the chief brazenly walked down Basin to Tom's saloon, where he loudly announced that he wanted Tom and Billy for questioning. Tom's guards barred the door. Hennessy blustered that *he* was the law and threatened to arrest anyone who interfered with his duties. Tom's men, who outnumbered the police, stood in a solid front, rifles and shotguns held upright and revolvers in plain sight.

The tense standoff eased a bit when Tom instructed that Hennessy be admitted, alone. In their private meeting, Tom pointed out that he was an innocent bystander to the shootout and that Billy acted to prevent the killing of Tubby.

"Witnesses say that Billy killed three men," countered Hennessy. "I need to take his statement."

"He's not in town," Tom replied.

"Make him in town or I'll issue an arrest warrant," Hennessy threatened.

Later that day, Hennessy released a statement that Mr. Anderson and Mr. Struve were cooperating with the police in the ongoing investigation.

Billy came back from his vacation and did answer Hennessy's questions. "You should talk with the Matrangas," he told the chief. "They can tell you about the Parkers."

Instead, Hennessy withdrew all police presence from Storyville to give Anderson and the Matrangas every opportunity to decimate each other, leaving Storyville to him.

But after a week it became clear that an unspoken truce had settled over Storyville and business returned to normal, for the time being. A new colorful sign announcing Josie's reopening above Tom's saloon was posted prominently at the foot of the outside stairs leading up the whorehouse. Henry the Magnificent made a final inspection of the Josie's now furnished temporary Arlington. As Billy and Ant accompanied him down the stairs, Billy handing Henry the key, they met Young Jack starting up the stairs. Henry excused himself and squeezed past.

"Here's our murderer," Ant whispered to Billy, "returned to the scene of the crime. Let's solve this problem for Tom right now."

Young Jack looked at Billy and Ant standing on the step above him, his face beaming with expectation. "Do you know where Laura is? She got out of the fire all right, didn't she?"

Billy gave Ant an 'Okay, Mr. Sheriff, make him spill his guts' look.

As the moments passed while Ant tried to devise a plan, Young Jack's expression lost its sunny outlook and clouded over. "Laura *is* here," he flat stated.

Billy glanced at Ant, who opened his mouth, but no words came.

Young Jack started to push his way up the stairs, but Billy put a staying hand on his chest. "They're not open for business until tonight."

"No matter. She'll see me now."

Billy didn't remove his hand but his touch had the softness of condolence rather than the firmness of resistance. "You don't know, do you?"

"What?"

"She died in the fire."

Young Jack stared slack-jawed, still not fully comprehending. He leaned forward as if to see the practical joke underlying Billy's somber face. "You mean Laura?" His voice so plaintive even Ant bowed his head in embarrassment.

"Oh," Young Jack managed, the faint sigh sounding like his last breath. He sagged against the building and ever so slowly collapsed on the steps.

Billy watched with arms folded across his chest, a former police reporter analyzing testimony. Then he reached down and helped Young Jack to his feet. "Come on then. You need a drink."

Young Jack wobbled like a sailor on shore leave, seemingly not knowing or caring where he was, not bothering to lift his head. He would've stopped entirely and sunk onto the dirt street if Billy and Ant hadn't supported him. They got him around the block to a bar on Franklin, which seemed about as far as he was capable of walking.

"This grief is just a show," Ant whispered to Billy. "Get him good and drunk and he'll start bragging about his perfect murder."

Then, I'll haul his ass to MayAnn and make him confess on his knees before her, Ant told himself. Show him to be a pitiful and broken man on the end of my leash. Is this what you want? I'll shout at her. You want to sleep with this gutted jackal? You want to have children by this sniveling coward, this spineless weakling? I'll kick him until he collapses at my feet. Then maybe I'll shoot him in the head.

Billy and Ant propped Young Jack at the bar and set a bottle of whiskey before him. Billy measured out three shots. Don't bother with a glass, Ant wanted to shout. Pour it straight down his gullet. Billy waited respectfully for Young Jack to lift his glass.

"May her soul rest in peace," Billy intoned.

Young Jack fumbled his drink and spilled a good portion on his way to wetting his lips.

He's overdoing the act, this heartbreak for a whore, thought Ant. Trying to make pity his alibi. I loathed him for the cheap trick.

"Who are you?" Young Jack asked, turning to Billy.

"Friends of Josie's." Billy introduced Ant. "We're trying to do right by the girl. Trying to find out who killed her."

"Killed her?" Young Jack's head snapped up. He was alert, eyes focused, no longer slobbering tears. "I thought she died in the fire."

"Crushed larynx," Ant injected. "You know how hard it is to crush someone's larynx? Takes lots of anger and brute strength to do that."

Billy gave Ant a swift look to 'Back off.' "No one knows the young lady's real name," he said. "We can't notify her people, can't lay her properly to rest. Who was she, Jack?"

Jack stared at Billy, blinking to clear his vision. Only his elbows on the bar kept him from falling down. Billy reached out to steady him, a brotherly gesture. To the casual observer, they were two friends, one helping the other maintain balance.

"Who was she, Jack?"

"My love," he sobbed, theatrically falling on Billy's shoulder. Billy gave him an awkward pat on the back and Ant applauded vigorously, asking for an encore. When the mockery registered, Young Jack spun to him. "Stop that!"

Ant gave two more slow resounding claps and said, in equally slow measure, "I saw you go up the stairs. During the fire. Go after her. And when you came back down, she was dead."

"Are you accusing me?" Young Jack cried, turning on Ant, fists balled.

"I'm stating a fact."

"You're stating a lie!" he shouted, his spittle hitting on Ant's cheek.

"You deny what I saw with my own two eyes? You're accusing me of being a liar?"

"I couldn't get up the stairs with all those men charging down."

"Do you want to send an apology to her parents?" Billy asked, taking Young Jack by the shoulders and turning him back to the bar.

"Apology?"

"For what you did."

"I didn't make her a whore. I was trying to save her."

"But your father wouldn't let you, would he?" Billy leaned in close, pinning Young Jack tight against the bar, his voice suddenly mean and aggressive. "Couldn't have a whore in the family. Gave you a choice, did he? Love or money?"

Young Jack shrugged out of Billy's grasp, using his elbows to gain space and, with surprising speed and aggressiveness, swung a short jab to Billy's jaw. Billy caught the fist in mid-air. For a moment, the two locked in combat; Young Jack quivering, Billy solid as a rock. Gradually, as if winning an arm-wrestling contest, Billy pushed Young Jack's hand to the bar. "Nobody need know, Jack," Billy murmured, his face just inches from his suspect's. "We can't prove anything. Don't want to. But her spirit is wandering the earth. She won't settle down and rest in peace until the truth is known, even if it's just between you and me."

Young Jack pulled his hand free. "Blackmail?" The word fierce with hatred. "Is that your game?"

"No, my boy," Billy now soothing as a priest. "Just trying to put things in proper order."

"I love her!" Young Jack cried out. "She was sweet and kind and funny…"

Then Billy drove in the spike. "A wild woman in bed. All those other men plugging her night after night. You hated that, didn't you, Jack? Other men's jissum soiling your girl. Had to put an end to it one way or the other?"

Young Jack threw his shot of whiskey in Billy's face. As Billy backed away wiping his stinging eyes, the enraged

Young Jack whipped his knife from its sheath on his belt. Ant saw the blade in slow motion, six inches long, the tip with a slight upward curve the better to rip the wound jagged as the knife came out. Billy glimpsed, or at least sensed, the attack and grabbed Young Jack's arm. The men on either side of them calmly went on drinking or staring in the bar's mirror or chatting, assuming that Billy was preventing a friend from falling down.

"Easy, boy. You don't want to get yourself killed," Billy murmured.

Ant stepped in and bent back Young Jack's wrist until he released the knife.

Unexpectedly, he crumpled. "I love her." Billy changed his grip to an embrace. "We would have been so happy… We were going to elope, money be damned."

"There, there, my boy." Billy turned him to the bar. "We'll find the killer, won't we? You'll help us, won't you? I know you will."

"Who was she, Jack?" Ant wanted a name to wave in front of MayAnn.

"Joan," he whispered. "Joan Stipton from Memphis."

Billy released Young Jack, all the fight out of him now. Ant kept the knife, a trophy to show MayAnn to prove he was her champion. Billy poured a round as if there was something to celebrate, but they slugged back the shot without joy.

When they left Young Jack a half bottle down, Billy asked, "What do you think? He didn't confess."

"He laid down a false trail of the bereaved. We're supposed to feel sorry for him," Ant replied with the heat of conviction.

"Come on, let's go tell Tom the girl's name," Billy said.

Chapter 6.

Tom stood behind his desk wearing a crisp white shirt and a well-pressed dark suit, indicating he'd be holding court for those who wanted to renew a liquor license or complain that a beat copper was trying to squeeze them for another nickel or get permission to hold illegal boxing matches in their saloon's back room.

When he heard the dead girl's name, he said, "Josie will rest easier the sooner the body is shipped back to the family. Billy, will you see to the undertaker? And Ant, you got a marching band to accompany the girl's body to the train station tomorrow? I'll pay well and there'll be the usual free drinks after."

Ant remembered that he'd forgotten to mention the gig to Buddy. "Ah, yes, I saw a man about that. I'm seeing him today to settle the details."

He hightailed to uptown to find Buddy. On the way, he planned to turn this trinket of a task into a golden nugget of a favor by handing Buddy a payday from the hands of the Mayor of Storyville. You're being noticed, Buddy, he rehearsed. You know who Tom Anderson is, don't you? This might lead to something big, like maybe a gig playing in his Arlington Café. Of course, Ant knew, and so did Buddy, such an invitation was as unlikely as the streets being paved with silver, given the Jim Crow segregation laws. But Buddy would owe him a favor. If he sat in with Buddy's band, well, Young Jack couldn't match that. MayAnn would swoon.

Ant crossed Canal and headed toward First Street, where Buddy lived with his mother. Seeing no one on the sidewalk, he practiced rolling the agate. White men, which Ant considered himself, don't have a natural instinct for putting on the agate. They tend to use their minds to conjure up expression; the Negroes use their bodies. For a white man to strut the agate is to risk ridicule and Ant did feel a bit foolish trying to roll his hips, which came out as a sashay. Remembering Buddy, he hooked his thumb in his pant's pocket and stuck out his index finger to troll for any sweet thing that tripped by. For a half block, he tried to twist his shoulders with the gyrations of his hips so they were beat and counter-beat. Hearing a snicker, he glanced over his shoulder and saw three black kids prancing along behind like fairy princesses.

They didn't know whether to run or not, and Ant didn't know whether to laugh or fake anger. He grinned and they grinned and Ant, properly chagrined, behaved the rest of the way to Buddy's. His mother, a tidy lady with a few gray hairs and tired eyes, answered the knock and said no, Buddy wasn't home. He's probably down at Louis's barbershop. The way she held her shoulders square gave the impression that she'd refuse to buckle no matter how heavy the burdens life heaped on her. Buddy's father had died when he was six years old, leaving his widow with three small children. The hardship still rode on her. A man had once courted her, Manuel Hall, a neighbor and cook at Nelson Quirk's Café on Royal Street. The only fruit of the courtship was Buddy getting his first horn lessons from Hall.

"Thank you, ma'm." Ant gave a bow of respect. "I appreciate your help."

Ant had, in the past, now and then, drop into Louis's barbershop for a shave and an earful. It was one of his listening posts, although at first he had trouble being accepted. The Negroes who hung out there considered him as a white man. But he had told them, I'm a Jim Crow white man. Louis liked

Storyville

Ant so the others were tolerant, if grudgingly so. Being light-skinned, Louis empathized with Ant's unease over trying to find a place in two conflicting worlds. Louis had enough tinge to be part of the Negro community, shading that Ant lacked.

Louis's barbershop was a pulpit, front porch, electioneering stump, card-n-checker clubhouse, gossip mill, job exchange for musicians and general refuge from the world of women. Cuss words and dirty jokes and disrespect for the fairer sex were standard fare, along with baseball and horseracing and politics.

Pushing open the door, Ant entered a garden in full bloom. Rose and gardenia and lavender and lilac scents oozed from the bottles of van-van water and hair tonics lined up along the shelf. Two barber chairs faced a larger mirror and behind them five plain chairs for waiting customers. The red-and-white diamond-shaped floor tiles were spotless; every time a head was shaved, Louis's underling swiftly swept up the cuttings. The proprietor looked, as usual, immaculate in his starched white doctor's jacket and shiny oiled hair. He sported a thin mustache, no more than a line but enough to give him a hint of debonair. With his light brown skin and thin nose and high cheekbones and expressive eyes that made women lean back to invite a kiss, he was the handsomest man—no, the most beautiful—Ant had ever seen.

Stropping a straightedge, he flashed Ant a smile. Only one chair was occupied, the bulky figure covered by a barber's cloth, the head wrapped in hot towels. Louis waved the razor. "Have a seat, Ant, tell me something wonderful, even it's a lie."

My love life is terrific, Ant said in his head. My prospects are better than those of the owner of a gold mine. My heart is so happy that it flies like a bird.

Instead, he asked, "Buddy been around?"

Louis was Buddy's best friend and his former drinking pal. Those two invented the color red just to paint the town.

When Louis tied the knot he put down his brush, but he still knew Buddy's schedule better than the cornet player himself.

"Not today." Louis lathered up a bowl of shaving foam. "But I expect him. He hasn't told me yet about the meeting with the hogs."

Speaking of the devil, before Ant could fill Louis in, Buddy came bustling through the door, cornet under his arm. He chucked his derby onto the hat rack and eased down in the empty chair next to the customer hidden under the hot towel. "How's you, Trombone Man? Bring your horn?" he said to Ant. "Always carry your horn."

"How'd it go?" Louis asked.

"Lived to see another day, but I've gotta do something better. Those hogs are ready to write my death certificate in my own blood." Buddy stretched out in the chair, clutching his cornet against his chest.

"Heard there's a woman looking for your blood, too," mumbled the hot towel.

"Did I hear something talkin', or just a bad rumor?" Buddy perked up and looked around with exaggerated head swings, his eyes big as full moons.

"Hattie she got an axe and she aiming to chop off your little man's head." The towel's plump belly pumped up and down in a laugh. "Hear tell she gonna hunt you down and demand child support."

Buddy popped out of the barber's chair like a flipped penny. "I think I hear jealousy having a wet dream." He stood stock-still, hand cocked behind an ear as if better to hear a faint cry in the wind. "Is that you, Jealousy? Or is that dried up Pickett say'n his prayer again? You know that prayer? 'Would Buddy Bolden be so kind as to give me the ugly ones he doesn't want because I'm poor as a priest.' What?" He leaned forward, listening intently. "Say what? If I can't hear the prayer, I can't answer it."

"How many women you got now, sweetback man?" Pickett's deep bass rolled out from under the towel. "You got enough fingers on one hand to count them?"

"I don't have enough fingers and toes to count'em. There's not enough beans in a five-gallon jar to keep track."

"Name me all the pretty ones you got, horn man. Start at the beginning of the alphabet, you know, at 'A', then go to 'B', if you know your letters that far."

Louis stopped stropping the straightedge to better watch Buddy. His friend had a long fuse, but once lit burned quickly to the dynamite.

Only Pickett's nostrils were clear of the towel soaking his whiskers. Buddy held a forefinger up in front of Pickett as if he might jam it up the man's broad nose. Instead, he started flicking his fingers open into a fan.

"Anita, Anna, Arabell, Antonia, Austina, Agnes, Abella, Alright. You always hunted after Alright, didn't you, hound dog Pickett? And right you should because she is more than all right. But you'll need more than that thin slat of yours to fence her in."

"You don't have them any more," Pickett laughed. "I hate to tell you, Buddy, but you ain't got any of the beautiful women any more."

Buddy moved around beside Louis, who shifted the straightedge out of Buddy's reach. "Where'd they go? Who took'em?" Buddy leaned down close as if to smell Pickett through the towel.

"You don't have them any more because I took'em." Pickett raised an arm to push him back. "You need some mouthwash, Buddy. No wonder the only thing you got to kiss is that horn."

Buddy made a quick move to grab the straightedge but Louis whipped the blade behind his back. "No, no, this isn't my dead man razor."

"Give it to me. Then you'll have a dead man to shave."

Louis whipped the barbering cloth off his customer. "Pickett, you best be going. Come back another time for your shave." He quickly unwrapped the towel from Pickett's moon face, eyes closed, a big toothy grin.

Pickett opened his eyes. "Been nice talk'n to y'all, Buddy." He sat up, a big fleshy man with sloping shoulders. "You better look out for Hattie. She say Charlie Jr. be missin' his daddy and she means to find him."

Pickett shoved out of the barber's chair and ambled to the door. Louis stood in front of Buddy, blocking his way until the door shut.

"I saw Charlie Jr. last week," Buddy called after him. "He knows who his daddy is. My mother wants to be grandma too bad to let that pass."

"Sit down, Buddy. Let me give you a shave."

Ant waited until the agitated Buddy calmed down under a hot towel before speaking up. "Got an offer for you, Buddy." and told him Tom Anderson was looking for a funeral band. "Pays cash. And free booze."

Buddy said something under the towel and Louis translated. "Give me the time and place and he'll be there with the boys."

The next morning the musicians gathered at Louis's barbershop to await the Grand Marshall, who'd lead them to the funeral home. Buddy had called together his core band but there were another ten or twelve musicians, including Ant, who stood next to Joe Oliver, a big fellow a bit slow on his feet. Ant had seen him at other parades and on occasion playing in some honky tonk or on a street corner. He was powerful but not gifted; didn't seem to understand the music but rather played like he was trying to remember which valve to press to get a particular note.

A neighborhood kid, Little Louie, also known as Sachelmouth because his gape was so big he could stuff in a whole chicken and have room for dessert, hung on the fringe.

He was always so damn eager with his like-me puppy grin and his big wide eyes pleading with folks to take him in. His horn looked like a Confederate bugle crumpled by a cannonball. But that didn't stop him from jumping into any opportunity to play, be it a spasm band or a marching band or just joining in a second line. He stood to the side like a kid who doesn't want to be noticed and chased off. Buddy gave him a wink and Little Louie damn near jumped out of his skin he was so happy.

Louis 'Big Eye' Nelson sauntered up, "howdy you, howdy do" to everyone, open and friendly as always. Big Eye, who had perfectly normal eyes, was a Creole, one of the few who associated with Negro musicians. On the whole, the trained Creole musicians considered themselves superior to the "unschooled" black musicians, who were mostly self-taught. They dismissed musicians like Buddy, who could neither read nor write music, and derided his "made up" music. But Big Eye had a deep appreciation for black musicians and Buddy in particular.

"You have to play real hard when you play for Negroes," he once told Ant after they formed a friendship from playing in funeral parades and the occasional jam. "You got to go some if you want to avoid their criticism. You got to come up their mark. If you do, you get that drive. See, these hot people, they play like they're *killing* themselves. With Buddy, it's like he's trying to figure out what he, and his people, are supposed to do with their freedom. And us, too, with these Jim Crow laws. He plays what a man does with his life when it's finally his."

Ant had a particular fondness for Big Eye because, although a much better horn man, clarinet, he always made Ant feel part of the musician's tribe. Ant once asked him how he got the moniker "Big Eye."

"My mother said that I always got 'big eyes' whenever I heard music as a toddler. The name stuck."

Ant wedged himself between Joe Oliver and Big Eye so whatever mistakes he made would be covered up by their superior playing. And he hoped that the mere association with the two musicians might impress Buddy. Ant didn't fool himself that he was in their or Buddy's class. Buddy played music like trying to puzzle out some great mystery, or create one of his own; Ant played the trombone because he could make jokes on it.

As the musicians stood in front of Louis's barbershop, sweat ran down Ant's back under his Sunday best suit, worn in honor of the occasion but also in anticipation of seeing MayAnn. Everyone dressed in proper black, though the mood wasn't somber. This was a payday with free drinks. Buddy seemed in particular high gear, talking so fast that you couldn't make sense of it, his smile a flashing mirror, and then, as if remembering the occasion, he'd slow down, try to rein in his fun and his face would go blank and a bit stiff. Then he'd laugh to himself and raise his horn, wetting his lips and his fingers ready to tap out the tune. Just when Ant thought he'd start to play, the Grand Marshall emerged from the barbershop.

Louis had done himself up in more glory than a war hero. He wore a shako made of beaver fur with a plume of white feathers, heron by the look of them, rising above the crown. Broad epaulets with a long fringe of gold rode the shoulders of his black shimmering silk jacket. Rows of ribbons, not war ribbons but strips of satin, covered nearly his whole left side. Every time he moved, the ribbons jigged. You'd think that he had fought in every battle ever waged from Luficer against the Lord up to and including the Union and the Confederacy. A wide band of red-purple, dark as a plum, ran down the deep-sea blue trouser legs. When he high stepped, the white spats gave the impression of doves lifting off.

"My man! My man!" Buddy whooped. "You put the Lord of Resurrection to shame!"

As the barber twirled around, the gold fringe and the colorful satin ribbons winked and waved. The musicians laughed in appreciation; his outfit put them in the spirit of joyful sorrow appropriate for a New Orleans funeral.

Louis moved to the middle of La Salle Street and the band formed up behind him. Raising his four-foot staff with a cockscomb of ribbons, he pumped it three times to give the beat to a sprightly marching song. The ad hoc band set off at a crisp military pace, Louis tilting his head back so far he saw only sky and arched his back to get his knees waist high.

The neighbors lined the street as soon as they heard the music coming. They didn't jump around and be carnival-time foolish but stood respectfully and waved and grinned. It was a time to "Cry at birth, rejoice at death," as the saying goes. Cry at birth because then you took on the earthly burdens that plagued you for the rest of your life. Rejoice at death because you had been released from those burdens and sent to your heavenly reward.

The funeral parlor was a half a mile away in the Garden District, a neighborhood of mostly Americans already several rungs up the ladder. That's where Tom lived; perhaps he felt Josie and the small group of mourners would feel comfortable among their own kind. At the undertakers, the band stayed in formation as the coffin was carried out to the horse-drawn hearse. Josie and Tom fell in behind the hearse and Josie, in billows of rustling black satin, took Tom's arm. Henry stood with them, looking like a dignified preacher in the well-cut black suit and Bible in one hand. Then came Young Jack, gloomy and downcast as an Edger Allan Poe caricature, dabbing his eyes with an oversized handkerchief. Billy stood at his elbow, despite having groused to Ant that Young Jack requested he be a pallbearer "like I'm his best man at the bride's funeral."

MayAnn slipped in at the rear as Louis raised his staff and the musicians hit the first low chord of "What a Friend We Have in Jesus."

The funeral procession trudged off to South Station to load the coffin on a Memphis-bound train. People stopped on the sidewalks and men removed their hats and women stood with bowed heads in respect for the solemn passage to St. Peter's Pearly Gates. Drays and hacks and wagons pulled aside, clearing the street, the drivers sitting patiently on their high seats with reins loose in their hands. The stillness that overcame the route seemed to make the torpid humidity sit heavier on everyone's shoulders. A waterfall of perspiration came down Buddy's shiny black forehead. Louis was so solemn as to be somnambulistic -- step, pause, feet together, step, pause, feet together -- his foot-dragging pace a symbolic reluctance to take the inevitable move toward the grave.

The cortege arrived at South Station weary and ready for a cold beer. Tom and Billy, with Young Jack and Henry, lifted the coffin from the hearse onto a baggage cart. Young Jack, a stylish cloak of black satin draped around his shoulders, hugged the coffin and cried out, "I only know we loved in vain. I only feel..." a sobbing gasp, "Farewell...Farewell." Ant recognized the snatch of Byron, although couldn't remember the poem. After an awkward moment, Billy led Young Jack away by an arm around his shoulders. Josie, Tom and Henry followed to offer condolences, with MayAnn last in line. Ant stepped in behind her as if to pay his respects, too.

Young Jack received each brief handshake and murmured words with his head bowed. MayAnn shuffled forward in an attitude of prayer with Ant nearly on her hem, rehearsing in his mind what he'd say. Certainly not, Sorry for your loss, but more like, If you so much as look at MayAnn, lay a finger on her, I'll feed you to a bayou gator bit by bit—while you're still alive.

She stood before Young Jack without moving. He waited for her to offer a hand and when she didn't, lifted his eyes a fraction. MayAnn remained motionless, her face obscured by the veil of her hat. As if to encourage her to get on with it, he tilted slightly forward. She extended her hand in a black-laced glove and he offered his fingertips. Instead of a perfunctory shake, MayAnn gripped his hand to hold him in place and said, "I'll be everything you want. You will be happy."

Young Jack cocked his head, as if to say, Did I hear right? He tried to pull his hand away but she kept a firm grip. With her free hand, she lifted her veil. He studied her with confusion before a flicker of recognition, and then, indignation flashed in his eyes. What was this impertinent parlor maid suggesting, of all the times and places? Before the angry rebuke formed into words, MayAnn released him, gave a slight curtsey and withdrew.

Ant, his heart roiled to a bubbling pot over MayAnn's words, didn't say anything to Young Jack, barely touched his hand. But Young Jack gripped him by the elbow. "Thank you for coming. You and me and Billy will bring this killer to justice." Ant twisted away, looking over the heads for MayAnn but she had disappeared. Just as he was about to dash down the street looking for her, Louis shot his staff in the air, the signal for the band to form up; the snare drummer rolled a measured march beat and the bass drum boomed three times to get the musicians on the mark. Louis called out, "Now is the time to give thanks and party," and the horns blared out the first notes of "Didn't He Ramble." Instantly, the funereal march became a fast-paced parade of snappy happy music as he led the swinging, high-stepping musicians to the designated saloon for free booze, courtesy of Tom Anderson.

The second line celebration party, uninvited but expected, fell in alongside. The ruffians, street kids and unemployed men carried concealed baseball bats, axe handles, knives and brass knuckles in anticipation of the expected battle royal with a rival second line for the free drinks at the saloon.

The second-line leader, a smart-alecky type, twirled a broomstick to mock the Louis's staff of authority and shouted, "Didn't he ramble?" and his rag-tag gang shouted back, "He rambled/rambled all around/in and out the town/didn't he ramble/he rambled/he rambled till the butcher cut him down." In a show to out dance, out prance, out strut the musicians, the second line gang lifted their knees so high they nearly hit themselves in the chin. Their arms shot up as if sending lightning bolts back to heaven. They leapt, legs pumping as if walking on air, and spun in full circles. Not to be outdone, Louis executed fancy steps like a show horse going through its dressage routine. He reared back, face straight up to the sky, elbows pumping like a quail gaining air speed.

And then Buddy let loose.

He might as well have lowered a battle spear and charged the interlopers, so brutal was his attack. The first blasting notes disjointed their prance as if they had tripped on barbed wire and came up crippled. They ran into a wall of sound, stopped cold, as Buddy and the rest of the band wailed on them. Joe Oliver threw big fat water balloons of notes bouncing off their heads as if he had figured out, for the first time, why he played the trumpet. Big Eye broke rank and ran at the second line leader with his clarinet raised as a cudgel. At the last second he put the horn in his mouth and hit high notes designed to pierce the man's eardrums.

The second line faltered; their feet stumbled; they couldn't hear their own rhythm through the assault.

Louis glanced over at the second-line leader and signaled to turn left at the corner. As the second line wheeled around the corner, the funeral band quick-stepped to the right, suddenly free of the barnacle. The second line, seeing it had been tricked, did a mad scramble to get back alongside for the final block to the saloon. Waiting in an alley, another second line suddenly charged out to battle for their place at the bar, the yelling, shoving, punching, baseball-bat-swinging men wrestling each other to the ground. The invited musicians sprinted for the safety of the saloon and barred the door.

"Don't you love New Orleans!" Buddy slapped Ant on the back and laughed as if he had earned from the Lord guaranteed forgiveness for all his sins past, present and future.

But all Ant heard was, *I'm what you want. You will be happy,* MayAnn's words to Young Jack chiseled onto the tombstone of his love. He liked the pathos of the sentiment. It made him feel important and doomed, and the more whiskey he drank, the nobler he envisioned myself.

"Buddy," he said, leaning on his trombone to keep himself upright, "Buddy, I'm down in the St. James graveyard of broken hearts." All around the other musicians hoisted their mugs and laughed and argued in merriment that teetered on the brink of a brawl.

Buddy, a good six inches taller, looked down at Ant and said, "No, you're in the graveyard of the blues. No better place to be."

"Why's'at? Why's a man lie down with the blues?" Ant hung on to Buddy's shoulder to hoist himself closer to his hero's ear. "A woman, disappointment, no money, no future?"

"You know what a bluesman is?" Buddy gave Ant the look of a man who knows all shades of blues, from robin egg blue to purple black bruise. "It's the person who, feelin' so low, lies down the train track waiting for the locomotive but, when the engine comes, he gets up off the track and goes back to livin' life. You got a woman problem, Ant? Or just a whiskey headache problem that seems like a woman pounding on you, wanting to turn your pocket and your soul inside out? Either way, you just keep walkin' and playin' the music."

"MayAnn...." The effort of explaining MayAnn seized up Ant's alcohol-ladled brain. "I'm a better magician than she is. I know the more deceptive tricks of love."

"MayAnn?" Buddy held him upright, nearly lifted Ant up to his height so to better hear. "You got a MayAnn problem?"

"I can break her heart with a snap of my fingers," Ant tried to snap my fingers but they slid noiselessly off each other, "and then fix her up. Magic."

Apparently only the word magic made sense to Buddy. "You preparing a magic act? Like sawing MayAnn in two?"

That hadn't occurred to Ant but why not? Give Young Jack half and keep half for himself. But then he'd still be a halfling. Ant laughed aloud at the absurdity of carrying around only half of MayAnn. Which half? His giggles made him a silly drunk.

"You've either got to drink more or sleep it off," Buddy said good-naturedly.

"I want to be on stage." Ant gripped Buddy's arm to keep from falling down.

"Like a magic opening act? In vaudeville?"

"No, Buddy, I want to play in your band. You owe me a favor now," Ant gestured to the barroom, "for this. I want to sit in with your band. What did MayAnn do in that fisherman's camp?"

"What camp?"

"Hot air balloon."

It took Buddy a moment to link the two, then he laughed. "That's a good story and all true. MayAnn, she's a spunky girl. I like her." He bumped into a little hole of sadness. "I like her the way I would have liked my little sister if she had lived." Then he bumped out of that hole on a laugh. "MayAnn riding up in that hot air balloon and never coming down. Scared shitless the whole time going up but never thinking to pull that vent rope. Says a lot about her."

"What happened with the fisherman?"

"Nothing happened with the fisherman, at least that she mentioned."

Well, maybe, Ant thought, but MayAnn always looks for adventure. He got out of bar while he could still walk and made his way to Tom's saloon, the distance made longer by two sideways steps for each one forward. The first thing he saw when entering the saloon was Young Jack sitting next to Billy at the back table. Ant held his arm out straight, cocked a finger and fired his hand gun right at Young Jack's head, who didn't fall over. Ant assumed that he must have missed. But

Billy apparently heard the bullet whiz by because he glanced up and called out, "Ant, come here. Jack has it all figured out."

Billy and Young Jack had obviously been holding their own wake, judging from their red eyes and hanging heads. "Tell him, Jack," slurred Billy. "Go on, tell him what you figured out."

"I know who killed my love."

"And who might that be?"

"That slut of a parlor maid."

Ant wanted to laugh at the joke and at the same time throttle Young Jack for his blasphemy. "And how did you come to that conclusion—in a revelation?"

"She'd been throwing me looks. You know how when a woman wants to send you a particular message, you know that kind of message I mean, when she gives an invitation without saying a word. An engraved invitation in the way she stands or licks her lips or puts come hither in her eyes. That's what that parlor maid has been sending me. And now, at the funeral of my beloved, she propositioned me."

"And why would she be doing that? To seduce *you*?"

Young Jack puffed his chest as if to say, Well, look at me. Handsome, dashing, rich and good teeth. "Because she was trying to earn a tip on the side, trying to divert some business her way. What else?"

"So she murdered your whore?"

"She wasn't my whore! She was my love. Besides, it can't be anyone else. She took Joan upstairs and when she came down, she left a dead girl behind. Just like you said."

"Well, that's a pretty compelling case, wouldn't you agree, Billy? A seasoned police reporter like yourself knows a solid case when you hear one." Billy didn't miss the smirk in Ant's tone, and neither did Young Jack.

"There's no one else," he shouted in protest.

"Only you and all those other men upstairs at the time."

"I wasn't upstairs. And all those other men were occupied." Young Jack rose unsteadily to his feet. "I'll prove it to you. I'll get her confession, in blood if I have to." He squared himself until his feet were solid on the ground and then staggered out the door.

Billy and Ant watched him go. "What you think he'll do?" Ant asked.

"Sleep it off."

"What about him, Billy? What does he do, other than grand gestures?"

"He plays about, a dilettante who writes poetry and spends his father's money chasing women and gambling."

"Poetry?"

"He and some other flops publish a 'literary magazine' for their rubbish, mostly about changing the world through love and revolution on a dewy morning."

"You ever publish in their magazine?"

"Apparently I don't do dewy mornings well enough," Billy said with contempt, which didn't completely mask his disappointment.

"What are we going to do about him?"

"Dawdle." Billy was in his lizard mood, lounging to soak up energy. He could be like that, near dormant, then suddenly snap into action and snatch a fly out of the air. "We can't go barging into Old Jack's house and accuse his kid of murder. And we can't mete out justice to Young Jack without some plausible evidence."

"I talked to MayAnn. She can put Young Jack upstairs at the time of the murder."

That was nudging the truth a bit off center, Ant admitted to himself, but, hey, in love and war...

"That's no proof he committed the murder."

"But it's the head of a nail to pound on."

Billy showed no sign of wanting to pick up a hammer. He tilted his chair against the wall, flicking a toothpick from one corner to his mouth to the other. A commotion at the front door brought the chair thumping to the floor as Sam Exnicio barged into the saloon snorting like a jabbed bull. The owner of the New Waldorf saloon resembled a bull, too, with his head of dark shaggy hair and heavy rounded shoulders.

"Goddamnit, Anderson's got to do something about Hennessy!" Exnicio shouted at Billy. "He just threatened to close me down. I pay Anderson to keep the coppers out of my place."

"What happened?" Billy asked.

As Sam recounted the incident, Hennessy, in full dress uniform, unarmed but flanked by two patrolmen wielding truncheons, busted up an illegal prizefight in the back room of his saloon. The room had been packed, maybe a hundred men yelling, bobbing, weaving, ducking left and right with each wet splat of fist on flesh. Sam, caught up in the story, acted out the action of the two men stripped to the waist whaling on each other, bare-fisted, toe-to-toe, blood flying from broken nose and split lip.

"The crowd roared so loudly that nobody heard Hennessy and his guys break down the alley door," Sam said, finishing up a roundhouse.

The police cleared a path to ringside while the two amateurs artlessly pounded each other with wild haymakers to the head, short uppercuts to the kidneys. One of the boxers was a copper trying to pick up extra cash for his family.

"O'Brien!" Hennessy shouted, standing outside the ropes.

O'Brien, distracted by his commander's voice, dropped his guard. Sam mimed how O'Brien's opponent, a known hold-up man, landed a vicious roundhouse. The cold-cocked copper spun around, bounced off the ropes and fell unconscious to the floor.

"Well, now," Sam straightened out of his fighter's crouch, "the crowd went wild. There was the chief of police looking at one of his own splayed out flat and the bad guy grinning, his foot on the fallen copper's head, like a big game hunter posing with his trophy. Hennessy climbed between the ropes and stepped on O'Brien's back as he made his way to the middle of the ring. 'Fight's over,' he shouted. 'Next time I find an illegal fight, everyone would be arrested and fined a week's wages.' But he might as well have been talking to the back of his hand."

The men paid him no heed as they collected bets and fixed up the next match. Hennessy pulled out his gold pocket watch and warned them to leave before the paddy wagons arrived, gave them ten minutes. Ignoring the cash bribes thrown in the ring, Hennessy kept looking at his pocket watch. Some men nervously edged toward the alley door and the crowd drained away.

As Sam recalled his customers fleeing, he got indignant all over again, his face flushed and voice boiling.

"Hennessy slapped me with a fine," he said through gritted teeth. "One hundred dollars to be paid on the spot. Tells me if I hold another illegal fight the fine will be two hundred dollars and he'll close me down. Who's running the show around here, Anderson or Hennessy?"

Billy assured him Tom was in control. The incident wouldn't happen again. Tom would be in touch and restitutions made, Billy promised, and escorted the still steaming Sam to the front door.

"Christ," Billy muttered as he returned to the table. "Maybe we should find a way to set Hennessy and Matrangas at each other's throats."

"How so?" Ant asked.

"Don't know. But they have to be distracted away from Tom."

Chapter 7.

Ant thought long and hard about what Billy had said about triggering a showdown between the Mafia and the police. And to throw Young Jack into the mix. And the murder. How to link them, make them a dog chasing its tail until it finally grabs on and eats itself.

He could start by manufacturing a connection between Young Jack and the Matrangas; that Young Jack was their agent, the inside man whose presence in the whorehouse wouldn't be out of place. Why the fire and the murder? Hennessy would most likely ignore arson, but throw in a body and he'd have reason to make a stink in Storyville. Ant felt the tingle of excitement as his scenario took shape. Convince Billy and Tom that Young Jack was the key to setting the Matrangas and Hennessy against each other. Put Young Jack on the murder scene and have Tom take the evidence to Hennessy. Make Hennessy believe that the Mafia had infiltrated the city's money/power circle by recruiting the son of one of New Orleans most esteemed families. And conjure up Tom's paranoia that the Matrangas are plotting to take over Storyville and, once they establish that base, well, they'll seize the city. By nipping the conspiracy in the bud, Hennessy would become a hero, the city's savior, a role he'd relish. The Matrangas would counterattack and they had more guns, and men, than the police. Imagine the bloodbath. If the Mafia did shred the New Orleans police force, then the mayor might request the army come in and wipe out the Matrangas once and for all.

By opening Tom's eyes to this conspiracy, Ant would be the hero richly rewarded—and he'd get the girl.

Never mind that the whole thing made no sense; this was New Orleans where people believed in magical powders, and spells, and voodoo dolls.

All I have to do, Ant told himself, is turn MayAnn against Young Jack so she'd swear that he was upstairs when the whore was killed. I'll tell her that Young Jack is going to turn her over to the police as the murderer, or kill her in revenge. Ant clapped his hands to celebrate his cleverness. After all, Young Jack had sworn before Billy that he'd get MayAnn to confess, by blood if necessary. No doubt MayAnn wouldn't believe him, but with Billy as a witness....

Damn, this is good! Ant did a hop-and-skip as he walked down the street, a little strut of joy. But he needed to bring MayAnn to his side and she wasn't being very receptive to him. Still, if he got to her in the right place, in the right atmosphere, when she had her guard down, and that would be, Ant realized, the coming Monday night at Lincoln Park when Buddy performed.

Lincoln Park became the Negroes' gathering place after all other city parks were declared off limits to them by the Jim Crow laws. At the start, it was just a large open field until a Mr. Andre Poree, who hauled garbage for the city and kept his stable at one end of the field, saw a business opportunity. Uptown blacks, with no other place to go for picnics or to play ball, congregated on weekends in the empty field of rough grass and dirt and no shade. Mr. Poree constructed a refreshment stand and sold soda and beer and fruit. He added a small dance floor, nothing more fancy than planks on the ground, and invited, not hired, uptown musicians to show their stuff. If a young man wanted to dance with a young lady, he'd present her with an apple or orange or, if he really wanted to impress with his sophistication, with an exotic mandarin.

Mr. Poree even sold watermelons, always refreshing on a hot Sunday afternoon.

City officials, glad the blacks had their own place, left him alone. He expanded and filled the two-city block field with a dance hall at one end, a bandstand across the lot from it and, at the far end, a diamond with bleachers for his Lincoln Giants baseball team. Other Negro teams, some from as far away as Texas and Tennessee, came to play in an informal league. The hometown Giants were the pride and joy of uptown and if they lost a weekend game, everyone dragged tail for a day or two.

Spread out across the field was a rink for roller-skating and a section for children's rides, including a miniature steam engine with a working whistle. Even grownups rode the train, knees drawn up to their chins, as it trundled around a loop of track. They could sit in any car of their choice without fear of being thrown off by a conductor. Nearby was a corral for pig catching contests for children and adults. A nickel entrance fee bought you the opportunity to chase the pig. If you caught it, you took it home for dinner -- a valuable prize for the poverty victims of uptown. To add to the challenge, the corral was watered down to create a mud pit. The little kids chased piglets but the adults tested themselves against a hundred-pound greased hog with a strong sense of self-preservation. If the hog wasn't captured within fifteen minutes, it lived another day. Then Mr. Poree hit upon the brilliant idea of a women's pig chasing contest. Women, especially those raising a family on their own, flocked to the chance. And men flocked to watch the risqué spectacular of women in soaked, mud-splattered dresses clinging to their bodies.

Rows of vendors selling food and drinks ringed the field and in the middle was the centerpiece, the hot air balloon ride. This was Mr. Poree's marquee, his advertisement that could be seen for miles away as the balloon rose. For a quarter, a brave soul sat on the wooden plank and gripped two ropes and rose up maybe a good fifty feet, swinging free under the balloon tethered to the ground. After ten minutes aloft, the balloon was hauled back down. The last ride of day cost one dollar and was reserved for the daredevils—a ride under an untethered balloon and you had to pull the vent rope to descend. MayAnn took that ride to the fisherman's camp.

On Friday, Saturday and Sunday, the dentists, teachers, shop owners, the professionals and the respectable working class came to Lincoln Park with their families. But Monday night was "adult night." Buddy played Monday nights at Lincoln Park.

Ant felt a twitch in the air as soon as he stepped through the entrance, as if everyone there was secretly a bank robber fidgeting to blow the vault. People put bustle to their hustle with sharp fast motions and flash dress. Prostitutes dolled up to attract attention treated the place as a job fair. Madams brought their entire stable to drum up business. The independent crowjanes and alleybats and strumpets acted like shop girls looking for fun. Pimps in St. Louis shoes with tiny mirrors embedded in the pointy toes made sly approaches to pretty girls.

Walking through the crowd, Ant heard one such shark man say to a girl, "I can open the Rich World for you, darlin'. I'll protect and guide you, sweet thing. I'll make sure no harm comes to you. You'll be my special best girl."

"What you'll do is beat my ass and steal my money!" The innocent-looking young woman had a razor in her voice. "Git out of here before I call my daddy over here to beat *your* ass and steal *your* money."

A fellow tugged on Ant's elbow. "You new?" Ant glanced at him. The man, dressed in dark plaids and a yellow shirt, didn't appear to be talking to Ant but rather stared off over the heads of the crowd.

"What?"

"We're paid up through the month. Go ask your captain," the man said without moving his lips.

"Who are you?"

"The Pimps Club. The Uptown Syndicate, man. Who are you? You so new you haven't got your ten dollars this month? And that's all you get for not being here, understand? If we see you around, you'd better be carrying a white cane. Understand?"

He slipped a folded square of paper into Ant's hand and disappeared into the crowd. Unfolding the ten-dollar bill, Ant understood he had been mistaken for a copper looking to put on the squeeze. The dix was a payoff. Before he could pocket the bill, a sweet candy man in a brown felt fedora, the broad brim hiding his eyes, sidled up and muttered, "Mexican cigarettes." He turned his back to the passing crowd and flashed a packet in his palm. "Cocaine, opium, morphine and hashish, too. You tell any girl, Just try, Little Darlin', this tiny bit and if you like, then come back for more at my Welcome Wagon. They'll be willing to pay any price for the taste. Five dollars and it's all yours. Two for ten."

Ant looked young and white, but he was no rube. Apothecaries sold cocaine over the counter. Chinese herb shops had opium for less than five dollars a gram. Hashish, too. He could get all he wanted from Chen the Chink at a much better price. But these street salesmen were getting their goods from someone. Must be the Matrangas. Chen would pay well for that bit of information, Ant thought

He brushed off the sweet candy man with a huff. "What do you think I am, some virgin frat boy? You must be a fool and I don't deal with fools." The man, taking no offense, turned away in search of a better sale.

Ant wandered past the makeshift stalls doing brisk sales in rum, whiskey, Red Eye Rye, bathtub gin and nearly any variation of hard liquor. A sign on a large wooden building, the Dance Hall, brought him to a halt: TONIGHT JOHN ROBICHAUX AND HIS CREOLE ORCHESTRA.

"May I help you, sir?" asked a portly Negro with close-cropped hair and a full round face and wearing a black suit. "Mr. Andre Poree, the proprietor of Lincoln Park. Pleased to meet you. A ticket to the dance tonight?"

"For the Buddy Bolden dance."

"Yes sirree bob, that'll be at the Bandstand." Mr. Poree pointed to an open-air pavilion a hundred feet away. "But I should warn you, Buddy's music is different. Not well understood by most folks. He appeals mostly to the younger colored bucks."

Ant handed over the ten-dollar bill and in return got a ticket and nine dollars and fifty cents in change. "You enjoy yourself tonight. That's what we're here for." Mr. Poree smiled at Ant as if he was a favorite son-in-law instead of an out-of-place white man.

It wasn't until the twilight deepened to night Ant caught sight of Buddy. A whirlpool of brightly colored dresses announced his presence. "Bud-dy! Bud-dy!" chorused the women. One brazen vixen shouted, "Let me blow your horn, baby!" At the center of this maelstrom of adulation, Buddy smiled and laughed and touched hands and kept his horn tucked safely under his arm. If MayAnn was around, she'd be somewhere near Buddy.

Ant was a jealous man about MayAnn. The way sin is necessary to know grace, so is jealousy necessary to know love, in his opinion. At times, that hot iron on the heart burnt him something terrible, worst than a gut full of bad whiskey. But just as whiskey gave him strength and reckless boldness, jealousy gave him righteous conviction of his just due. Ant reasoned that if he allied with jealousy's power, then his force would be invincible. MayAnn's ambition and Young Jack's wealth would crumble under his onslaught of slight-of-hand and brute force. A Faustian pact, he realized, but one worth making.

Only, he hadn't bargained on the inexplicable ambushes he'd suffer, like suspecting that Buddy and MayAnn had more going on than they let on. Seeing Buddy surrounded by all those women, knowing that MayAnn hopped, skipped and jumped after him, that Buddy knew things about her, like the balloon ride, and by his own admission he had special feelings for her, the 'spunky" girl, and knowing Buddy treated women like ripe fruit, and who was juicer than MayAnn, 'Well', Jealousy shouted in Ant's ear, 'what else does he know about MayAnn? The lovely curve of her breast? That special laugh/ sigh she gives when you hit her spot just right?'

They lived around the corner from each other, so it would be easy to drop by through the midnight window. The image of Buddy and MayAnn tangled together made Ant's stomach heave, forcing him to bend over, hands on knees, and nearly puke.

When he straightened up, Buddy was coming right at him with one arm out like a bowsprit parting the crowd. He sailed passed and called out, "Mr. John Robichaux." Ant turned to see the handsome Creole in a suit and a stiff white collar.

"Mr. Robichaux, I heard that you called me and my band a routineer bunch. Is that true, sir?"

Robichaux stopped and gave Buddy a haughty appraisal. Like most Creole musicians, he held Negro musicians in low regard, especially Buddy. The popularity of Buddy's new hot music threatened the livelihood of the classically trained Creole musicians. "Christ, you playing at the Bandstand tonight?"

"Sir, what's a 'routineer bunch'?" Buddy stood with feet apart, rocking from toe to heel, chest puffed out and chin high to appear taller, like a man trying to bluff a bear. "I know it's an insult but I don't know how I've been insulted, so I don't feel insulted. Therefore, your insult is wasted. I'm giving you another chance to make me feel bad."

"You're a fake, Bolden," Robichaux sneered. "You and your 'musicians' can't read music. How in the hell do you know how the music is supposed to be played? You just get up there and hoot and toot any old which way and make a lot of noise. You're no better than a spasm band on a street corner. Monkeys could play your music. Just bang and blow."

"Sir!" Buddy held up his cornet in one hand and a sheet of music in the other. "I challenge you to a duel." He slapped the sheet music against Robichaux's cheek in lieu of a pair of gloves. Then he leaned forward as if to kiss him. "We'll eat you alive tonight," he said in a friendly tone. "Even brought some special sauce along, extra *hot*."

Robichaux dismissed Buddy with a flick of his hand and continued to the Dance Hall. Buddy sent him off with a *toot-ta-toot*, getting laughs from the crowd around him, including Young Jack standing at the edge of the crowd.

Ant spotted him and felt a shock of disbelief. How did he know to look for MayAnn here? Did she tip him off so she'd get the thrill of having Ant and Young Jack and Buddy sniffing around each other? Lining up to battle for her favors? He was a man looking through a jug full of water, everything all wavy and distorted. That's what jealousy did to him. And he thought that he had perfect vision because he had two jugs of water for eyeballs.

As soon as he set eyes on Young Jack, he remembered his nemesis's words: *I know who killed my love...I'll get her confession, in blood if necessary.*

Buddy played some 'Come on' music and led his fans to the Bandstand, where the wooden floor filled to overflowing with a young crowd eager to dance new ways to Buddy's jumping music. Ant trailed after Young Jack, all the while searching for MayAnn.

At the opening chords of Robichaux's first song, a nice waltz, Buddy aimed his cornet in the insulting Creole's direction and launched the minstrel "Jump Jim Crow," a musical slap to remind Robichaux he, too, rode on a blacks' only trolley. Then Buddy segued into snatches of songs, hymns, dance numbers, street calls, popular arias all jumbled together and embellished with twists and twirls and sudden plunges into slow slides. The young people leapt into action, jumping and shaking, heads back as if howling at the moon like people about to have sex if only they could get out of their clothes. Some of the music wasn't recognizable at all, just patterns of notes made up on the spot, wide open without reservation, emotional, rebellious and wild.

The music caught Ant. His hand tapped against his leg, hips wiggled and shoulders twisted and twitched. Much to his astonishment, he bounced straight up and down and jerked about like a baby bird struggling out of its shell. A single dancer in front of the stage jittered as if she was being electrified, if the stories about the dangers of electricity were true: spasms shook her shoulders; hair fanned straight out as she swung her head from side to side; fingering wiggled as her arms reached for the heavens. MayAnn. Ant started towards her, then spotted Young Jack twenty feet closer and already on the move.

"MayAnn!" She didn't hear Ant. "MayAnn!" Diving into the crowd, his arms and legs thrashing, he tried to swim over heads to her. Young Jack pushed within ten feet of her. No way Ant could beat him. "MayAnn!" Buddy lifted his horn to start the next song. Ant lunged onto a man's back with the idea he'd stand on his shoulders and run, in his madness imagining himself hopping from stone to stone across a stream. His stone gave a violent shrug, "What the fuck you do climbin' on me?"

Tumbling through the air, Ant saw Buddy reach down and pull MayAnn onto the stage with a big smile of welcome. Ant bounced off a head and fell to the floor. Scrambling on all fours through the thicket of legs, he butted open a woman's legs with my head. "Nasty man! Nasty man!" she yelled and whacked her assailant. Ant curled into a fetal position, afraid of being trampled, when Buddy struck up the fast number,

"If You Don't Shake It, You Don't Get No Cake." A fat lady pulled Ant upright and wrapped him between her legs and jammed his face into her sweaty breasts. He squirmed free and staggered out of the crowd, his shirt torn and right eye starting to swell shut. But he could see MayAnn on stage doing a pure out-of-the-mind lightning storm show. She shimmied like a raindrop going down a windowpane; stomped as if killing a snake; marched and strutted, knees high, elbows swinging, like a flambeau carrier in a Mardi Gras parade. And she got down dirty on a phantom lover.

Young Jack watched her from the corner of the stage.

After the last song, Buddy called out, "Go on home, all my children. Go on home and keep the fun rollin'."

By the time Ant bulled his way to the stage, Buddy and MayAnn were coming down the stage's stairs arm-in-arm, laughing and enjoying each other. Right in front of them stood Young Jack. Ant heard him say to her, "I want you."

"MayAnn." Ant stepped between them. "Billy needs to talk with you. Business."

"I got no business with him." MayAnn kept her eyes over his shoulder on Young Jack.

"Josie business. I'm just looking after your well being."

"You bring me a bushel of money then, maybe two?"

"Billy and I are looking for the man who killed that girl," Ant said low so Young Jack wouldn't hear.

"What's that got to do with my well being?"

"Because Young Jack killed that girl and he's going to kill you, too. Billy heard him. I'm here to save you from yourself."

"I don't know what you're talking about, Antoine."

"You know the story about the dog who bites himself because he's hungry? You know that one?" Ant reached out and gripped her arm hard to make her look at him. "Well, I'm the dogcatcher. I'm here so that dog doesn't eat itself."

"Antoine, you're so clever you're stupid." She twisted out of his grip and put him in a stare down, eyes as hard and fierce as he'd ever seen them. "You ought to go out an' catch yourself a mutt or two, Mr. Dogcatcher, to keep yourself occupied elsewhere."

"I saw your Young Jack go up those stairs and when he came down, he left behind a dead girl. He's a killer, MayAnn, and you don't want to go chasing after that. What was going on with him and the dead whore? You know something."

"He was a john and she was a whore. Business as usual." Ant could always tell when MayAnn played the innocent—her face took on a plaster saint look, all smooth and blank eyed, like it was now.

Young Jack edged around into Ant's line of sight and semaphored indecipherable eyebrow signals. When Ant didn't respond, he made furtive hand motions as if they should what? rope a calf? Then it dawned on Ant that Young Jack intended for him to help snatch MayAnn.

Buddy pushed MayAnn along and Ant stepped in beside her. Young Jack fell in right behind, surprisingly agile considering his clubfoot. "Billy wants to ask you about the killing." Ant kept my voice barely above a whisper so Young Jack couldn't overhear.

"I don't know anything." MayAnn tried to push him away with her attitude. " I told you, get out of my business."

Without warning, Young Jack grabbed Ant by the shoulders and twisted him aside to get at MayAnn. Ant recovered and wrapped his arms around Young Jack to pull him off balance. In his rush to get pass, Young Jack shoved Ant's face under his armpit to slip around him. Ant's hand searched for the knife on Young Jack's belt as they spun once, twice, tripped and fell.

"What?" Surprise put a croak in Young Jack's voice.

Ant lay on his back, arms pinned, helpless. People stepped around them, indifferent now that no fight was in the offing. Young Jack pushed up with his hands on Ant's chest, putting his full weight on Ant's heart. As he rose to his knees, then upright, Ant clung to his coat.

"What!?" He grabbed Ant's wrists to pry him off.

In answer, Ant rammed his head into Young Jack's nose and drove him backward into the dirt and hit him and hit him. "FIGHT!" People circled around, making a dog pit, and called out bets. Young Jack squirmed to free his knife. The crowd, now five deep, cheered for blood. "Bite him in the throat!" "The eyes! Get his eyes out!" They rolled over and over, legs kicking, short punches doing no damage. Finally, spent, they settled for a tactical truce.

"What the hell are you fighting me for? She got away. I had her and you helped her escape," Young Jack accused.

In truth, Ant didn't know why he'd picked the fight. To help MayAnn escape was the easy answer. But, he had felt something so irrational, so powerful, so true, so much a rage that he had only two choices—destroy the cause or be reduced to an insignificant fool. That scalding geyser had erupted in him. He was being tossed aside, left behind, left out, no value, a fetch boy, unworthy for the woman he loved, no place to call his own without her, no stake in life except what he stole from others, a shadow man, insubstantial, used, cast aside, abandoned, called an ant, stepped on, robbed, imprisoned by all he was denied. And this white guy, this rich white guy, who had everything, who made Ant hate myself...

Instead, Ant told Young Jack, "Wrong place to assault her. The crowd would've torn you apart, a white man jumping a black girl in their park." Then he helped Young Jack to his feet. The crowd muttered their disappointment and called them cowards.

"We live to fight another day," Ant said, dusting off his shoulders.

"Never took you to be a fighter, a man of spirit," Young Jack replied and gave Ant a thoughtful look. "I have some friends you should meet." Then leaning close he whispered, "Week

Thursday. Ten p.m." and gave an address not far from Chen the Chink's opium den. "Don't tell anyone on your mother's heart or you'll put us all in danger."

Chapter 8.

"I know how to get the Matrangas and Hennessy going at each other," Ant told Billy the next day. He'd thought of a new wrinkle overnight.

"How's that?"

"Start a drug war."

They were walking down Basin Street, Billy seemingly not paying much attention to anything but occasionally stopping to look at the worn down buildings that lined the street from Tom's saloon to the far corner.

"How's that?"

Ant told him about the drug sellers at Lincoln Park. "Those aren't Chen's men. So they must be Matrangas. Chen can be mighty touchy when it comes to competition. I'll build up the threat with Chen until he starts feeling profits slipping through his fingers. There's nothing a Chinaman hates more than having someone taking money he believes belongs to him by birthright, especially by an interloper like the Italians.

"If Chen is tipped off about a drug shipment on the docks, he might make the business decision to destroy, or steal, his competitor's supply. The Matrangas will naturally fight to protect what's theirs. A huge blazing gunfight on the docks will attract the police. The Matrangas, with enough men to take on both Chen and the police, will have the upper hand."

"How will you know about the drug shipment?"

"Makes no difference if there's drugs or not, as long as Chen believes there are. A crate of bananas can look like a crate in cocaine in the dark."

Billy stopped at the last building on the block, a grimy, blank-faced three-story hulk, and stood, hands behind his back, examining it like someone assessing a piece of machinery. "What about Hennessy?"

"When the police are driven off the docks, as they will be, Hennessy will have to put all his attention on the Matrangas in order to save face, leaving Tom alone in Storyville."

Billy turned away from the building and started back towards Tom's saloon. "Think so?"

"Either that or lose his job. You encourage your newspaper buddies to write stories about an army of drug-crazed Italians poised to overrun the city. Whip up the fear. The mayor will have no choice but to order Hennessy back into battle. After all, the mayor put him in that job to clean out the criminals, right? Hennessy has declared the Matrangas his blood enemies." Ant, very pleased with his cleverness, had to restrain from prancing along side Billy.

When they reached Tom's saloon, Billy gave Ant's shoulder a squeeze. "Let me buy you a drink to celebrate the bonus Tom will surely give you for thinking up such a cockamamie story. But, hell, it just might work."

That night, Ant met with Chen in the privacy of the opium den's back room, without Little Flower in attendance. "It's true, dear friend," Ant said. "One of Matrangas' men at Lincoln Park told me a big supply was coming in tomorrow night on a ship from Columbia. The *Santa Clara*. The drugs will be hidden in crates marked banana."

Chen, sitting on a silk pillow opposite Ant, sucked on his long teeth and rocked slightly back and forth, staring at a spot on the floor between the two men.

"The running dogs Italians are disrespecting you." Ant couldn't sit crossed legged like Chen, so sprawled to one side. "They're stealing from you."

Gradually Chen became motionless, as if he had sunk into the quietude of mediation. The long silence made Ant anxious but he knew not to overplay his hand. He straightened up on the pillow, stiffing his spine to mimic Chen as a show of respect.

Chen appeared to be asleep. Ant stretched a leg that was going numb. He rustled on the pillow. Chen showed no awareness. Finally Ant couldn't restrain himself any longer.

"How do you like your dog prepared?" he asked in a quiet voice. "With a side dish of rice, steamed or fried?"

Chen lifted his eyes. "I thank my good friend for his advise." And then seemed to truly fall asleep.

The next night, night of the expected battle on the docks, Billy and Ant sat anxiously in Tom's saloon. They intended to tell Tom of their plan and uncork a bottle of champagne at the first sounds of gunfire. At ten o'clock, with still no action, Ant said, "Give it a while longer. By midnight, Chen should make his move." At midnight, when Ant and Billy had drunk too much so to ease their anxiety, Ant said, "Chen must be waiting until Matrangas' men leave the dock. Maybe he plans to ambush the cargo when it's taken elsewhere." At three a.m., when the bartenders were serving last drinks, Ant said, "What the fuck happened?"

"So much for your bright ideas," grumbled Billy, a couple days after the failed showdown. Accompanied by Ant, Billy was once again strolling Basin Street to survey the buildings.

"Chinamen are crafty. Chen will go after the Matrangas, just you wait and see," was Ant's only explanation.

Not until months later did Ant learn what went wrong. The Chinese coolies part of the Matrangas dock gangs were also members of Chen extended family, if not by blood then by loyalty. In the bustle of unloading the *Santa Clara*'s cargo, the men set aside crates marked 'banana' and discretely threw them overboard to cohorts in rowboats waiting to pluck the crates from the water. The Matrangas saw no reason to go to war over a couple crates of bananas.

Ant had been puzzled why, on subsequence visits to Chen, he was always presented him with a banana.

"Well, Tom has his own strategy to keep the Matrangas off Basin Street," Billy said, "and the strategy starts with these buildings and Josie."

As Billy explained it, Tom planned to convert the shabby sporting palaces on Basin Street into first-rate brothels. He'd invite Storyville's classiest and most successful madams to relocate their establishments to his Golden Row. And he'd help finance their renovations and cover moving costs.

"Here's his thinking. He's going to spiff up his Arlington saloon. Put in electric lights, a new bar with a fancy mirror. People will come just to see the lights. Then he's going to rebuild Josie's burned down Arlington as the most modern elegant whorehouse in the country. It'll be the model of his sincerity and goodwill to the other madams. He wants his Golden Row to be such an asset to New Orleans' financial well being the politicians and business leaders won't want it to fall into the wrong hands. When push comes to shove, no matter who's doing the shoving, whether Hennessy or the Matrangas, the savvy business interest, the real power in New Orleans, will protect him rather than let a bad wolf in the door."

"When's he going to start," Ant asked.

"Soon. He hasn't explained all this to Josie yet and he needs to get the other madams on board. But soon."

Ant saw an opportunity to further his cause with MayAnn—and the Matrangas.

"It isn't good to have a whore killer on the loose. Might scare people away from Basin Street when Tom's trying to make it his castle."

"The girl's murder might have been a one-time deal. An aberration," Billy answered.

"Or it might have given Young Jack a taste for the dark side exotic. Satan's wine."

Billy stopped walking and looked at Ant with askance. "Why are you so convinced it's Young Jack?"

"You know what MayAnn said—she saw him upstairs during the fire. And you yourself accused him of a money-love-family triangle. Opportunity and motive. You don't need to be a Sherlock to figure it out. You as good as Sherlock, Billy?"

Billy considered the challenge and then said, "I need to talk with MayAnn."

They continued to the end of the block and turned back towards Josie's burned out Arlington.

"Why Josie?" Ant asked. "Why is she so important to Tom?"

"Why does a pig like mud," Billy replied. "They're comfortable with each other. Like war buddies, they trust each other. They recognized the other's grit to battle for their dream and mutual respect is a large part of what holds them together. Tom wants a partner on Basin Street whose loyalty he can count on. In Josie, he's found someone as determined as he is to fight for a better life. And Josie, she sees Tom as a pair of strong shoulders to stand on while she reaches for the brass ring."

He waited a couple seconds and then added, "Let me tell you a true story."

Josie was a nasty piece of work in her early days, according to Billy, angry as a hornet, foul-mouthed, crude, always picking fights, even with other whores. "Always think of Josie as a wolverine with the sharp teeth and instincts of that animal," Billy cautioned.

Josie's street fight with Beulah Ripley, a Negro competitor, made her reputation. Beulah outweighed her by a good forty pounds, was four inches taller and had a longer reach. The match was a heavyweight against a lightweight. But Josie knew more agony than most people, even people like Beulah, and that made her dangerous in ways not considered rational.

Billy didn't know firsthand how the brawl started, probably something Josie said. As soon as the two whores tore into each other, right in the middle of Burgundy Street in broad daylight, a crowd circled around. They fought like boxers -- knees bent, shoulders hunched, feigning and dodging, parrying to find an opening. Beulah got a hold of Josie's long hair and yanked hard to throw her off balance.

"She hoped to fell her and kick her in the face, stomp on her ribs, put a toe into her spleen," Billy said, "but that's not what happened. Josie lunged forward and grabbed a fistful of Beulah's dress. She aimed to chomp on Beulah's bread loaf of a breast. Might have got a nip in, the way Beulah yelped. They shuffled with arms around shoulders trying to trip each other. If you didn't know better, you'd think they were embracing while dancing a slow waltz. Beulah tried to smother Josie with her flabby weight. But Josie kept her feet moving and worked her inside game, the way a boxer pounds on his opponent's kidneys."

Beulah scored a point by tearing out a hunk of Josie's hair by the roots, exposing a patch of raw scalp. At the sight of blood, the crowd hollered for more. "You'd think that John L. Sullivan and Jim McCormick were going at it bare knuckled the way the spectators were carrying on," Billy smiled at the memory. "Josie landed a haymaker on Beulah's right eye and people screamed 'Kill her'. Every time Beulah's or Josie's fingernails clawed bloody streaks down the other's cheek, the loonies whooped. Two drowning cats trapped in the same bag couldn't have been more vicious with each other than those whores as they wrestled in the dirt, spitting in each other's face.

"Now, Josie is a smart fighter," Billy reminded Ant. "She thinks on her feet. When Beulah had her in a bear hug, Josie appeared to faint away. Beulah leaned forward eager to snap her spine but Josie grabbed her by the head and clamped her teeth into Beulah's ear. Fierce as a terrier on a rat. Josie gnawed and shook her head back and forth. Beulah shrieked and tried to put her thumbs in her opponent's eyes."

Suddenly, the fighters fell free of each other. Josie stood in the middle of the street, satisfaction in her bloody grin, with what looked like a hunk of chaw bulging her cheek. She took a couple chews and puckered up as if to spit out a stream of tobacco juice. Instead, she slowly pulled out half of Beulah's ear and threw it to a mangy mutt, which gave it a sniff and quickly gobbled it up. Beulah reached up and felt her jagged wound. Howling in pain and rage, she leapt at Josie, fingers in claws, her large front teeth bared. Josie ducked under Beulah's swinging arms, then shot up and bit down on Beulah's large lower lip. For a moment it appeared as if the women were kissing mouth-to-mouth. Beulah savagely tore at Josie's hair but Josie kept burrowing into the lip.

The crowd shouted whoops of insults and pounded each other on the shoulders at the sight of two women lip-to-lip with their clothes half torn off, blood streaming down their faces.

Josie released her grip and gave Beulah a hard shove backwards. The Negress grabbed Josie's head and gave a vicious jerk. Josie howled and bent double as Beulah triumphantly waved a hank of Josie's hair.

"She put a curse on Josie's cunt so it would close shut and she'd starve to death," Billy told Ant. "But her words tumbled out in a slur. Josie reared back and spit a chunk of Beulah's lip in her face. You'd do well to remember that if you ever get into a pissing contest with Josie Arlington. Tom shouldn't lose sight of that either."

The next day Tom summoned Billy and Josie to his office. Pacing before his desk, rubbing his hands together with excitement, he came to a stop before her and hooked his thumbs in his vest. "Your new place will be the first pearl on my Golden Row. I'll loan you the money to make it absolutely without question the most sumptuous sporting palace in America, a palace fit for a king to get laid in. Your sparkling mansion will be the showcase, the diamond."

If he expected Josie to clap her hands in glee, she disappointed him. "On what terms?"

"Favorable. I'll give you a low-interest loan. And I'll finance, at reasonable rates, the refurbishing of the other rundown mansions along Basin. *We'll* control who is allowed to open a house on *our* street."

Josie held back for a moment longer as the idea of being the Empress of Basin Street settled in. Then her face flooded with delight. "You delicious man!"

"There's just one little thing." Tom edged forward gingerly, a man venturing out on thin ice. "I want you to drop the name Arlington from your new establishment. You know—new place, new name, new start. Besides, it's confusing to have both my place and your place called the Arlington, especially that we're next door to each other."

"I had the name first, Tom. Why don't you rename your place Tom's Café and Saloon or the Mayor's House or some such thing?"

"Now, Josie," he said, plunking down on the sofa next to her, "it's hard to say who got the name first. But I'm putting up the money to rebuild your place, so I should have naming rights."

Josie locked her arms over her bosom and sat straight, a knot of determination rippling along her jaw. "I'm not giving up the name Arlington, Tom."

He leaned forward with elbows on knees, an affable smile on his face. "Josie..."

"It's *my* name. I'm not giving up my damn name." She sounded as if she were clutching rocks, ready to pitch them at the least provocation.

"We can't have two Arlingtons, Josie! It'll confuse the customers." Tom still smiled but a pinch of anger showed at the corner of his eyes. "You'll have the grandest whorehouse in New Orleans because of my the money. I get the name in return."

Josie leaned forward until she and Tom sat nearly nose-to-nose, working her lips into a pucker, reminding Billy of when she had bitten off that chunk of Beulah's ear. Tom bared his teeth, in either a challenging smile or a snarl.

For Josie, the name Arlington was the cornerstone upon which she had rebuilt herself. After being shunned by other whorehouses for being a foul-mouthed street fighter and a troublemaker, she joined forces with three other renegade whores and opened the tawdry brothel Chateau Labrano, named after her pimp/lover. A sporting man about town, John Thomas Brady, came to the bagnio for a quickie. He liked what he got enough to take Josie on a vacation to Hot Springs, Arkansas, a popular tourist spa with curative waters, fine restaurants, nightly dancing to orchestras, legal gambling tables and a horse track where Brady spent his afternoons. They presented themselves as a respectable married couple basking in the optimism and good life that buoyed the American middle-class at the time.

The centerpiece of Hot Springs was the elegant Arlington, a sprawling, posh hotel. When Josie returned from the vacation, she renamed her whorehouse, and herself, Arlington. She set about remaking her image from a low-class whore to the madam of an establishment offering gracious, amiable foreign girls who would service only gentlemen of taste and refinement. She began reading popular magazines featuring tips on manners and stopped swearing in public.

About the same time, Tom opened his Arlington Café, a resurrection of his failing Anderson's Cafe. He had chosen the new name for its high tone, the ring of class to take the edge off the accent of "bare arse" Irish. Arlington had an English upper crust tone connoting old family, culture, respect. As he was putting the finishing touches on the establishment, which quickly became a neutral ground for dealmakers, legal and illegal, Tom heard about Josie's newly christened Arlington. Two Arlingtons within blocks of each other could confuse his customers, so he went to investigate. Josie mistook him for a client.

Even then, Josie refused to sell her name when Tom offered. He decided if he couldn't beat her, he'd join her and invested in her whorehouse.

The name Arlington represented Tom and Josie's coat of arms, a bit of camouflage to hide their Irish Channel roots, where they had grown up as poor immigrants kids. In their Corduroy Alley neighborhood, bashing a person over the head was considered a friendly greeting. The infamous residents of that slum were never content unless drunk and fighting strangers, spouses, children, friends, it didn't matter. Tom often described his birthplace as a neighborhood disguised as a pirate ship with everyone living there trying to take over the ship. It wasn't enough to plunder the outsiders; the crew sought to eliminate the weak among them.

Watching Tom and Josie huddled on Tom's sofa in a face-off over the name Arlington, Billy put his money on Josie. He wouldn't be surprised if she bit Tom's nose as to put "teeth," so to speak, into her non-negotiable position.

"Call yours' the Arlington Annex," Josie said, unblinking.

Tom held his stare. Josie kept working her lips. He edged back an inch. "That's something to think about."

Josie eased back. Her lips relaxed. Her arms dropped so she could be embraced. Tom reached out and took her hand, either in affection or as a business handshake. In the gesture, Billy understood the solidarity between them: protecting their self-esteem was key to their survival.

Now they had reached a tenuous agreement over sharing the name Arlington, Josie and Tom sat shoulder-to-shoulder turning the page of the *Blue Book* to select madams worthy of their Basin Street Golden Row.

Countess Willie Piazza, the Grand Dame of Storyville madams, topped their list. Her high-toned sporting mansion, considered the most elegant in New Orleans, was a must stop for visiting European royalty and well-heeled gentlemen. A French count became so enamored with her he proposed marriage. When she turned him down, he threw in a chateau in southern France to sweeten the pot but she remained steadfast in her refusal. Every suitor, and there were many, received a polite but firm "no" in French, German, Spanish, Dutch and Deep South, all of which she spoke fluently.

When in public, she wore a diamond choker and smoked black Russian cigarettes in a two-foot ivory-and-gold holder. Despite her profession, the society women acknowledged her as the fashion doyenne for her stylish self-designed clothes. The opening of the Spring Season at the Fairgrounds racetrack was not complete without Countess Willie appearing in her latest creation. The St. Charles Avenue matrons and their seamstresses followed her around to note, sketch and copy her designs. The matrons' husbands also followed her because she brought her most beautiful girls as advertisement.

Yet for all her high visibility, Countess Willie was an enigma. No one knew her origins. There was no record anywhere of her working her way up from the street, the ladder to success climbed by most madams. The ad in the *Blue Book* pointedly said her house was "the place to visit, especially when one is hopping about with friends—women in particular," which caused all sorts of speculation.

Her whorehouse was known for the best library in New Orleans. Men went there just to read the unexpurgated *1001 Arabian Nights, The Anatomy of Melancholy, Lettres de Mon Moulin, The Nabob* and *Sapho*.

"Imagine going to a whorehouse to read a book," Josie said. "I have a book." Tom didn't hide his look of surprise. "And I've read it," she added rather defensively. "*The House of Mirth* by Edith Wharton. I won't be so foolish as Lily Bart. She should have married any one of the rich men who loved her. Better to snag a prince than scheme for the king you'll never get. Look where she ended up, falling down the social ladder, a failure at each step. The poor fool had no skills, couldn't even make a decent hat. At least me and my girls have a skill we can live by. I don't intend to die like Lily, poor and in despair."

Tom innocently asked, "How about Emma Johnson?"

Josie shuddered theatrically, the spasm rippling off her shoulders and down through her fingertips. "Heavens NO! That mangy dog should be mercy shot. She's a sideshow, Tommy, and her girls are equally crude. They're pancake flippers. Cook'em and toss'em. Faster turn over that way but they take no pride in the profession. She'd give Basin Street a bad name."

Emma Johnson had a reputation as notorious as Countess Willie's, but for very different reasons. Her French Studio featured infamous live sex shows involving every combination imaginable, including animals and vegetables. She offered a "sixty-second plan"—any man who, after penetrating her, didn't climax for one full minute got a free ride. If they lost control, they paid double. She made a good deal of money on the trick.

Billy, who had visited the French Studio, didn't understand why anyone would want to ride her, free or be paid to do the deed. She was old, so old that her rivals gossiped she had done tricks in the mud with Confederate soldiers while serving as a Union spy. And ugly. Her dewlaps, bulldog jowls, swayed every time she moved her head. She plastered her face with white powder, drew on eyebrows with a black grease pencil, smeared her mouth with scarlet lipstick so it looked like a leaking tomato, and always wore a wig of brilliant pink curls. Her detractors claimed she was bald.

Costumed in a red circus swallowtail coat, no trousers, with fishnet stockings held up by a black garter belt over her flabby thighs, she acted like a ringmaster and the whorehouse her private circus. The French Studio was the most successful in Storyville, one reason being her French Challenge. In the foyer hung the framed notice: "Mme. Emma Johnson, the Parisian Queen of nations, has set the world record of performing oral sex on thirty men non-stop. She challenges anyone to break her record. A $100 dollar prize is offered."

Every Wednesday was open challenge night. A woman sat in a barrel and the man stuck his cock through a knothole. Rumor had it, probably spread by Emma, not only whores sucked in the barrel. Respectable woman took their place incognito either for the thrill or out of dire financial distress. Savvy Emma knew the possibility would get men lined up. On a busy Wednesday, she might have three or four barrels in business with thirty men, who paid ten dollars, at each barrel hoping to be part of a record setting event.

And she had another lucrative sideline—procuring underage virgins. The *Mascot* had caught Emma red-handed selling unspoiled girls. A reporter, posing as a prospective customer, went to the French Studio and asked about "the special."

In his exposé, the journalist wrote Emma presented him with a ten-year-old girl woozy on brandy.

"I took the unfortunate into a bedroom where she tried to climb onto my lap. When I stayed her wandering hands, the girl cried out, 'But we must have fun. Otherwise she won't give me candy and five dollars.'

"Shocked by the proprietress's shameful manipulation of the innocent, I informed the infamous Emma Johnson I was unable to perform.

"'Why you're foolish!' she said. 'You won't get another chance like it in the entire city. The girl's a virgin!'

"I returned within the hour with a policeman who arrested the madam of the French Studio. The still virginal girl was taken to the House of the Good Shepard and entrusted to the care of the good nuns."

The *Mascot* didn't report Emma got off with a warning. In fact, she never spent a day in jail during all her years dealing in the dark side of the sex trade.

Taking Emma's rejection in stride, Tom pointed to another ad. "There's Minnie White. Her house is as much of a clubhouse as a whorehouse. Domino and checker matches in the front parlor, along with the occasional strip act by one of the girls. Minnie's like the unofficial headquarters for conventioneers because she encourages male horseplay and camaraderie. She makes more money on the sale of alcohol than on the sale of sex. She'll give Basin a wholesome, fun aspect. And she has Marguerite Griffin, who knows more bawdy ballads than a boatful of sailors."

Josie put a tick beside Minnie's name.

Tom turned the page to Antonia Gonzales. "I hear she sings opera."

"She plays the cornet naked, that's what she does," Josie corrected. "Often accompanied by the Negro homosexual Tony Jackson. She goes after the common trade."

"You hire Tony."

"Because he's the best piano professor in all of New Orleans. You can't do better than Tony. You should sign him to an exclusive to play only at my Arlington. And Sammy Davis and maybe that Ferdy boy, too—you know, Ferdinand Morton."

Josie ruled out Sappho. "We can't have lesbos on the street."

"Why not? Bring in a new class of customers, the ladies. And it would titillate the men."

"Basin Street shouldn't be about perversion, Tom. Rule number one. Our Golden Row must be about class and elegance and respectable sex."

When the list was completed, Tom asked Billy to get a contractor working pronto on the renovation of his Arlington *Annex*—his lips twisted around that last word as if eating bitter fruit—and Josie's new whorehouse, the Arlington.

Chapter 9.

Later that evening at his house, nestled into his favorite club chair with a glass of good Scotch in hand, Tom smiled and sipped at the prospect of his new and improved Arlington *Annex*. Why in the hell had he ever agreed to that? He held the high cards, for Christ sake. Annex. Sounded like a hospital wing. Or a government building, which, upon reflection, Tom decided was not far from the truth; his saloon was Storyville's City Hall.

The soft light from the kerosene lamp cast muted shadows upon the living room's sofas and armchairs, always empty; the copies of famous paintings he never looked at; the expensive carpet. The room gave the impression of comfortable domesticity. Tom made a rueful toast to his solitude and swallowed his abiding sadness with another gulp of Scotch.

This room represents is what I've worked for, fought for, sacrificed for, he reminded himself, ever since I was a newsboy in the Swamp. Now I'm 'The Mayor'. I'm rich. People fear me. And I'm lonely.

Even after fifteen years, Tom missed his life with Emma Schwartz, whom he "married" at the age of twenty-one without a marriage license, or sanction of the Church, or registering the union with the Orleans Parish Marriage Records. All that cost fees. Tom longed for, as he did nearly every night, the first two years with Emma. She'd be there when he came home from work, the piquant smells of dinner on the stove, fawning over him, adoring him. Oftentimes, the chicken in the oven became overdone because Tom swept her into the bedroom, scattering their clothes, her laughter of joy and pleasure all the nourishment he needed. He missed loving her; he had placed his entire being in service of their relationship.

But most of all his heart wept for his daughter, Irene, whom he hadn't seen for most of those fifteen years. When Emma left him, she took their three-year-old daughter with her. Curly dark hair, startling light blues eyes that sparkled with love for him, a clear and pure laugh that almost had him believing in God, or at least Higher Goodness. Her absence was the one bright spot of regret in his life.

Damn, Emma, I tired so hard for us. Tom finished off the Scotch with an abrupt, nearly violent slug back and swore, yet again, that he'd forget her once and for all.

The union with nineteen-year-old Emma, a beauty who wanted out of the apartment above her father's butcher shop, was to be part of Tom ticket into the respectable middle class. Lightly educated but with a quick mind for figures, he got a job as a bookkeeper with Louisiana Lottery Company. He was proud to have a job that required a white collar and a suit. It made him a responsible man with a responsible job, a way out of his father's Irish working-poor class. He went to the office every day so Emma could have her Madagascars on overstuffed horsehair chairs and proper plates and good food to put on those plates. They just barely managed to scrape by.

From the beginning, the lack of money plagued the couple. When the bloom of young love began to fade, Tom felt Emma expected more practical things, more accruements to show that her station in life had risen. Her increasingly ill-disguised disappointment made him feel guilty. Dinner was always waiting but Emma might sidestep him or be busily sweeping with the broom between them, especially after she became pregnant. Her smile became a tight purse of the lips, a pout of reproach: her terms of endearment took on a sardonic twist. He started avoiding home and the nagging and stayed out drinking with his friends, which made Emma even more the shrew.

The final straw came when he took all their savings, without asking Emma, and invested in a restaurant, the original Anderson Café, with his friend David Heller. When the restaurant failed to thrive, he quit his job and spent fourteen, sixteen hours a day, seven days a week trying to bail out the sinking ship. After the first month, Emma stopped pleading; after the second month she stopped the angry shouting; after the third month she went silent, a perfunctory, wooden figure in the bed beside him. He came home one early morning and found a note and an empty house.

Tom saw all his efforts to improve her station as the expression of his love. So when Emma walked out, well, it was a humiliating failure for him. From then on, he devoted himself to business, where he could succeed.

He met Billy soon after Emma left. At the time, Billy worked as a police reporter and was as poor as a starving dog with no prospects of getting a steak. Tom had resources and an understanding of money. Billy had friends in the world that didn't like sunshine and who would patronize a clubhouse where they could relax and do business. He and Tom saw a mutual benefit in joining up. Besides, they liked each other. So Tom decided to transform the Anderson's Café into the Arlington Cafe and Saloon. He installed leather booths for a touch of luxury. Politicians, police officials, businessmen and criminals appreciated the privacy of the booths. Tom, known for his discretion, became the trusted go-between to arbitrate negotiations and payoffs.

And now it's the Arlington *Annex*; like Josie's is the main Arlington and his saloon a mere add-on to her whorehouse. Well, he'd make sure that impression didn't take hold. The grand opening of his *Arlington* would happen first, an event all of New Orleans would envy.

Emma will be sorry she ever left me, he muttered, half drunk on his third glass of Scotch. She'll hear about my success and wealth, and the things she aspired to, even if she lives in St. Louis or Chicago or wherever she is with Irene. News of *my* Arlington, *Anderson's Arlington*, will travel far and wide as the grandest, most modern saloon in the South, hell, in the entire country.

Tom went to put another shot of Scotch in his glass but the bottle was empty. He stood looking at the bottle in his hand and thought; Life is like an empty bottle. You can fill it up. If not with a wife and a daughter to love, well, then lots of other things can be poured into the bottle.

Rarely did Tom sink into such a maudlin mood, a condition he disliked as a sign of weakness. The lapses, which happened only when he drank too much alone, he attributed to his Irish nature, the poet behind the fighter.

Blowing out the lamp, he made his way upstairs to bed. Lying under the blanket, he recited, as was his habit, the nightly prayer: Tomorrow I'll do everything within my power to rule my world, with or without the grace of God.

And, the next day, perhaps by the grace of God, or, in Tom's opinion, by his own acumen, he devised a jab back at Hennessy.

Sam Exnicio, owner of the New Waldorf saloon, stilling smarting over Hennessy having closed down his illegal boxing match, came to see Tom.

"You promised retribution against Hennessy, Mr. Mayor." Tom heard a hint of disrespect in Sam's tone. "I need to make my profit back."

Tom put an arm around the man's shoulder and handed him a cigar. "Here's what we'll do. That jerk threatened to close you down for illegal prizefights, right?"

Tom held a wooden match to Sam's cigar. After a couple puffs, Sam replied, "Yeah, so what you going to do about it?"

"He didn't say anything about other kinds of fights, did he?"

Sam studied the tip of the glowing cigar. "No."

"Then you sponsor dog versus rat fights." Tom patted Sam on the back and beamed like a proud father. "Rats spread the plague, you know that? Rat bites kill babies. Proven cases, just go down to the morgue. Rats spread yellow fever. You'll be doing a civic duty by ridding the city of the germ-infested carriers of disease."

"What?"

"You sponsor events where rats are killed to stop the Saffron Scourge from rearing its ugly head again. And provide entertainment for men who might otherwise be raising the crime rate. How can Hennessy object? You get to be the first to hold such an event, Sam, because of what Hennessy did to you. After you, all the other saloon owners can do their civic duty."

The next day handbills plastered the city:

GRAND NATIONAL RAT KILLING MATCH.
New Waldorf Saloon
Sunday 4 PM
$100 to any dog that can kill 12 full-grown rats per minute
for 5 consecutive minutes
Admission 50 cents   Reserved seats $1

Word on the street had it Hennessy ripped down the first handbill he saw and vowed to run Anderson out of New Orleans.

Tom told Billy the police chief was getting too big for his britches and needed to be put in his place.

Tom's Basin Street strategy was a coin burning a hole in Ant's pocket. The valuable tip of the real estate opportunity on Tom's Golden Row would buy him a corner lot of Mantangas' good grace.

By all outward appearances, the Matrangas were businessmen supervising the commerce of the port; only if you didn't do business their way, they'd put you out of business. Ant liked them. They didn't decorate themselves with pretensions or deceive with sweet talk. Take it or leave it, they'd say, but don't try to jew us. If you want to prosper and have a peaceful life, then mix blood with us. They were family men who loved children, including those they made fatherless through a business deal gone awry. They provided nice clothes so the kids could attend the dearly departed parent's funeral in style. A stipend to the widow, an educational fund, gifts at Christmas and food baskets flowed from their benevolent hands.

When Ant entered their office, Charles, the dapper one, sat adding columns of figures at the far desk. Black sleeve protectors covered the cuffs of his crisp white shirt. The green eyeshade didn't ruffle his pelt of black hair, shiny and slicked back with scented oil. Ant had thought of him as prissy, the accountant, until the time he heard Charles dispassionately order the man standing in front of him to be given a "big sendoff." The man fell on his knees begging for his life. Charles turned his back and the bravos dragged the crying man out of the office.

Tony stood at the window to keep a watchful eye on the comings and goings on the docks below. The brogans, the twilled pant and heavy work shirt he wore were dock ready if he needed to jump in and personally solve a problem. The more gregarious brother, an arm-around-the-shoulder type of guy with expansive gestures, he greeted Ant like a big-hearted friend; yet Ant felt the camaraderie could easily be a pillow with which to smother him.

"Ant," Tony enveloped him in a paesano bear hug. "How good to see you. Come sit. Some wine? To what do we owe this pleasure?"

Ant didn't expect the warm greeting, not after the Parker brothers killings.

"I have news you'll find interesting, " and told them about Tom's plan to consolidate his Storyville stake on Basin Street. Perhaps if they bought a lot or two on Basin they could pluck a plum from Tom's pie.

"Why not steal his pie?" Tony snickered.

"City Hall won't let you. You're the Mafia. They'd sooner close down all of Storyville than let you run the place."

"We don't want to steal Storyville," Charles injected. "Let Mr. Anderson build his fine whorehouses. And have our madams run them."

"You don't have any madams," Ant reminded him.

"Perhaps not now. Do you know his Golden Row madams?"

"No, not yet."

"When you do, come see us."

Now Ant put his mind back on MayAnn. Young Jack was hunting her; Buddy might be bedding her; she was shunning him. How was he to gain her favor?

Be her shining knight disguised as a best friend, Ant told himself. Use the old magician's trick of creating an illusion to disguise the reality.

However, Ant had a big hurdle to clear before he could convincingly present himself as a guileless friend—jealousy. That red-eyed demon ate at him. But Ant knew, in those rare moments of self-truth, that a far more powerful monster stood behind the jealousy demon. He had appointed MayAnn as his lifesaver, the cork ring he'd cling to so not to sink without a traced into the sea of indifference around him. Jealous was just the flame he danced around but the real heat came from his desperation not to be discarded as a throw-away man, a man without a legitimate place, a helpless powerless man.

Yet, he was irrationally powerless to banish jealousy. Which is why he found himself loitering on MayAnn's street, imagining Young Jack lurking in the shadows and sneaking to her window on tiptoes and jimming the window open. Then Ant would pounce, the scene real in Ant's mind, and put that pretender, that *privileged* man, in a chokehold and squeeze with all his might until Young Jack gurgled and yelped for mercy. MayAnn would come to the window, her nudity glimmering in the moonlight, and her eyes would lock in adoration on Ant's as he choked the life out of his unworthy rival. Ant saw himself as the hero he always imagined, a broad-shouldered man who feared no other, a man who didn't have to ask anyone for permission to live as he sees fit.

In his fantasy, while leaning against the building opposite her house, Ant imagined that MayAnn would pull back the curtain and see him guarding her and her heart would burst with love for him. She'd wave, shyly at first, and then thrust open the window and urgently motion for him to dive through. Then she'd fall upon him and cover him with kisses.

But, in reality, her window remained dark and the curtains never moved.

After an hour or so, with no sign of Young Jack, Ant drifted down the street. At the end of the block, he flattened himself to the corner building and kept one eye on MayAnn's house, the other on Buddy's around the corner, in case she was tomcatting with him.

Nothing stirred on the street for the rest of the night. At early light, a few people drifted out of their houses and headed off to work. Ant walked a half block, crossed the street and came back, putting purpose in his stride to avoid suspicion. His feet were swollen. His back hurt. The black eye from the Lincoln Park kafuffle felt hot and bruised. By eight o'clock, hunger served up another distraction. The street settled down, with only an occasional passerby. Then mid-morning, MayAnn stepped out her door with a shopping basket on one arm. Ant didn't show myself. Once certain she was headed for the market, he took a short cut to intercept her.

"MayAnn," he called out in a voice mistaken for Young Jack's.

She turned and, seeing that she had been fooled, exclaimed, "Antoine! What are you bothering me for?"

Her question stunned him so much he couldn't answer. He waited for a quip to come, like, Why does the sun shine? But he had the good sense not to be flip.

"You must believe me when I say Young Jack thinks you killed his whore. He wants revenge."

She pishawed him. "He's a dandy, all show. So I'll be part of his show, the candy on his arm." She laughed, shifting her basket. "Jack may be stomping around just now but I can tame him. I have no fear of him, Antoine. You know I'm a wily woman, and I can get what I want. What I need, Antoine. What I need to live."

"At least get some protection."

"You mean a bodyguard, Antoine? You want to be my bodyguard?" she teased.

Ant had an answer but instead replied, "You know Eulalia Echo?"

Prostitutes paid Eulalia for talismans to attract luck and money and love, and for potions to ward off disease and unwanted children, and for charms to deflect the evil eye cast by jealous wives and envious competitors. But she also had the reputation as New Orleans' high priestess of *vodun*, the real spiritual work from Africa, not the Royal Street tourist voodoo. Black and white, rich and poor, consulted her about everything from jealous lovers to the mysteries of the soul.

Once, a friend of Ant's who had a love problem confided that Eulalia's advice had completely changed his life. He had been swooning in unrequited love. Eulalia told him he could not create love, either within himself or anyone else. All he could do was create a space for love to enter. Love comes not from a state of mind but from outside the mind, from Oloddumare, the Almighty Creator. If the man stood in the way with all his chattering and desiring and feeling sorry, then he might as well tie himself in a poke and jump into the Mississippi River for all the happiness he'd find.

"And here's the secret, the key to happiness," he had told Ant. "I had to forgive. Not just myself or the other person, but this place and this time and all that has created it. Not to forgive is to cling to the emotions of the past and that's to fear the future."

Ant hoped Eulalia might help MayAnn forgive herself for not being what she wanted to be. If she could get free of the burden, she wouldn't need Young Jack. Then maybe she'd relax enough to be happy with him.

"You want Eulalia to give me a charm to ward off danger, is that it, Antoine? I know about her voodoo powers."

"No harm in asking the gods for help. If not a charm, then hang a prayer book around your neck."

In New Orleans, even rational people didn't dismiss the mystery of voodoo. Some people went to the racetrack and gave away their money because they had a "feeling" about a particular horse. That's what prayer is, isn't it? A feeling. And voodoo is a form of prayer. If you believed in magic and love, you believed in voodoo. It might be a sideshow or the high altar, depending on if your fear spurred mockery or worship, but you genuflected nevertheless.

"I don't believe in that stuff, Antoine, not really."

"Maybe she'll give you a charm to keep me away."

"Now that'll be worth the visit." She looked serious but Ant heard the mock of humor of her voice.

He guided her through the center of gun-slinging uptown, deceptively peaceful in the morning hours, and across Rampart Street, where the furniture emporiums and second-hand shops and good clothing stores were opening for business. A steamboat whistle, shrill as a hawk, came from the river six blocks in front as they crossed Magazine Street, a high-tone shopping street, one of the few cobblestone streets in the city. On the other side of the street lie the Garden District, where millionaire cotton brokers, bankers and steamship owners lived alongside Italian, German, Irish immigrants, poor Americans, whites and blacks in a mish-mash of stately Southern-plantation style mansions next to shotgun shanties and smelly stables. Eulalia's small-whitewashed shotgun with red trim was wedged into a row of similar houses.

As soon as Ant knocked Eulalia opened the door as if expecting them. "Come in, my child," she said, taking MayAnn's hand.

Her brightly colored five-pointed *tignon*, a defiant statement of style and independence, warned she was not to be trifled with. Over a hundred years ago, the city's colored women created flamboyant homemade hats with more creative flair than the Parisian pretensions worn by the white women of the ruling class. The upper-class women complained to their husbands their serving girl's crowns upstage them, show disrespect, and that reflected poorly on their menfolk. The husbands went to Louisiana's Spanish governor, who decreed lower-class women could wear only a bandana as a head covering. The ingenious women of Eulalia's lineage transformed the humble bandana into a fashion of rebellion.

The tignon was her fair warning; her big-boned heft of her otherworldly power the enforcer.

Eulalia ushered Ant and MayAnn into her tidy front room. A simple wooden table with four chairs stood in the center. Against one wall was a horsehair sofa under a painting of a solemn African chieftain surrounded by leaping dancing figures. Bundles of dried herbs hung from the rafters. On the opposite side of the room, in front of a window, sat a light-complexioned Creole, handsome save for his big nose. "Can I borrow this for tonight, Lalee?" he asked, draping a diamond necklace around his neck. She ignored him and gestured for

143

her guests to sit at the table. MayAnn couldn't take her eyes off the dandy as he fastened on diamond earrings and tilted his head from side to side, the gems glittering in the light from the window.

"What can I do for you?" Eulalia asked.

Ant launched into an account of Young Jack and how he had murdered a woman and now wanted to get MayAnn, when the young fellow sauntered over to the table and held a diamond up against his front tooth. "What do you think, Lalee?"

"I think you're intruding. My godson," she explained, "Ferdinand Morton. I named him for the king of Spain but he calls himself Ferdy, like some street-boy American."

Ant had heard of, but never met, the latest whorehouse piano professor whiz, later better known as Jelly Roll Morton. At the time his nickname was Windin' Boy because he could get himself wound up and go like bunny with the women all night long.

"I'll have one of these in my tooth when I'm rich. And have them sewn on my sock garters." He gave MayAnn a big wink and drifted back to Eulalia's jewelry box to try on rings and bracelets.

Again Ant started to explain the situation but Eulalia held up a hand to silence him. "I want to hear the *orishas*." She took a handful of cornmeal from a covered bowl and dribbled a line around three candles—black, white and red—on the wooden table while mumbling an invocation in a language Ant didn't recognize. Then she lit the candles, closed her eyes and reached her hands out, signifying MayAnn and Ant should join hands to close the circle with her. He didn't expect to feel anything special, no visitation of spirits. But, the longer they clasped hands, the quieter the room became; even the presence of Ferdy disappeared. After long minutes passed—Ant began to wonder if she had fallen asleep—Eulalia squeezed their hands to signal they should open their eyes.

Eulalia's eyes were all white, as if her orbs had rolled back into her head. A glow infused her face and she smelled different than when Ant and MayAnn had entered, sweet and smoky. MayAnn, transfixed with her mouth hanging open, tried to take her hand back but Eulalia tightened her grip, although she let go of Ant's hand. Without looking at either Ant or MayAnn, her chin dropped to her chest as if she was truly asleep. They waited for a minute, then another. MayAnn mouthed, What's happening? Eulalia didn't appear to be breathing. Ant was about to alert Ferdy when her head jerked up. She slowly turned to look at MayAnn.

"The white man is not your savior nor your doom." Her look had such intensity Ant could fairly hear the air crackle between them. "Your soul is in great danger. You must surrender."

"To the police?" squeaked MayAnn and jumped to her feet. Quick as a thought, Eulalia pulled her down to the chair.

"We're concerned with the soul, not the body. But this white man is a danger to you." She gave Ant a sidelong glance.

Eulalia leaned toward MayAnn and sniffed her, the way one does to determine if meat has gone bad. "All right." She patted MayAnn's hand. "All right now, lovely. We can fix things. Let's start with the first step and that'll carry you to the second. Then all you have to do is surrender to the journey."

With great deliberation, she blew out the candles one by one, saving the red for last, which she pulled to her. She dug out some of the soft wax and, with deft fingers, shaped a small heart and held it up for MayAnn to see. "Look like you?" and laughed when all MayAnn could do was flap her jaws. Eulalia carefully, tenderly, set the tiny heart on the table and rose to fetch a jar from a shelf. Settling back into her chair with a satisfying grunt of comfort, she placed the jar next to the wax heart. "High John the Conqueror Root for power," she explained. She took a pinch and sprinkled it on the heart, which she placed in a red flannel mojo bag. "He'll come at you with hatred and revenge. Don't be afraid. Keep this close to your heart while you open his heart."

She handed the mojo bag to the mystified MayAnn and swept the cornmeal off the table with the edge of her hand. Sound flooded back into the room -- from the house next door came an oddly offbeat piano hobbling along like a three-legged horse trying to canter. Ferdy stopped fooling with the diamonds and listened intently. A woman's plangent voice sang, "I stood on the corner, my feet was dripping wet/I asked every man I met, Can't you give me a dollar, give me a lousy dime/Just to feed that hungry man of mine."

"That's Mamie Desdoumes," Eulalia explained. "I call her Maimed Mamie because she's got only two fingers on her right hand and a big hole in her heart. He's hearing his dream." She nodded toward her godson, oblivious to everything but the music. "That's what he comes here for, and to borrow my diamonds." She took MayAnn's hands in hers. "You don't want your spirit to be maimed, dear. The purpose of life is different from what you think. If you need further guidance, come see me."

On their way back uptown, MayAnn tried to outpace Ant, damn near running. He dragged her to a halt. "Billy wants to talk about the night of the fire. But first you and I need to be in agreement about what we saw."

"Leave this alone, Antoine. I got nothing to talk to Billy about."

"You're in danger, MayAnn."

"I have protection now." She fingered the mojo bag with a look of sideshow amusement and high altar sincerity. "You don't need to be hanging outside my window at all hours no more. And I can do my own shopping."

She wrenched the shopping basket from Ant's hands and hurried away.

As she fled around the corner, Ant thought, Maybe I should kill Young Jack and be done with trying to put him in the frame. But he wanted MayAnn to conspire with him, to be bound to him by complicity. Love needs more than passion to endure. It requires ineffable magic, a grand sleight-of-hand to conjure a reality so desirable as to justify any means. Is that not the definition of love worth dying for? Total surrender to the heart. The duel between the mind and the heart, the tame and the wild, the rational and the irrational is the apex of love, the climactic moment when you put the gun to your own head and pull the trigger. You die yet you live, are reborn in the bliss of no return. The old is new, the imagined is real, the improbable is possible.

Love requires cunning. Taking MayAnn to Eulalia Echo was an act of deft cunningness, or so Ant thought. *Now she'll see him as a caring friend looking after her protection. She'll lower her guard and I'll slip back into her bed and all that stood for. My heart has more value than Young Jack's money. She can take that fool's money and live in the nice house he'd provide, and we'd still find our time together. That would require cunning on both our parts. A bond of conspiracy would be created between us, a bond of cunning.*

Ant valued cunning for two reasons: he could operate in full view and not be seen; and he could operate from the shadows but his effects were seen.

But he didn't have the confidence of a skillful cunner. Compared to Tom or Chen, the most skilled and opaque cunners in all of New Orleans, he was an amateur. One reason he had put himself at Tom's service was to learn first hand how the vice lord operated in the open but behind the scenes simultaneously. A great survival skill, Ant thought, one worth learning.

The Matrangas weren't good at cunningness. In a way, their undisguised use of power was an attraction for Ant. They were, in an odd way, a model of Old Testament rightfulness; this is who I am and if you spit in my eye, I'll club you over the head. Ant thought by being around them some of their self-assuredness might rub off on him, or at least he'd learn a trick or two.

Chapter 10.

After the scuffle in Lincoln Park over MayAnn, Ant hadn't seriously considered going to Young Jack's mysterious meeting. But on the appointed night he thought, Why not? Maybe I'll come upon another way to skin that cat.

As he neared the address, a sinister and foul-smelling back street two blocks from Chen's opium den, a man suddenly materialized, grabbed Ant by the elbow and muttered, "Keep walking." They slid around a corner before Young Jack said, "Just a precaution to see that you weren't followed."

He steered Ant into an alley so dark nothing could be seen beyond an arm's length. "Don't mind the rats," Young Jack said, while guiding Ant to a door recessed in the wall. Glancing over his shoulder, he scanned the alley before giving a coded rap. Pause. Then two more knuckle knocks. The door eased open and an eye appeared at the crack. The door opened wide enough for Young Jack and Ant to squeeze through by turning sideways, a move that made them defenseless. The guard briskly ran his hands over them, searching for weapons, before leading the two down a completely dark hallway but for the thread of light beneath a door at the far end. There the guard said a password and waited for a reply before opening the door. Inside the room a kerosene lantern on a plain wooden table showed the dim figures of three men standing in the shadows. As Young Jack entered, the men stepped forward and sat at the table on simple straight back chairs. Young Jack gestured for Ant to take his place at the table.

"This," he pointed to the man across the table, "is Santa Claus."

The slight clean-shaven man looked nothing like Santa Claus. He nodded without offering to shake hands. Although he appeared benign, Ant sensed the readiness of a quick-draw gunslinger in how the man sat, slightly forward with weight on the balls of his feet and his hands near his hips.

Young Jack motioned to the man on Ant's right. "Machine Gun." The bull of a man with no neck clasped his arms crossed his barrel chest and stared, as if daring Ant to take him on.

"And may I present," Young Jack's tone became reverential, " El Presidente." The brown-skinned man rose to shake Ant's hand. Unlike the other two, he wore a formal black suit and smiled. "Manuel Bonilla, President of Honduras. Pleased to meet you."

"Mr. President and his associates are here on a secret mission of international importance," Young Jack explained. "The success, or failure, of their effort will have political and business significances for our country. As an emissary of those interests, I've been assigned to assist President Bonilla in every way possible. My compatriot," he gestured to Ant, "with his connections in the shipping business will be able to help us."

Ant couldn't hide his look of surprise. Was this some elaborate joke? Dilettante Jack creating theater? Why was he being dragging into this, this hoax?

"I thank you," said President Bonilla solemnly. "My country thanks you. The poor peasants of my country thank you. We are here to return justice and freedom to Honduras."

Then he launched into a long and convoluted speech about the history of Central America, political chicanery and corruption, and the untrustworthiness of allies. "When that Nicaraguan son-of-a-whore Zelaya invaded, I escaped to the United States on the U.S.S. *Chicago*. Now Davila, once my trusted general, is Zelaya's puppet in the presidential palace.

My heart cries with the suffering of my country. My people beg me to come save them."

"We are preparing an invasion to liberate Honduras," the man called Santa Claus said. "Machine Gun and I are President Bonilla's American generals helping him procure supplies and ships to carry those supplies. We need cover operations to get the guns into the country. This must be very very clandestine so not tip off our enemies."

"And this is where you come in, Ant," Young Jack said.

Ant truly didn't know what he was talking about. "I don't see how..."

"You have connections to certain parties in shipping, right? Bringing fruit from South America. The ships load bananas in Honduras and could leave things behind."

Ant thought to deny any connection to the Matrangas, but obviously Young Jack knew something. And, if he presented himself as Innocent Joe with nothing to contribute, Ant may well be an expendable liability.

El Presidente leaned over the table, his chubby face within a foot of Ant. "For your associates support, no banana will leave Honduras except on their ships." Bonilla's gaze bore into Ant's eyes with the sincerity of a gold digger proposing marriage.

Ant placed his hands flat on the table and counted to ten to give the impression of careful deliberation. "And?"

Bonilla half stood to better lean over the table and get nearly nose-to-nose with Ant. "I will pay a reservation fee in advance and a goodwill commission to you."

Ant and El Presidente had a stare down, that moment in poker when the player decides to raise, call or fold. "Perhaps I know someone."

"Yes, you know someone," Bonilla replied, settling back in his chair. "You talk to someone, then you give Mr. Bohomme a message for us."

Young Jack stood and shook hands with Bonilla. "You'll hear good news soon," he reassured El Presidente and nodded to Santa Claus and Machine Gun.

Back on the street, Young Jack offered to buy drinks and discuss details.

"A place where no one knows us," Ant said, more anxious to ask questions than discuss details.

Young Jack, with a surprisingly good working knowledge of the seamier side of Storyville, led Ant to a plank bar. A plank bar was the lowest of the low, often nothing more than a dirt floor, planks laid across kegs for the bar, a mongrel mix of tables and chairs and benches, and, in the finer plank bars, an out-of-tune piano. For five cents, a patron could take a glass tumbler, or an earthenware mug, from the communal bin and fill it from a spigot of any barrel lining the wall. The barrel marked "Irish whiskey" contained neutral spirits flavored with a pint of creosote to give it that bite of hard liquor. The rum was made from cast-off sugarcane stalks, molasses and raw alcohol, which also formed the base of the gin flavored with a dash of turpentine and juniper. The mixture of three parts water to one part alcohol with port prunes, cherries and burnt sugar—with a slug of olive oil for a tawny taste—constituted the wine.

"This is my favorite bar because it's called 'Fare Thee Well'," Young Jack said. "The owner told me that he named it after Lord Byron's poem. Can you believe that? The owner of a place like this," he made a wide gesture to the roofed over a section of an alley, the front and back of the rectangular box made of rough lumber, "being well enough read to know Byron's poems? He's also a terrific singer with a heart rendering tenor. Knows hundreds of ballads." Young Jack set two full mugs of the Irish whiskey on the table and offered a toast. "To the success of our enterprise."

Ant raised his mug, tentatively touched his tongue to the "whiskey" and set the mug down. Somewhere in the skein of Young Jack, Bonilla, Matrangas was an opportunity that Ant could just barely sense. If he could place Young Jack in cahoots with the Matrangas. If Hennessy was tipped off the Mafia was scheming with international revolutionaries—no *bandits*—to import drugs—no drugs and *guns*—to set up a base in New Orleans from which to launch an attack on a friendly country, an invasion that might drag the United States into a Central American war, well, how could Hennessy resist such bait. The provincial chief of police would become a national hero overnight for thwarting the conspiracy. And Young Jack could find himself in prison, perhaps even shot as a traitor.

And then MayAnn will beg for forgiveness and pledge eternal fidelity to me. The thought put a smile on Ant's lips.

"You know the man I admire the most?' Young Jack broke into Ant's revelry. "Lord Byron. A man of feeling and action," he raised his mug in a toast, "and one randy son-of-a-bitch."

Young Jack lifted his chin and recited:

" 'Tis to create, and in creating live

A being more intense, that we endow

With form our fancy, gaining as we give

The life we image even as I do now.'

Childe Harold. That's my creed, to live intensely for honor and love."

Ant also raised his mug, not in a toast but rather a challenge, and countered with:

" *'But sweeter still than this, than these, than all,*

Is first and passionate love—it stands alone....' from *Don Juan*."

Young Jack watched Ant for a moment over the rim of his mug. "You're a man of many surprises, Ant. An educated man, as I now discover. A man willingly to risk a knife in order to prevent a friend from endangering himself, as I found out at Lincoln Park. And, as I've learned since our last encounter in the dirt, a man of nefarious connections."

Young Jack equally surprised Ant. A man of his class would be educated but Ant didn't expect his nemesis's enterprise in sniffing out Ant's connection to the Matrangas. And how did Young Jack's fall in with Central American renegades?

"How did you find Bonilla and his "generals"?"

"My father. He has far flung business interests in banking, investing, import-export. He's a friend of J.P. Morgan. Did you know that? And with the men who own United Fruit. They have a vested interest in a stable, and friendly, Honduras. The present president, Davila, is weak and the target of rebels supported by Guatemala and El Salvador. El Presidente Bonilla, on the other hand, is a strong man who knows how to rule with an army. So I'm helping my father. That's how I earn my keep."

"Why bring me in?"

"You can make a handsome commission, a thanks for helping me bring that murdering parlor maid to justice. When you saved me from a rash move at Lincoln Park, I realized that you were loyal to your friends. You know what Byron once wrote to his future wife," Young Jack asked, taking a healthy slug of whiskey. "Sensation is the great object of life. A man should jump into the 'craving void,' his term which I call the 'wild yes', with a ringing affirmation to life whether it leads to the gambling tables or into battle or to the beds of many women." He waved his hand over his head with the flourish of conducting an orchestra. For a moment he held perfectly still, arm upraised, face pointing to bare-beamed roof and eyes closed in concentration. "Us poets have a duty to seek out Sensation and plunge into the Wild Yes, the seat of our inspiration, the friction between the doing and the accomplishment. The doing, that agitation of the spirit in action, leads to TRUTH."

He held the noble pose, which Ant took as self-satire but quickly realized Young Jack believed the hogwash. Yet, Ant liked him in that moment because, despite the pretentious affectations, this foppish fool did put himself into direct action for "honor and love." But at the same moment, Ant hated Young Jack because of his advantage. It wasn't just his pure white linage or his easy wealth but his confidence to leap into his wild yes. He was a shining man, a complete man, a man Ant wanted to be but found so elusive.

"How did you find out about me and the Matrangas?"

"My father's business tendrils reach into dark holes wherever profits can be found."

"And," Ant hesitated so not to seem too interested, "this parlor maid business? What should we do?"

"Lady Justice carries the scales and a sword in the service of love and honor."

"What exactly..."

"Make her my prisoner while I decide the punishment."

Eulalia Echo had told MayAnn: "He'll come at you with hatred and revenge." Well, Young Jack is certainly determined to hunt her, Ant thought.

The journey of life is a walk across a bog of quicksand, in Ant's opinion. What looks like firm ground can, without warning, turn into a quagmire. He had thought MayAnn was his firm ground upon which to build the life he wanted. He hadn't doubted that his white skin was a safe pass into a society of advantages and privileges. And look what happened. Betrayed. What's a man suppose to do? Be on guard every waking moment? Do what has to be done became Ant's guiding principle. Extreme measures in some cases, the Civil War a case in point. When the stakes are high enough, all rules will be broken and a man has to answer back in like terms.

"What do you expect me to do with the Matrangas," Ant asked.

"Present Bonilla's business proposal to them. It could be a very lucrative and long-term deal."

Ant pushed his mug aside without pretending to take another sip. "I'll let you know," and left the plank bar.

Tom sat with Billy at a back table of the Arlington saloon working on a jigsaw puzzle: how to make all the pieces fit so

Hennessy and the Matrangas neutralized, if not eliminated, each other. "The Matrangas are the hard bit." Tom moved his forefinger around the table as if actually pushing pieces of a puzzle. "We can't, as you suggested, Billy, burn down the docks. That would be shooting ourselves in the foot, if not worst. The commercial loss to the city would be ruinous."

The Matrangas seemed impervious to any damaging attack. Their protection business centered mostly on fellow Italians, especially the illegal immigrants living in Little Palermo, on the other side of the French Quarter from Storyville. For less than a fifty cents a week per person, the Matrangas guaranteed those Italians that the police would not raid their homes and throw them in jail to wait for deportation. And, the Matrangas would help them find work, either on the sugar cane plantations outside the city, or on the docks, in the markets, or, if the man was big and strong, as a soldier in the Mafia.

Their business on the docks was locked up tight as a strong box, so no way for Tom to pry that open.

"Maybe their drug trade," Billy thinking back to Ant's botched attempt to have Chen go after the Matrangas.

"I want nothing to do with drugs," Tom replied forcefully. "Sex is a more powerful addictive than any drug." He glanced up at a flutter at the front door of the saloon. "As long as we control prostitution, that is Storyville, we don't have to worry about losing customers. We need to get Hennessy and the Matrangas out of our hair, that's all."

Billy followed Tom's gaze to the well-dressed and startlingly beautiful woman who had entered the saloon, announced by the white plume fanfare on her black broad-brimmed hat. A tumble of dark luxurious curls framed her face that positively beamed good will and good times. My God, she could get a smile out of a dead man, thought Billy. Poets would describe her blue-green dress as a mist of gossamer sea spray clinging to her bodacious figure. Every man in the place fell silent and stared. She paused and graciously drenched everyone with her sunny cheer and glided over to Tom's table.

"Mr. Anderson," she said, extending her hand. "I hear you're looking for business partners." Tom rose and took her hand. And didn't let go.

"Sit down, Miss…."

"Hilma Burt, lately of St. Louis."

"My pleasure." Tom stared, his cheeks stretched in an idiotic grin. Still holding her hand, he came around the table and pulled the chair out for her. "Would you like a refreshment?"

"Perhaps later. Mr. Anderson…"

"Call me Tom."

"All right, then, *Tom*." She made the name sound like their intimate secret. "I have business experience you can capitalize on."

When in negotiations, Tom always maintained a stoic front as if nothing ever, ever surprised him. Unflappable. He could keep a straight face in the gale of the funniest joke, which made him a hard man to read. Alert even when resting, he'd take in a person —the tone of their voice, how their body moved—and wait patiently for them to reveal themselves. He kept his sense of humor carefully under wraps lest his competitors perceive such humanness as a weak point in his stolid façade.

But this woman, this sprite, had him behaving boyishly. He grinned like a six-year-old who had a crush on his teacher, squirming in his chair, fawning over her. A blind man could see Tom was smack-gobbed smitten.

"Billy, would you please excuse us."

Billy graciously stood, not sure if he was piqued over being dismissed or amused at Tom's befuddlement. He politely nodded to Hilma Burt and received a dazzling smile in return. He glanced around and spotted Ant sitting at a nearby table.

"Mind if I join you? Seems Tom needs to conduct some business in private."

"Please do." Ant was stilling trying to work out how to put his own puzzle together. Billy might be able to make a contribution.

"Now would you look at that," Billy said, beaming at Tom and Hilma twittering together. "Our boy may have found his heart again."

Ever since his "wife" Emma had left him years ago, Tom had been guarded about intimate relationships. He had "friends" and "business partners" such as Josie, but never a lady friend, someone he could relax with and have fun. But this young lady sitting across the table clearly beguiled him.

"Who's that?" Ant asked.

"Tom may well have found another "associate" for his Basin Street Golden Row. But I'll wager she'll be more than a business partner."

Later that night, Tom, in a buoyant mood, unabashedly admitted, "I have no idea what happened. It was like someone pulled the cloth off a statue and I was struck dumb by its beauty. Did you ever have anything like that happen, Billy? Me either. It feels like grace. Do you know what that feels like, Billy? Me either, but it must feel like this."

"How's the Basin Plan going?" Ant inquired, innocently.

"Tom and Josie have drawn up their list and sent out invitations. There's interest. If Countess Willie comes on board, then the deal is good as done. All the other madams will follow."

Countess Willie's reputation made her the de facto arbitrator not only of fashion but where it was fashionable to get laid. Her high class of clientele would raise the profit level for all the madams as her neighbors.

"How soon is this grand strategy going to shape up?" Ant asked.

"I've already talked to the contractor to begin work on this place." Billy waved a hand at the well-worn saloon. "He'll start tearing it apart next week to build anew."

"It'll be something to look forward to," Ant replied, finishing his beer. "Time for my sleep."

But instead of going to his boarding house, Ant took a roundabout way, cautiously keeping to the shadow wherever possible, to the Matrangas "clubhouse." Located a couple blocks from the docks, the nondescript wooden single-story building was where the Matranga bothers could be usually found when not at their official office. Ant was one of the few outsiders allowed in the clubhouse, closely guarded by armed Mafia soldiers.

The man on the door frisked Ant, even though he was a familiar face. The Matrangas were in the main room, a lounge/game room with dartboards, chess and checker tables, and shelves stacked with newspapers from Italy. Four burly men were shooting pool at the table in the center of the room. Charles sat near a lamp reading one of the newspapers, while Tony slumped comfortably in an overstuffed armchair nearby.

The understanding was that Ant would never hang out in the clubhouse. He'd conduct his business briskly and leave.

He stood in front of Charles, waiting to be acknowledged. Charles unhurriedly rustled through the pages before lowering the paper and looked at Ant, who drew a sheet of paper from his suit coat. "The name of a madam Mr. Anderson is trying to recruit for his Basin Street Golden Row. Countess Willie Piazza. An Italian name, right? Perhaps you share a kinship."

Charles nodded for Ant to set the paper on a table and went back to reading his newspaper.

Chapter 11.

The following day Ant went to Louis's barbershop in search of Buddy with the intent to cash in the funeral parade favor, and use it as a chip in the gamble for MayAnn.

He hadn't been there but five minutes when Buddy stumbled in looking like the night, and morning, he'd want to forget. Someone must have danced on his suit jacket the way it was crumpled; lip red and cheek rouge and what smelled like throw up smeared his grimy shirt; his eyes, what you could see of them behind the swollen lids, looked like cracked marbles.

"Buddy, you feelin' sick?" Louis asked as he guided Buddy to a chair.

"Yeah."

"You got a fever?"

"Fever in the heart." Buddy gingerly lowered himself into the barber chair.

Louis snapped a cloth over his client, turning his nose away from the sour smell. "Threw up, huh?"

"Cleared myself out twice," Buddy groaned.

"How's your eyes? Got a yellow tinge?"

Louis suspected the Saffron Scourge wasn't the cause of Buddy's misery, but given New Orleans' history with yellow fever, prudent men inquired when someone looked as sickly as Buddy. With the mere mention of yellow fever, citizens of New Orleans crossed themselves in hopes of warding off the disease. In the near past, yellow fever epidemics had killed tens of thousands of New Oleanians. Mention yellow fever and a person would run home to take a bath or gulp an iodine tablet imprinted with a cross to ward off the killer. Some people sprinkled gold dust in their drinks and on their food to give their internals a protective lining. Those with less money ate pickled apple peel suspended in laudanum.

"Naw, my eyes are red," Buddy replied. "All I'm suffering from is bad whiskey and worse women. I ran into Leda on the corner of North Liberty and Conti. Went looking for her, to tell the truth. Knew she'd be at her stand and I took her off her feet for the night. The girl needs a rest now and then."

"By the looks of you, if she was resting I'd hate to see the result of her working." Louis chuckled in relief that only a common suffering afflicted Buddy.

The cornet player lay stiff as a dead man while Louis wrapped his face in a hot towel. He hadn't noticed Ant sitting in one of the waiting chairs. Buddy, his voice muffled under the towel, said, "I got a big worry, Louis. That's what's behind this headache and fever."

"What's that?"

"Tonight I'm playing Kenny's Hall and Sweet Lovin' is going to be there. The hogs have arranged a cuttin' contest between us."

"Here then, you'll need these." Louis gave Buddy a handful of plasters, the ones he used to stop shaving nicks from bleeding. "When it's all over, you stick these on Sweet Lovin' and his boys before they bleed to death."

Buddy gave a grateful laugh followed by a worrisome sigh. "Sweet Lovin's band is so hot they can light fire a mile away."

"Sweet Lovin' plays the mandolin, Buddy. That's a foreign lady's instrument. It has a plink-ca-di-plink sound. What's that? How can people dance to that?" Louis the corner man pumping up his fighter.

"He can switch to the fiddle, the devil's own instrument, if you believe the preacher."

"Back hills," scoffed Louis. "This is New Orleans. You're the only person playing new music in this entire city. Don't worry about Sweet Lovin's campfire when you're setting the whole town ablaze."

"He's got that trombone man Frankie Dusen. I need two trombones just to sound like one Dusen."

Ant jumped up and stood by Buddy's side. "I'll be your second trombone."

"That you, Ant?"

"I'll put my slide right in Dusen's ear and clear him off the stage. You know I can play. You heard me in the funeral parade," a reminder that Buddy owed a payback.

Buddy took a moment to think it over. "All right. Be at Kenny's Hall at eight."

Kenny's Hall, once a church, was the Union Sons Hall, a benefit society run by Mr. Kinney. The squat wooden building didn't look like a church but a workingman's place, plain and no nonsense. Inside, the pews and pulpit had been cleared out, leaving one big room, a hall for meetings and potlucks and wakes and, on weekend nights, dancing and music.

Ant was so damn nervous he showed up half an hour early and paced in the alley talking confidence into his quickly fading courage. Buddy had to cut Sweet Lovin' at the knees or the hogs would give him a thumbs down. He might well end up driving a dray, as his father had done. Why had he, Ant anguished, promised Buddy he'd blow the city's best trombone player off the stage? Hell, the only thing he could play were marches by rote.

Just as he was about to flee, Buddy appeared surrounded by a flock of women hoping he'd invite them on stage to dance. He paid them no mind, not even a smile or a tease. The man had the look of a person whose mother had just died. Spotting his nervous second trombone, Buddy called out, "Ant!" and pulled him through the stage door. "You full of steam tonight?

You be as loud and fast as a champion racing sidepaddler. This is life or death tonight, and death is a hard way to make a living."

Over in a backstage corner, the rest of the band shared a bottle. Buddy took a big swig. "Enough now. We got to be loose, but sharp. If you want them women to keep loving you, you've got to win their hearts tonight, you hear me? We don't want to walk out of here poor pockets."

Sweet Lovin' and his band was nowhere in sight backstage, and he couldn't be missed any more than a clown in a funeral parlor. "Maybe he's not comin'," suggested Buddy's guitarist.

"That's like saying the sun ain't gonna rise," Buddy replied. Then he put on a big smile and some shine in his eyes. "Don't us worry about Sweet Lovin'. Let's go out there and blow off some knickers. Come on, boys, the pearls are just waiting to be picked up."

Buddy stepped out on stage blowing his horn. Triumphal blasts. Archangel blasts. "Callin' all my chillun!" he shouted and his fans erupted in cheers.

Ant had no choice but to follow the band onstage, but he was too scared to blow his trombone. Instead, he faked it, pulling the slide back and forth, puffing his cheeks but not even a garbled note came out. A sheet of paper couldn't be slipped into the dancehall so packed was the place and Ant felt all those people looking at him, expecting him to hold up his part in the Buddy Bolden Band. Not even MayAnn seemed worth the humiliation of being exposed as a fool.

Aaron Harris and the hogs stood at the edge of the stage, a panel of judges.

Buddy got up a head of steam, some march-stomp-jump only he knew how to play, and the other band members blazed along, somehow making sense of the whole thing. The piano player gave Ant a look, Blow that damn thing! so Ant made a sliding swoop and no one seemed to notice. Watching the other trombone player, he mimicked his movements and was getting the hang of it when, without warning, came a bellow of sound. Sweet Lovin', hidden in the curtains on the other side of the stage, led his band out in a full swing march of "As the Saints Go Marchin' In."

The rule of a cuttin' war was one band played a song, then the other band answered. In a mean cuttin' war, the bands interrupted each other, butted in, sent mocking challenges right in the middle of a passage. Ant saw right away this wasn't the only thing to worry about with Sweet Lovin': his music told the audience, Be Happy for nothing else is worth a damn. A natural showman, he wrapped his arms around the crowd and whisper dirty ditties in their ears. His band had the filthiest, foulest mouths, always your mother that, I know your wife, your wife did this, I did this with your grandmother, mother, sister, wife's sister, your lover and with your dog. Your grandpappy didn't use a shotgun to get your parents to the altar; he had to use a Civil War cannon. His fans stomped so loud the hall shook and boomed as if a stampede coming through the front doors. Sweet Lovin' high stepped, waving his arms as if to lift the cheering and hollering through the roof.

If Buddy didn't do something, he'd be drowned out, washed right out the door on the wave of Sweet Lovin's music.

Buddy sauntered over to Sweet Lovin', put his horn right in his face—and waited without playing a note. Sweet Lovin' kept on his grin, but a nervous grin. Both bands stopped playing. The crowd held its breath waiting to witness a murder, or at least a blown-out eardrum.

Buddy started low, barely heard, giving Sweet Lovin' a chance to step away. Everybody strained to hear the note. Buddy sobbed, or his horn sobbed, the same thing. He dipped the cornet and turned to the audience and poured warm honey over them to calm down the fevered pitch inflicted by Sweet Lovin'. He held their hand tenderly as a lover. Just when they became restless with the foreplay, he squeezed their hand and heated up the honey.

He didn't play particularly loud or fast. Rather, he oiled them up. Then patted their loins with aching gutbucket so their hips rocked in desire. He swung the dancers around with long looping notes, lowdown blues that slit them open to the lust for life, every bit of it, the highs and lows because if you had to march to that swing, and you did, then you might as well have a good time. The crowd moaned with his phrases, pitch perfect, and moved like snakes standing on their tails, wiggling as to fly.

Knowing Buddy was winning over his crowd, Sweet Lovin' cut in with "Let Me Be Your Li'l Dog Till Your Big Dog Comes," breaking Buddy's grip. Frankie Dusen's trombone growl like a dog in heat.

"Let him be the li'l dog," Buddy told his band. "We'll show them how the big dog bites."

He raised his hand and Ant got ready, lips a puckered embouchure and eyes squeezed shut so he wouldn't pop them out of his head; that's how hard he intended to play. He'd be a mastiff to Dusen's mutt. He'd be a roar from hell, but melodic, as Buddy launched into "Stick It Where You Stuck It Last Night." Ant didn't know the song so he did what the foolish do whenever they bumbled into a contretemps—cover it with brashness. He imagined Dusen was a brass door for him to melt with his blowtorch horn.

Sweet Lovin' cut in with "All the Whores Like the Way I Ride," Dusen and the other horns going like a locomotive and paddlewheeler combined, chugging along while splashing the dancers with sparking notes. Ant barked back with three crisp yelps. But if Dusen felt challenged, he didn't show it. The whole hall was thumping and vibrating, dancers leaping like frogs in boiling water, uptown whores, friends of Buddy, shaking down on the floor, not caring what dropped off as they danced. Ripping shirts open, men began doing their version of the African dances once seen in the old slave market of Congo Square. They shook their arms over their heads as if banishing spears and stomped in a steady one-two, one-two, advancing on an enemy, but added a twist and slide to turned the aggression into a graceful ballet.

Ant saw MayAnn right in front of the stage grinning at him. A dancing flame, hell, the whole city ablaze, couldn't have been more dazzling than MayAnn as she soared on her private passion. Ant imagined all her burning desire aimed right at him. He could feel it, see it in her eyes, begging him to take her back, to rescue her from the white jackal. Ant let out a powerful orgasm of sound. No other way to describe it. Then he saw Young Jack not ten steps from MayAnn, half hidden behind a jumble of gyrating bodies.

Both bands stood facing each other, horn bells nearly touching. The musicians reared back to heave big blocks of crushing chords and shards of phrases sharp enough to cut down anyone's melody and darting notes of mockery. Ant, in an attempt to warn MayAnn of the Young Jack danger behind her, let out a bray on his horn, the sound overriding Dusen. Buddy arched his eyebrows in appreciation and cut back in with "Pretty Pretty Mama, Open Your Legs One More Time."

The couple hundred people inside the hall jumped like walking barefoot on hot sand. Sweat poured down their foreheads and ran down their necks and the crevasse between breasts and dripped from armpits. To cool off, they waved their arms above their heads and a thick cloud of stink wafted over the stage. Buddy, fanning the air in front of his face, shouted, "My chilluns here. I know because I can smell 'em. Whew, it smells like a funky butt in here." The piano player immediately changed the tempo to fit the words and sang out, "I thought I heard Buddy Bolden say/Funky Butt, Funky Butt/ Take it away." The rest of the band joined the improvising, "I thought I heard Buddy Bolden say/Funky Butt, Funky Butt/ Take it away/ Let Mr. Bolden play."

The crowd took up the chant and guffawed when Buddy played outhouse music, his cornet making obscene farts. He put a stomp in the ragtime, went racing with the horses, a fast one-two-three-four gallop, slid into a strut and did whatever to keep up with his manic vision, no thought, no plan of phrases and bridges. His band barreled along with him, hanging on to his coattails with no choice but let the music tell them what to play.

Sweet Lovin' tried to cut in but no one heard him. Turning directly to Frankie Dusen, Ant sprayed him with noise and got a surprised 'What the hell's that?' look. Before Dusen could retaliate, Ant pounded him -- BLAT! BLAT! BLAT! -- like driving a stake through a vampire's heart, at least he thought so.

Ant looked in triumph to MayAnn. And saw Rough Nuts, one of the hogs with a reputation for ill-treating women, grab her by the arm. He dragged her toward the alley door when Young Jack, violently shouldering people out of the way, came directly behind Rough Nuts in a low crouch while reaching back under his jacket. Rough Nuts howled in pain and clutched the back of his thigh when Young Jack knifed him. For a moment MayAnn spun free. But Young Jack caught her by the back of the dress and shoved her out the alley door.

Rough Nuts came up off the floor with a long-barreled revolver raised above his head and fired two shots into the ceiling. As he spun round looking for someone to shoot, Ant fell flat on the stage with the rest of the musicians. Women's screams ricocheted around the hall like zinging bullets. Men bellowed to cover their fear. Everyone bent low, or curled on the floor with arms over their head, leaving Rough Nuts alone upright, his gun looking for a target. People scrambled to escape, punching, pulling hair, stepping on each other as they fought to get out the front door.

Buddy stood on the front of the stage, legs apart like the Colossus of Rhodes, and described the scene with his horn: fat *blaps* for a fist landing in a gut, a long loop of sound for a haymaker, a *rat-a-tat* for a swift combination. From the corner of his eye, Ant caught Sweet Lovin' and his band scurry off to safety. Ant fled after them out the alley door, hoping to catch MayAnn and Young Jack before they disappeared. Running down the alley, he heard Buddy playing his signature closing song, "Get out of Here and Go on Home."

From that night on, Buddy was known as "The King" and Kenny's Hall was called the "Funky Butt."

In the street in front of Kenny Hall, Ant felt the sensation of popping awake from a vivid nightmare, his mouth dry, breathing fast as if trying to outrun death, disorientated in the darkness, not knowing where he was, a sense of doom sitting on his shoulders. People rushed from Kenny's Hall and milled about, laughing with the relief of having escaped a grave danger. Calling MayAnn's name, Ant elbowed his way through the crowd. Dismay as stiff and heavy as cold tar stopped Ant in his tracks when he saw no sign of her.

Buddy found him slowly spinning with one foot stuck in place while he tried to divine which direction to search for MayAnn.

"Ant, you did great," Buddy laughed and clasped him on the shoulder. "Chased Dusen right off the stage, just like you said you would. Come on, we're going to celebrate."

"Buddy," Ant's voice hoarse, "MayAnn's been … taken." He couldn't get out another word.

The dark hours spent searching for MayAnn that night were the most miserable of Ant's life, although, in hindsight, he ranked it as the second most miserable, given what was to come. A chicken with its head cut off would have had a better plan than his random running around Storyville's back streets; going back to the plank bar hoping to find anyone who might know places Young Jack favored; searching alleys while quaking with fear of robbers and thugs, but even more afraid that he'd find her body. He braved St. Louis Cemetery No. 1, nervously peeking behind the mausoleums, dreading what he might discover, and, with scattered nerves, thankful for finding neither her corpse or a ghost.

He scanned the dark Mississippi for a boat carrying her away, or for her body. Standing on a levee, Ant told himself, MayAnn's not dead, not until I have her cold body in my arms. That quiver of hope stopped him from throwing himself into the river. When his mother died, Ant had felt a wooly numbness and stumbled about drunk with grief. The mere possibility of MayAnn's death caused a searing pain, a red-hot poker stabbing his heart.

It occurred to Ant that maybe Young Jack had taken MayAnn to Billy to force her confession of the whore's murder. In desperate hope, Ant ran the ten blocks to Tom's saloon, where he found Billy sitting by himself.

"Young Jack here?" Ant panted, "with MayAnn?"

Billy paused with a beer to his lips, puzzlement furrowing his brow.

"He grabbed her."

Billy set the beer down and wiped the foam off his upper lip, waiting for Ant's explanation.

"We've got to organize a search party. Get every ruffian, thief, mugger, low-life snitch, anyone who thinks like a criminal, who knows where a murderer might hide out. Offer a big reward if she's found alive."

Billy held up a hand to slow down Ant's breathless panic. "Whoa, now...."

Ant hopped from foot-to-foot like he was about to pee in his pants, so high was his anxiety, when Tom appeared.

"Mr. Anderson," Ant chose the formal address to emphasis the seriousness of the occasion, "I have a personal problem of utmost urgency. The problem may cast a shadow on you."

"How's that?"

"It's about that girl who was murdered at Josie's."

Ant looked like his own ghost as he gushed the story about MayAnn and Young Jack and how that vain man probably killed the whore and if MayAnn turned up dead Hennessy might put two and two together and close down Storyville until the "WHOREHOUSE KILLER"—can't Tom just see the *Mascot*'s headline—was caught.

Tom poured Ant a shot of whiskey to calm him down. "What do you think, Billy?"

"We got no proof. Jack Bohomme's family is powerful and rich and would make for a bad enemy. On the other hand, Ant's right. If two girls, both associated with Josie, turn up dead then Hennessy could cause headlines. That might risk the investment you're making on Basin Street."

After a long thoughtful moment, Tom said, "Send some of the boys to ask around, quietly."

"Thank you. Thank you." Ant would have kissed Tom's hand if, sensing Ant's gratitude, he hadn't put it behind his back.

Ant's panic next sent him barging recklessly into the Matranga's clubhouse. Charles and Tony stood with three other men examining a map spread on a table. At the sight of wild-eyed Ant, the brothers turned to face him, shielding the map behind their backs.

"What'd you want?" Charles demanded. "Why are you here?"

Ant, hesitant to lead in with a request for the personal favor to have the entire Mafia army search for MayAnn, opened with the Honduras gambit, emphasizing the profitability of the banana monopoly.

"Santa Claus?" Charles asked. "What's this guy look like?"

After Ant described him, Tony broke out laughing. "That's Lee Christmas, the color-blind locomotive engineer. He used to drive a sugarcane train, until he wrecked it. Couldn't tell the green signal from the red and ran smack into an oncoming train. You'd think a man named Christmas would know red from green. He went to Honduras as an engineer for United Fruit and got caught up in gun politics. Considers himself a soldier of fortune."

"And Machine Gun," Charles added. "He's a local boy, Guy Molony, who fought in the Boer War as a machine gunner. He's so stupid he once blew up an arms despot while standing on top of it."

Charles and Tony threw each other calculating glances. "Bonilla was the president of Honduras. If he got back into power..." Tony said.

"We don't have any ships."

"But you know ship owners," Ant injected.

"With those clowns, the ship could be lost, which is a high probability. Not worth the bananas."

The brothers bantered the pros and cons back and forth until Ant blurted out, "There's something more important."

Charles and Tony fell silent. Again Ant gushed out the story about MayAnn being kidnapped. "If she's killed..." "Hennessy..." "Could cause trouble..." "Any excuse..."

"Sounds like a thorn for Anderson," Charles said. "Maybe we want him worrying about that thorn so not to think about us."

Ant pointed out that Hennessy was a common enemy who had his own ambitions in Storyville. Finding MayAnn alive was in their and Anderson's best interest. Still, Charles and Tony were not inclined to help.

Ant, grabbing any straw to jab into their attention, blurted out, "I know your enemies who want to stop your drugs. Help me find MayAnn, then I'll tell you who has a knife at your back."

"You trying to extort us," Tony stepped forward, a look of threat and amusement on his face. "That's our business, Ant." He placed a heavy arm on Ant's shoulder. "You remember the story I told you your insect namesake and the elephant? The ant ran up the elephant's hind leg with rape on its mind. The elephant waited in anticipation and, just at the right moment, let out a big poop and buried the ant in shit."

Tony laughed and pulled Ant closer to him, tight, like getting in position for a strangle hold.

"Please," Ant pleaded, the sob in his voice hooking Charles; he hadn't heard such pitiful sorrow since he had wept at his father's funeral.

"All right," Charles interrupted. "Some men. For a few days. You're in our debt, Ant."

Chapter 12.

The Young Jack/MayAnn distraction didn't divert Tom's attention from rushing the renovations to his saloon. Mr. Poutan, the contractor, claimed it was impossible to complete the work by the beginning of the Madri Gras season, but Tom mercilessly hounded the man. "And I want Josie's Arlington finished by then, too," he demanded.

"Impossible. Even the pyramids didn't get built overnight," protested the contractor.

"Well, hop to it," Tom replied. "Put on double crews. Triple crews. You're racing against the clock. Imagine yourself a poor man digging a gold mine."

"You're crazy," sputtered the contractor. "Even if we get the lights installed, the city has to inspect the wiring."

"The wiring is approved, Mr. Poutan," Tom assured him.

"What are you going to do if all those lights cause your customers to go berserk?"

"Hell, how could I tell from their normal behavior?"

"Electricity is not well understood," Poutan stated with authority. "Electricity can throw off the sleep cycle and make a person irrationally irritable. Scientists fear that electric lights in a house might lead to an increase in wife and child abuse. With electric lights in your saloon, people can stay longer in a place bright as day and not get the sleep they need. Sleep-deprived people might commit suicide or murder. Do you want to risk that?"

Tom dismissed the man's warnings with a wave of his hand. "Make the deadline or I'll find someone who can."

Poutan put aside his reservations and drove his crews nearly around the clock at an impressive pace, as if in fact building a Great Pyramid to meet the deadline of a pharaoh's impending demise. As an extra kick in the butt, Tom plastered New Orleans with flyers announcing the "miracle of the modern age," a sight to "dazzle your eyes," an event "never been seen in New Orleans." In bold black letters:

THE NEW ANDERSON'S ARLINGTON ANNEX GRAND
OPENING
Customhouse and North Basin
8 o'clock
Don't be a moment late for the big surprise.

"Now we don't want to be disappointed, do we, Mr. Poutan," Tom said.

The contractor put on a fourth crew, at his own expense.

Miraculously, Tom's place was ready by the deadline, although Josie's still needed work. On the grand opening night, two hundred people filled the street out front for Tom's big surprise. Inside his new showplace, he paced like a nervous groom, inspecting the bartenders in their starched white aprons, rubbing an imaginary spot from his gleaming new bar mirror, straightening a chair and then moving it an inch to one side and then setting it back.

Billy paced and wiped his palms on his trousers.

Tom pulled the heavy curtain aside and peeked through the front window. When he judged the darkness significant for optimal dramatic effect, he called out, "All right, boys!"

The bartenders and waiters and musicians hurried to their posts.

"Billy, you ready?"

Billy, at the front door, raised his hand.

The curtains were pulled back and Tom flicked the switch. One hundred light bulbs blazed from the white pressed tin ceiling. The first electrified saloon in New Orleans! The crowd roared its delight. Putting lights in the saloon was more than a convenience for Tom, and more than a gimmick. His belief in the future—in a strong, vital, exuberant America with a booming economy—blazed in Edison's glowing filaments. Tom was determined to march at the front of that parade. The electric lights would show all of New Orleans he was no upstart Irish opportunist but had arrived. Electric lights would be the declaration he, Tom Anderson, controlled his fate. He'd be the only saloon owner in Storyville who made light his servant with the flick of a switch. Imagine what he might do to mere mortals who challenged his authority.

The men stepped through the front door as if entering a fine home. Some actually wiped their shoes before crossing the glistening tile floor of white squares with a single large brown hexagon in the center. No one spit in the polished cuspidors shining like golden pots meant for a king's chamber. But the men bellied up, six deep, to the thirty-foot long cherry wood bar with its brass foot rail. Eight bartenders in spotless aprons lined up behind the massive rococo bar with serried ranks of rum and whiskey, rye and bourbon and gin reflected in five arched mirrors.

Representatives of the big breweries and the wine companies pumped Tom's hand. "Marvelous!" "Fantastic!" And stuffed order forms into his suit pockets. More than a hundred cases of champagne were sold in four hours, the patrons outbidding each other for their favorite vintage.

Tom climbed on the bar and called for attention. The band fell silent. A respectful hush settled over the room. Chest puffed out, he pulled a piece of paper from his breast pocket. "I have here a telegram," he announced, "from my good friend." He waved the telegram. "John L. Sullivan, boxing champ and fellow saloonkeeper in New York City, wishes this enterprise the greatest success. And he buys a round on the house!"

Men cheered and threw their hats as if Sullivan had regained the championship by a knockout. The all-white band blasted out ragtime and stomps and marches and popular Tin Pan Alley tunes.

Billy wasn't expecting trouble from the Matrangas, or from Hennessy, but he kept watch at the front window so not to be taken by surprise. Shortly after Tom flaunted John L. Sullivan's congratulatory telegram, Billy saw a crowd of trouble marching up the street. Shoving through the boisterous crowd, he found Tom and shouted over the din, "Carrie Nation and her Smash Ladies are about to invade."

Tom, half drunk on booze and excitement, carelessly exclaimed, "Invite them in."

But he was sober enough to help the bartenders place the liquor bottles out of harm's way.

The crowd parted for Nation and her troop, renowned for charging into saloons wielding hatchets or baseball bats chanting, "Smash, ladies, smash!" as they busted up hundreds of dollars' worth of liquor. Nation's husband had been an alcoholic; apparently she held a grudge.

Tom waited by the bar. "Good evening, Mrs. Nation," he called out jovially. "I'm honored you came all the way from New York to help celebrate my grand opening! The evening wouldn't be complete without you."

Nation looked like she could take on John Sullivan and give him a good round or two. Six-foot two, perhaps one hundred eighty solid pounds, she carried an axe handle with grim determination. She stood feet planted apart, a home run hitter's stance, holding the axe handle in both hands: the Preacher of Doom in her long black full-skirted dress, buttoned to the collar. Her face, severe as a granite crag, lacked any feminine charm or beauty, an effect heightened by the tight bun of dark hair. Whatever she was mad about had set her face in permanent outrage.

"You, Mr. Anderson, are condemning these people," she swept an arm majestically over the crowded barroom, "to a crippling life of degradation. You might as well cut out their livers and eat them."

Nation glared, daring him to contradict her.

Tom smiled amiably. Men along the bar stopped their conversations.

Nation drew herself up like a diva about to deliver her best aria. "We know by absolute, incontrovertible twentieth-century science that alcohol, considering its ultimate effects on the human system, is incomparably the most virulent and far-reaching poison known to the medical world. It has the same power to addict as cocaine and morphine. We are not only talking about a moral issue, Mr. Anderson, but a health issue. We shall banish this harmful poison once and for all.

"Listen to me, friends." The axe handle rested on her shoulder as she turned to address the barroom full of men. "Alcohol is preeminently a brain poison that first and most disastrously poisons that part of the brain wherein resides reason, conscience, judgment, and self-control. When the human race understands the nature of alcohol, they will no more consent to alcohol shops wherein this deadly, narcotic-irritant poison is dispensed in highballs, cocktails and mint juleps than they will consent to opium dens and cocaine joints."

"Hear, hear!" called out a merry voice. "I'll drink to that."

"For your own good we will destroy the liquor traffic!" In full evangelical stride, voice fervent, she aimed her eyes over the heads of the crowd as if reading a vision on the horizon. "We will destroy liquor making, liquor importing, liquor selling" -- with each "liquor" she chopped the air with the axe handle -- "in saloons, hotels, public houses, private houses, on railroad cars, on shipboard."

"Even in the still!" someone called out.

"We have called upon the Episcopal Church to use unfermented wine at the sacrament of the Lord's Supper."

She stood on tiptoes, arm outstretched as if to receive a tablet directly from God's hand.

"The Lord didn't serve up that swill at the wedding feast," called out a voice. "He wanted people to have a good time."

"We abolished slavery!" Nation shouted. "Now we will abolish the curse of liquor! Then, with clear thinking, we must turn our attention to how to reconcile the sorrows of life with God's love and providence." She struck a pose, chin lifted like a figurehead on a ship pointing the way to the Promised Land.

Tom shouted, "A round on the house," to the men's ringing "Hoorah!" Standing on a chair, he directed the musicians in "Onward Christian Soldiers." The barroom choir of besotted men linked arm-in-arm swayed back and forth singing in god-awful out-of-tune harmony.

"Lemonade, ladies? Sweet tea?" Tom offered.

Nation regarded him with a cold eye. "Mr. Anderson, you are the devil himself," and gripped her axe handle as if ready to do battle with that very evil.

Without taking his eyes from her, Tom raised a hand. Twenty of his thuggish men materialized from the barroom crowd and surrounded the Smash Ladies. "I made you a gentleman's offer." He spoke in a polite even tone but his eyes glinted hard and mean. "I expect a civil reply."

For a couple of minutes Tom and Nation arm-wrestled with their eyes, testing each other for a weakness. People swore that they could damn near smelled sulfur coming off Tom, so intense was his threat. Without a word, Nation spun on her heel and led her troop out.

From that night on, Anderson's Annex became a drinking parlor-cum-tourist bureau-cum-informal city hall, the gateway to Storyville. Tourists started their tour at the Annex with a jovial drink and perhaps a quick thumb through the *Blue Book* with all its appealing promises.

In the following days, Ant pestered Tom for a greater effort to find MayAnn. "Too much on my mind right now." Tom, preoccupied with the final details of completing Josie's new Arlington, due to open in two days, brushed Ant off. "Wait until after Josie's grand opening. Then we'll find MayAnn and deal with Young Jack."

But Ant tirelessly searched the city twisting the arms of everyone he knew for information and got nothing but people trying to sell him false tips. He spent hours at Louis's barbershop listening for a whisper on the jungle drums, and cautiously, very cautiously, probed MayAnn's mother, who was concerned but not alarmingly upset. MayAnn had spent time away before, she confided. Work, you know.

The grand opening of Josie's new Arlington was last straw to clutch; MayAnn might be there, but then a pig might learn to sing. Nevertheless, before opening time, Ant walked up to Henry the Magnificent standing at the front door dressed in two-foot busby, a double-breasted frock coat fastened by gold frogs, tight riding britches and black cowboy boots with silver Mexican spurs. Ant paused to admire his new costume. "Feeling better now, Henry? The boots are an improvement."

"My feet don't hurt, that's an improvement."

Ant raised his arms for the weapons check. "You find out anything about who killed that girl?" Henry asked, giving Ant a perfunctory pat down.

"No. Young Jack thinks MayAnn is involved and threatened to kill her. Both of them have disappeared. You heard anything, Henry?"

Henry gave Ant a quizzical look and held open the door to the foyer. A larger-than-life faux-marble nude Venus on her clamshell greeted Ant. This Venus didn't modestly shield her pubis and breast—she had her arms wide open and her hip cocked.

"Isn't she fetching?" Josie, wearing a high-collared green satin gown with long sleeves and antebellum hoops, breezed up to Ant. Loops of silk roses sewn around the full skirt suggested a fluffy bush. The hair piled high with two long curls falling on each side of her oval face gave Josie an unfortunate pointy-headed look.

"I'm doing the final inspection now." She led Ant into the Vienna Parlor "in honor of that fellow Freud everyone's talking about. He's in the sex business, too."

The room looked unfinished to Ant. An upholstered bench stood against one wall. Opposite were two stiff utilitarian chairs, the kind reserved for guests you didn't want to be comfortable. Between them was a floor lamp with a fringed shade. Tom had ordered the contractor to wire Josie's, too, making it the first electrified whorehouse in New Orleans. The room's back wall had been painted as a formal English garden rigid with respectability. Three swoops of golden silk gave the impression of looking at the scene through a window.

"This is my 'modern' room," Josie said with pride. "Out with the cluttered and stuffy, that's what *The Decoration of Houses* book recommends."

How was this supposed to get anyone in the mood to fornicate, Ant wondered.

Her "foreign" girls filed in and stood in a line. Josie minutely examined each one, the general looking for an out-of-place ringlet, a smudge of makeup, an unsightly wrinkle. She insisted her girls wear elegant gowns, complicated to remove, which was part of their show. No daring neckline plunges or breast-boosting bustier or flashes of thigh. Other houses had the women dress in jockey outfits or as schoolgirls or other fantasies, but Josie insisted on high-class decorum.

"Now let's hear your accents." Some of the bayou girls spoke passable French. One girl's parents were German so she could do the hard consonants. The Texan spoke limited Mexican Spanish with a completely wrong accent. Several of the girls made up gibberish, but it sounded great, soft slurs with lilts and swoops and throaty whispers. Very sexy.

179

"We're a high-toned *maison de joie* with manners," she reminded them, "where a man can fantasize he's cavorting with a sophisticated foreign society lady living out her secret sex life."

She paused before her star attraction advertised as "a bona fide baroness, direct from the court of St. Petersburg. The baroness is at present residing at the Arlington and is known as La Belle Stewart." Circles of bright red rouge on each cheek and blue eye shadow made her look more clown than royalty. Previously, this bona fide baroness had performed as a hoochy-koochy dancer at Chicago's World Fair.

"Chin high and look down your nose." Josie told her big ticket item, striking the pose. "Look imperious. Tonight you play hard to get and go for only the top dollar."

La Belle nodded and tried on a haughty look.

"Don't look at the tip of your nose," Josie corrected. "It makes you cross-eyed. Try staring down at your tits."

Josie glanced at the clock and clapped her hands. "Everyone to her station." The girls scattered to the various rooms. She took up her position next to Venus, smoothed her skirt and nodded to Henry to admit the first guests.

Ant found Tom and Billy rubbernecking in the Turkish Parlor: a tent of silk walls made a room-within-a-room, an inner chamber, an intimate hideaway, a place to keep a prisoner or to be made a prisoner. The bank of votive candles cast cunning light that turned solid figures into flitting shadows. Large cushions, some long and wide enough to serve as an impromptu bed, squared a low round brass table on which *The Arabian Nights* lay open as the centerpiece.

"This must be Josie's library," Tom said with a smile.

The next room was smaller, even proper, with two wooden sitting chairs on either side of an octagonal table before a pristine fireplace. From the center of the ceiling hung an eight-foot diameter waxen umbrella chandelier with painted scenes of stylized birds perched in Japanese brush-stroke trees.

The room may as well have been painted in prim, suitable for having tea with your mother or aged aunt. Perhaps this was where virgin boys were introduced to their seasoned seductresses for a birds-n-bees lesson.

They wandered into a "den" furnished only with a settee. In a corner stood the breastplate and helmet of a suit of armor mounted on a pole. "What happened to the legs?" Tom asked.

"Perhaps it's meant to symbolize an emasculated male?" Billy replied.

Curlicues richly inscribed the breastplate. Poems written in the fanciful style of Arabic lettering? Doodles? The helmet looked very conquistador. Tom gave it a ping. Behind the settee hung a round shield with spokes of sword handles and axe heads radiating out. Battle of the sexes? Perhaps Josie knew her clientele better than Ant imagined.

The downstairs "public" rooms, and the upstairs "boudoir" rooms, filled with men in proper attire—suits or evening dress, no open collars or scuffed shoes. Ernest Bellocq set up his awkward camera in an alcove; Josie had hired him to document her triumph. Black menservants wearing white jackets and red gloves circulated with trays of drinks. The gentlemen and ladies chatted and laughed and no one openly leered or grabbed or asked for money. The mood carried the patina of a soiree rather than a whorehouse's grand opening. But the titillating undercurrent of possibility was palpable; the goods were on the table if you wanted to nibble.

Ant's heart jumped when he caught sight across the room of a flash of brown skin and a twirl of long silky black hair. He twisted through the crush of bodies to follow the woman's pale golden gown. A man stepped in front of her and gave a slight bow. She offered a gloved hand, which he gallantly kissed. How could this be MayAnn? Ant edged closer. She smelled of rosewater and jasmine. The woman turned in profile and Ant saw Josie had hired a new caramelized tart for her array of desserts. He slid on past, disappointed she wasn't

MayAnn, yet also relieved: MayAnn might be dead but at least she wasn't a whore.

Piano music came from the "American Parlor" with tufted deep red leather chairs and sofas grouped beneath the blazing light of the cut-glass chandeliers. Tall mirrors lining the walls reflected couples twirling around the polished dance floor. The room looked like a cross between a London gentlemen's club and a Viennese ballroom. Tony Jackson sat at the piano wearing a gray pearl derby, checkered vest, ascot with a diamond stickpin and garters to hold up the sleeves of his pale pink shirt. He pounded out a dramatic crescendo as Josie entered the room, clapping her hands above her head like a Spanish dancer.

"Now," she announced, "the special performance of the evening, the grand event of the grand opening, Olivia the Oyster Dancer!"

A naked woman stepped from behind a black curtain. She leaned back, a position that thrust out her bosom and pelvis, and balanced a slimy raw oyster on her forehead. Tony played a lilting rhythm of daffodils swaying in the breeze. Olivia tilted her head and the oyster slid down her cheek, then alongside her neck to rest in the hollow of her collarbone. Her shoulders shook and the oyster slipped down to her ample well-formed right breast. And balanced there. Then seemingly leapt to the left breast.

Men applauded.

The oyster bounced from tit to tit as Olivia swung her breasts as if twirling nipple tassels.

The audience whistled in appreciation.

The sea creature shimmied down between her breasts and rested in the spoon of her right hip. She slid the oyster across her pelvis with an obscene hip thrust. An undulating belly-dancer motion made the oyster disappear into her pubic mound, then squeeze out onto her thigh and slip down to top of her right kneecap. Olivia slowly raised and cocked the leg in the pose of a Hindu temple dancer and the oyster dripped down her extended leg into the cup of her instep.

The men cheered.

With a deft kick, she flipped the oyster into the air and caught it on her forehead.

"By God, order me a dozen on the half shell!" someone exclaimed. "Oysters and Olivias!"

From that night on, Oyster on Olivia, shortened to O-on-O, became a code word for the outrageously exotic in Storyville. It wasn't long before other houses began to advertise a "Double O Special."

After her no-hands demonstration, Olivia took three bows on demand, demurely refused an encore and disappeared behind her curtain. Tony took the last gulp from his ever-present glass of whiskey and struck up a waltz. As couples crowded the dance floor, the serving help again circulated with trays of drinks. Ant caught a glimpse of brown skin as he drifted towards the bar, but assumed it belonged to one of Josie's "Brazilians." Then, on second look, saw that the woman wore the plain black dress and white apron of a maid.

He dodged around people to get a look at her face. To his astonishment, there was MayAnn. But a different MayAnn. Gone was any sense of the parlor maid. She looked everyone in the eye and offered no polite submissive bob of her head. Rather, she moved brusquely, even contemptuously, so people had to grab their drink off the tray as she went by. Her entire bearing said, Make no mistake, I'm not your servant.

When she turned, Ant popped up in her way. "MayAnn, thank God you're alive!"

"Shouldn't I be?" The blaze in her eyes, the shield of her stiff shoulders, warned him to stay away.

"Where you been? I thought Young Jack had put you under for sure." The apostles couldn't have been more joy struck at the sight of the resurrected Christ than Ant was at seeing MayAnn alive. She looked over his head, as if he were a nuisance little boy, and said, without looking at him, "I'm moving on now, Antoine, and I don't want you following me. You hear. This is my last night working."

"You can't get away from me. You're what I want." Ant meant to sound like a lover but, even to his own ear, he heard the flat declaration of a buyer.

She moved to go around but Ant didn't give ground. "Please, Antoine," pleading in her eyes, "Please give me this chance." Then she pushed into the crowd and disappeared.

For the rest of the evening Ant skulked after MayAnn determined not to let her out of his sight. But by three o'clock, when the crowd had thinned, she was nowhere to be found. Henry shooed Ant out, "I'm locking the front door now. We're closed except for the overnight guests."

"Where's MayAnn?"

"Can't say I know." Henry dropped his customary sternness and looked at him with sympathy. "Time for the weary to rest. Give the Lord your hand and He will lead you."

That surprised Ant, coming from Henry; Ant had always thought Henry would mug Christ given the chance. Certainly throw Him out the door for wearing sandals. Henry gently placed a hand on Ant's back and guided him out. Ant crossed the street and waited hidden in a shadow for MayAnn to emerge. When the last lights in the house winked off and still no sign of her, he thought of the back door and dashed around to the alley. Empty.

But he knew she was alive and in the city. Finding her again was inevitable; after all, New Orleans wasn't a big place.

Chapter 13.

The next day, the Matragnas summoned Ant to their office. He was aflutter with hope that their men had discovered MayAnn's hide-away.

"Whose knife is stickin' in our back," Tony barked.

"What?" Ant didn't know what he was referring to, having forgotten his panic-driven promise to reveal the Matrangas' rival in the drug trade.

"For our help in your personal matter, you said that you'd tell us our enemy," reminded Charles.

"Ah, ah..." Ant was so attached to the idea that MayAnn had been found he couldn't nimbly switch thoughts. "Ah," grasping at the first desperate thought, "ah, remember the Honduras deal? Jack Bohomme and his father have their thumb in that pie. Now, I don't know for certain but, you know, I've heard, maybe, they're looking to expand their business interests. If they can arrange ships to help the revolutionaries, then Bonilla and his gang might put something extra besides bananas on those ships, you know, something secret no one knows about." Ant felt his story slipping away into the implausible, his voice hesitating as he snatched any stray idea to bolster his story.

Charles and Tony watched Ant fumble away his credibility, Tony's face clouding with anger for being taken for a gullible idiot while Charles sat with his arms folded, an impassive judge waiting for Ant to finish putting his head through the noose of his own devising.

"You're lying," Charles declared. "You're protecting someone."

"Remember my parable about the ant and the elephant? You remember that, *Ant*?" Tony emphasis, and its implication, caused Ant's stomach to clench in fear.

"It's your Mr. Anderson, isn't it, Ant?" accused Charles. "No one else can contest us."

"No. No, you're wrong." Ant, not expecting this unfortunate turn, spoke with earnest conviction, as if that might douse the spark he had inadvertently laid in the Anderson-Matranga tinderbox. A blazing battle between the two could well destroy Storyville. "Mr. Anderson wants nothing to do with your drugs. Sex is a more powerful aphrodisiac, in his opinion. He just wants you to stay out of his turf."

"And what better way to keep us out of his whorehouses than to distract us by disrupting our business?" Ant recognized the look in Charles' eyes, the flat glaze that stopped any plea for reason or mercy from reaching his consideration. Ant had seen that same look when Charles had sent condemned men to their death.

"You're completely mistaken." Ant, anxious as a little boy who had set the bed on fire by playing with matches, glanced at Tony to intercede. But Tony, a glint of amusement tugging his scowl into a smile, had the look of a man anticipating the entertainment of a fighting cock tearing apart a hapless chicken.

"Then who?" Charles demanded. "And no more of your lies. There's no one but Anderson. We cannot stand by and let him threaten us."

The Mafia didn't have any real rivals in the New Orleans drug trade. Maybe Chen the Chink, but he wasn't trying to move into the Matragnas' street trade. Chen had the opium and heroin market cornered with the supply coming from the East, so he didn't concern himself, overly, about the Matrangas' South American source. Still, who else would be a plausible threat?

Ant breathed out the thought before even realizing he had formed the words. He felt the puff of air slide down his tongue, tried to swallow the injustice before the Matrangas heard it, yet failed to stop the almost inaudible, "Chen the Chink."

Charles cocked his head back to better assess Ant. The little man before him was truly afraid, head bowed to hide the shame of his fear. Yes, Chen was a possibility. He was the only other major player in the New Orleans drug trade, although they'd had no trouble from him before. Still, Chinamen have a lust for money. And they are sneaky to the point of being invisible.

"Go," Charles gave a dismissive wave of his hand, "before I gut you."

Ant forced himself not to run from the room. But once out the door, his legs trembled so violently he had to sit down on the sidewalk, back against the building.

When he finally regained his feet, Ant walked on automatic to Tom's saloon. Should I warn Chen, he wondered. About what? The Matrangas hadn't issued a threat. They probably wouldn't do anything about the Chinaman, who, after all, wasn't a real threat. Chen had opium dens; the Matrangas dealt in Mexican cigarettes and South American cocaine. No conflicts. Best I keep out of sight on this one, Ant decided, as he walked into the saloon.

Tom, in his role of Storyville's mayor, was a receiving petitioner at the City Hall table. A man, hands clasped between his knees under the table, sat with shoulders hunched as he spoke to Tom in a faltering voice about his sick little girl. "I need money for the medicine," the man said humbly. "I fear she will die."

Tom, whose relationship with Hilma Burt opened his heart in ways that made him tender, showed sympathy by reaching over to pat the weeping man's hand. Tom had become so giddy over Hilma that he bought the building between his Arlington Annex and Josie's Arlington and made renovations to install Hilma. His Basin Street Golden Row was falling into place: in addition to Hilma and Josie, Minnie White had moved onto the street as did Julia Dean, Flo Meeker, Lollie Fisher and Ella Schwartz. Two empty slots remained.

Tom asked a few questions, at first out of civility and then, hearing the sad man's answers, probed for details. With each answer, Tom leaned in closer so no one could overhear until his head was bowed to the man's mouth, like a father confessor listening to a sinner's agony. Tom gave the man a wad of money and spoke urgently to him, gripping him by the arm to focus his attention. The man nodded several times, crossed himself and attempted to kiss Tom's hand.

When the anxious father hurried out of the saloon, Tom motioned Ant to his table. "I want you to go down to Little Palermo and poke around. Seems that yellow fever might be getting a grip. I want to know how bad."

Ant nodded, his mind regulating the risky task to one of his runners.

"No one is to know about this," Tom said in a low voice. "I don't want to start a panic."

Yellow fever, colloquially known as Bronze John, had terrorized New Orleans with five previous epidemics, with thousands of deaths. People mentioned its name in a fearful voice appropriate when whispering the name of a serial killer.

The Italian ghetto of Little Palermo stood on relatively high ground, its streets wide and sunny, open to river breezes. The breweries and mills occasionally gushed their waste down the streets, flushing the gutters. But Storyville, tucked down and behind the French Quarter, simmered in torpid humidity.

If Bronze John nibbled in Little Palmero, it would feast in Storyville.

Ant left immediately to walk to the dilapidated neighborhood, populated mostly by Sicilian immigrants, nestled against the riverside of the French Quarter.

On the way, he thought, How can I save MayAnn from the ravages of the disease? Force her to leave the city with me?

I'll present myself as her friend looking out after her welfare. I could support us in Chicago as a musician until the danger passed. During those weeks or months, she'll realize that I'm her Prince Charming, the Provider of Her Future, Husband and Father of her children. The first step, the abduction, might be a high hurdle. I could truss her up in a trunk and ship her north on a paddle wheeler. I'd be there giving her water and food every day and at night I'd let her out for fresh air and we'd sit on the bow of the boat and I'd hold her hand and explain how I was saving her life, giving her a new life, and she'd come to understand so by the time we reached Memphis or thereabouts she'd voluntarily stay in the cabin with me and we'd call the trip a honeymoon. But trussing up MayAnn and shutting her in a streamer trunk would only make her spittin' screamin' mad. I'd have better luck reconciling with a raving polecat than I would repairing our relationship ripped asunder by such rash action, no matter how noble the intent. So I'd have to fool her, deceive, lie for her own good. A poor way to start a life together but I'd bring her around. I'd forgive her for jilting me and she'd forgive me for my relentless pursuit. And I'll live happily ever after.

Ant, deep into his fantasy, didn't realize he had entered Little Palermo until he stepped into a pool of stagnant water, ideal breeding grounds for mosquitoes, in the rutted and holed street. The old buildings abutting the street with patches of plaster facades flaking off had the presence of tombs. There was no sound, no one on the streets, not even stray dogs. Ant spotted a black-shrouded woman standing in the doorway of one of the crumbling French mansions. When she saw him coming, she quickly disappeared through the thick wooden door. Running fast, Ant managed to stick a foot in before it closed.

"May I see?" She looked at him blankly. "We need to know how bad the disease is."

The woman didn't move, tense as a deer facing unknown danger. "I've been sent to help. Do you understand English? Is anyone sick here," Ant attempted in rudimentary Italian.

Whether she understood his words or not, the old lady let Ant slip in to the building's interior subdivided into ten-by-twelve cubicles. Ant poked his head into one of windowless boxes contained a table, six chairs, a bed and a charcoal-heating pit. Clothes on nails flowed in soft dribbles down one wall. The mother immediately swept her four children behind her. Ant asked in faltering Italian after the father. The mother stared terror stricken. Finally the old lady said *morte* and drew a finger across her throat.

She made Ant understand two people, a child and a man, had died in the house that day. More were sick. Deeper in the house, Ant found fourteen people living in three rooms, with only the front room having a window. No running water. Kerosene lamps or candles provided dim light. Five members of the families had died of yellow fever. In another room, so dense with grief that he didn't try to push in, sat a girl, maybe sixteen, holding the hand of her dying husband. The sadness in her eyes, the hurt and fear so deep and incendiary that it had hollowed the young bride, made her black eyes peepholes into her personal numbing void. Ant turned away, embarrassed that he had seen her so nakedly exposed.

In the enclosed courtyard stood two stinking outhouses. Mosquito larvae floated in uncovered barrels of drinking water.

Ant had seen enough and retreated back to Storyville. What he found had put the fear of God and Satan as evil twins in him.

Tom wasn't in his office.

Billy stood by the bar in a saloon. "Where's Tom?" Ant asked.

"Where do you think? Touring the Burt property," Billy smirked.

"Come with me. I've got bad news."

Billy followed Ant next door to Hilma's "sporting palace," which Tom had shelled out a fortune to fix up with rooms so sumptuous as to put a railroad baron's palace to shame. Tom and Hilma stood in the reception room, fingers entwined, when Ant and Billy entered.

"Would you look at these, Tom?" Hilma pointed to the stained-glass windows letting in a soft bouquet of light. "It's so calming, don't you think? Gives the place an atmosphere of a cathedral—of pleasure." She had a way of holding his hand with the comfort of an old friend and the teasing promise of a lover.

Billy watched Tom in the gilt-framed mirror (five thousand dollars at least) above the marble mantel (eight hundred) as Tom watched Hilma glided across the oriental carpet (twelve thousand) graceful as a swan on a calm pond. Later, Tom asked Ant to find a top-quality jeweler to make him a diamond brooch in the shape of a swan. Swans mate for life.

Ant caught Tom's eye with a subtle nod that said, I need to talk with you. Tom beamed as if he had totally forgotten the mission he had sent Ant on.

"Welcome, boys," Hilma said. "I was just starting to give Tom a tour. Will you join us?"

She led the three men through the double doors of her library and said, with a mischievous smile, "I have a special surprise for you, Tom."

Scattered about the book-lined room were comfortable sink-in armchairs and loveseats made for reading niches, or trysts. Hilma led Tom pass lunettes with bronze sculptures on pedestals and the paintings on the walls but gave no hint of the promised surprise.

"Countess Willie has been over several times and we've exchanged books," she said, leading Tom by the hand to an excellent copy of the painting "September Morn" that had caused such a scandal when unveiled in Paris. If the painting, of a nude veiled in mist while bathing in a lake, was the surprise it failed to astonish. Hilma moved on to an open book of nudes, "Willie and I share the same taste for anything dedicated to beauty," she said.

Whatever the surprise, she was being an artful stripper in revealing it.

During the languid tour, Ant got right on Tom's shoulder. "I've got news." But Tom put all his attention to a sketch of entwined lovers Hilma pointed out. Finally she guided Tom, more accurately led him by the nose, to a particular bookshelf. "And here it is," she said with delight. The trio of men stared at the row of books searching for a clue. Billy leaned forward to read the titles. Tom rocked up on his toes ready to be thrilled by anything she produced, even a dictionary.

Hilma gave the bookshelf a gentle push to reveal a hidden doorway. "Marvelous!" exclaimed Tom and followed her into the secret room. Two enveloping leather chairs and a long, wide sofa were in the center of the small space. Glass-top display cases and several closed wooden cabinets lined the walls.

"The objects, and the books, are from my personal collection," Hilma said with pride.

Tom stepped closer to examine prints hanging on the wall that showed a couple, East Indian by the furnishings, in various positions of the love act. "From the Karma Sutra," Hilma explained, "a very ancient spiritual practice."

"If that's spiritual, I'll become a churchgoing man," Tom quipped.

Several small-carved pieces of ivory looked like frogs until Tom noticed woman's leg clasped around the man's back.

"What's this?" he pointed to a slightly curved ivory stalk.

Hilma took it from the display case and handed it to him. Tilting it back and forth, he looked at her quizzically. "Rolling balls?"

"Japanese women invented this no-hands johnny to amuse themselves while they sat around knitting or drinking tea or whatever Japanese women do when alone, or with each other. You know about dildos, don't you, Tom?"

He obviously had no idea from the way he handled the object. But his expression said, Anything good for you, Hilma dear, is excellent for me.

She pressed against him and breathed into his ear, "This is our special room, Tom. There are many marvels here I'll show you."

The intimacy was so personal Billy and Ant looked away in embarrassment. As they started to shuffle out of the secret room, Tom seemed to notice Ant for the first time. He caught the fright in Ant's eyes and called him back.

Ant spoke in generalities so as not to panic Hilma. "Dazed and miserable, that's what they are. Cornered. No hope in their eyes. Food's hard to come by. They have no idea how to stop themselves from dying."

"Jesus, Mary and Joseph," Tom sighed.

"I suspected there was something behind the increase in business," Hilma said. "Fear of death is always good for the sex trade. People want to reaffirm life and what's more reaffirming than the very act that creates life? That's why wars are always a boom time for us, Hooker's camp followers being the latest example. It's not a coincidence whorehouses go with military camps like fleas on dogs." She spoke with a lighthearted touch, the way someone who hadn't fought at Gettysburg or Bull Run might joke about war.

"You Northerners have no idea what a voracious killer Bronze John is." Tom slouched on the sofa, momentarily overwhelmed.

"What symptoms do I look for?" she asked, her concern piqued.

Fever, chills, rapid heartbeat, headache, back pains, nausea, stomach cramps, constipation, kidney failure, hemorrhaging and jaundice, Tom ticked off his fingers. Bleeding into the skin dappled the victims with bruises. Uncontrolled bleeding from the nose, mouth, eyes and stomach, delirium and coma, often followed by death.

"Shouldn't be too hard to miss," she replied, more subdued.

"There's no cure. The last time this disease hit the city, eighty-five percent of the people who got it died, Hilma. When I was a boy, five thousand people in New Orleans died in a yellow fever attack." He sat with his head in hands. "How many dead," he asked Ant.

"Hard to say as the people in Little Palermo are hiding the disease," Ant answered. "They're scared the authorities will deport them if they are discovered. I saw twenty-three dead in a couple hours. I suspect there's been a couple hundred."

"If yellow fever gets into Storyville it'll be more trouble than the Matrangas or Hennessy." Tom pushed himself up of the couch. "This is one enemy you can't out smart. Go back and do a thorough survey, Ant. I need to know what we're up against."

For two days Ant prowled Little Palermo, handkerchief over his mouth to filter the stench, each step more and more hesitant to enter another stifling, fear-filled death box. The disease had spread so fast through the Italian ghetto that a special mortuary chapel dedicated to St. Anthony of Padua was constructed next to St. Louis Cemetery No. 1 to better facilitate quick burials.

In the evenings, Ant searched uptown for signs of the disease. In the Red Onion it was impossible to tell who was healthy and who was unhealthy, so he didn't inquire. The hogs were at their usual back table. He didn't tip off Harris and the others. Buddy wasn't there so Ant walked to his home.

"Buddy's out," his mother said.

"An illness is about," Ant told her. "Best to stay indoors for a few days."

He went around the corner to MayAnn's house and made an inspection of the small back garden, empting out several pots of standing water. "You want to keep mosquitoes away,"

he explained to MayAnn's mother. "They give you irritation."
He asked if she had seen MayAnn.

"Yes, she came by the other day. Said that she had a new
job that was keeping her busy."

"She didn't say where that was?"

"Some rich folks house. She seemed awfully happy."

"When you see her again, tell her that I have important
news she needs to know right away."

People became twitchy as the citywide death count
rose to eight hundred in two weeks with no sign of abating.
An ordinary inquiry about one's health took on ominous
overtones. Friends and strangers stared frankly into each
other's eyes, looking for the telltale yellow in the irises. Some
refused to shake hands on the misguided belief the "strangers'
disease" was passed through touching. Others, who believed
it was airborne, carried a three-foot stick used to keep people
at a distance. Nearly everyone wore a cloth mask across the
nose and mouth when out on the streets. The city looked over
run by bandits.

Business conventions canceled as word spread of New
Orleans' infection. Rail and river service from New Orleans
to all cities north was suspended, which put a serious crimp
in the city's commerce. Despite the precautions, the disease
spread to Texarkana, Pine Bluff, Arkansas City, Helena and
Newport. The Arkansas Board of Health placed these cities
under quarantine, allowing no one in or out. Spiriting MayAnn
out of New Orleans may have been impossible, even if Ant
could find her.

New Orleans' mayor ordered pots of tar and pitch burned
on street corners in the belief the smell and smoke would drive
away the mosquitoes. In hopes of "purifying" the atmosphere,
the local militia fired salvos from cannons.

In his spare moments, Ant searched the city's hospitals
and visited the quarantine camps, tent facilities the health
authorities set up in empty fields away from the city. The

hospitals were a cesspool of disease, no healthier than the fetid courtyards in the slums. Overcrowded rooms forced patients into the corridors, many on the floor instead of in a bed. The smells of unwashed bodies, piss, vomit and rank fear gagged Ant as he went from bed to bed, fearful he'd find MayAnn feverishly tossing in her death throes.

Bronze John made its first inroads into Storyville via the fetid backstreets, ravaging the crib girls along Robertson and Villere. Still, the denizens of Golden Row remained untouched. This lulled Tom into a false complacency—until Hilma took ill. In the first few days, she was only lightly touched with fevers and sweats and cold chills. Jaundice gave a faint yellow tinge to her eyes. Other than headaches, she suffered no other pains. She remained rather cheerful, when her teeth were chattering, so Tom didn't take attack seriously. Sitting with her in shifts, Tom and a temporary nurse bathed her brow in cool water, fed her soup, tended to her personal cares and read to her. Josie and Countess Willie came to entertain her.

Bronze John's attack on Hilma, and the city, made the disease Tom's personal enemy. "We need to fight this head on," he told Billy. "Firing cannons won't hit even one mosquito."

After a couple days, as business continued to precipitously decline and the death count steadily climbed, Tom reluctantly reached a decision. He sent Ant to see the Matrangas with the message, "We need to join forces to stop this epidemic."

Ant found them in their dockside office. Despite the urgency of the situation, Tony and Charles were suspicious of Tom. "Why's he willing to help Italians?"

"He doesn't care about Italians," Ant replied. "The city is at risk and he's losing money."

The brothers spoke back and forth in rapid Italian. Ant knew enough words to understand the disease had hit their community hard and they needed help.

"Okay," Charles said. "Tell Mr. Anderson to meet us at the Italian Relief Committee on Decatur Street tomorrow morning, nine o'clock. Sharp."

When Ant reported to Tom, Billy raised a cautionary flag. "I don't know, Tom. That's enemy territory where you have no control. Any sort of unexplained accidents could befall you."

"That's a minor risk compared to what we're up against. I'm going."

Billy arrived at the meeting first to make sure Tom's wasn't walking into a trap. Mr. Patorno, the relief committee's director, sat behind a battered desk in a suit with a vest and a clean starched collar. Before him a young woman sobbed, face buried in her hands, a black mourning veil covering her hair. Mr. Patorno patted her arm and pressed an envelope into her hand. The woman stood, "*Grazie, grazie,*" and left the room.

Mr. Patorno leaned back in his chair and sighed. "That woman, Maria," he said in heavily accented English. "Her husband, Salvatore, was sick in the emergency hospital. Bad sick. They had given him a boxful of capsules to help with the fever. But he was very suspicious. Aware that Italians were liked less than Negroes, and afraid of being poisoned. He gave Maria the pills and told her to feed them to their goat. If the goat lived, he would take the pills. She fed the pills to the goat and waited overnight. In the morning, the goat was still alive. She rushed back to the hospital with the good news. But Salvatore had died. Now she has only the goat. She lives on goat milk and sells a little. She has no money to feed the goat. If the goat dies, she'd be truly ruined."

The Matrangas entered the office wearing formal black suits to underline the seriousness of the situation. They kissed Mr. Patorno on both cheeks, muttered in Italian, and sat on two straight back chairs against the wall. Moments later Tom knocked and pushed the office door open. Mr. Patorno rose from his desk and nodded his greeting. Tom took the only vacant chair, next to Charles. The rivals didn't shake hands but stared straight ahead, stone faced, hands on knees.

After a few uncomfortable moments, Charles gave Tom a quick look. "Good day."

Tom ventured an unsure "*Buon giorno.*"

Tony leaned around his brother to address Tom, "I hope you are well," in careful English.

"Yes, thank you."

Charles said something in rapid Italian. Mr. Patorno started to reply in kind, then switched to English. "We need kerosene to pour on stagnant water and screening for the top of cisterns. Food. Clean water. Medicine. I have widows, young children, families to feed." He sagged, his head nearly touching the desktop. "How are we to survive such suffering?"

"We'll send wagons of food from the markets," Tony said.

"I'll have my men bring you gallons of kerosene," Tom added.

"Fresh fruit, we'll send tons of fresh fruit," Charles promised.

"I'll have the mayor send city crews down here to burn off the stagnant water," bid Tom.

Charles raised the ante. "We'll set up a special social fund of a thousand dollars."

"I'll add another thousand," Tom countered.

Mr. Patorno held up his hand to silence them. "I need men."

Tom and the Matrangas looked at one other. Billy gave a slight nod. "All right," Tom said. "I'll send men."

"Our men will come," Tony promised.

"No funny stuff," Tom said.

"We are honorable men," Charles replied.

Tom started to say something but thought better of it.

The next day, city workers spread oil and kerosene on every spot of standing water. The Marine Hospital Fumigating Corps sprayed and smoked the rooms and courtyards of Little Palermo.

While the city now had hope of fighting off the disease, Hilma took a turn for the worst. She hardly ate and what she did she couldn't keep down. The lost of weight stretched the skin tightly over her cheekbones and rimmed her eyes with shadows dark as bruises. But even in the worst of her times she remained cheerful. Her innate generosity of spirit made Tom fall even more deeply in love with her. He sat at her side ten, twelve, fifteen hours a day, even as others did their turns, stroking her face, brushing her hair and, when the stomach cramps curled her into a tight ball, he'd climb into the bed to hold and comfort her. Billy and Josie urged him to take her to a hospital but he refused. Instead, he converted the rooms above his saloon into a sick bay where she could be tended to around the clock.

Despite being distracted to the point of near madness, Tom made true to his promises to Mr. Patorno. Billy browbeat every business owner in Storyville to contribute money, goods and men for neighborhood cleanups. He often crossed paths with Matrangas' men distributing fresh fruit from the docks. Even the madams joined the campaign by offering special discounts to the "malaria troops." Some prostitutes volunteered to nurse the sick at the tent hospitals; others washed soiled bed sheets and linens that laundresses refused to touch for fear of contamination. Minnie White and Josie's girls took the fresh bedding into sick homes and administered to those too ill to seek help. A sense of wartime alliance united the city as blacks, whites, Creoles, Italians, Germans, and Americans -- the native born of English stock who considered themselves the true "first sons" -- cared for each other in their common suffering.

Every day Ant asked Josie if any of her volunteers on their rounds had come across MayAnn. She, too, thought it odd MayAnn had disappeared, especially at a time when all helping hands were sorely needed. "She's always been such a dependable girl," Josie said. "Perhaps she has been taken, or left the city, or is caring for family."

One night, while Tom napped next to Hilma's bed, she began thrashing and throwing off the blankets. Her fast breathing, as if she was in a desperate race, woke him. With a strangled groan, she strained to raise her head to say something before slumping back into the pillows. Tom thought she had died. In absolute panic, he could think of nothing to do but breathe life back into her and clambered onto the bed, straddled her and, holding her mouth open, put his lips on hers and blew. When she didn't respond, a grimace of grief bared his teeth in a grotesque square grin. He looked wildly around the room and broke into a sob. Shaking his head back and forth in denial, he gently arranged her into a more comfortable position and stood for a long moment over her, hand on her heart. Then he felt a faint beat and heard her ragged intake or air. He fell to his knees and, for the first since his mother had knelt with him in their nightly act of faith, said a prayer.

Two days later, an unexpected cold snap killed off the mosquitoes and, as if she only needed a signal, Hilma came out of her coma.

Slowly the city regained confidence. The facemasks disappeared. People were at ease with one another again. The travel ban was lifted and commerce flowed once more. Hilma, weak but recovering at her own house, announced Bronze John had been too much of a man for her: she was leaving town. If I stay, I fear for my life, she told Tom. He begged her reconsider, even went on his knees and cried. He assured her yellow fever episodes didn't hit New Orleans but every thirty or forty years. You're safe now, he promised. I'll keep you safe. But Hilma had already arranged for Gertrude Dix to take over her establishment. She was returning to St. Louis now that transportation had been restored.

After her departure by train, Tom sent telegrams pleading with her to return and she wrote letters to him. Sometimes Billy would catch him reading one of her lightly scented missives, his eyes brimmed with tears. One day, when Billy popped into the office on some business or other, Tom sat behind his desk, hands flat on each side the lilac-colored paper Hilma used for her letters. An unlit cigar protruded in the middle of his mouth. He didn't respond to Billy but stared straight ahead, as if in a trance. Billy waited a minute or two before saying Tom's name again. Tom's lips parted around the cigar held firm by his teeth. He chomped down hard, biting the cigar in two.

"She married a banker," he said flatly. "Has a respectable life now, a new name and wishes to remain undiscovered." He carefully folded the letter and put it in a desk drawer. "Time to get back to work."

Finding MayAnn became Ant's main business. He asked Tom if his men could take up the search again, implying MayAnn would lead to Young Jack. "You still need him gone as a threat to your Golden Row."

Ant intended to ask the Matrangas to put their men back on the search when they unexpectedly summoned him to their office. Perhaps they had come to a decision about helping Bonilla invade Honduras. If so, Ant would put out an urgent call on the underground telegraph for Young Jack to contact him. Young Jack would be the string leading to MayAnn.

But the brothers had another matter to discuss. They had approached Countess Willie about being their silent partner on Tom's Golden Row, and she hadn't shown them any respect.

"We offered her a very good deal," Tony complained. "And a bonus if she'd bring the other madams to us. You know what she did? How does she know these things, these words? She told us in choice Sicilian curses what to do with ourselves. Those words would get a man's throat cut, his family slaughtered, his house burnt." Tony huffed and puffed, pacing up and down the office. Charles, sitting at his desk, motioned Ant closer.

"Now, Mr. Ant, you tell us why we shouldn't take this Anderson business into our own hands? We appreciate he helped us with the yellow fever but now it's business as usual. Mr. Anderson did us harm when our friends were killed over the Tuxedo deal."

"He didn't kill the Parkers," Ant protested.

Charles gave him a long cool stare. "Mr. Anderson, the Mayor of Storyville, must take responsibility."

"Business, right? You want into his business? A wedge to pry open his vault? All right." Ant gave them another name. "Anderson thinks she's poison because she sells virgins at special auctions in her French Studio. He's afraid that sooner or later the churches will force the city's mayor to crack down on her and that may trigger a crusade against all of Storyville. You want to put Anderson on the hot seat, encourage Emma Johnson to relocate to Basin Street. There's still a house or two available. If you persuade her to stop the virgin auctions, Mr. Anderson will be a grateful and accept your presence."

Ant was bluffing with an empty hand. Emma Johnson, the most infamous and successful madam in New Orleans, didn't need the Matrangas. But it would take the brothers some time to find that out and by then the whole situation might have blown over.

Charles leaned back in his chair and gave Ant an appraising stare as if assessing a cow for choice cuts of beef before butchering it. "This Emma Johnson, she's a home run, yes? You hope she puts me on home plate." Then he dismissed Ant with a flick of his hand.

"What about Bonilla and his ship?" Ant asked before leaving.

"No one's interested. The risk's too high and the return too low."

Ant sent out a street message for Young Jack: he had real news for him.

Chapter 14.

Ant had every eyeball and ear in his network looking and listening for MayAnn and Young Jack, but to no avail. Not a peep. Then, three days later, a vegetable vendor informant spotted Young Jack coming out of a house on Tchoupitoulas Street.

"He usually leaves by mid-morning."

"And the girl?"

"Sometimes I don't see her all day."

Ant went to Tchoupitoulas, which paralleled the river, early the next morning, edging around the corner from Clio Street. Big clumps of river fog concealed him as he slipped from doorway to doorway until he spotted the house. In its day, the two-story had been a mansion of an ambitious merchant. Instead of the row of Grecian pretense that distinguished the truly impressive Southern plantations, this structure had only a simple column on each side of the front door to support the porch roof. Once white, the scabbing paint had turned gray from neglect. Wood rot etched decay into the façade. Veiled in river mist, the house gave the impression of an impoverished widow trying to maintain her dignity by sitting stiff-backed behind a lace curtain, half hidden but refusing to disappear.

The doleful place looked like what it was, a third-rate house of assignation.

Ant settled into a doorway where he could see the entrance but not be seen. He thought of abducting MayAnn, spiriting her away to some safe place out of sight. *In the security of our refuge she'd come to her senses and accept me*, he told himself.

I'll protect her from Young Jack and from the false pride of rising above her station. The refuge will be our walled garden; our love will blossom in that blessed place and protect us from the vulgarities and cheap tricks of ordinary mortals.

Such fantasies helped the hours go by as he waited for Young Jack or MayAnn to emerge from the house. By and by the river fog burned off, leaving behind a harsh glaring heat. A few people appeared on the street to do errands or go to work or go home. Over the levee, the funnels of a steamship glided pass. The street, away from busyness of the city, was a cat stretched out in the sun.

Ant's feet ached from standing so long; he grew thirsty and removed his suit jacket and, with his handkerchief, wiped his neck and face. No sign of life came from the house, no flicker of the heavy drapes on the front windows. The house appeared dead.

Why wait? Why not launch the assault, Ant asked himself. *Why not just kill Young Jack before MayAnn's eyes and be done with it? I'd be a hero for rescuing an innocent girl and for ridding the city of a killer.*

But he knew that such rash action would forever lose MayAnn's trust. He shifted from foot-to-foot to relieve his lower back pain. An increasingly persistent thirst tempted him to find a drink. Then the front door of the house opened and Young Jack stepped out and casually strolled away, whistling with the air of a self-satisfied man.

Ant waited another twenty minutes before going in. The "concierge" who guarded the door and collected the tariff, an unshaven beetle-browed with the look of a washed-up boxer, pocketed Ant's five dollar bribe. The once large ground-floor rooms had been partitioned into smaller spaces on either side of the central corridor. The guardian/enforcer pointed up the dilapidated staircase leading to the second floor. The banister wobbled under under Ant's hand as he started up. Reaching the top, he tiptoed down the hallway to the last door and paused to calm his breathing.

"I need a quiet heart," he said under his breath. "Be the good friend, the helping hand here to rescue."

The door wasn't locked. Ant quietly pushed it opened. MayAnn, her back to him, stood with arms reaching over her head as she pinned a picture cut from a magazine onto the wall. She wore only her chemise.

"Making a little love nest here?" Ant said, as if picking up a conversation they'd had the day before.

MayAnn spun around, her eyes wide in surprise. Her tousled hair looked like the upheaval of sex, all twisted and bunched where, Ant imagined, Young Jack must have hung on, held her down, forced her under him.

"Antoine!" He gave a mock bow. "Why are you here?"

Ant closed the door. The room was like being under the muddy Mississippi; even the sunlight was dirty. The wallpaper, the color of tea, stained from ceiling leaks, hung in strips; musk of old cigars seeped from the peelings. Stuck on the wall were magazine pictures of Paris, of women parading the latest fashions, and of prim and proper English gardens. A large swayback bed, neatly made up, dominated the space.

MayAnn crossed her arms to shield her breasts; the gesture of exclusion made Ant suddenly furious. He had come to save her! She, who had once so enthusiastically and completely given herself to him, now made herself untouchable. Ant's hands balled into fists as he fought the nearly overwhelming impulse to beat her. To make her ugly so no man would want her. His arm muscles twitched and bunched. To kill her so no man could have her. Ant looked away until the madness faded from his eyes. Then he smiled at her with his entire being, face open in a beam of goodwill, hands relaxed at his sides, his very presence saying, Would you like ice tea? Please, sit and tell me about your adventure. You're looking well.

"What are you doing here, MayAnn?"

"Don't concern yourself, Antoine."

"Did he hurt you?" His solicitous tone softened her. She dropped her hands and her shoulders relaxed.

"Not much." She sat on the bed; the springs sounded like rusty hinges. In Ant's mind, he tried to change the bed into a patch of grass and the squeaks into cricket chirps. Otherwise, he couldn't tolerated the sight of where Young Jack must have defiled her.

Ant cautiously eased down next to her. "We must go now, before he returns. I'll protect you."

MayAnn shook her head, not looking at him.

"What happened to make you so afraid? What happened the night he kidnapped you?"

At first, Ant didn't think she'd talk, so long was the silence. She kept her head bowed, looking at her fingers fidgeting in her lap. Then, with a small sigh, she said, "He brought me here and tied me to the bed."

Ant waited for more, but when she remained tight-lipped, he reached over and placed a hand reassuringly on hers.

"He said that I owed him my life for killing the love of his life. He started telling me all the ways that he could kill me." She spoke so softly Ant barely heard her. "He'd shoot me so many times I'd look like wormwood. Or cut my head off and feed it to the crows. He threatened to garrote me, strangle, hang, drag me to death behind a horse. Or behind one of those new-fangled automobiles. Poison, hex, curse, drowning, set me on fire. Beat me with a hammer. Impale me on a stake. Wall me up and let me starve to death. Seemed like he couldn't make up his mind."

To Ant's surprise, she gave a little smile. "Poor boy, he didn't know what to do. I could tell he had to do something, some action so he'd feel manly. He reminds me a bit of you that way, Antoine."

Ant sat back at the insult but she took no notice. "So I said I'd help him if he'd untie me."

"You'd help him kill you?"

"He didn't want to do, not really. I've never been afraid of him, Antoine. You know that."

"So?"

"You don't want to hear, Antoine."

"Come on," he grabbed her wrist, "we're getting out of here."

But she resisted, forcefully pulling her arm free and looked Ant directly in the eye. "When he untied me, I took off all my clothes, laid out on the bed and told him to tie me up again."

If she had wanted to stun Ant, she pole axed him good and proper. The entire construct of his life, the wobbly platform of his identity, tilted. Only with a Herculean effort of denial did he prevent his hope for an acceptable life from collapsing.

"Now do you see, Antoine?"

"He's vowed to kill you. I heard him. Billy heard him. He said he'd get your confession to the murder, even by blood." Ant shouted more to hear his strength, to reinforced himself, rather than intimidate MayAnn. "You tried to bribe your way free. I can understand..."

"He won't kill me, Antoine."

"What makes you so sure? He murdered one woman."

MayAnn looked away to the pathetic magazine pictures pinned on the drab wall. Her hands were folded primly in her lap, her back straight as if at afternoon tea in a society matron's best sitting room. "I've won him over," she answered, demurely.

"Like winning over your executioner? He'll kiss you just before chopping off your head." Ant tried to make a joke but didn't successfully hide his bitterness. "Look, MayAnn, Billy believes Young Jack killed the girl. If he killed a whore once, he can kill again, and that makes him a problem for Basin Street. Billy solves such problems for Tom. I'm afraid when Billy closes in, Young Jack will use you as a hostage or worst. You have to come with me—*now*."

"No, Antoine. If you love me, if you've ever loved me, leave this alone. Tell Billy to stop."

"There's no stopping Billy."

She gripped his wrist, digging in her nails. "Nothing's to happen to Jack, do you understand me, Antoine? He didn't kill the whore."

"How do you know?"

MayAnn released him and turned so he couldn't see her face. A held breath foreshadows certain momentous times—the acceptance of a marriage proposal, the announcement of a tragic death. That stillpoint enveloped them. And stretched out. And longer until Ant wondered if MayAnn wasn't slyly teasing him. His hope revived. This was a game of who could hold their breath the longest. Just before turning blue, she'd burst out laughing and say, Wasn't that fun, all this foolishness.

Ant didn't hear her words. They came out as a breath, not spoken. He leaned forward to catch the trace of a word. The breath came again, a whisper this time. MayAnn's head bowed. Her shoulders sagged. She folded down, forehead to her knees. The whisper became a ragged sob. "*I* killed her."

Of course Ant didn't hear her right. He took MayAnn in his arms and rocked her. It's hard to hear properly through a waterfall. The words were muffled, thrashed about in the cascade of her tears.

"I did it, Antoine."

A trick of an amateur magician, Ant told himself. The old standby of distracting with one hand while pulling a coin from under the nose with the other. She is trying to save Young Jack by offering herself, knowing I'd never let Billy kill her.

MayAnn sat up and shrugged off his comforting embrace. "I'm shameful about killing her. I pray every day to her and to her family and to God for forgiveness. But, Antoine," she faced him, both hands gripping his, "I deserve a better life. My children deserve a better future. A war was fought to give our people that chance. This is my private battle, one soldier to another. You understand, don't you, Antoine? This is my chance for emancipation."

Ant didn't believe her any more than when she told him they'd never be lovers again. He couldn't believe such a thing about her. She wasn't a murderer. Even if she did kill the girl—let's suspend disbelief for a moment—even if she did, it wasn't craven murder. She acted from noble motivation. Our entire nation had fought that war. Brothers killed brothers, but it wasn't murder.

She separated herself from Ant and took her hands back. "Jack had this romantic notion of avenging the woman he loved. Or thought he was in love with." MayAnn spoke with more assuredness now. "He had to believe with all his heart or he'd be nothing but a joke on himself. But he was really in love with the notion of love. I knew that, Antoine. Getting that girl out of my way was a gamble I'd win.

"He didn't hear his precious Miss Laura talk about him with the other girls. He was her big jackpot. All she wanted was to make enough money to open a millinery shop back in Memphis. She was willing and eager to be with twenty slobbering idiots a night -- men, dogs or goats—just for the money. She didn't have a romantic bone in her body. If getting a better life meant selling herself for a while, then she'd make it as pleasurable as possible for everyone. He never knew her *desire* was to design *hats*, not to be some bauble on his arm. He was nothing more than her big bonus, a bankroll, but he made the mistake of thinking he had bought her heart. But he wasn't special. Make the money and run was her plan all along. She didn't want any trace of her New Orleans life following her back to Memphis, including Jack. I've made him understand that truth."

Ant didn't know whether to laugh at the outrageousness of her confession or recoil at the truth she was a stone-cold killer or dismiss the fact as a mere inconvenience.

Did it make any difference, he asked himself. First thought: no, not at all. He loved her. Second thought: hugging her might be clasping an asp. She had proven herself capable of drastic action by crushing a woman's throat for her own gain. That gave him pause, no matter how much he loved her. Say he'd deny her something she wanted and they had an argument. He might find it difficult to get a restful night's sleep next to her.

Yet, he wasn't repulsed. This MayAnn was someone he'd want by his side in the battle of life. She'd be a cutthroat in striking down adversaries. Shoulder to shoulder, they'd hack out their paradise from the wilderness of an unjust society.

We'll win, he silently cheered. I'd win! This new MayAnn thrills me -- the way playing Russian roulette sharpens your lust for life.

"He doesn't have to tie me to the bed, never did, Antoine. Although he sort of likes it." She couldn't, didn't want to, hide the mischievous flash in her eye. "He's coming around. Even promised to buy me a new dress. Jack's innocent, Antoine. You have to protect him. If Billy kills Jack, it's the same as killing me. I hold you responsible for his safety."

MayAnn had him tied in knots. The more Ant thought about it, the more he realized she was a powerful trickster who had managed to turn him against himself, like when the magician removes the belt off the gentleman on stage without him knowing it—until his pants fall down. Ant found himself with his pants down around his ankles, hobbled.

But, perhaps his situation wasn't so impossible. Billy had never believed Young Jack was the murderer. He wants to talk with MayAnn about the killing so all I've to do is put them together, Ant told himself. She'll confirm Young Jack's story that he never reached the upstairs and he'll be free of suspicion of murdering the whore.

But I'll still have the problem of Young Jack. He keeps her in that ugly room on Tchoupitoulas. No fancy dresses. No white picket fence in sight. No sweet little cottage on St. Ann Street. That wasn't her dream of raising her station in life. I can offer her better once he's out of the way. Ant imagined himself as a hero and an avenging angel.

An accident can be arranged, or a brutal mugging, or a mysterious death with clues pointing to Central American revolutionaries. MayAnn would eventually get over her loss. But, she has made me Young Jack's protector.

The irony was laughable, if Ant had a sense for gallows humor. He realized that for him to remain in her confidence as a heart companion, he'd have to kill his dream of having her. He'd have to give her up as his refuge; stand alone to whatever vulgarities white society and laws hurled at him. He'd have to be brave on his own, which, he knew, wasn't his nature.

However, the more Ant thought about the knot MayAnn fixed him in, the more he saw possibilities to slip free. Crossing Canal Street on his way back to Tom's Arlington, he had something of a St. Paul conversion. Struck blind by the revelation, oblivious to the wagons he stepped in front of, not hearing the curses of the drivers, bumping into people without apologies, even nearly knocking over a careless child, Ant had a new plan to win MayAnn.

He'd always believed deception, lying, and slight-of-hand as legitimate means to protect himself: do whatever it takes to get what he needed to protect the person he had the right to be. That's the survival of the self, man's highest responsibility. He had been using tricks to win back MayAnn and nothing had worked. But what if he made the lover's ultimate sacrifice: give up his desire so MayAnn could find her happiness.

"If I could throw away the urge to trace my patterns in your heart, I could really see you." He had read that somewhere.

Well, if I make the effort to stop writing my desires on her heart, Ant told himself, *maybe I would see her differently, and she would consider me differently. I'll stand by her for no other reason than she needs my support. I won't use misfortune as a side door to slip into her embrace. I'll conduct myself in a fine and honest manner. Altruism, not self-interest no matter how justified, will be my guiding principle.*

He truly believed himself that in the moment.

When Ant stepped into Tom's saloon, Billy, looking grim, signaled him over to his table. "Sit down, Ant." Billy hunched forward, elbows on the table, and spoke under his breath. "There's been another murder. One of Minnie White's girls was strangled in her room."

"When?"

"Two nights ago. Tom's concerned. You know Minnie is popular with conventioneers. He wants this nipped in the bud *now*. You may've been right about Young Jack getting taste for this thrill. He was there that night. We need to deal with him."

"But we have no proof."

"We have him on the scene of two murders of Storyville prostitutes. More than a coincidence, I'd say."

"But he might have been at Minnie's for a card game or checkers or a fun time over a beer with other men. Minnie's was known for such diversions as much as for the girls. We can't accuse a member of New Orleans most prominent family. You yourself had said the Bohommes would be a bad enemy."

"My job is to relieve Tom's anxiety," Billy replied. "Your job is to find Young Jack."

All right. Simple. Ant knew exactly what he'd have to do -- have MayAnn vouch for Young Jack on the nights of both murders. What better proof that he was Young Jack's protector? If Young Jack happened to disappear later or be the victim of cruel fate, MayAnn wouldn't suspect him.

"While you're snooping around for him, Tom has another job for you."

Countess Willie had shown no enthusiasm for joining Tom's Golden Row. In fact, she hadn't even bothered to reply to his offer. If she didn't join Tom's coalition, other madams would shy away. Tom had started obsessing about her Italian name and the possible link to the Matrangas.

"He sees shadows in shadows," Billy said. "So he wants you to put light on Countess Willie's shadow. He wants you to find out everything about her."

For a moment Ant wondered if the Matrangas had gotten to her and made a blood pact. But then he remembered their wounded pride at her rebuff. So what was Countess Willie's game?

He began his inquires with Josie and a few of the other madams. But they didn't even know her real name, assuming Piazza was her *nom de plume,* as many women in the profession hid their true identity. His copper contacts said she had never been arrested and never would be, given her sterling reputation. Ant visited men with direct knowledge; they confirmed she was well educated, had superb taste and ran a five-star house. "Wish I could move in permanently," one gentleman said wistfully. "She has the best library in the city. Her ladies are sophisticated and delightful. If only my wife would take lessons from them."

Several clients claimed they visit her house as much for her parlor concerts as for the company. "She's a patron of musicians like Tony Jackson and Sammy Davis and Ferdy Morton. She bought a white upright piano inlaid with mother-of-pearl for them and has a tuner come in once a week. I heard she might invite that Buddy Bolden fellow."

Where did she come from? Ant asked. Hard to say, everyone answered. She speaks Spanish, French, Dutch, Italian and several Basque dialects fluently. Her English is mellifluous Deep South.

Dutch? Who speaks Dutch in New Orleans? Where did she learn Dutch?

Maybe she had a Dutch lover, some men guessed, although if she had a lover, male or female, it was the best-kept secret in Storyville, where secrets never remained hidden for long.

Yet, the real Countess Willie was apparently a secret.

What about the countess title? Ant asked. Surely it's made up, a bit of gold foil to attract the right clientele?

Well, she is awfully imperious, the men replied. Always proper and gracious, even a bit aloof, never a pal-around gal.

Although, one man added with a smirk and wink, she does let her hair down with special friends.

One client of long-time standing revealed a startling bit of information. "She killed a man, you know. It was covered up, never reported. He had brutally sodomized one of her girls and she shot him through the heart right there in the room."

"Sounds like a tale to me," Ant said.

The gentleman gave Ant a dare-call-me-a-liar look. "I was there. Countess Willie is a good friend." He refused to answer any more questions.

Countess Willie's whorehouse/residence stood on the corner of Canal Street and Claiborne Avenue, on the far edge of Storyville. The imposing three-story house with four columns supporting the portico had the look of a St. Charles Avenue mansion-- old-time money, respectable society and impeccable discretion. She encouraged the impression that her establishment was an independent republic superior to her déclassé competitors.

Needing an inside source, Ant staked out her place from across the street and waited for the kitchen maid to emerge for errands. On the second morning, a young black girl with a shopping basket on her arm came out. Ant tailed her to the shoemaker and then to apothecary, gradually closing the distance while waiting for the opportunity to approach. At the sidewalk fruit stand, he stood next to her as she plunked a melon.

"How do you know when it's ripe?" Ant asked, playing the dumb male needing help.

"If it sounds rich," she replied, "and smells fragrant."

Ant steered the conservation to she worked in a rich house; his discreet bribe made her a little richer.

After they became ten-dollars friendly, she admitted to working for Countess Willie for about a year.

"Does she have family?"

"Not that I know of but there was that cute French count," giggled the maid. "They've corresponded for years. My nephew collects stamps and Countess Willie gives me the French stamps. He was wild about her, truly was, according to the girls in the house. Gave her expensive jewels whenever he came all the way from France to visit her. When she refused to join him in France, he said he would move to New Orleans and make her an honest woman. She said she was an honest woman."

"Is she a drinker? Drugs?" Ant probed for any weakness to exploit.

"Oh, no. She's a proper lady, although she can have a salty mouth and swears like a sailor when she's upset."

After several more days of inquiries around town, Ant didn't know anything about the real Countess Willie -- until the night his guardian angel Serendipity graced him.

He was in a backstreet dive going on his second whiskey bemoaning the impossibility of persuading a strong willed, independent, mindful woman—he was thinking MayAnn as much as Countess Willie –to do something against her will, when the stranger on the neighboring bar stool volunteered, "That's no puzzle. Find her shame, or secret desire, and threaten to tell the world. Women will eat out of your hand if you hold that velvet switch over them."

"What shame does a woman like Countess Willie have?" Ant asked. "She runs a whorehouse. Doesn't care who knows."

"Countess Willie, you say?" The stranger spoke in a slow Mississippian drawl with more cotton field than New Orleans slur. He wore the dusty jacket of a man on the road. "I know a *Countess* Willie and she has plenty to be ashamed of."

Ant ordered a bottle of good whiskey and set it before the stranger, an older man with gray at the temple. His callused hands told of a workingman but the quality of his suit jacket signaled discerning taste. He didn't say another word until Ant poured.

"Tell me about your Countess Willie."

"I heard she settled here." The man took a sip of whiskey, not slugging it back in the manner of an impoverished drinker.

The man, "Harlan," he said, offering his hand, was from Vicksburg and on his way home after taking care of some business in New Orleans. "Willimae was always a cut above the crowd, even as a girl. She came to stay with her daddy, Vincent Piazza, in Vicksburg when she was a teenager. She was the oldest child. The other two stayed with their mother somewhere around Belzoni after Vinnie left them."

A half bottle later, Ant had learned Belzoni was little more than that a short stretch of saloons along the banks of the Yazoo River. "Not even a church," Harlan said, "although we had a preacher until he became the town drunk, an honor earned by drinking Hell dry."

The number of Italian inhabitants earned the town the sobriquet "Greasy Row." Why they settled there was unknown other than the town had been named after Giovanni Belzoni, an Italian engineer, circus performer and explorer of Egyptian antiquities.

Harlan had a plantation on the Yazoo when Vincent ran the Belzoni dry goods store and cotton exchange.

Over a second bottle, Ant learned Vincent had left the "Dark Corner of Washington County" for better opportunities in the big city of Vicksburg. But he stayed in touch with his family, not abandoning them as much as just moved away.

"Can't say I blame him," Harlan said, now nearly nose down in his whiskey glass. "Man's got to improve himself whatever the sacrifice. So it was no surprise when Williemae came to stay with him. She had ambitions, just like her daddy. And she had a high opinion of herself."

"So how did she get from Vicksburg to New Orleans?" Ant asked.

"On a boat. A steamer carrying bales." Harlan looked at Ant like he was an ignoramus for asking such a foolish question.

"Do you know why?"

"There was talk."

But Harlan didn't volunteer anything further.

"Com'on, Ha'lan." Ant rested his head on his hand to keep upright.

Harlan gave a curiously high-pitched snort. "She bamboozled him."

"Who?"

"That prig Conti. Count Conti, so he called himself, didn't have a cent to his name after Willimae was done with him." Harlan slapped the bar and bellowed with laughter.

A couple more drinks and the story slid out.

Seemed Willimae made herself attractive to the Count. He was nothing but a pompous blowhard, heaven's high fart, in Harlan's opinion. Educated in Italy, or so he claimed. Traveled the world, or so he claimed, snorted Harlan. Could sing opera, if you call that caterwauling singing. So why was he hiding in backwater Vicksburg? He had money, lived in a mansion the Yanks hadn't burned.

Willimae was nothing more than a country girl but smart as a whip. The count took her on as a pupil, sort of, a lump of clay to mold. He didn't have much else to do so the challenge of shaping her into a refined lady amused him. Talk got going she was an apt pupil in more ways than one. Then one day she jumped aboard the steamboat without saying goodbye to a soul, not even telling her daddy where she was going.

"The count made accusations she'd stolen a great deal of cash from him. But he quieted down after Vincent conferred with him. Maybe there was a child on the horizon. That was part of the talk."

"So what's the shameful secret?" Ant asked. "There's not much shame in stealing. The robber barons made it respectable."

Harlan reared back his head and looked at Ant with bloodshot eyes. "Her mama," he took the last gulp of whiskey, "is a nigga."

Ant bought Harlan another bottle as a thank you gift.

By mid-afternoon the next day, Ant had made himself presentable and rang the bell at Countess Willie's establishment. His friend the maid answered the door. Ant handed her a note to deliver with a dollar bill folded for her. The note read, "Your middle name is Vincent."

The maid left Ant standing on the doorstep but returned moments later and ushered him into the foyer. Deep green wallpaper patterned with fluers-de-lis covered the walls. A vase with an enormous bouquet of gladioli and roses stood on a table before a large mirror in a gilded frame. The house was silent, none of the tinkling piano or flights of teasing laughter heard in whorehouses. Instead of taking him into the house, the maid opened a nearly invisible doorway in the foyer's back wall.

"Countess Willie will see you in her personal sitting room," she said, escorting Ant up three flights of narrow stairs.

They emerged into a large room fit for a queen with literary taste. A built-in bookcase containing a couple hundred volumes covered one wall. Ant recognized what appeared to be a Renoir and next to it a Corot. During his education in Germany, he had visited the Paris galleries and had been very taken by the Impressionists. A baby grand piano occupied one corner. Groupings of winged reading chairs gave the room the atmosphere of a salon.

Countess Willie sat in a chair, more a throne with its high back, in the center of the room. Ol' Jack Frost would have greeted Ant more warmly than she did. He had never seen her in person: she had a dusky Italian complexion, a small pert nose and a rounded face with fleshy cheeks. Her lips had a full arch, which made them a shade too big for her face. Jeweled hairsticks held her black hair artfully piled on top of her head.

"That's a very fine Manet," Ant said gesturing to the painting, hoping to impress with his educated eye.

She didn't reply. Holding her cigarette holder upright as a scepter, she scrutinized Ant with the distain of a queen for a beggar. Minutes dragged by as she kept him standing like a servant before asking, "Why have you come?" One of the charms of a Southern accent is it sounds courteous, even when dismissive.

"Tom Anderson requests your presence on Basin Street."

"Why should I uproot my establishment to please Mr. Anderson?" She slowly lit the black cigarette in the holder, dragging out the moment with a long plume of smoke.

"Because I know about your mother." For one breath her nostrils flared. Ant involuntarily edged back a half step from the tight coil of her hatred.

For her entire career in New Orleans Countess Willie had passed as a white woman of European descent. If her true identity were discovered, she'd be in violation of the Story ordinance banning blacks from living in or operating a business in the sanctioned downtown vice district. She'd be forced out. Her options would be to close her business or move uptown, to black Storyville. Wealthy white men and European royalty didn't venture there.

"I'll keep your secret. Not even Mr. Anderson will know," Ant promised as his first step in his avowed self-reformation. By not using trickery or other underhanded means, he'd find the strength to build a mansion of true unselfish love for MayAnn.

"And who are *you?*"

"A much aggrieved person like yourself trying to make his way."

She took another puff on the cigarette and assessed Ant from behind the scrim of smoke.

"Mr. Anderson worries you have connection to the Matrangas."

"The Matrangas are shit beneath my shoe," she replied with distain. "They are dirty Italians not worthy of the name."

"What you do is your choice. But Mr. Anderson is a powerful friend to have in your corner in case unpleasant things do happen."

She turned her face in dismissal without replying.

That evening, Ant told Tom he shouldn't concern himself about Countess Willie. She had assured that she had no loyalties to the Matrangas.

"But is she moving onto my Golden Row? That's the assurance I want."

"Her complicated situation will take time to resolve."

Tom took Ant's non-answer for whatever he wanted to hear. Then he asked, "What about Young Jack?"

"I'm working on how to best deal with him," Ant replied, glad to get back to the heart of the matter.

Chapter 15.

Ant hadn't seen or heard of Young Jack or MayAnn since the yellow fever outbreak. To find one would be to find the other, and his best chance was to find MayAnn.

But how?

The obvious place to start was with Buddy; wherever he played, MayAnn would show up. But Ant had another reason to seek out Buddy and that had to do with his vow of self-reformation: if he was going to be straight in his dealings, he had to address his music.

Until then, music had been one of Ant's means-to-an-end, a double bet. By playing with Buddy, he had a presence in the Negro community, a home-away-from-home so to speak. Music also had been to ploy to ingratiate himself with MayAnn. But now Ant felt he had to be honest with music; did he have a real love for it like Buddy or Big Eye or the others?

Ant found Buddy at Louis's barbershop getting a shave. Without preamble, Ant stood at the side of his chair and said, "I want to play in your band."

Buddy didn't say a word until Louis wiped the last of the shaving cream off his face. "Frankie Dusen is my trombone man now. Needed the work after Sweet Lovin' left town."

"I'm not asking for anything permanent," Ant clarified. "Just to sit in a few times to see if I'm in love for the right reasons."

Buddy gave him a righteous look and sonorously pronounced, "A love castle built on deception will crumble." He let that hang between them. "If you ever do that to music, play with a false heart or cheat or lie, I'll never talk to you again." He paused. "I'm playing Frank Mangetta's tonight. You stand *behind* Dusen."

"Want me to make you shine?" asked Louis as he took the barber apron off Buddy. Ant settled in the chair feeling smug.

Mangetta's occupied the corner of Marais and Canal, on the border between uptown and downtown Storyville. By day, Frank Mangetta sold imported meats and provolone, tins of Sicilian olive oil and other home country food out of his back room. By night, the accomplished violinist and uptown padrone turned his high-ceiling front room into a music hall. When Ant sauntered in with his horn, college boys from Tulane and Loyola universities, dockhands from the deep delta, St. Charles Avenue patrons of hot music and uptown rowdies jammed the bar and tables around the hardwood dance floor. Mangetta had pasted up signs advertising "Buddy Bolden's live jass tonight at Mangettas." A newspaper reporter had described Buddy's playing as "jaser," French meaning "to chatter." On his way to the show, Ant had noticed a poster altered to read "live ass tonight at Mangettas."

He pushed through the crowd and onto the stage. Buddy nodded a greeting. Dusen ignored him. Ant didn't know for sure if MayAnn would show up, but the sun always shines. Buddy shouted out, "Callin' all my chillen," and the band launched into ragtime, which Buddy used as a starting place to make the melody nervous, jumpy, as if trying to hop out of a box. Then he'd forget all about the melody and let it disappear underneath an improvised cascade of blues, Celtic folk songs, jigs, hymns, African foot stomps and hand slapping and stuff nobody knew where it came from, including Buddy. He'd throw in waltzes and schottische to give people an anchor, make them feel safe with the familiar before leading them into wilderness of his jass. The crowd loved it.

Musicians from around the city—black, white and Creole—always showed up to study what made Buddy so popular.

Whoever figured it out got spillover jobs Buddy didn't have time for. Ant wasn't surprised to see Big Eye Nelson and the kid Sidney Bechet listening intently in the back of room. He hadn't seen Big Eye, a big affable horn player, since that fine time they had had at the funeral parade beating up on the second line. Freddie Keppard also stood against the wall. A Creole, he was darker than some blacks but acted like his shit didn't stink. Always with his ladies, flaunting; always with the flask, drunk or going there. Keppard regarded himself as the superior horn player to everyone, especially Buddy. After all, he was a *trained* musician. Buddy didn't like Keppard, claimed he was a thief who played with a handkerchief over his hand so other horn players couldn't copy his technique. That was stealing the tradition in Buddy's opinion, taking and not giving back.

And in the middle of the crowd there she was, dancing like a raindrop on a hot tin roof. Ant stepped from behind Dusen so MayAnn could see him. To get her attention, he blew an emphatic swoop—which got Dusen's attention. He half turned towards Ant so their trombones nearly touched as they sawed away. The faster Dusen played, the faster Ant played. Their slides pinged off each other a couple times, as if in a fencing duel. Buddy gave Ant a get-back-in-line glare. Instead of retreating, Ant stepped forward and aimed his horn right at MayAnn.

Only then did he see Young Jack, who was, much to Ant's astonishment, dancing! or, more accurately, jerking around like a puppet on unskilled strings, hopping from foot to clubfoot, arms akimbo. MayAnn laughed and twirled about him and he spun with her enjoying his foolishness.

Ant hated him with all his heart.

MayAnn wasn't a trickster or a magician; she was a WIZARD, Ant thought. Young Jack wanted to punish her, maybe kill her, and she had him dancing with her! Damn brazen of her to flaunt him before me, Ant fumed. On the other hand, maybe she was powerless. Maybe Eulalia Echo's High

John the Conqueror Root powder had worked, but on the wrong man.

Ant put all his anger right through his horn and told the couple, You can't disrespect me like this! FAIR WARNING!!

His fortissimo blast got Dusen up on his toes and he attacked like he was trying to put out Ant's eye with his slide.

MayAnn and Young Jack didn't even look at Ant, treated him like he wasn't there.

Fury ignited in Ant like a benzene bomb. He'd put Billy on Young Jack's scent. He'd send the Hounds of Hell after that lame man who had stolen his girl. I'll be the Hounds of Hell, Ant shouted through his mouthpiece, blowing threats at Young Jack, barking out short sharp notes. Ant used his horn as a revolver to fire off six fast shots aimed at Young Jack's head. To hell with his vow to be MayAnn's unselfish friend.

But MayAnn and Young Jack ignored him no matter how loud and furious Ant made his horn scream at them. The rest of the band stopped playing and Buddy stared at Ant in amazement. Then he gave Ant a big smile and the band jumped in to improvise around Ant's disjointed anger.

After Buddy closed out the set, he watched MayAnn and Young Jack walk out the front door. He turned to Ant, who expected a tirade about his abusing the music and disrespecting Buddy's main trombone man and how Buddy never wanted Ant on stage with him again. Instead, Buddy said, "I see she's been found. Now what are you going to do about that?"

Ant didn't know what *he* was going to do about Young Jack but Billy had ideas on how to rid Basin Street of the whore killer. Ant went to Tom's saloon to find Billy and by chance followed Chief of Police Hennessy, dressed in his high command uniform, through the front door. The police chief strode directly over to the piano player and ordered him to stop.

"What? You want a different song?" the pianist asked. "Maybe Irving Berlin? Something out of Tin Pan Alley?" He started tinkling a tune.

Hennessy slammed his palm down on the keys, the loud discord turning heads at the bar. "You're breaking the law," Hennessy barked.

The piano player gazed at him in disbelief.

"Get out!" ordered the police chief.

Tom, alerted to the trouble, emerged from his back office. "Officer?"

"Chief of Police Hennessy to you." He held out a folded piece of paper. "That's a citation for violation of the Gay-Shattuck Law. First time, pay the fine. Second time, do the time."

Tom didn't reach for the citation. "The knight always hand delivers news to the king. That's his role, right?" Tom smiled to smarten up the insult.

Hennessy tapped him on the chest with the citation. "You know what happened to the Roman Empire and to pretenders in togas."

Men at the bar stopped talking and turned to watch. Billy positioned himself at the front door, a lookout for Hennessy's reinforcements.

Tom hooked his thumbs in his vest, rocked back on his heels, then slowly forward onto his toes, and again on his heels, each time coming an inch or two closer to Hennessy. "May I offer you a drink, officer? Or a dime for your time?"

Hennessy slapped Tom on the chest with the citation, then higher so the next would be a dueling challenge across his cheek. "An official court order to be obeyed."

Tom, thumbs still hooked in his vest, rocked forward as if to head butt Hennessy. One more inch and they'd be chest-to-chest.

The saloon was absolutely still.

The two bulls were locked in, unable to back down without losing face.

Billy signaled the piano player to roll out a barrelhouse.

Hennessy let the citation fall to the floor.

Tom stepped on the paper as if grinding out a cigarette butt.

"My men will come around, often, to check that you are in compliance." Hennessy spun on his heel and marched out.

Tom watched him out the door. He didn't pick up the citation.

The new Gay-Shattuck state law was a stunt to counter the prohibition reformers, God bless Carrie Nation. The law prohibited the serving of alcohol to women, girls and minors in any barroom, cabaret, coffee house, café, beer saloon, liquor exchange, drinking saloon, grog shop, beer house or beer garden. This included such places, to quote the law, as "any apartment where intoxicating liquors are sold to girls or women, or minors, or to permit girls or women, or minors, to enter or drink in any such apartments."

The law also banned musical instruments in saloons.

A powerful group of New Orleans' businessmen had backed the law to forestall the reformers' total ban on alcohol. The tactic was meant to buy time while the pro-liquor interests launched an offensive to shore up public support for the time-honored tradition of a friendly relaxing drink.

Nobody took the law seriously. Imagine New Orleans without music in the saloons? Imagine a world without gaiety? Impossible!

But, the day after the Hennessy-Anderson confrontation, coppers began enforcing all aspects of the law with unprecedented vigor. Hennessy's men systematically closed the "ladies rooms" that connected to barrooms, which gave the night ladies and their clients' easy access. The *Daily Picayune* accurately reported that the "police put the lid down on Storyville, and saloon men and dive keepers raised a howl which vibrated from one end of the district to the other."

After a week, saloon owners told Tom they were losing money faster than a donkey pissing. Why pay him a mayoral fee if he couldn't keep the police chief out of their business? Tom assured them Hennessy's harassment would be short lived. He'd talk to the city's mayor.

When the pressure didn't let up, Tom called Billy into his office and announced, "We're closing down the Annex."

Billy stared with disbelief and began to protest but Tom held up a quieting hand. "I've called a meeting tomorrow night for all the Storyville owners of places where liquor and women and men are served in the same room." He pulled a copy of the Gay-Shattuck Law. "It states here the law doesn't apply to the sale of liquor in hotels, boarding houses or restaurants where malt, vinous or other liquors are sold in connection with the service of meals supplied to guests."

Within days after the meeting, menus posted on the front doors of every Storyville liquor establishment announced their conversion to a "fancy restaurant." Tom's menu for his Arlington Annex & Café featured Mardi Gras Doubloons, Stuffed Okra, Rich Shells, Shrimp Ceviche, Oysters Bienville, Peachy Chicken, Andouille and Potatoes, gumbo and steaks. Some of this could actually be prepared and served, given enough advanced notice.

The 101 Ranch and Fewclothes and the Big 25 and other back-street dives offered only peanuts and snacks. Nancy Hank's, which already had whores' beds in the upstairs rooms, declared itself a hotel.

Josie's and the other Basin Street sporting mansions posted menus as diverse as sandwiches—"no fuss to slow you down"—to full meals with linen tablecloths. Countess Willie, who had, much to Ant's astonishment, relocated to Basin Street, hired a French chef for her dinner parties; a "beautiful companion" came with the five-course meal. Minnie White boosted a community table at her "boarding house." Josie's menu featured the code "stewed fruit": constipation being a professional hazard, the madams kept a ready supply of stewed prunes for their employees.

Saloon owners installed raised platforms in their "dining rooms" for performances. A sign invited any and all to come up and entertain, with the understanding the singer was available for a "date" after her song. Storyville prostitutes quickly got in on the game. They learned songs whether they could sing or not—humming was a big hit—and reclassified themselves as entertainers.

Rightly suspecting a scam, Hennessy came unannounced to the Annex in hopes of catching Tom out. Tipped off, Tom greeted him at the front door with a towel draped over his forearm.

"Table for one?" Tom asked with a mock bow.

Hennessy hesitated, then gave a curt nod. Tom led him to a table next to the busy bar, handed him a menu in French and poured a glass of water, slopping it over onto the tablecloth. "A drink? Or are you on duty?"

"Bring me everything on the menu," Hennessy said, "warm and prompt."

"Do you have a favorite song? I'll have the cabaret songstress entertain you."

Hennessy whipped open his napkin without answering. Within twenty minutes the soup arrived, much to Hennessy's consternation, followed by plates heaped with steaming, piquant food prepared by Countess Willie's French chef hired for the occasion.

"Will you be wanting dessert?" Tom inquired.

Hennessy sat with his fists balled, eyes straight ahead, back ramrod stiff. "Anderson, you are being too clever by half," he said, grinding his teeth so hard the porcelain practically squeaked. "And half clever people are fools." He stood up abruptly, toppling over his chair. "I'll run you out of town and into ruination, mark my words, Anderson." Without warning, he chest-butted Tom and stomped off.

"Now you've wounded his pride," Billy commented. "He'll come charging back and we'd better have a plan."

"You're right," Tom replied. "Time to put some thought on that."

The very next day more trouble arrived, and Josie the irate messenger.

"Goddamn, Tom, you know what's going on at 331? A squatter moved in! She ripped out a wall to create a "ballroom" and had her girls working before the dust settled. I don't think she even has beds upstairs yet. Doesn't make any difference from what I hear," Josie said, stiff necked. "Her girls do it standing up, on the floor, sitting on a window sill, hanging from a trapeze, on a pony, with a pony. Goddamn Emma and her circus."

As she plopped onto Tom's office sofa, her face crumpled in distress. "There goes the neighborhood," she wailed. "Everything we've worked for."

Ant, who was in the office to tell Tom that he had spotted Young Jack and they needed to get the posse on the hunt, moved towards the door. Tom motioned him to stay.

"Emma Johnson?" Tom asked.

"Yes, goddamnit, Tom. EMMA JOHNSON, the Cocksucker Queen."

"I never heard she was moving in. How did that happen? Had you heard anything about this, Ant?"

Ant looked surprised and perplexed. "Not a whisper." He never believed Emma would actually throw in with the Matrangas. But, not being a crystal chandelier type of madam like Josie or Countess Willie, she would do it just to thumb her nose at them. Emma was, to say the least, earthy; if you could imagine it, Emma would provide it.

"Why would she uproot her French Studio and disrupt her business?" Tom asked. "It's a landmark for the outrageous."

"The disgusting," injected Josie. "She'll ruin us, Tom." Josie's anger brought her out of despair and off the sofa. She stormed up to him, her nose no higher than his top suit button. "She sells virgins. You think those reformers are on the warpath with that prohibition law, just you wait until they sink their righteous teeth into the ruination of young girls for money."

"All right, Josie." Tom put a hand on her shoulder to keep her from jumping at his throat. "I'll see what I can do."

"Don't see what you can do," Josie shouted. "*Do!*"

"Yes, Josie." Tom gently steered her out the door. "Yes, Josie."

He paced the room, head down, hands clasped behind his back. "This Johnson woman is a poison spear aimed at us, Ant. I want to know who's behind her. Poke around and see if the Matrangas are hiding under her bed."

Ant was afraid that he already knew the answer but he had to find out for certain. So he went to see his friend Cawzi, who performed in Emma's sex circus giving ten exhibitions per week, twice daily except Tuesdays and Thursdays, screwing prostitutes and amateur volunteers before a salivating audience. Emma paid him $150 per week and she made a handsome profit on those private shows. Cawzi, a remarkable man, pulled in double his salary by selling his own brand of pep pills. He'd been doing the gig for twelve years; sent his four children through college with his earnings. He was a man who loved his job and kept his wife satisfied. "Anyone can do it if they know the trick," he once confided to Ant, but wouldn't tell him the trick.

When Ant knocked on Cawzi's door in a respectable part of town, he was greeted with a bear hug. "Ant, so long. Come in, come in." The full head of black hair slicked back, the soulful dark eyes that invited everybody to drop into his arms, and the rakish pencil mustache gave Cawzi the look of a dangerous, but fun, lover. The sinewy body had remained strong and supple over the years.

His wife, Suz, who had the exotic look of a gypsy, greeted Ant with a peck on the cheek. As a couple, they did private events with straps, belts, pinchers, razors, hoods and other tools of the trade for those so inclined. A little something towards the retirement fund, Cawzi had explained.

After sweetened tea and cakes and preliminary chitchat, Ant asked if his friend was performing at Emma's new place.

"She's a bit nervous about moving to Basin Street with those uppity neighbors," Cawzi confided in a confidential voice. "For her official opening, she's planning a special theatrical show. Something more high toned and literary than her usual fare. An enactment of a reading from Marquis de Sade. You should come, Ant. I've got the starring role. It'll really be something, very rousing."

"I heard that she and the Mafia partnered up," Ant probed.

Cawzi laughed and slapped his knee. "They're peas in a pod but can you imagine Emma being anyone's partner? Or anyone wanting to be her partner? I'd just as soon fight a wildcat blindfolded. No, Emma's just moving to a better address. There're rumors the city might put a trolley line right down Basin. You heard that? If so, customers will be dropped off at her doorstep."

"You know Tom Anderson controls Basin Street. It's impolite not to confer with him."

"When has Emma conferred with anyone about anything? Hell, I'd fear Emma more than I would the Mafia. She's damn good with that bullwhip of hers."

"So, no whispers about the Matranga brothers?"

"Emma doesn't whisper about anything. Full shout all the time. Why you asking, Ant?"

"Tom Anderson likes to know his neighbors."

"You come see the show, Ant," Cawzi said, seeing him to the door. "It's like nothing you've experienced."

The Matrangas might be behind Emma, whether Cawzi knew it or not. Ant would have to ask them.

But a note, a space-filler really, in the afternoon newspaper caused Ant to tremble at the very thought of the Matrangas. A father, mother and son had been murdered, shot in the head execution style. Family name Chen. No other details.

Ant stared at those simple words and waited to be filled with guilt, remorse, anger, revenge. He didn't know what. But something. Chen deserved something from him. A tear. He couldn't muster up even a simple tear. Somehow the murders seemed like business as usual. What else would be expected of the Matrangas? He did feel regret. Chen had been a friend, of sorts, and the rest of his family certainly didn't deserve to die.

Ant sat at the table in Tom's saloon staring at the newspaper when Tom stopped by while making a glad-hand round of his customers, clapping shoulders, laughing at nothing, jollying the men up so they'd buy another drink. "You find out anything about Emma Johnson?"

Ant drew a thick line around the death notice with his pencil. "There's trouble."

Tom bent to read the small print. "Don't know'em. Don't know any Chinamen. "Were they killed on Basin Street?" He peered closer for a missed detail. Then remembering Young Jack, he asked, "Any sighting of that Bohomme fellow? We have to be careful handling that one."

"I saw him the other night. He must have gone out of town for the duration of the yellow fever epidemic. He won't be hard to find but this," he pointed to Chen's death, "this ranks with Josie's fire."

Tom gave him a startled look and examined the notice with greater intent. "There's no Chinese working in the houses, at least that I know of. Don't see how that's trouble for me"

Ant explained that Chen owned several opium dens in Storyville. "Somebody's has created an opening to take over Chen's business, and get a toehold in Storyville. They tried once with the Parker brothers."

Tom eased down into a chair at the table, no longer interested in finessing his customers. "You think the Matrangas are behind this?"

"Know so," Ant answered.

"What's happened at Chen's place?"

"Don't know. Haven't been around. Perhaps the Matrangas have moved in their own people. Maybe they'll wait a while until they work out a deal with Chen's suppliers."

"Go around, will you, Ant, and take a look. Good of you to spot this. There'll be a bonus this month for you."

Ant went to Chen's passageway, after carefully checking the vicinity for Mafia-looking types. Funeral money was pinned to the black door, along with dabs of opium, a paper ship, a card printed with the image of traditional Chinese house and a pair of chopsticks. At the foot of door lay a bowl of rice, some raw vegetables and a bottle of rice wine; everything the Chens needed for their journey to the other side.

The door was locked. No answer when Ant knocked. He knocked harder and waited, ear pressed to the wooden door. He pounded on the door and listened. Someone was on the other side.

"It's a friend," Ant said. "I've come to help."

When there was no reply, Ant spoke louder. "I'm a friend of Chen's." And for the first time he felt sorrow and his voice stumbled on a choke. Perhaps that's what persuaded the person on the other side to open the door a cautious crack.

A sliver of a frightened eye stared at him. Ant didn't' recognized Little Flower until she opened the door enough to show her face. Ant pushed in and locked the door behind him. Little Flower unexpectedly clung to him and began sobbing. Ant held her awkwardly for, despite their sexual encounters, he had never felt a personal connection to her until now.

"Oh, Mr. Ant, I so scared."

He never knew she spoke English.

"Come now," Ant patted her back and led her back to Chen's private room. The rest of the place was empty with no lights. Little Flower told him, in halting English, that she had been hiding in the opium den for two days, ever since the killings, without food or water.

"What happened?" Ant asked, solicitously settling her on one of the large floor cushions. Instead of the seductive dress always worn with Ant, she had on wide-legged trousers and a long over top, which made her look like a very young girl, younger than Ant ever suspected.

"Men came and took them away." Little Flower controlled her sobs but still trembled at the memory.

"What men?"

"European men."

Ant held her as one would a quivering bunny to calm her. Laying her head on his shoulder, Little Flower eventually stilled into regular breathing.

"Did they say anything?"

"I saw guns and hide."

"You're safe now. Little Flower, I want you to stay here and keep the door locked. I'll bring you food and water, but you're to let no one in but me. Understand?"

She nodded.

"You'll be my little guard dog. I'll get you some food and water." Ant disengaged himself and started for the front door. "I'll be back soon."

But first he reported to Tom. "The Matrangas had been there and took the Chens away. I have a guard in the place now, but something else has to be done."

"I'm thinking on it," Tom replied.

Chapter 16.

Ant still had the problem of Young Jack. Tom was preoccupied with the greater Matranga threat and Billy was seemingly satisfied to let Ant shoulder the responsibility of finding Young Jack. Ant's network of informants hadn't turned up any news and MayAnn's mother hadn't seen her daughter since the yellow fever scare. So Ant went back to the honey pot MayAnn could never resist. If Buddy didn't have news, then Ant would go to his next gig and wait for her to show up—with Young Jack.

Ant had hoped to find Buddy at his mother's house on First Street so to avoid the public forum of Louis's barbershop.

Buddy's mother cracked open the door.

"Mrs. Bolden." Ant lifted his hat respectfully. "Is Buddy home?"

"He's feeling poorly."

"A hangover?"

"No..."

"Not the yellow fever, is it?"

"No. No, he's been acting funny." The poor woman looked worn out. Bags of worry sagged under her eyes and gray hair frizzled around her face, a halo of fright.

A younger woman appeared over her shoulder. "May I help you?" she asked, taking charge. Mrs. Bolden, relieved, slipped back into the house. Ant introduced himself and said that he was a friend of Buddy's, played in his band.

"I'm Nora." She opened the door to invite him in.

My, my, Buddy, what have you been hiding under your bushel basket, Ant thought, appreciating the young women color of

235

a cinnamon bun with a fresh-out-of-the-oven glow. She was graceful as a greyhound, slim and elegant.

"Mrs. Bolden said Buddy's not well?"

Her hair, more wavy than kinky, pulled back in a bun emphasized her high cheekbones. "He's tired, that's all." Anxiety made her eyes look older than she deserved.

The sight of Nora uplifted Ant. Buddy appeared to have a woman in his house, which meant MayAnn wouldn't be crawling through his midnight window. Buddy might be greedy but he's not a fool. This woman was a winning lottery ticket. You don't tear up such a ticket or treat it carelessly.

"What's wrong with Buddy?"

"He has things on his mind." Her arms hung at her side with the thumbs tucked tightly into her fists. "Business things with everyone after him and all." She looked away, brusquely crossed her arms over her chest, looked down the other way, bit her lip in indecision. "You said you play with Buddy?"

"I have a few times."

"He's been talking about musicians lately. You know Bunkie Johnson?"

Bunkie, the self-style "Prince," imagined he stood next in the line for the crown of King Bolden. And, like many princes, he had shown impatience in claiming the crown, sometimes coming up on the bandstand uninvited to jam with Buddy. In fact, Bunkie's brother-horn bonhomie was a cutting contest in disguise. Others, too, were mastering Buddy's style and challenging him, greenhorn gunslingers looking for a reputation by blowing him away.

"Buddy's fearful they're trying to kill him," Nora said. "Foolish, isn't it?" She paused, chewing her lower lip. "Only... it's like sometimes he jumps from light to dark, back and forth, laughing then angry, loving then lashing out. I don't understand it."

"May I see him?"

She checked if he was asleep, then motioned Ant into the bedroom. Buddy sat on a ladder chair next to the window holding his horn. A dreamy look, the same he had when wandering lost in music, gave him a sweetly happy aura. Ant tiptoed in and was taken aback when Buddy shouted, "Ant, you got sore feet? Come here. You got your horn? Never be without your horn."

Ant didn't sense anything wrong with him. Expansive, a bright spark of humor in his eyes, he rose and put an arm around his second trombone man. "Glad you're here, Ant. Glad you're here. Nora, bring us some sweet tea, will you, darlin'. Sit, Ant, sit." He motioned to the chair by the window.

"How you doin', Buddy?"

"I'm still here."

They chatted over tea about this and that as Ant edged the conversation around to MayAnn, but Buddy hadn't seen her since that night at Magnetta's. "I got a worry," he confided to Ant. "Supposed to play over in downtown Storyville tonight. At Nancy Hank's Saloon just across Canal Street."

Apparently Frank Magnetta had bragged to his friend John Exnicious about how much money he made when Buddy played. Exnicious, owner of Nancy Hank's, chose profit over prudence and invited Buddy to cross Canal Street — in other words, to break the color line.

"That's dangerous, you know," Ant reminded him.

"It's just the other side of Canal," countered Buddy. "If I smell trouble, I'll scoot across the street to safety."

"You'll need insurance."

"Going to see my agent this afternoon. You play with me tonight, Ant. I need another white man besides Dusen in the band to look, you know, integrated."

Buddy quickly dressed in a suit and expensive shoes polished so bright you could see sunshine on a cloudy day. At the door, he tapped a derby onto his head, hugged his mother, kissed Nora and with his customary good cheer set off for the business meeting at the Red Onion with the "agent." On the way, a small gang of kids spotted him and came running. He played some happy skipping music as they danced around him.

Aaron Harris, Steel Eye, Chicken Dick, Rough Nuts and the others sat at their usual table playing cards when Buddy strode up exuding confidence. "Mr. Harris," and removed his hat with a flourish. Harris played out his hand before looking up. "Got a business deal for you," Buddy said.

Harris looked like hell; a five-o'clock shadow, hair a pile, eyes outlined in red, his clothes crumpled like he'd slept in a hayloft for a week. His gang had been on a crime spree; stole a top-of-the-line carriage with its brace of four high-stepping bays; broke into three mansions and carted off the silver, rugs, everything of valuable. Two of the homes they stripped while the owners were away; the other, they had to tie up an old man and his wife. The gentleman needed a bruise or two to calm him down, a big mistake.

The victim was the leader of the Ring, the Democratic machine that controlled city politics; the same Ring Harris occasionally worked for to turn out the vote. Abusing the man was like spitting on the King of Politics. The mayor got a blistering personal order; the mayor sent a red alarm to Chief Hennessy; the chief threatened his captains, who guaranteed the beat cops their families would be well taken care of if the man-of-the-house died in the line of duty. The order of the day: get Aaron Harris's head on a pike.

Harris, tipped off, went underground, actually sleeping in a hayloft until things cooled down.

Buddy spoke low and earnestly into Harris's ear, holding his derby behind his back clear of Harris's filthy shirt. "What?" grunted Harris. "You want what?"

"You be my security manager. You watch my back when the band plays downtown. I'll pay you better than the average mugging."

Harris pushed back in his chair to glare at Buddy's boldness in suggesting he'd stoop so low. A new round of cards dealt out. Harris focused on his hand. "Tonight at Nancy Hank's, you say." Harris lined up his cards, "See you there," and won on a full house.

Later, became clear why Harris agreed to Buddy's proposition: he had to show his face to keep face—deliver a counterpunch before some coppers started to believe they could take him.

Buddy's band, including Ant, got a bit soused before venturing across Canal, the separating line between black and white Storyville. Courage requires fortification, whatever the battlefield. Once it got good and dark, the musicians gathered up their instruments and walked way to the edge of Canal, one hundred and eighty-seven feet wide, designated for a waterway never built. Canal was more than just a street: it represented hopes dashed by the failed Reconstruction; it was the line drawn by fearful and resentful whites that darkies didn't dare crossed, except in the expected humble bow. Canal Street was a bald statement: you don't belong on our side. Stay over in uptown with your own kind or we'll slap you down—again -- and again if you get uppity.

As the trepid band stared across the vast street, a space without shelter that looked wider than the Mississippi, their courage seized up and to the man they hated themselves for involuntary quaking -- despite the fact each band member carried a gun.

Prudence dictated they arm themselves. Colored musicians played in white whorehouses as piano professors but never as professional musicians in white saloons. As a professional wearing a white collar and suit, the black man posed more a threat than a band of drunken field hands. But, despite being armed, Buddy and his band were scared to use their guns. An armed black man was a mutiny. Unless you were prepared to go to war, you kept your weapon to yourself, at least against a white man.

They hung in the shadow of a building taking short nips to get a firm grip on themselves. Ant, as a white man, or one who passed for white, shouldn't have been scared to venture into white territory. But he was with black musicians. If this had been a crap game, he would have taken favorable odds of the band getting killed that night at Nancy Hank's.

Bunched on the curb like boys daring the other to be the first to step into a cold river, the musicians made a sorry attempt at jostling and joking to ease the tension. "It's okay, I told you I've got us covered," Buddy reassured for the hundredth time. "We survive this and we eat off gold plates. Come on, boys, let's give them something they've never heard before."

Ant peered into the darkness for Harris and hogs, the insurance policy. As far as he could tell, the band was alone. Buddy stepped forward, his fingers drumming the valves of the cornet in his hand. The other band members hesitated for a beat before Dusen followed and then the rest moved in a small tight knot, soldiers on a dangerous patrol. All the way across the street Buddy kept repeating, "We're okay. We're okay." Instead of an inspiring leader, he sounded more like a little boy convincing himself there were no monsters under the bed.

Safely on the other side, the band stayed close enough to touch each other as they walked single file, hugging the storefronts in case they had to jump into a doorway for shelter. Buddy brought them to a halt in front of Nancy Hank's. "No turning back in any way," he said. "If we gonna die, let's do it playing the goddamn hell out of the music." He gathered himself up, standing tall. "All right, let's play for all my children."

He busted open the door and let out a blast meant to blow a hole through the crowd inside. The musicians came in like a flood gushing through a levee, bellowing for all they were worth, cheeks bulging, pointing their horns to create a protective perimeter against the wall of white faces three feet away. To Ant's surprise, he spotted Louis, who started a rhythmic clap to march the band through the crowd, his face a lighthouse pounding out beams of 'You're fine. You're safe.' Then Ant picked out other familiar faces from Magnetta's and the Battlefield, Buddy's friends and neighbors, and from Lincoln Park, the whores and Buddy's fans. Although he didn't spot her, Ant knew MayAnn had to be near at hand.

Ant figured playing with Buddy was a straightforward approach to MayAnn. No more being clever with voodoo or being two-faced about his intentions. He'd stand up on stage in front of her and everyone else and lay it out best he could. This is me, flaws and all. I may not hit all the notes just right but I'll reach for them and try to blow true. You hear me, MayAnn? I'll stand here exposed fearful and trembling before judgment and I won't be ashamed. I'll do the best I can at the moment and hope to do better in the next moment.

For Ant, the declaration was like a turtle coming out of its shell; unburdened, but even the weight of light hurt. He had no experience in showing his naked heart; doing so had always been the dumb thing, asking to get his ass shot off. It would like going to Tom, or the Matrangas, and saying, I'm the other fellow's ace up his sleeve. Or going to Young Jack and telling him, I've been trying to put a stake through your heart and I'm going to keep trying because I need MayAnn more than you do. May the better shot win.

No more trickery or subterfuge. Just stand up in a face-to-face duel, take aim and fire. And hope that he and MayAnn would remain standing.

The audience took up Louis's steady one-two, one-two clap as the band marched through the press of smiling faces. With each step, the musicians became more confident, looser, and began to swing the music. By the time they reached the stage, everyone was on holiday, ready to dance and hoot and rip off their collars. "Callin' all my children," shouted Buddy and damn near shattered front windows with the opening notes of "When the Saints Go Marchin' In." The whole crowd rose in a single voice as if cheering their favorite team to victory.

That night Ant crossed over from playing the notes to understanding how to play the feel of music; he understood, for the first time, the ethereal power of music. An hour before, the band members had been shaking with anxiety and fear about crossing Canal to play in the overseers' territory. And now, inspired by the music, black and white, men and some women, made fools of themselves. Everyone danced with everyone; men making silly moves with other men; blacks showing whites smooth glides; women dancing with two, three men in a prancing circle; old and young dropping all judgment; the whole room an embrace of acceptance. Buddy called out, "The coming of the second Reconstruction," and took off into some dazzling concoction that could come only from his personal revelation.

Ant spotted in the teeming mass on the dance floor a twirl of white, no more than the flutter of a moth's wing before it disappeared. But he knew that dancing dervish. He kept shifting around without getting in Dusen's way or catching Buddy's attention as he spied on MayAnn. A flash of her white dress, a glimpse of her brown arm, the tail of her black hair flying like a horse at full gallop made him overjoyed, even when he spotted Young Jack with her. Give the boy credit, he was the biggest fool of all on the dance floor. He couldn't dance a whit with his lame foot but there he was hopping and twirling and jigging, laughing his damn head off.

In the corner by the front door sat Aaron Harris, arms folded across his chest, a hat pulled low over his forehead. Rough Nuts would have come with the other hogs. The night could become more complicated than a crooked card game if Rough Nuts recognized Young Jack as the man who had stabbed him and stole MayAnn away; and if Ant attempted to steal her from Young Jack; and if some jerks tried to punish

Buddy for his audacity; and if the police caught wind that Aaron Harris was out of his uptown safety zone.

Ant edged forward toward to the front of the stage in anticipation of a hullabaloo. Dusen kicked him in the shin, thinking Ant was rising above his station. The sharp pain caused Ant to blow a flat note and Buddy threw him a warning glance. An overly excited man burst through the front door shouting. The people around him became agitated, but they didn't look much different than the people dancing. Harris took his hat off and waved it once over his head, then move to the door.

As Ant was rubbing his shin, the saloon's doors slammed open. A phalanx of coppers charged in led by Police Chief Hennessy. Buddy, thinking they had come to arrest him for breaking the color barrier, let out a squeal of alarm on his horn. At the sight of the cops, the band went into high, high gear as if the sheer force of the music would protect them.

The blue coats fanned out on either side of the doors. Hennessy took up station in the entrance, his brass buttons shiny as freshly minted coins, hat cocked over his eyes, for all the world looking like a commanding general on the verge of claiming victory. People near the front door surged toward nearby windows for a quick dive out.

Harris elbowed his way over to Hennessy and said something in his ear. The two men, head to head, looked like they were comparing notes. Recognizing Harris, some of the cops moved to seize him but Hennessy raised a palm to stop them. With little chin motions, a flip of the hand, Harris pointed out his men, hands under their coats, some openly displaying the butt of shotguns hooked there. Hennessy looked at Harris with hatred that would have caused Satan to beg for forgiveness on a bended knee.

Menace hung heavy over the room, palpable as a Gulf storm poised to slam the city. The bar owner, John Exnicious, eying Harris and Hennessy, stashed liquor bottles out of harm's way. Those near the front door slipped around the top cop and the notorious killer and the ebb become a steady flow as the saloon emptied. Young Jack, sheltering MayAnn with an arm around her shoulder, moved forward with the stream, everyone silent, eyes down as Buddy launched into a dirge-like version of "Auld Lang Syne."

Ant leapt off the stage and set off after MayAnn.

People pooled outside in the street, torn between wanting to see the showdown and the compulsion to seek safety. As Ant scanned both directions for MayAnn's white dress, Harris and Hennessy came out of the saloon. Street murmurings hushed as the crowd, maybe fifty or sixty, flattened themselves against the buildings to be out of the line of fire. Harris strode to the middle of Marais Street and stopped. Hennessy stayed on the banquette with his men huddled behind him. The hogs walked brazenly past them and took positions along the street, flanking Harris.

A half block towards Canal, Ant caught sight of a flutter of white dodging into a doorway.

Harris, with a sloppy mock salute to Hennessy, walked down the middle of the street towards Canal, his men drifting along on either side, guns drawn, wary of a betrayal of whatever agreement reached by Harris and Hennessy. Cocky as a bantam rooster, he flagrantly showed the cops his back, a clean target, a boast he had nothing to fear from them.

Ant saw the flutter of white accompanied by a dark figure scurry towards Canal. He began to run, not wanting lose sight of MayAnn. One of Harris's men broke out of the protective formation and slammed him down, holding his shotgun tight across Ant's throat. "Mr. Harris goes first." Then he jumped up and hurried back to escort Harris's victory parade.

By the time Harris and his men reached Canal, MayAnn and Young Jack were nearly on the other side. Harris stopped and his gang formed up behind him, guns pointed back at Hennessy and the coppers twenty feet behind. MayAnn and

Young Jack disappeared into uptown. To dash across the broad street would invite a certain bullet in the back, so Ant stayed, crossing with Harris and the hogs, fuming, wondering where MayAnn and Young Jack might be headed. Once across Canal, Harris and the hogs lined up facing Hennessy's men on the other side.

The shadows and side streets behind Harris leaked his Battlefield cronies, twenty or thirty, maybe more, to line up with the hogs. Each man carried a weapon: those with pistols and shotguns only to be noisemakers but others with long-barrel rifles, even one or two sniper guns from the Civil War, that could kill at that distance. Many of the police also had rifles, although it was difficult to see exactly how many given the darkness and distance across Canal. The street became eerily silent, as if everyone was waiting for a ceremony to begin. Torn by indecision, Ant had one foot going after MayAnn and the other rooted in place waiting for the show. The hogs, on some unseen signal, raised their guns to their shoulders. A rustle of motion showed the police also taking firing positions. Then the thugs and the coppers fired volley after volley at each other, aiming high, blasting away like a Fourth of July fireworks display.

The next morning, the *Daily-Picayune's* headline would announce a fierce gunfight between the police and Aaron Harris's gang as the brave police, led by Chief Hennessy, made a valiant effort to capture the vicious killer in a daring raid.

At the first shot, Ant dashed in search for MayAnn and Young Jack. He guessed they would turn on Tulane Street, cross Basin and head toward the river into the Garden District, where Young Jack would feel safe among his own kind. As for MayAnn, the Battlefield, a block straight beyond Tulane, was a deadend with no cottage and a white picket fence for her. She'd gladly follow Young Jack into the neighborhood of white respectability.

People, curious about the barrage of gunfire, crowded Tulane. Ant ran into the middle of the street for a more sweeping view hoping to catch sight of MayAnn's white dress. A block away a hack pulled back into traffic and he broke into a full sprint after it. When another hack pulled up to let off passengers, Ant jumped up on the seat with the driver. "Follow that but don't be seen," he ordered, pointing to the red lantern disappearing down the street. The fellow gave a look like Ant had leapt off the pages of a dime novel, but whipped his horse into a trot when Ant handed him a generous bill.

At Basin, they followed the hack upriver on Carondelet Street, then left on Napoleon, across St. Charles to Magazine Street, the main shopping street. Ant could see the foliage of Audubon Park ahead when the hack in front turned into a small lane easily missed. He hopped down and covered the remaining block on foot.

At the lane, Ant peeked around the corner in time to see Young Jack and MayAnn disappear into a house. He slunk forward when their cab clattered away. To his surprise, the house was charming, not big, nothing fancy, no room for a yard but well maintained, the wood front painted forest green with light gray-green trim. Red geraniums in the window boxes made for a happy domestic smile. The black window shutters on either side of the pale yellow door were open. A lamp flickered on. Standing across the narrow lane, Ant glimpsed MayAnn through the window.

The house was a hidden place, a secret hideout. It felt safe. *It could be our love nest, our perfect cottage*, Ant fantasized. *I'll play music and she'll dance in the parlor. I'll go to work and she'll make dinner. Our children will take after me but have her appetite for life, the fierce drive to better herself.*

He pulled himself out of the dream with the admonishment. If you want to be the greater magician, the wizard, who pulls the Grand Rabbit out of the hat of life, well, pull.

Ant pushed out of the shadow with a sigh of dread; nothing he disliked more than direct confrontation. The weight of the revolver tugged his pocket down. The only light in the house came from the front room. They must be there, right inside the door. *Wonder if they were kissing or doing it on the floor? One shot for the double-backed beast?* Ant resisted peeking in the window and pounded on the door with authority he didn't feel.

He sensed the house curl upon itself and play dead when he banged on the door with his revolver, the way police or angry cuckolded husbands announce themselves. Nobody home so he banged all the harder. A man of action would've shot the lock and kicked in the door. But to fire the gun was a commitment to action Ant hadn't fully decided on.

As Ant raised the revolver to thump again, MayAnn opened the door. "Where do you think you are, Antoine, in the Wild West?" She stood with arms tightly folded across her body, trembling with anger. "Why are you banging on my door? Ruining the paint."

For a moment, Ant was dumbfounded. The last thing he expected was a schoolmarm giving that stern one-more-word-and-I'll-whip-you look.

"I…" MayAnn tapped her foot impatiently. "I've come to rescue you," Ant blurted out, reaching for her.

She stepped back, still blocking the door. "Rescue me from what?"

"The police." The words surprised him as much as they did her. "I saw you at Nancy Hank's tonight," Ant hurried on, "and I overheard one of the coppers saying they'd arrest you for killing that girl. So I followed you here to rescue you."

"You betrayed me, Antoine?" MayAnn's voice so steely he could have built a bridge from it. "Only two people know that…"

"No, no," Ant interrupted. "It wasn't me. I just overheard the cops…" trying to backtrack from his mistake.

He heard a shuffle behind the door and reached to snatch her. She leaned away as the door swung all the way open and Young Jack aimed his gun between Ant's eyes.

"And it wasn't me," Young Jack said. "So that leaves you."

With a flick of his head he told Ant to drop his gun, then motioned him in. "Sit and tell us your story, Ant."

Ant glanced around the room: the furniture appeared more heirloom than secondhand and the patterned carpet centered on the oiled wood floor looked expensive. He eased down on the couch, keeping a wary eye on Young Jack's gun. MayAnn took a chair across the room. Ant could feel the heat her smoldering anger, bright as a blaze in a fireplace. On the wall behind her hung a needlepoint, "God Bless Our Happy Home." Young Jack stood at her side, the gun held loosely in his hand.

"I see you've captured her." Ant meant the remark to be ironic but instead it sounded defeated, the verve punched out.

"And now you've sicced the coppers on her? Why did you do that, Ant?" Young Jack asked.

"Because he wants them to capture you. Isn't that right, Antoine," MayAnn butted in. "He's been plotting all along how to make you fall for the girl's murder. He's even got Billy after you."

"Billy," said Young Jack in surprise. "Billy's on my side."

"Is that right, Antoine?" MayAnn accused, daring him to lie. "You've been making *suggestions* to Billy and wanting me to tell him I saw Jack upstairs when the girl was killed." MayAnn's voice hard and cutting, a judge condemning a criminal.

Young Jack gently slapped the barrel of the revolver in his palm.

Ant remembered seeing him the first time at Josie's, his theatrical pose with the dueling pistol, a man of no searing experience to give him starch. He'll fold, Ant assured himself, given a way to save face while appearing heroic.

"Billy and Tom Anderson think you killed the girl at Josie's and the one at Minnie's place. They have witnesses placing you there. They want you gone." Ant paused for the sudden flash of cleverness to form up. "You got the message I spoke with the Matrangas?"

The shift confused MayAnn and she looked to Young Jack for an explanation.

He nodded, the gun barrel resting in his hand.

"Maybe you should go into hiding. Get on that ship to Honduras."

No matter the Matrangas had rejected Bonilla's offer. Ant wanted MayAnn to see that Young Jack could abandon her.

"Here's your chance to shout the wild yes, to follow the footsteps of your hero Byron into battle," Ant's voice on the verged of a taunt.

Fear flitted across MayAnn's eyes as she turned to Young Jack. "What's he talking about, Jack?" She gripped the arms of the chair, ready to push out and confront him.

"I'm already in hiding," Young Jack said. The revolver stayed in his palm, his finger hooked around the trigger. "My father wants to send me away until I 'recover my senses.' He could tolerate my dalliance, given his own indiscretions, but I've vowed to marry MayAnn and give her full rights of a married woman, which include our children bearing the Bohomme name. That's when he threatened to have the Pinkerton men seize me and put me on a ship to Europe."

He was going to *marry* her! Ant silently shouted in surprise. Surely he couldn't be so stupid. He was only a stool for her to stand on to elevate her position in life. "Look now, Jack..." Ant intended to expose the perfidious MayAnn. She'd be left dangling: he'd be the only one willing to cut her down and take her in. "Now, Jack, you see... "

"That she only wants someone to take care of her," Young Jack cut in. "Well, it's nice to be asked. To be wanted."

"Now, Jack, discretion is the better part of valor." Ant's old self came charging out of the shadows and ate up his resolution to be MayAnn's faithful friend. "You can slip away before shots are fired and Billy will shoot you on sight. Europe or Honduras, either way you can create your own Byronic exploits, memorialize yourself in poetry to live through the ages. A much better legacy than bedding a black girl."

"She killed for me!" Young Jack bellowed and came at Ant, his revolver pointing at his chest. "What greater show of love is there? Isn't that what God demanded of Abraham, that he kill to prove his love? I will never NEVER abandon MayAnn. She's my WILD YES. She's my epic to love and honor!"

MayAnn lifted her chin in triumph.

Ant felt a visceral, vigorous detestation for Young Jack. He rose from the couch and said *sotto voce* to MayAnn, "The cops aren't coming. You're safe." At the door, he stooped to retrieve his gun and, as leaving, told Young Jack, "Be careful of Billy -- and of her."

Chapter 17.

The next night Billy waylaid Ant on his way into Tom's saloon. "Come on, we've found Young Jack." He spun Ant back out the door as one of Tom's goons fell in behind them.

"Where?" What?" Ant tried to drag his heels to slow this down. Had Billy followed him last night?

"We know where Young Jack will be in about ten minutes," Billy said, hustling Ant down the street. "We're going to set up an ambush. You're the lookout." He stuck a revolver in Ant's coat pocket. "Just in case."

Giddiness sent Ant to the verge of giggles at the prospect Young Jack would no longer stand in his way. Simultaneously, dread nearly sank him to his knees. MayAnn would never forgive him if Young Jack were killed. She'd know Ant had a hand in it somehow.

"Billy, he is innocent. I have a new lead, a witness who can vouch for him when those girls were killed."

Billy brushed aside Ant's protest. "The guy's a problem and I'm solving the problem."

According to Billy's tip, Young Jack would soon leave a card game run by one of Tom's associates. "We'll make it look like a mugging," Billy said, pushing Ant along at a near trot. "Our man will testify that Young Jack left with a large winning. When the robbers accosted him, he resisted and paid for it."

Three blocks deep into Storyville, where even on a full-moon night you couldn't see for the gloom, Billy slowed to a stop. "Big John and I will wait in that alley," he pointed. "You stay here on the corner. When you see Young Jack coming, wave your handkerchief."

Ant edged around the corner out of sight and fought down the impulse to run. But if he disappeared, Billy would hunt him down. He peeked around the corner. Billy watched from the alley, his gun held in both hands against his chest.

A door opened at the far end of the block and a figure emerged from the slab of light. Ant shrank against the building, praying the man would go the other direction or return for one more hand or a friend would come out and accompany him. The clump of a crippled foot told Ant that Young Jack was headed his way. In the unlit street, the intended victim was barely seen, a bulk of black in the dark. Billy shifted in expectation at the footsteps. When Young Jack was about thirty feet from the alley, Ant reached into his pocket for the revolver and the handkerchief.

He didn't actually make the decision to fire the bullet. As he started to wave the handkerchief, the revolver went off. The man stopped dead and then scrabbled away at a surprisingly fast run in the opposite direction. Billy stepped out and fired.

The dark form hunched low. Ant lost sight of him. Billy stood in the street, gun poised, waiting to take a second shot, then fired again. Ant spotted a blur of black duck around the corner at the far end of the block.

Billy came at Ant, gun swinging at his side, fury in his run, fists pumping. "What the hell! Why'd you warn him?" He grabbed the revolver from Ant's hand; Ant genuinely feared Billy would shoot him on the spot.

"It went off accidentally," Ant stammered. "The motion of signaling must have caused my finger to tighten on the trigger."

"Goddamnit to hell!" Billy made as if to hit him over the head with his gun. "Now he'll be as skittish as a rabbit." He jabbed a finger in Ant's chest. "You'll answer to Tom for this."

252

A flicker of contempt flashed in Billy's eyes. Ant knew he could never trust Billy again.

Billy stalked off. Ant started after him wanting to explain about his changed heart, how he was a new man, a man serving love rather trying to steal it. Instead, he decided to get the hell out of there before Billy changed his mind and did shoot him. But, a wave of euphoria washed the fear out of Ant. Next time he saw MayAnn, he'd tell her how he'd saved Young Jack's life. Ask him, he'd say, about the warning shot when he left the card game. There's the proof I'm looking out for your happiness.

But right then Ant needed to disappear for a few hours, get out of sight and hopefully out of Billy's mind. Some place with people who knew him, who'd be a protective circle around him. He scurried across Canal and into the Battlefield, heading for a joint where white men didn't go.

At one corner, Ant spotted a poster advertising the next music night at Mangetta's. But instead of reading "live jass at Mangetta's" the spelling of 'jass' had been changed to 'jazz' to deny the wits while keeping the sound of the word.

Ant headed down a narrow unlit passageway between a sagging wooden fence and an equally dilapidated building, more or less feeling his way to the door of the after- hours joint. No sign marked the entrance; a person had to have the interest to find it. The large room was so dim and smoky the unaccustomed would damn near believe he'd stumbled into a farmer's smoke house and all those dark forms hanging about were hams and slabs.

Ant recognized one of the figures and threaded his way to the table. "Big Eye, you through for the night?"

The musician looked up at the greeting. "Ant!" with genuine pleasure. "Sit yourself. You got your horn?" Big Eye's clarinet lay in the middle of the table, and Ant remembered leaving his trombone on the Nancy Hank's stage.

Ant explained about the gig and Hennessy and Harris and the fake gunfight, but left out MayAnn and Young Jack.

"Mighty brave of you all to play across Canal in a public place," Big Eye said. "But when there's a crack in the dam, you might get a flood."

They drank in silence, no hurry. Finally Ant asked, "Big Eye, you hear anything about Buddy not being well?"

"How's that? I haven't seen him since the funeral parade."

"Acting funny, thoughts wandering."

Big Eye stared off to the empty stage as if sorting through scraps of paper in his mind. "No, can't say that I have. Heard he messed up some gigs. Not showing up or wrong place wrong time. Happens to all of us if we live long enough and drink to forget."

He looked up and waved at someone at the bar. "Windin'Boy!"

Ferdy Morton waved back and started for the table. This wasn't the same green boy Ant had meet at Eulalia Echo's. This one was dressed like a St. Louis hustler enjoying his high roll with a cocky walk and a smile meant to con the world. The brim of his white fedora with a scarlet band dipped over his eyes. The suit must have been tailored to fit so well and get that flare on the back. His shirt shone like a snowfield under a frosty moon and the tie had the glimmer of silk. In the glimmer was a star, a diamond stickpin bigger than anything he had been trying on at his godmother's.

"Windin' Boy, haven't seen you around for a few weeks," Big Eye said as Ferdy settled at the table. He gave no sign of recognizing Ant.

"Been traveling on the Gulf. Little vacation. I got me a new name now."

"What's that?"

Ferdy ducked his head and paused to set up a good punch line. "Jelly Roll!" He glanced up without raising his chin, a sly grin sharing the joke.

"JELLY ROLL!" Big Eye slapped the table in gleeful disbelief. "Why don't you just get a big penis hat and wear it on your head? You know, one of those old-fashion stovepipes?" He pantomimed a two-foot top hat, then made it three feet. "How'd you come on that?"

In the slang of the day, a "jelly roll" implied 'lover' or 'spouse' or a 'vagina'. A ladies' man like Morton would boast about being a good jelly-roll baker. A jelly roll could also be an outsized penis.

As Ferdy told it, he had judiciously taken a vacation after upsetting a few too many sharks in the pool halls. "Those boys just don't have a sense of fun," he said. "Threatened to break my hands. I decided to visit the Gulf Coast. Sit on the beach, stare into space, work some tonks and felt tables around Biloxi, Gulfport and other little towns until things cooled off."

Ferdy had a reputation around New Orleans as an ace pool player, equally adept right or left-handed. He'd play someone proud of his game, lose a few, propose a bet, lose, jack up the stakes and then clean house. He'd offer to play left-handed to give the sucker a chance to win back his money, and clean house again.

"Slow goin' in slow places. I couldn't afford to get my shirts and suits cleaned. One night I got drinking with this fellow, Sandy Burns. He was out of work, too. He did blackface vaudeville but his partner had quit, so he needed a straight man. I've always been a funny guy, right, Big Eye?"

"Yeah, funny as a sick baby," said Big Eye but Ferdy took no offense.

"Burns proposed we team up. I didn't tell him I was a piano player, since he needed someone to bounce jokes off. So we're up on stage in this dive theater in some backwater town and I'm winging it, mugging like a field hand fool, when Burns says, 'You don't know who you talking to?' I thought it was the set-up for a joke but I didn't know who I was talking to. I'd just met the guy a week before. I sensed there was something behind his patter, like he was telling me something he couldn't say to me face-to-face when we were off stage and he was trying to cover it now as part of the routine. I said, 'Well, who are you?' And he said, 'Sweet Papa Cream Puff.'"

Ferdy paused to take a sip of his drink, letting that sink in. Tony Jackson was a cream puff, a faggot. "Burns got a big laugh with that. You know why. So I thought I'd better come back with something about a bakery shop, too. I said to him, 'You don't know who *you* talking to. Do you to want to get acquainted?' Now the audience hung on the edge of their seats waiting for the big slam. I had 'em, and I had Burns all turned around. 'Who are you?' He had to say it but he knew he was walking into a put-down trap. I says, 'I'm Sweet Papa Jelly Roll with stovepipes in my hips and all the women in town just dying to turn my damper down.' The audience went on the floor. I called out for women's names and addresses and Burns goes beet red. I turned him down and branded him, like hitting two birds with one stone."

Ferdy sat back with a big open laugh. Big Eye, guffawing with him, banged the table so hard their whiskey jiggled and splashed.

Big Eye caught Ant's eye and motioned to Tony Jackson ordering a drink at the bar.

"You going to be playing in the houses again, Jelly Roll?" Big Eye testing the name on his tongue.

"Don't know. Be a way to pick up some quick cash and reacquaint myself with a few friends." Ferdy winked. He'd always had a "girlfriend" in each whorehouse where he played. "But I've got another game on the front burner right now."

"Not back to sharkin'?"

"No, I manage a fine pool player, the best. Will be world champion one day. We give people an honest chance to test themselves against him. Since I know players here who think highly of themselves, we came up to give them some self-evaluation, somebody to measure themselves against."

Big Eye slid a quick glance to Tony knocking back a whiskey. "Why don't you play us a few tunes, Jelly Roll? Rest of us guys have been working all night and have tired fingers. I'd like to hear you again, hear anything new you've discovered."

Big Eye walked to the piano on the small stage and held up his hands for silence. "A favorite son has come home," he shouted. "All of you with an educated ear, and that's all of *you*, know this man's sound. Nobody's faster on the ivories, as inventive with the rhythms, as clever with the words. Bring him on up with a big hand. Put them together for JELLY ROLL MORTON!"

An uncertain silence filled the room. Jelly Roll? But a smattering of applause broke out as Ferdy made his way to the stage. He slid onto the piano stool with a wave of acknowledgment and adjusted his suit coat. His left hand started pounding a march while the right hand flew off on its own into a rag. Then he stopped abruptly.

"You should fix up this thing. You want a piano to cry a bit. You want it to play the pain because if it knows the pain, then it can give the joy, too. Those come together, like good and evil. Like you and your reflection. You can't know one without the other."

Old pros shifted in their chairs venting a whiff of resentment stirred by this pompous ass giving them a lecture.

"Get me paper, old newspaper will do." He ran off a fast riff. "And some strips of burlap. That'll give some muffled crying, some moans, some gutter talk. Then you'll have a rum shop piano, the only kind to grind out "Barrelhouse Women"."

After fixing the piano to his liking, he played some flash, a bit of stomp on the rag, showing off his "Spanish tinge" rhythm, a syncopated beat. He didn't see Tony Jackson move away from the bar.

"Uh-oh, here it comes," Big Eye said.

Jackson he set his glass of whiskey on top of the upright.

"Get up from that piano," someone called out. "You're hurting its feelings. Let Tony play."

"You don't need no burlap or tricks, Ferdy," Jackson said. "You just need to do it right, the New Orleans way."

Ferdy stood up, a big grin hiding his embarrassment. "Mr. Jackson, my pleasure," and stepped aside. He came back to Big Eye's table only to mutter, "I'll get you back, you motherfucker."

Big Eye nearly fell off his chair laughing.

Tony Jackson played a few songs and then retreated to the bar to drink in solitude. Musicians came onstage, experimenting with new ways to put together old music. Big Eye took a turn with a piano player, testing snatches of phrases, working new verbs into old phases. Whenever a bit showed promise, the other musicians shouted out, "Be brave!" and "Roll it out!" and "Feel it. Feel it!" Bunkie Johnson took a turn and Ant could hear why Buddy worried about him. He was no imitating rooster; he had a feel for taking the music apart and building it back new. That night, the musicians lit a fire that burned up old notions. Ant heard the future, though it wouldn't come for another twelve years or so.

The next day, an urchin, a scrap of a boy, brought Ant a note from MayAnn. 'URGENT! Meet me at Lincoln Park. Noon.'

A meeting in broad daylight in a public place didn't promise a tête-à-tête. Still, she wanted to be alone with him, urgently. Hope springs eternal, and without reason. Ant let himself believe she had finally seen the light. Young Jack was a violent man, a possessive jealous man, a rapist who had once kept her prisoner. No doubt she wanted Ant to help plan her escape and what better place to avoid suspicion of betrayal than a public park in the middle of the day.

Tremors of excitement made him jumpy. Early by a good half hour, he paced the circuit between the dance hall and the open-air pavilion where Buddy had performed. The crowd, mostly mothers and young children, would give perfect cover. The pig-chasing corral was empty and the hot air balloon concession closed, but the toy train ran, as did the merry-go-round and other kiddie rides. Every two or three minutes Ant looked to the entrance, jittery with joy. He hummed to calm his nerves.

Memories of making love with MayAnn, the coltish bucking of her body and his pride of ownership, gave Ant the sweats and a hard-on, which he tried to hide by ramming his hands into his pockets and puffing the pants out. Wouldn't want the mothers, or the kids, to take offense. He'd tell her about saving Young Jack's life, which would make his victory all the sweeter. See, no ulterior motive, he'd proclaim. I only want the best for you with no strings attached. The implication being, which she would recognize, that he was the better man for it.

She came through the park's gate at a near run, the exertion putting a beguiling flush on her cheeks. Don't overwhelm her, Ant told himself. Be contained, pose as a caring friend, and don't gloat.

"I have disturbing news," she said without an embrace or a peck on the cheek or a warm smile. "I visited Buddy last night. He was in a dreadful state." She clutched Ant's arm, which wasn't the hug of affection he'd hoped for. "He stood in the parlor, eyes frantic, shaking and yelling that there was two of him, sometimes three. How do you do, he'd say, sticking out a hand, not to me but to shake hands with one of his phantoms. He started boxing, slugging away with an invisible heavyweight champion. We—me, Nora and Buddy's mother—ran behind the sofa and he tried to climb over it to get us. I shouted at him to stop and for a moment he appeared to have taken a punch on the chin. Dazed. Nora said that he'd been like that for hours, ranting and dazed. Sometimes he'd go into a calm spell and they'd try to sooth him, but he'd rear

259

up again and start flailing. It's been sunshine one day and thunderstorm the next, she said."

As MayAnn told it, Buddy raved there was another him watching the other two hims. And he didn't know any of those other guys.

"He'd shout he was a funhouse mirror, all wavy and distorted. I see myself but don't know that person, he yelled. So confusing, so confusing, he kept repeating, and he didn't want to be any of those guys. I just want to sit still and not exist, he told us, and went into his room and barred the door. I'm so worried about him, Antoine. What do you think he was talking about?"

"Was he drunk?"

"No. But he looked like it, staggering about, shouting gibberish nobody could understand. Said that he's talking to the voices in his head. Go over there with me, will you? Maybe we can help him."

"Now?"

"Not a moment to lose."

"But..." Ant began to protest, "I have important things to tell you, revelations of the highest order that will change our lives."

She had already set off for Buddy's house. As Ant skipped and half ran to keep up, she told him her theory why Buddy acted so strange. "Dusen fired him from his own band. I think the shame damaged his mind."

A couple of nights before, MayAnn and Young Jack had gone to Kid Brown's to hear Buddy play. Two, three hours went by and no Buddy. Dusen and the band entertained the best they could but people had paid money to hear Buddy. The crowd became restless, then agitated and, at each passing hour, more and more angry, shouting insults and throwing coins at the band with the intent to hurt. When Buddy finally did push through the front door, calling out "All my children," arms outstretched to embrace the whole room, the people were sullen: they didn't make kissing sounds back to him.

"Where you been," shouted out one man.

"Why, on my way," answered Buddy, reeking of alcohol. "Now I'm here. Right on time."

He made his way through the hostile mass of bodies, horn hanging from hand, looking for a way to get on stage. Dusen stood at the front of the stage damn near quivering with rage. The insults, the empty bottles hurled at the band, the apple that had hit Dusen, had pushed him beyond caution and into a fury.

"He let Buddy have the full load of resentment and anger," MayAnn told Ant, getting short of breath as she walked faster the closer to Buddy's house. "He was cursing and swearing, saying things even that dance hall crowd was embarrassed to hear. Ranted about Buddy letting the band down, missing jobs, wrong times, wrong places, people wanting their money back, about how Buddy's gotten sloppy, how he can't even make up the music anymore, it coming out all chopped up and garbled and wandering."

She stopped in the middle of the sidewalk, suddenly tired. "It was awful, Antoine." Head bowed, arms straight at her side, she looked as if she had suffered a personal defeat. "I felt so bad for Buddy. Dusen up there on the stage taunting him there are better players than him. People go hear Keppard and Oliver, half a dozen other horn men who show up. Musicians who are actually on the bandstand behaving like musicians who know what the hell they're doing."

Ant made to put a comforting arm around her but she pushed past with renewed determination.

"He wanted to get on the stage but no one offered him a hand. 'The King is here,' he called out, but it sounded like question. Dusen squatted down to talk to him face-to-face and told Buddy if he showed up and played like the old Buddy, they were his band. That's how they made their living, he said, being better than all those other bands, having Buddy up front, sober, dressed like he's proud. But right now, the band didn't need him anymore."

A couple of blocks from Buddy's house, she broke into a trot. In-between pants, she said, "I was there, right beside Buddy. He stood slack jawed like a dumb cow shot between the eyes. He didn't say anything. Perhaps he didn't hear. I waited for him to get angry and go stormin' on stage to take back what was his. But Buddy looked at Dusen as if not understanding he had been fired. How could a man do that? Take another man's band away from him?"

Two doors from Buddy's house MayAnn slowed to finish her story. When Dusen's words sunk in, Buddy got the look of a shamed dog, tail down, head down, eyes begging for mercy and another chance at acceptance. He turned around; his shoulders slumped and he started to shuffle away. "I plucked his sleeve and told him that I'd dance for him if he'd please play for me. But he just smiled and patted my hand and said, 'You're a brave girl, MayAnn'. The crowd parted for him, no one asking him to stay, not a word of encouragement."

She stopped in front of Buddy's house and asked, a pleading for reassurance in her voice, "Is he just having bad headaches, Antoine? Last night, he said his head didn't hurt so much as it forgot. Just went blank. Like he was walking around in a pitch-black room that was himself. He was afraid of falling into that blackness and disappearing. You think Eulalia Echo might be able to help him?"

"We should talk to her. Maybe somebody had a spell cast on him. I wouldn't put it past Bunkie Johnson or Freddie Keppard. They're looking to claim his crown as king."

Mrs. Bolden answered MayAnn's knock. Ignoring his nod of greeting, she stepped aside to let them in. She looked like a stick of ash, gray, all vitality burned out of her, held together only by the wan hope her son would recover. Nora came out of the back bedroom calm but somber.

"How is he?" MayAnn asked.

She didn't answer except for a flutter of hands. MayAnn clasped her with the strong love men have never mastered. Males mistake bravado for strength. In the simple holding of hands, MayAnn and Nora assured each other they wouldn't let the house fall down; if necessary, they'd hold up the sky itself to protect their loved one.

"I can't really say," Nora replied. "Go in and see for yourself."

In the dim room Buddy sat in a straight-back chair with his cornet standing on its bell at his feet. He smiled at MayAnn and beckoned her to him. "Ant," he said in welcoming. "You got your horn?"

Ant shook his head, relieved to see that Buddy wasn't raving and foaming.

"I'll dance for you, Buddy, if you'll play for me," MayAnn said in her coy teasing way.

Buddy motioned to his cornet. "I'm afraid to pick up it. It'll be too heavy."

"Aw, Buddy, you've floated that horn to your lips without any effort plenty of times. It's just a little ol' thing." MayAnn stood next to him, bending at the waist with her lips nearly touching his cheek. The smile in her voice put some brightness in the room but Ant couldn't shake the feeling that he was in a hospital, or a jail.

"Come on, pick up the horn and play," she sounded like a lover inviting Buddy to bed.

"I'm afraid that if I so much as twitch an eye, my head'll explode."

MayAnn wrapped her arms around Buddy's shoulders to wipe the tears out of his voice. "Aw, Buddy…"

In a burst of fury he twisted away, knocking over the chair. MayAnn reeled back, dumbstruck.

"You're stealing my music," he shouted, his eyes darting around the room to find the thieves.

MayAnn reached to him but he flung himself on the bed, wrapped himself in a blanket, and lay there, still as a corpse. Ant couldn't even see the blanket rising from his breathing.

Before Ant could react, Mrs. Bolden came into the room with a bowl of hot soup on a tray. She set the tray on the bedside table and spooned out soup to blow it cool.

"Charlie," she said, holding the spoon to her son who appeared comatose under the blanket. "Come on, honey, have some soup."

As she leaned closer, Buddy reared upright and fought free of his cocoon. "No!" He scrambled out on the opposite side of the bed. "Stay away! You're trying to poison me," nearly knocking the porcelain water pitcher off the nightstand.

"Charlie." She took a step to embrace her son, a loving gesture of a mother willing to walk through the gates of Hell and eat the Devil raw to save her baby boy. Tears flowed down her cheeks. She held out the spoon of soup as if offering her milk-laden breast. "Charlie, it's your favorite soup." Her sweet coaxing smile told her little boy everything would be all right; she'd take away the pain.

She took tiny steps around the bed, the soft swoosh swoosh of her cloth slippers on the wooden floor, cooing to Buddy, the spoon in one hand, the other hand beneath to catch any drops. Buddy shuffled one way, then the other, his arms swinging as if he might break out in a buck and wing routine. His eyes, big as eggs, rolled from side-to-side. "No, Ma, no!" A mercy plea to avoid a whipping.

Mrs. Bolden blocked his escape route so he retreated back to a corner at the head of the bed. "Charlie, lovely Charlie, let mother help you," in a tender lilt.

Buddy stood with his back against the wall, hands pressed flat to the wallpaper, and stared over his advancing mother's head with the intensity of a man willing himself not to break under the exorbitant pain of torture. Mrs. Bolden offered up her spoon of soup with a smile of happiness. Mother knows best. Buddy grabbed the porcelain water pitcher and swung, the glancing blow knocking his mother sideways.

MayAnn's scream brought Nora rushing into the room. Ant leapt to Mrs. Bolden. Nora bounded across the bed and shoved Buddy onto the tangle of sheets and blanket. He didn't resist, didn't try to get up but lay on his back, feet on the floor, staring at the ceiling. Only when Nora shifted his feet up on the bed and covered him did Ant notice the tears streaming down Buddy's cheeks.

Dazed but conscious, Mrs. Bolden struggled to sit up. Blood seeped from the bump and cut.

"I'll get a doctor."

"I'm fine. Get Charlie some help."

Buddy appeared to be dead, rigid as a corpse again, hands folded on his chest and eyes wide open. When MayAnn brought the doctor back, Buddy made no response to his questions. His heart rate was normal. He wasn't running a fever. The doctor shone a light in his eyes. Dull as a market fish. Buddy didn't blink.

"Has he been violent before?" the doctor asked.

Nora shook her head.

"Is he a mean drunk?"

"He's not drunk," she said. "Something's wrong in his head."

"Maybe," replied the doctor. "But this may be the effects of alcoholism. Could be dementia."

Taking no chances, he summoned the police. "He could become violent again," he told the sergeant. "He struck his mother."

They all followed when the police took a docile Buddy to the Twelfth Precinct station. "What's the charge?" asked the desk sergeant. The arresting officer shrugged. Buddy stood there, smiling a bit, dreamy.

"Keep him in a cell for a couple of hours. If nothing happens, send him home." The desk sergeant wrote Buddy's name in the ledger but no charge.

When the police released him, Ant and MayAnn escorted Buddy home, which was like walking a dead horse, a crazily leaning weight that had to be prodded and shoved and hauled along. With Nora's help, they gently settled him in his bedroom, the drawn shades making the room a box of musty shadows. Buddy refused the bed and sat in the straight-back chair. Mrs. Bolden, her head wrapped in a white bandage garish as a fresh scar, hung back in the doorway wringing her hands. Then, inexplicably, Buddy said, "Ant, bring me my horn." His eyes were clear and his face cheerful. He seemed normal as day. "What you looking at?" he asked Nora, a tease in his voice. "I always come home to you."

For the next two days he played almost without pause. Beautiful music, not romping but sweet blues, call-and-response between himself and himself. Neighbors paused outside his bedroom window to listen and forgot their errands and their lunchtime, stopped doing the laundry to come listen quiet and respectful.

Nora, his mother, MayAnn and Ant took Buddy's playing as a sign of recovery. Word went out Buddy was back on his horn. When musician friends stopped by, he acknowledged them not with words but a musical phrase, part of a tune they had played together.

"He's comin' back," they reassured each other.

Ant was sitting with MayAnn, Nora and Mrs. Bolden on the Thursday morning when the playing stopped. They waited expectantly for the next note. Or for Buddy to come out of the room smiling, a joke in his eyes, as if he'd been playing them, too. Silence filled the house, as if a hole had been dug in the air.

From behind Buddy's closed door came the sounds of a chair splintering. Mrs. Bolden's hand flew to her mouth in alarm. Nora half rose off the sofa. A violent banging came from the room, like Buddy was beating the walls with his horn. Ant started for the room when Buddy lurched out and charged past him, arms flailing as if swatting bees from his head, and ran out of the house. On the sidewalk, he veered toward young girls in the crowd that had gathered to listen. They scrambled away when he tried to grab them. Ant ran to catch him but Buddy turned with a smile and held up his hand. Without a word he shambled, peaceful as a lamb, down the sidewalk, occasionally raising his head as if playing his cornet, the Pied Piper he used to be for the neighborhood kids. Nora, MayAnn and Ant followed and the older kids trailed behind, watchful.

At the neighborhood bar, Buddy had two quick shots and started shouting, not at anyone in particular, just issuing threats in general. Belligerent, laughing as men backed away from him, shouting for more whiskey or he'd smash every bottle over the bartender's head.

The police came and carted him away. The police captain, recognizing Buddy from before, had him taken to Charity Hospital to be examined.

The doctor asked the five questions to determine if the Negro had a weak mind.

"Do you like fried chicken?"

"Yes, fried chicken. My mother makes tasty chicken. You want to come home with me, doc? And she'll fry us up a mess of chicken."

"Do you like watermelon?"

"No, I like mandarins. A girl can't put a watermelon in her headscarf, now can she? You'd never get her to dance with you by offering a watermelon and a slice of watermelon would be an insult. Show you up as being too poor to afford the whole melon."

The doctor wrote down Buddy's response without reaction.

"Do you like gin and whiskey?"

Buddy grinned. "Yes, yes, love to drink with my friends. Drink and play the horn, have a pretty girl to pat my sweaty forehead. Yes, that's a good night's pay."

"Are you scared of ghosts and spirits?"

Buddy said nothing, his face blank. The doctor was about to repeat the question when Buddy answered, "No, sir. The spirits and ghosts are my friends. Except when we fight."

"When you die, will you see St. Peter at the Pearly Gates and Gabriel blowing his horn?"

Buddy burst out laughing. He laughed so hard he couldn't breath, couldn't get a word out. The doctor, thinking Buddy had gone into hysterics, called in attendants when Buddy, struggling for control, sat up straight and said, "It won't be Gabriel. It'll be Freddie Keppard." He started giggling. "And on the other side of the Pearly Gates will be Joe Oliver." Hilarity pushed Buddy off his chair. "And those two motherfuckers trying to blow each other to hell." Buddy was on the floor with the sheer joy of those two playing his jazz in Heaven.

If a patient answered "no" to any of the five questions, he was suspected of being insane. The doctor ordered Buddy kept under observation for a week.

All of Buddy's friends dropped by—Ant, MayAnn, Louis, Dusen, other musicians who played with Buddy—for vigils by his bedside, talking about old times. When Nora wasn't in the room, they reminisced about old girlfriends and the wild parties in the whorehouses. Do you remember, Buddy? they asked hopefully. Buddy looked at the ceiling and said nothing. Dusen sang softly in Buddy's ear, "I thought I heard Mr. Bolden say, Funky Butt! Funky Butt" but he couldn't call out a smile. He made trumpet sounds but Buddy might as well have been a wooden Indian.

After a week, and not another word from Buddy, the doctor signed a document declaring him insane and a danger to others, a condition, the doctor opined, caused by an addiction to alcohol.

Orderlies dressed Buddy; completely listless, unable or unwilling even to put his arms in the sleeves of the shirt, he moved in a daze, half alive, half dead, apparently not caring which half he lived in. He seemed to know what was going on around him, but not the meaning. The women weren't allowed in but Ant hovered, made sure they treated Buddy tenderly and with respect. They fitted his feet into his shoes and carefully lifted him from the side of the bed. Eyes glazed over, he was led to a van and taken to the Louisiana State Insane Asylum in Jackson.

Chapter 18.

Ant had hoped the experience with Buddy, the shared grieving for a lost friend, would strengthen and deepen the bond between MayAnn and himself. Who was at her side, holding her hand, being strong and supportive? Sure as hell wasn't Young Jack. He hadn't shown his face the whole time.

Looking back on the catastrophe that followed, Ant couldn't help but wonder if God and Satan are not the same Almighty Omnipotent Evil. He'd been raised to believe God is good and merciful, despite the overwhelming presence of injustice, grief, brutality, sorrow, hatred, greed, violence, nasty meanness, conniving backstabbing, plain wrongness and the depravity of those made in His image. The explanation for such self-evident contradictions: God acts in mysterious ways. No one ever says Satan acts in mysterious ways. He's a straightforward guy. No deception there—he tears your heart out without asking that you suspend judgment or believe in his mystery. There are no contradictions in Satan; he's just plain bad through and through. You know what you're up against. He gives you a clear choice—you're for me or against me. But with God, the whole thing is ambiguous. He lets something evil happen to you and you're supposed to turn the other cheek, to say, 'I love You no matter.' You're to joyously embrace someone who clearly dislikes you.

If God didn't personally hate me, why did He cause the devastation I experienced, Ant later asked himself repeatedly but he never found an answer.

A blackest day on Ant's calendar was the Monday Tom summoned Billy and him to the office. Tom sat behind his desk puffing up a blue cloud, the open box of cigars an invitation to join him. The three men smoked in clubby companionship for a few minutes before Tom announced, "I'm running for alderman from the Fourth Ward, Storyville. The mayor, and his pals who run the city, won't dare let Hennessy or the Mafia mess with an elected representative of the people." Leaning far back in his high-backed chair, Tom, enormously pleased with himself, added, "We'll be killing two birds with one stone."

At the time, neither Ant nor Billy knew he meant that in a literal sense.

"Ant, I have two assignments for you. Go fetch Aaron Harris. He's been helpful to the Ring in bringing out voters," Tom paused, "dead or alive." He gave a knowing smile and Billy grinned at the quip. "I want to discuss my upcoming campaign, the future of Storyville, so to speak. And Ant, nobody is to know about the meeting, understand? The second assignment—burn down Emma Johnson's French Studio."

Tom's order may as well been an immense thunderclap, the kind that causes a person to involuntarily duck as if a cannon ball was coming directly to rip off their head, and after the boom there's a reverberating silence that shakes the air.

"You mean on Basin Street?" Ant stammered in disbelief. "But the fire might spread and burn down the whole Golden Row."

"I don't want a conflagration. Just a campfire, not a bonfire. A flame bright enough to deliver a message and put her out of business."

"But the Matrangas—the Matrangas will…"

Tom held up his hand. "The Matrangas, as businessmen, will assess this as a balancing of the bottom line. A tit for tat. Josie had a mysterious fire. Emma has a mysterious fire. Now we're even."

Ant wasn't so sanguine. Charles and Tony didn't play by reasonable rules. If they had invested in Emma, then protecting that investment as well as their pride meant a showy retaliation. "But we don't know for sure they're connected to Josie's fire."

"I know even if I don't know," Tom replied, a bit testy.

That night Ant surreptitiously made his way to the Matrangas' office on the docks.

"Ant, you been climbing any elephant's leg lately?" Tony laughed.

He told about Tom the elephant and how Tom planned to step on them.

"Who's Emma Johnson?" Charles asked.

He took Charles' deadpan as being disingenuous. "Your piece of Tom's pie. The slice I told you to take."

"She's a bitch. Has a worse mouth than that Countess Willie," Tony responded. "We'd teach them both a lesson if we weren't such gentlemen."

"You're not behind Emma moving onto Basin Street?"

Charles and Tony gave Ant a dead-mackerel look without answering.

"You tell Mr. Anderson that tomorrow he should walk down the street to this Emma's place of business," Charles instructed, "and then act prudently."

When Ant delivered the message, Tom look perplexed. "What does he mean?"

Ant shrugged. "Who knows?"

"I won't give them the satisfaction. You go look."

In the morning, Ant strolled down Basin. Posted on the sidewalk in front of Emma's were two burly men, each holding an Italian flag on a long staff, like honor guards. Four policemen pointedly lingered on the street corner. Had Hennessy and the Matrangas reached an agreement—Tom was their common enemy?

Ant recognized one of Matrangas' thugs. "What's going on? This Italian national day?" hoping a lighthearted opening would crack the sternness on the henchman's face.

"So to speak. We're showing the flag."

"Will there be a band?"

"There might be fireworks if proper respect isn't shown to our dear friend Emma Johnson. You tell Mr. Anderson that."

Ant returned to Tom in his office and repeated the message. Tom slammed his hands flat on his desk as if killing flies, jumped to his feet, promptly sat down, doubled over in rage, his face turned red and, looking up under his bushy eyebrows, his eyes flared in a declaration of war.

"They dare to plant their flag on my Golden Row! They dare such … such brazen impertinence!"

Impertinence had the ring of a politician's word.

"And Hennessy blatantly allying himself with the criminal element! How can we trust a chief of police who sends our city policemen, the force we pay to protect us from those very criminals, to stand shoulder-to-shoulder with the Mafia?"

Sounded as if Tom was practicing a campaign speech.

"They might look like different problems," he went on, "but they are part of the same solution."

"I take it your plans for Emma are called off," Ant said.

Tom answered with a question. "You set the meeting with Aaron Harris?"

Ant gave him the time and place with an assurance the two wouldn't be disturbed or seen.

Ant didn't know firsthand what was said between Tom and Harris but, based on what happened two nights after the meeting, he made an educated guess.

On that night, according to the trial testimony of Captain William O'Conner of the Boylan Protective Police agency and the chief's close friend, the two men shared a beer at day's end before walking towards their homes; they lived a couple of blocks from each other.

"River fog filled the streets so you could hardly see more than ten feet," O'Connor testified from the witness stand. "At Rampart and Girod, where we usually went our separate ways, I asked Chief Hennessy if he wanted an escort home seeing that he'd gotten a slew of death threats ever since he cracked down on the Storyville saloons. But he joked that a mugger couldn't find a victim in the fog and waved good night. As we parted, I heard someone across the street whistling, but I didn't put any significance to it at the time."

Reporters later had him hum a few bars and identified the song as "La Marcia Reale," the anthem of the Kingdom of Italy.

"After I'd walked a block, I heard the boom of a shotgun followed by three revolver shots. I ran back where I'd parted from Chief Hennessy. The smell of gunpowder hung in the air but I didn't see anyone. Then I heard some moans and Davey calling for help. I found him lying at the mouth of an alley. 'They've given it to me, Bill, but I gave them the best I could,' he said, clutching his side. I pulled aside his hand covering a gaping wound. He was bleeding something terrible, going into shock. I made a pillow of my jacket and put it under his head and told him that he'd be fine. He spit blood trying to say something. I put my ear down close and he said, 'Dagoes. The shooter said *'arrivederci.'* Those were his dying words."

The police, when investing the crime scene, found a Luparas, a double-barreled sawed-off shotgun with a retractable stock that folded like a jackknife for carrying on a hook concealed under a coat. The Mafia favored the Luparas. Aaron Harris's men had armed themselves with such a gun in their facedown with Hennessy.

The morning after the murder, Tom called Billy into his office. "What'd'ya think of that?" He tossed the newspaper across his desk. "The coppers say a Mafia gun killed Hennessy."

"There'll be hell to pay. By someone," Billy replied.

Hell roared a day later when Mayor Shakespeare, standing on City Hall steps, issued a resounding public statement: "Heretofore, the scoundrels have confined their murderings among themselves. Now they claimed their first American victim. We owe it to ourselves and to everything that we hold sacred in this life to see to it that this blow is the last. We must teach these people a lesson they will not forget for all time."

The mass of people, nearly five thousand men, lustily cheered and waved their hats in the air, slapping, then pounding, each other on the back, some shouting, "This is the beginning of the hunting season." City aldermen took turns delivering xenophobic rants and the crowd, now worked up, red faced and sweaty, became eager. Impromptu speakers took over from the politicians to scream ad hominem slogans that swerved into racial diatribes until the crowd became a mob, a sea of men whipped by an emotional storm building from a gale to a hurricane.

Billy and Ant stood on the edge of the crowd as observers for Tom, who didn't want to be caught unawares if things spun out of control. Billy hadn't felt such concentrated hatred, even at the few launchings he had witnessed. "What we need is a marching band," he said, "to led these mad-dog idiots around a parade ground so they'd blow off steam."

"Have Tom throw a beer party," Ant suggested. "Free booze until they fall over drunk. That's one way to stop this unruly army."

"Not a bad idea. If this continues, we'll have a riot on our hands and who knows what'll get burnt down. You wait here and keep an eye on things," Billy said and slipped away.

Within a half hour, word spread through the crowd that the Storyville saloons were offering free drinks. "Consider it insurance, a fire policy," Tom had told the saloonkeepers. "An investment in your future. Those men slopping up your profits will come back later and repay you ten times over."

The entire stock of Storyville booze was depleted within two hours. Now the bloodthirsty mob was a drunken bloodthirsty mob all the more bold and reckless. When night came, the darkness gave the men the mettle of bravery to take them beyond their boosts and brags. White men carrying revolvers, shotguns, knives, clubs, chains prowled the streets intent on beating or murdering anyone who wasn't one of them. That meant Negroes for the most part. The hell-raisers and provocateurs targeted uptown, reasoning they'd find Negroes thick as cherries on a tree.

A gang of men, rooting and hollering as if giving each other permission for mayhem, came across a lone black man, who, seeing the danger, immediately ran toward St. Charles Avenue, where only black servants were allowed. The drunken men, baying like hounds on a coon, charged after him. They lost sight of their target when he rounded a corner. Moments later the pursuers skidded around the same corner but their intended victim had vanished. The wide St. Charles was empty but for the horse-drawn trolley trundling down the center of the street. The knot of the drunken men stood in the street and grabbed the reins, bringing to trolley to a halt. Inside sat a single white woman, broad shoulders and wide-hipped, wearing the usual long skirt. The suspicious men boarded the trolley and began looking under the seats.

The formidable woman sat staring straight ahead until the men reached her. "You're drunk stinking dogs," she accused. "Don't come near me."

One man, accustom to ruling his womenfolk with an iron hand, stepped forward to push her skirt aside so he could see under the seat. "Shut yer glob," he snarled, "or you'll be smilin' without teeth."

"Don't you dare!" cried the woman, as he bent down to look. "Trying to see my privates!" and vigorously slapped him about the head.

The startled man backed off a bit and raised his hand hit her. Another man grabbed the hand on the downswing. "This is not our sport," he said. "Leave the white women alone. It's the others we're after," and dragged the man off the trolley.

Four blocks later, the white woman said, "It's safe now."

The black man, who had wet himself with fear, slid out from under the seat. "Thank you, ma'm. Thank you, ma'm. Jesus will welcome you to His home. May you have a long life." He backed off the trolley, holding his hat to cover his wet crotch.

Ant sprinted to warn Buddy's mother and Nora of the approaching danger. They assured him they'd remain behind locked doors. Then he went around the corner to MayAnn's mother and pounded on the door.

"Where's MayAnn? Is she with you?" For once he hoped she was with Young Jack safely out of harm's way.

MayAnn's mother was so scared she wouldn't answer the door.

Ant ran to the Red Onion to see if Harris and the hogs had prepared to defend their territory. All the saloons, even the gambling dens, in the Battlefield were locked and the lights off. He suspected armed men crouched behind the dark windows. The nearly palatable taste cordite hung in the air waiting for a spark to set it off. White men in impromptu gangs, coteries of friends, spontaneous alliances, roamed the streets to take advantage of the lawlessness. Ant drifted along the edge of the crowd propelled by fear and curiosity, and something oddly sexual that bubbled just beneath the surface: the brutal excitement of a gang rape.

The intersection of South Franklin and Gravier streets filled with men spoiling for a fight. Random shots fired in the air kept them primed for action, if only they could find someone to attack. A Mardi Gras mood floated through the crowd, the grim gaiety seen when the bands of Mardi Gras

Indians probed their rival's territory in anticipation of a street fight. Ant half expected a second line to suddenly appear and everyone beat on one another in rhythm to the music for lack of anything better to do. Men hollered in each other's face, whether exhortations or threats was hard to tell, and punched each other on the arms to stir up the battle blood.

From down the block came a whoop and the rabble surrounded a dray trying to turn around in the street. The two frightened horses shied away, kicking their forelegs, as men grabbed the reins. The driver on his high box pulled hard to keep them under control. Ant couldn't see much more than that the driver was a small black man. White men swarmed up and lifted him over their heads as he struggled, twisting this way and that. They held him high, showing off a trophy, then threw him into the cheering crowd. Eager men caught him and flipped him into the air, arms and legs flailing, a rag doll as he rose and fell above the crowd, tossed about like a ball. One part of the crowd held the screaming man above their heads and attempted to run through their spontaneous opponents to score a touchdown. The other side charged forward fighting to wrestle the man away. Ant saw him buck upright then disappear down into the mass of men shouting Rah! Rah! Rah!

Ant had had enough and turned away to find his way out of the mob. Walking close to the buildings, he saw ahead, standing alone, Young Jack. He watched the street scene as if at a parade, hands in his pockets and what looked like a wrapped loaf of bread under one arm.

What's he doing here and where did he find bread at a time like this, Ant wondered in surprise.

In that moment, Ant had no conscious intent in mind. He was, however, aware of an absolute certainty, a deep and chilling calmness, as he came up behind Young Jack unseen. In one swift motion, Ant drew his gun and shot MayAnn's lover in the back of the head.

Young Jack's knees buckled and he flopped face up at Ant's feet. He was still alive and recognized Ant, at least his brows clenched in questioning puzzlement. The package rolled free of his arm and the paper wrapping unfolded. It wasn't a loaf of bread but a dress.

In that moment, Ant realized he had failed MayAnn. He'd taken an oath to change his ways when she ordered him to protect Young Jack. He'd sworn to himself he'd be being forever more an honorable man, even if he couldn't win her heart. His only motive would be to serve her happiness and she'd love him for his nobility. But, in the moment of truth, Ant couldn't do that, couldn't leave himself. Not to claim MayAnn by any way possible would be to condemn himself to be always on the outside, always at risk, always vulnerable. Such a life would eventually drive him insane, or turn him mean, or make him such a bitter man as to be irredeemable. Not to claim her would be an act of disloyalty against himself. You can't expect that of a man. Tom, Josie, the Matrangas, Buddy, MayAnn all stayed true to their vision for themselves. He wanted to be as worthy so MayAnn would accept him as an equal.

"Now MayAnn and I both have blood on our hands earned in the Battle of Love," he said aloud to the corpse at his feet. "I have finally seized my claim with bold action and with it the responsibility for MayAnn's future happiness. For the first time in my life, I feel the full power of a man worthy of his woman. We have the right to lie in each other's arms as heroes."

He stepped over the body, brimming with confidence MayAnn wouldn't hate him once she accepted him as her station in life. Besides, Dead Jack was just an unlucky victim of a stray bullet.

When informing her of the tragedy, he'd explain there as nothing he could've done to protect Young Jack. He wasn't even there. MayAnn would accept the lie after a suitable period of mourning.

The murder drew no attention. Ant slipped into a pack of perhaps fifty men leaving uptown and threw the revolver away so to be free of accusing evidence. When the hollering swarm crossed Canal Street into white Storyville, Ant realized they were headed to the backstreet clubs where Negro musicians gathered after hours ever since Buddy played at Nancy Hank's. The downtown bars and saloons and whorehouses had remained open on the reasoning a race riot wouldn't invade their white territory.

Ant knew Big Eye was playing at Fewclothes, two blocks ahead of the mob, as the featured "hot" clarinet player with the Charles Payton band. He raced ahead to the club, banged through the door and charged the stage. "Get out! A mob is coming."

Big Eye gave him a quizzical look without taking the clarinet from his mouth. "White killers are coming," Ant screamed over the music. Big Eye missed a beat but he didn't abandon the song. "Big Eye!" Ant reached up and grabbed his friend's clarinet. The other musicians, Negroes, paused, ready to defend him from this madman. In that moment of silence, they heard the mob storming down the street.

The horn section knocked Big Eye over as they pelted off the stage. Ant helped the now panicked big man to his feet and shoved him toward the back door jammed solid by bodies fighting to get into the alley. Ant went to a sash window to jerk it open but it didn't budge.

Big Eye, wielding his clarinet like a pole, broke the window and cleared the frame of jagged glass. He put one leg through and bent double to squeeze his bulk out. From the front room came the sounds of bottles shattering and tables and chairs being smashed. Big Eye got stuck in the window frame. Ant heaved a shoulder into him. Big Eye tumbled out and Ant dove headfirst after him into the alley full of black men confused about where to run for safety.

Grabbing Big Eye, Ant pushed him down a narrow passageway that cut through the block. At the end of the passage, Ant poked his head out to check for danger. "Come on." He shoved Big Eye ahead and they ran as if their lives depended on it, which they did, three blocks to Josie's back door. The last light in the house went out as Ant rapped on the door. Then pounded. Then beat on the door with both hands.

"Who is it?" The voice on the other side of the door sounded frightened. "What do you want?"

"Ant. Let me in. The mob is on my tail."

Josie cracked open the door, saw Big Eye and started to slam the door close. Ant jammed his foot in and yelped in pain.

"Josie, let us in," he pleaded.

Big Eye leaned over Ant and steadily and gently forced the door.

"Josie," Ant panted, "please. There's a mob looking to kill anyone with so much as a tan." Big Eye easily qualified. "Let us hide here for the night."

Ant didn't know why she relented; perhaps because of his association with Tom; perhaps because of the terror in his voice; perhaps because Big Eye had already pushed him inside. Whatever the reason, Ant and Big Eye spent the night safely in an upstairs room.

"I never thought I'd find myself in a white whorehouse on Basin Street," Big Eye said with a chuckle. "There must be a God in Heaven after all."

In the morning, Big Eye decided to venture out to see if his aged father was safe. Ant went with him on the theory that having a white man at his side might stave off trouble.

They cautiously, very cautiously, crept down the sidewalks, staying in the early morning shadows as they made their way toward uptown. Hesitating at every intersection, Ant poked his head around the building's corner to check for any hint of danger. If he saw more than three white people together, he kept Big Eye hidden until the way cleared. After a nerve-

281

wracking hour, they arrived at Big Eye's father's house in uptown.

When no one answered Big Eye's knock, he pulled his key from his pocket and opened the door. "Father?" Emptiness echoed back. "It's me, Louis."

He and Ant searched every room, even under the beds, Big Eye calling out, "Father. Father!" distress pitching his voice higher each time. "I'll ask the neighbor," he said, and returned with worry plastered across his face. His father hadn't been home since the rampage started.

"Now what?" Ant asked.

"We check the hospitals."

At Charity Hospital, a nurse recognized Big Eye's description of his father. "The man was brought in last night severely beaten. He died this morning. I'm sorry. He's at the morgue."

Big Eye didn't tear up. Rather he went grim, jaw set, his throat muscles working. "Let's go get him. He's all the family I got."

The morgue, a holding pen for dead bodies, was at the rear of the hospital so hearses could access the alley. Big Eye and Ant pushed through the swinging double doors and entered a large white-tiled room. The smell of cloying decay and harsh chemicals—formaldehyde and what all they didn't know—made the room a vat of death. At the far end were four tables on which laid corpses, all but one covered with a sheet. A doctor had his hands inside the chest cavity of the exposed body. Along one wall sheeted mounds waited on six gurneys. Ant immediately tried to back out of the room but Big Eye held him by the elbow. "Don't desert me now, Ant. Not in this valley of death."

Ant, feeling Big Eye tremble, resolved to be steadfast.

Holding his hat in both hands, Big Eye shuffled forward, timid as a scare little boy. "Excuse me, sir."

The doctor didn't look up.

"Sir, I'm looking for my father."

The doctor continued doing whatever inside the body; it looked like he was tying a knot the way his arms twisted and pulled.

Big Eye stood respectfully waiting, watching and not watching, then watching with morbid fascination as the doctor finished. "And who is your father?" he asked with kind consideration.

"Mr. James Nelson."

"When did he come here? We've got a pile up because of the trouble the last night."

"This morning. He was beaten to death." The sob of sorrow put a chokehold on Big Eye's voice.

"Look in there." The doctor nodded to the door of a side room. "The toe tag will have the name, if we know it. Otherwise, we'll need visual identification."

Big Eye's eyes got wider and wider, and his eyebrows rose higher and higher, and his breathing became fast and shallow. Ant thought the poor man was going to pass out at the thought of stepping into the room of dead people and reached to support his friend by the arm.

"If he's not in there, look on these tables," the doctor motioned to the bodies on the gurneys waiting for his attention.

"All right. All right," Big Eye said to himself. "I love you, daddy. I won't leave you now."

He started toward the storage room. Ant took a step with him but couldn't go any further. "It's all right, Ant. You don't know what he looks like. You stay here. Maybe check the toe tags of those out here."

Ant thought he'd drift away, maybe go stand in the corner with his face to wall and imagine being some place else, any place else. He edged along the six gurneys towards the door, but stopped.

"I can at least help my friend by reading the toe tags. I didn't have to look at the faces."

The first body was the size of a child. Ant didn't bother there and passed on to the second, identified as Elmer Block by the toe tag. He had an inexplicable urge to look at the dead Elmer's face, maybe to get over the strangeness of a lifeless body. Ant lifted the sheet away from the arm but only got as far the shoulder before losing his nerve.

'John Doe' said the tag on the third body. Ant took a deep breath, two then three, before slowly folding the sheet down the forehead, past the closed eyes and the mouth slightly open of the young man's face. It occurred to Ant how odd how a person is both here and gone in death. The body had the look of somebody but it was nobody. It appeared as if it could still move, but looked too dull to move again. He bravely touched the chin, rough with beard stubble, and nudged the head, telling himself, It's like buying fish in the market. Check the firmness of flesh for freshness.

The fourth body was, by it's shape, of a female. I can get a free peek at bare breasts, Ant thought. When he saw their covered shape on a woman walking down the street, he'd speculate, have a male fantasy of uncovering the tits for no other reason than men are insatiably curious about women's breasts. Ant glanced around at the doctor still occupied with his work and, even if it was sick in the head, lifted the sheet. The dislocated jaw made her face lopsided. One eye only a slit, the other swollen shut. Ragged edge of a broken front tooth showed through the torn upper lip. Blue/purple bruises edged with a reddish/yellow hue nearly hid her true color.

Ant didn't recognize the balloon-swollen face. But the silky black hair matted with blood.... He breathed fast and hard through his open mouth to flush out the shock and became dizzy. To keep his balance, Ant leaned heavily on the gurney. His hands floated over the body. He imagined that he'd make her levitate and then leave her in midair as he waved a cane to prove wires didn't suspend her. The audience would gasp in wonder and disbelief at the miracle of magic. With a flourish, he'd whip off the sheet and there would be—nothing. Stunned silence. Impossible. He'd face the audience and shake out the sheet. Nothing. No bouquets of flowers or linked flowing scarves or doves flying to the ceiling. Then, looking around and, with a shrug of puzzlement, he'd beseech the audience for an explanation. For a long moment he'd stand there, letting the tension build before holding up a hand and MayAnn would step from the wings with her seductive smile.

Had Young Jack been on his way home to her with the promised dress and stopped to watch the street yahoos? When he didn't show up, had she gone out looking for him?

Big Eye found Ant with a strand of the corpse's hair wound around his finger. "Somebody you know?"

"Ask the doctor about this body. Who is it?" Ant didn't look at Big Eye. Stared into space. Didn't see the walls of the room or smell the disinfectant or feel his heart or hear his breathing.

Big Eye came back, edging towards Ant as if he was a pane of glass with a big crack clear through. A faint breeze and it would shatter. "They don't know who it is," Big Eye said in a whisper so his words wouldn't be that breeze.

Ant was humming so loudly he didn't hear.

"She was found in the street." Ant saw Big Eye's lips move. "The mob must have beaten her."

Ant refused to hear the words. The humming filled his head to bursting. He let nothing else in: no thoughts, no acceptance, no feeling, no awareness other than that dense buzzing—a barricade between the heart and the mind—coming from his throat.

Big Eye touched him on the shoulder. "Ant?"

Ant nodded and his head began to bob faster and faster and his feet moved like he was tap-dancing and he began shaking so Big Eye held him in a tight hug.

"Ant?"

After a minute or so, Ant managed, "Tell the doc I'll come back for her."

Then, "Did you find your father?"

"Yeah."

They left the hospital together, two men slowed by grief but manly keeping the appearance of not being cowed, rather having the strength and presence to accommodate death. In the street they parted, Big Eye to a funeral home to make arrangements and Ant, he didn't know what he did. He had no recollection of the missing hours until he knocked on MayAnn's mother's door.

She still wouldn't open the door even though he cried out, "It's Antoine. It's safe. I have news."

Ant slapped the door palms flat with the slow beat of a dirge until she finally opened a crack, perhaps just to stop the noise. "MayAnn's not here."

"I know. Please let me in."

Ant could see it in the way she kept her head bowed, hands twisting the white handkerchief, that she suspected the worst. "I sorry," he said. "I'll bring her to you if you like." She nodded without looking up.

Afterwards, Ant didn't go to Tom's saloon or seek out Billy but spent the night in the dark refusing to let go of his numbness. In the morning, he rode the train to Jackson and walked the dusty couple of miles to the state insane asylum.

"You're the first visitor he's had," the male orderly said, leading Ant to Buddy's room.

The cube had blank walls of putty color, a single iron bed with crisp sheets, a window with no curtains that looked on flat green land good for sugar cane. Next to the window on a straight back wooden chair painted, for some reason, bright orange Buddy sat hands on knees staring at the horizon. Ant found his cornet under the bed, its bell full of dents. When he offered the horn, Buddy didn't move a muscle.

"He's likes to sit outside sometimes," the orderly said. "Would you like to take him out?"

They guided Buddy by the elbows down the corridor and out the front door and to a bench under a spreading oak bearded with Spanish moss. He shuffled amiably along, docile as an aged dog. Whatever his eyes were watching, it wasn't in this world. The only sign of awareness was a glint of humor deep behind the glaze.

Other visitors might have mistaken Ant for an inmate he sat so still next to Buddy. Two life-size clay figures that's what we are, Ant thought while screwing up his courage. He honestly didn't know if he could say the words. Two guys sitting together like we had nothing on our minds. Sitting in the sunshine on a muggy Louisiana day, perhaps dreaming about fishing. Pals sharing an afternoon with no worries. This isn't so bad, sitting in the sunshine with Buddy, deaf and dumb to the outside world.

He had to say the words for myself.

"MayAnn's dead."

Buddy gave no indication that he heard or understood.

"MayAnn…"

The fingers on Buddy's right hand, his horn playing hand, moved.

They sat there all afternoon without saying a word. When the evening cool rose from the grass, the orderly came and said, "Time for dinner, Mr. Bolden." Buddy stood and shuffled inside without looking at Ant.

Back in New Orleans, Ant went to the morgue to claim MayAnn's body and had her taken to the Moss Brothers funeral home. Then he contacted every musician he knew to arrange for the biggest, most boisterous, most booming funeral march and celebration New Orleans had ever seen. Word went out that the entire city was invited to the second line.

Ant told Tom that he was expected pay for the first-class coffin, MayAnn's new dress, the musicians and the party. And Tom and Billy would walk behind MayAnn's mother in the funeral procession as a show of respect. Tom balked but Ant explained why it was in Tom's best interest to be so magnanimous—after all, he didn't want to risk Aaron Harris spilling the beans, did he?

"Not Harris," Tom bluffed. "No one intimidates Harris."

"I know his enemies, as I know yours. Break a man's kneecaps, snap his fingers, put his balls in a vise. No matter how mean the man, he hurts like all other men."

"You wouldn't. You can't," Tom said with the confidence of a lion tamer.

"I know people who can."

The absolute flatness of Ant's voice made Tom assess this different Ant and then, with a slow nod, understand that he had become a dangerous man of conviction. "What time does the funeral march start?"

On funeral day, Ferdy, Big Eye, Dusen, Bechet, Tony Jackson, Sammy Davis, Joe Oliver, Little Louie, even Keppard, and another fifty or sixty musicians Ant didn't know formed up behind Grand Marshall Louis in front of the big black car, one of two motorized hearses in all of New Orleans. Tom and Billy were duly solicitous of MayAnn's mother, although she was puzzled why the two white men were even there. Nora and a contingent from her church came and sang hymns. Bringing up the rear was Josie with Henry the Magnificent, dressed in a dignified formal mourning coat.

Most of the couple hundred or so people who lined the route didn't know the person on her final journey. But a funeral parade that big, that loud, had to be for someone important. MayAnn's spirit was sent off on a big gust of joy so God wouldn't miss her coming. He'll see her brightness rising up and get off His throne to personally open the Pearly

Gates, Ant said to comfort himself. Anyone arriving with such a celebration of life must be the fulfillment of His love.

At the wake—the first time a mixed colored crowd had been served in a downtown saloon—Ant danced until his brain jiggled, until blood came out his nose. He couldn't catch his breath because he cried so hard.

Chapter 19.

Sixteen people died in the race riot following Hennessy's murder—all Negroes—and no suspects arrested, including the police chief's killers. Everyone in New Orleans, from the mayor down to the street sweeper, believed that the Matrangas were behind the killing. A front-page editorial in the *Daily Item* stated, "We need to cleanse our city of Sicilians whose low, receding foreheads, repulsive countenances and slovenly attire proclaim their brutal natures. Their very name means crime. They must be flushed off our streets."

In the following days, the police snatched up every Italian they could find. Italian mothers kept their children home from school and hoarded food. A house-to-house search swept through Little Palermo. Ships backed up at the docks because all the Italian dockhands were either in jail or in hiding. The fruit-and-vegetable markets closed because most of the vendors were Italians. Attendance at daily Mass sharply increased as the innocent prayed for protection. Even the men got on their knees, so the police raided Catholic churches.

Emboldened hooligans and ordinary people assaulted any unfortunate Italian they found. Tom sent friendly advice to Storyville's Italian saloonkeepers: close down and to stay off the streets. Keep your families behind locked doors until I say it's safe to come out.

The cops hauled in a hundred Italians, but the Matrangas were not among them. Rumors swept the city that the brothers were plotting to send their Mafia thugs throughout the city to cause mayhem in retaliation for how the Italians had been treated.

Tom called Ant into his office. "I have a matter of utmost confidence to discuss with you, Ant." Wearing a black suit and crisp white shirt, his serious business dress, Tom was somber as a hanging judge. "New Orleans is faced with a serious threat to its safety as long as the Matranga brothers are a large. I've been asked by the mayor to help with this crisis. He's prepared to offer the brothers accommodations, perhaps amnesty, if they agree to a secret meeting to arrange a truce. I want you to get word to the Matrangas."

"How am I to do that? I don't know where they are."

"But you have ways to find out, don't you. You've always been close to them, in their vest pockets as it were." Tom's tone turned ominous and the flaying look came into his eyes. He held Ant in that stare for long moments, the unspoken accusation hanging over him like the Sword of Damocles. "Disloyalty is the worst sin, in my book. Worst than murder or thieving."

Ant's throat became so dry that he couldn't swallow, couldn't work any words out.

"See what you can do, Ant, and do it soon," Tom said in dismissal.

Ant put the word out that he needed to meet with the Matrangas. He spent his days walking around Little Palermo to make himself visible and accessible. On the third day, he stepped into a bar where only Italian was spoken and ordered a glass of wine. No one paid him any attention, in fact studiously ignored him. Half way through his second glass, a man settled next to Ant.

"My friends do not trust your friend."

Ant looked straight ahead but nodded his head that he understood. "They are prudent men."

The man leaned with his elbows on the bar, head lowered so he couldn't be overheard. "Our community is suffering from needless cruelty, even innocent women and children. We had nothing to do with Hennessy's killing."

"The mayor wants to clear up this misunderstanding and everything can return to normal."

"What guarantee?"

Ant didn't know what to say. "Your terms. Name the place, time and conditions. I can't offer any more than that."

"Be here tomorrow night." The messenger stood away from the bar. "Enjoy your wine."

Ant sat at the bar for a long time, pushing invisible pieces of a puzzle around in his head. He was certain that Tom had arranged Hennessy's assassination and for the gun left behind as damning evidence pointing to the Matrangas. MayAnn had died in the resulting riot. Now, how could he use the Matrangas to get back at Tom?

He still hadn't figured that out when he arrived back at Tom's saloon to deliver the instructions.

"They'll meet us at the bar?" Tom asked.

"I doubt it. Probably just give a message on the details for a later meet."

"All right," Tom agreed.

"I'll go alone. They don't trust you."

"Billy should be in the shadows to watch your back."

Ant didn't trust Billy after the botched attempt on Young Jack's life. "No. I don't want to give any reason for distrust. This has to be on the up and up."

"Nevertheless," Tom replied.

The next night, as Ant walked to the rendezvous, a hack pulled up alongside him. The door opened and a man ordered, "Get in."

The same man from the night before sat in the far corner. He didn't say a word as the horse pulled the cab through the dark streets for another fifteen minutes. Then the man rapped on the roof of the cab. The driver made two more turns and pulled into an alley.

"The Matrangas will meet only with you," the messenger said. "They want a public statement from the mayor to be published in the paper stating they are innocent of Hennessy's murder. And all Italians now being held will be released. Then they'll make a public appearance with the mayor on the steps of City Hall to call for calm. Otherwise, no deal. Only trouble."

"When and where?" Ant asked.

"Just take your evening stroll tomorrow night." The man opened the cab's door for Ant to get out.

Twenty minutes later, he sat in Tom's office. "Impossible!" Tom exclaimed. "The mayor will never be seen in public with the Mafia and certainly not in a partnership."

"Take it or leave it. That's the message."

"I'm giving the orders, not those murdering dagos. You take your stroll tomorrow and tell those arrogant bastards the mayor will not meet with them in public, but accommodations will be made to meet in private. Demand you meet with the Matrangas immediately to get all this set. Time is running out."

"You're going to kill them, aren't you?" Ant asked point blank.

"No, I'd never do that. I'm working in the best interest of the city, and the Matrangas, too. I give you my word. We worked together to defeat Bronze John so I feel a certain alliance with them."

The next night Ant took his stroll and again the hack stopped beside him. When he delivered the ultimatum, the same messenger adamantly refused to take him to the Matrangas. They rode apparently aimlessly around city, not really arguing their cases but stating the positions in simple declarative terms, over and over. At one point, when they were alongside the Mississippi, Ant was sorely tempted to jump out and leap aboard a boat, a ship, anything that floated, to take him across the river, up or down the river, anywhere away.

Finally Ant said, "Look, take me somewhere, blindfold me, tie me up, gag me and then take me to the Matrangas. We've got to finish this."

The man sat silent for a long time. Then he rapped on the roof of the cab and it pulled to a stop. The man used three matches to light a cigarette. When he blew out the last match, another man appeared outside the cab. They spoke quickly in Italian and the outside man hurried off. At another rap on the roof, the cab started another meandering journey.

Twenty minutes later, another hack came alongside and Ant was ordered to change over while on the move.

"What!" he protested. The maneuver would be like crossing from one ship to another while rolling about on the high seas.

"You go now." The man opened the cab's door and pulled on Ant's elbow.

Ant stood in the doorway, his hands gripping the frame so tightly he thought he he'd never be able to let go. The gap between the cabs was only a couple of feet but to Ant it may as well have been two hundred yards. He tentatively stretched a leg towards the other cab, swaying precariously above the rough cobblestones and then, in a desperate moment, lunged in a split second free fall across the space. Hands grabbed him as he scrabbled into the cab.

A man handed Ant a blindfold. "Put this on."

Despite all the precautions, Ant sensed that he'd left a trail behind, a scent, a shadow to be followed.

Taking a serpentine route, the cab pulled up at a dilapidated warehouse stinking of decaying fruit where Charles, dressed as dapper as usual, and Tony waited surrounded by armed guards.

"Well, Ant, whose elephant's hind leg you running up now?" Tony asked, putting his death-grip hug around Ant's shoulders.

"The mayor wants to make a deal but in private."

"We had nothing to do with Hennessy's death," Charles said.

"Your innocence or guilt has nothing to do with this. Anderson is setting a trap. You need to strike first. Without Anderson, Storyville will be wide open for the taking. You have more guns than the police. What's anyone going to do to stop you?"

"The mayor, the American bankers, the people with influence will not allow us. We would be a threat to their power. That's the worst sin," Charles said, stating the obvious.

"If Anderson is gone, you'll have no trouble finding a friendly beard to be the face of Storyville," Ant replied.

"How about you, Ant?" Tony asked. "You want the job? You want to be our puppet?"

"I'm not the right man. Maybe Billy. He stands to lose everything without Anderson. With you as a new partner, he'll gain everything."

"Who killed the police chief, Ant?" Charles asked. "Who used the Luparas?"

"I have no proof but probably Aaron Harris on Anderson's orders."

"Anderson is the worst kind of assassin," Charles said. "His left hand pushes the killer forward while his right hand makes the sign of the cross."

Suddenly, a lookout rushed in shouting, "Coppers!"

Charles grabbed Ant by the head and forcefully kissed him on both cheeks. "We're innocent but you're dead."

The armed guards automatically clustered in front of Charles and Tony, their guns pointed toward the warehouse entrance. From outside came shouts of "Police! Police! Surrender!"

"Out the back way," Tony ordered but additional commands told them that the police also blocked that escape route.

"We fight to the death," Tony shouted and the twenty men took up firing positions.

But Charles ordered the men to lay down their guns. "We have faith in the courts, like all good Americans. No reason to risk the lives of our people."

Tony stared in disbelief. "If you believe that you're a fool! A dead fool."

"We're innocent. They have no proof."

"They don't need prove, Charles," Tony pleaded. "They only need our bodies."

"We'll show them that we are good citizens," Charles replied.

The warehouse front double doors cautiously edged open and a sacrificial policeman poked his head in.

"We will not shoot," Charles called out. "Do not murder us in cold blood." He motioned for Tony and the others to lay down their weapons.

"No, no," Tony cried out.

Charles put a hand on his brother's arm to prevent him from raising his gun. "Have faith, little brother. Otherwise we die on this spot."

A steady stream of policemen slipped into the warehouse and fanned out to surround the Italians.

Later, Ant learned Tom had set the ambush by using Billy on a bicycle. Following Ant at a discreet distant, he dropped pages from his notebook as markers for the police.

The Matrangas and twenty-one Italians were charged with Hennessy's murder. An instant grand jury indicted nineteen of those, eleven as principals and eight as accessories to the crime. Fourteen-year-old Asperi Marchesi was accused of being the whistling boy who signaled the gunman, despite his mother's vigorous protests her son had been at home in bed that night.

At the quick-march trial, no solid evidence was presented against the accused and no witnesses to the actual shooting took the stand. The murder weapon couldn't be linked to any individual. The prosecutor relied solely on circumstance, rumor and the well-know animosity between Hennessy and the Matranga brothers.

The jury acquitted the nineteen men.

"What'd'ya think of that, Billy?" Tom asked when hearing the news.

"There'll be hell to pay. By someone."

The Italian community celebrated the acquittal as a victory for the underdog. Sicilians decked their vegetable stalls in the French market with green-red-white bunting, the colors of the Italian flag. They sent wine to the men still in jail waiting release.

Rumors flew that Mafia gold had bought off the jury. Fear rippled through the Americans, who saw the tide of foreign scum as a threat to their newly found middle-class prosperity. "The assassination was part of a plot by 'alien criminals' to take control of the city," railed Mayor Shakespeare. The unfounded accusation that the Mafia had targeted the mayor and the new police chief heightened the hysteria sweeping the city. Sixty prominent citizens called for a mass meeting to protest the injustice. On nearly every lamppost in the city a poster appeared announcing

MASS MEETING!
All good citizens are invited to attend a mass meeting on Saturday, March 14, at 10 o'clock a.m. at Clay Statue, to take steps to remedy the failure of justice in the HENNESSY CASE. Come prepared for action.

Two days later, thousands of white men dressed in suits and hats filled the streets and pushed purposefully toward the Henry Clay statue at the intersection of Canal and St. Charles, on the edge of the French Quarter. Ant went out of curiosity, expecting a bit of a lark. The men shouted and laughed and sporadically broke into song—drinking songs or Civil War marches or popular ditties—but the light heartedness didn't diminish their deadly intent. Many of them openly carried rifles and shotguns and clubs. Pistols were tucked into belts and jacket pockets sag with the weight of a revolver.

Speakers climbed on the statue's plinth and shouted out patriotic hatred about duty to protect home and hearth against foreign heathens. Only the men in front of the crowd could hear the words but whenever they cheered in approval a yell rippled through the thousands behind them. With each speaker, the men became more festive and combative, pumping their fists in the air and calling for action, any action.

"The justice of the courts has failed us but the Lady of Justice and Liberty is on our side," shouted a rabble-rouser standing by Clay's feet. "We cannot, must not, let our fair city be taken over by mobsters. Let's lynch those dagos!"

The jury of thousands roared its approval.

The self-appointed leaders hoisted a banner of red-white-blue bunting and led the now howling crowd up Canal Street towards Parish Prison at Beauregard Square. Rage of men defending their way of life against the great unwashed boiled away the light-hearted Fourth of July mood.

"We de-mand jus-tice! We de-mand jus-tice!" The chant set a cadence, menacing as an executioner's drumbeat, to the marching feet. Ant was carried along, at times lifted off his feet, in the densely packed mob, the men around him ranting just to hear their outrage. The surging power of the voices filled the street and rebounded off the buildings, the roar drowning out all reason. A man marching next to Ant carried a young boy on his shoulders. "You watch now, son," he called out. "You'll see American justice defending our God-given rights."

At Beauregard Square, Ant worked his way to front of the hoard. If the men charged the prison's doors, he'd rather be carried on the crest than trampled by the following mob. One of the leaders, William S. Parker, a prominent politician who later became mayor of New Orleans, pounded on the thick oaken double doors and demanded the Italians be turned over. Ant was close enough to hear the captain on the other side shout back his refusal.

"We'll blow the doors open with dynamite!" Parker threatened.

"And we'll shoot the first of you through the door," retaliated the captain.

Later, the newspapers reported that when the sheriff of the prison learned a mob intended to seize the acquitted Italians, he hurried to the new police chief and asked for reinforcements. The police chief said he wouldn't put his men in danger to protect the killers of his predecessor. The sheriff ran to the local militia commander for help but he refused to involve himself in a police matter.

Ant spotted Billy leading a group of apparently handpicked men down an alley next to the prison. He followed, curious that Billy seemed to have his own plan. At the door used by guards to enter and leave the prison, Billy rapped a code. The door opened and Billy led his men inside.

Ant squeezed in at the rear before the door closed.

They were in a narrow corridor used by the guards to get around the prison unseen by the prisoners. Billy held up his hand for quiet as he led the band of armed men, Ant now seeing the pistols and shotguns, forward. At the end of the corridor, Billy cautiously opened the door. The captain could be heard furiously shouting at the mob on the opposite side of the front door.

Billy raised his arm above his head and waited for a moment. Then he yanked open the corridor door and the armed men charged forward, taking the prison guards by surprise. Ant acted as if he was part of the gang, while careful to stay out of Billy's sight.

"Let them in," Billy order, his men leveling their guns at the guards.

The captain turned to face the unexpected attack and saw that his ten men were outnumbered.

"Stand down," he commanded.

The guards backed away from the prison's front doors.

"But I'll not open the doors to let in a murderous mob," the captain said.

"Turn the Italians over and there'll be no rampaging mob tearing your prison apart," Billy answered, tucking in his gun as a sign of goodwill.

"They've been released from their cells," the captain replied, "and told to find their own safety."

"Drop the cell keys on the floor. Take your men to a room and lock yourselves in. We're not after to harm you."

When the captain hesitated, Billy added, "Unless we have no choice."

The captain unhooked the keys from his belt and threw them down.

Billy picked up the keys and shouted, "Parker, it's me. I'm going to open up. Control your men so they don't trample us."

When the doors opened, Parker stood calmly flanked by his second-in-command. "Thank you, sir," he said. "Your service will be rewarded."

The entrance foyer of the prison was a large square room with tables along one wall where guards checked visitors, and their parcels, for contraband. At the far end, a single door led to the interior cell blocks arranged in tiers around a central walkway. The mob, lead by Parker, entered the foyer in a surprisingly orderly fashion.

"The Italians have been let out of their cells to hide wherever in the prison," Billy told him.

"All right then." Parker instructed his lieutenants to divide the men into search parties. "We want only the guilty."

The men were formed into groups of fifteen to twenty and the group leaders handed a piece of paper with the names of the wanted Italians.

"Do not harm anyone not on the list," Parker ordered.

He assigned each search party a section of the prison. As the groups filed through the single door into the prison proper, Ant saw Billy take his gang on their own search.

He ran after them. "Billy." Ant grabbed him by the arm but had no idea what to say. Perhaps stall him, give the Mantrangas every chance to find their way out of the prison.

Billy looked down at Ant in surprise. "What you doing here?"

Before Ant could answer, a hubbub broke out in the stairwell nearby.

"Got'em! Got'em!" and a blaze of gunshots.

When Billy and Ant arrived, the search party was pulling two bullet-ridden bodies from the large box in which the captain's bull dog slept under the stairs.

"Cross'em off the list," ordered the squad leader.

"Who are they?" one of the men asked.

"How in the hell am I supposed to know," the leader answered.

Billy bent down to examine the blood-soaked dead men. They didn't have agony on their faces but rather looked startled, as if someone had jumped out from behind a door and shouted BOO!

"Shame about the dog," one of the men said.

"Serves the captain right for not turning over those dago killers to us. He deserves a little pain."

The dead men were not the Matrangas.

Two of the Italians hiding in the kitchen storage room were captured and passed over the heads of the jubilant men like sacks of grain to the mob outside the prison. By the roar of the crowd, the uninformed would have thought that the War of Independence had been won again. Everyone fought to get their hands on the Italians, climbing over backs, pushing and shoving, the whole mass heaving and recoiling as an unruly tide. The helpless Italians were more dead than alive when delivered to the lamppost at the corner of Treme and St. Ann, where a rope was put around their necks, the noose meant to slowly strangle rather than snap the neck as they were strung up. The mob clapped as if calling a dance as the victims' feet kicked the air, hips jerked to jackknife the weight upward to relieve the choking pressure. Shoulders furiously twisting, their heads stretched back and neck red raw from the coarse rope. Then they did a slow spin. The crowd cheered for a good five minutes after they dangled lifelessly.

Inside the prison, Billy and Ant heard loud shouts from the woman's section across the interior yard. When Billy and Ant arrived, the yelling rabble dragged eight Italians into the courtyard. Trying to protect their heads, the Italians raised arms to ward off the blows. In the struggle, their suits, worn in anticipation of their homecoming celebration, had been half torn off. Two of the men were bloody about the head. Three had managed to keep on their soft-cloth caps.

"Give as good as Hennessy got," shouted the crowd. "Against the wall! Against the wall!"

The Italians huddled in a tight group, not fighting back, hunched against the blows—except for Charles and Tony. They got right in the face of their tormenters, shouted and waved their arms, defiantly cursing the men, their families, their first-born. The armed men steadily back the Italians to the wall. Suddenly, Tony charged followed by Charles and the other Italians fighting pell-mell into the crowd. Four of them were instantly clubbed to the ground and beaten to death. The Matrangas grappled for the rifles until they were overwhelmed.

"Looks like ants at a picnic, doesn't it?" Billy said to Ant. "Don't you want to join in? Get a piece of the cake?"

Gradually the mob backed away from the heap of mangled bodies twisted in their black suits. Charles lay on his back, arms and legs splayed as if he had been dropped from the top of the building. One arm bent back on itself. His hair, always so carefully in place, covered his eyes. Blood came from his nose and mouth. Tony lay next to him. Whereas Charles looked, despite the damage, almost peaceful, Tony had rage on his face, his lips curled back, a mad dog ready to bite. A rifle barrel had smashed open his skull, the split oozing blood and grey matter. His face was a battlefield, the cheek gashed, teeth broken, nose twisted to one side and flattened.

All the innocent Italians were killed within thirty minutes of the mob entering the prison. The celebrating men carried the leader Parker on their shoulders back to the Henry Clay statue, where he declared, "The instinct of self-preservation made necessary the extra-legal measures to stamp out the existence of the Mafia in our midst. The Italians took the law in their own hands and we had to do the same. This was a justified action conceived by gentlemen and carried out by gentlemen."

Chapter 20.

Ant left New Orleans immediately after the prison murders. For years he roamed the country as an itinerant musician, even played with Tony Jackson in Chicago and with Ferdy Morton in New York. Occasionally he'd pass through New Orleans, on business or tugged by memories, and visit with Buddy. Never once did Buddy talk or act like he knew Ant. In his last years, Buddy walked around the institution with a hand always brushing a wall, a man desperate not to get lost. He had violent spells, tearing off his clothes and yelling at whatever only he could see. His words were, like his music, powerful and wild.

Buddy died at the age of fifty-four in 1931. Ant missed his funeral, being on the road at the time. When he did get back to New Orleans, he went to pay his respects and had a devil of a time finding Buddy's grave, a simple stone slab with his dates. No mention that he was the first man of jazz, a visionary whose spirit showed other musicians ways to create an original American art form. Ferdy Morton claimed the title of Father of Jazz and perhaps rightfully so; he wrote the form down so others could follow along and build on it. But Buddy got the bigger kudo: the word "jazz" was named after him, at least that what Ant maintained.

Etymology of the word "jazz" is vague. Attempts to trace the origin to an African word for "hurry" are not convincing. It's equally doubtful that the word derives from *chasse*, a dance step; or *jazib*, Arab for "one who allures"; or the Hindi *jazba*, meaning "ardent lover"; although jazib and jazba share an affinitive for an early use of "jazz" as a verb for having sexual intercourse. A "jazzbow" was slang for a local Don Juan.

The word may also have a direct link to Storyville. The ladies of the evening favored a jasmine scent and would ask a prospective customer if he was looking for a little "Jass" as in jasmine. The sexual "hot time" in the brothels was known as "playing jazz," an easy association with "playing hot music".

The clincher for Ant is found in the *Oxford Dictionary of English Etymology,* which states jazz is "a pet form of Charles, name of a Negro musician, has been suggested." Buddy's given name was Charles; Chas is a pet form of Charles.

Ant broke all contact with Tom and Billy considering, in his opinion, Tom had ordered Hennessy's assassination and planted the clues of blame toward the Matrangas, which led to the riot and MayAnn being brutally killed. He heard through the grapevine that Tom died a rich and respected businessman, although a reprobate to the end. Always the resourceful entrepreneur, he sold the Arlington Annex in 1917, when the Storyville whorehouses were ordered closed by U.S. Secretaries of the Army and Navy. He founded three oil companies: Record Oil Refining Company, an independent refiner, Protection Oil Company in 1917 and the Liberty Oil Company in 1920, which he later sold to Standard Oil. He even served two terms in the Louisiana state legislature.

The year he sold Liberty Oil he was charged with keeping a house of disorder, which he maintained was only a restaurant. An undercover agent testified up to forty "shady ladies" posing as waitresses or cabaret entertainers met prospective customers in the restaurant. After a brief trial, Tom was acquitted.

Tom survived a serious illness in 1928 and found religion, that is, he started going to Mass and gave a large endowment to the church. In that year, at the age of seventy-one, he married Gertrude "Gerty" Dix, his companion for many years and the Storyville madam who took over Hilma Burt's establishment when she returned to St. Louis. The newlyweds moved into Gerty's house on Bourbon Street between St. Ann and Dumaine where they lived happily and quietly until his death on December 10, 1931. Neighbors remembered Gerty, who survived Tom by nearly thirty years, as "that nice little old lady."

And there was one other choice tidbit. Tom left Gerty $120,000 in his will but a Mrs. Irene Delsa, widow of George Delsa, the former manager of Anderson's Rampart Street Café and Chop House, contested the will. She claimed to be Tom's legitimate daughter by Emma Schwartz and challenged the will on the grounds that Gerty lived in concubinage with him and, by law, could not inherit the estate. Gerty produced her marriage certificate and won the court case. In an act of generosity, Gerty, once satisfied Irene was Tom's real daughter, voluntarily gave her a substantial part of the inheritance.

Billy had been a bartender in Kansas City before he passed. Ant always avoided playing clubs in Kansas City.

Josie did rise above her station. Using John Thomas Brady as a front man, the same man who took her to Hot Springs, Arkansas where she discovered the Arlington Hotel, she purchased numerous properties in New Orleans, including a house and twelve lots on high-toned Esplanade Avenue. The alderman and wealthy businessmen Sidney Story, Storyville's namesake, also lived on Esplanade.

The semi-rural property, where she kept chickens and horses, served as a buffer between her Storyville life and her reincarnation as a respectable woman. As Mrs. Tom Brady, although she refused to marry him, she acquired the accouterments of a wealthy matron -- private doctors, dressmaker, a corset maker and maids—and a country house in Pass Christian, where the other fashionable families vacationed.

She still owned the brothel and maintained the liquor license under Josie Arlington, but she leased the property to Anna Casey on an annual basis and no longer oversaw the business. Her health deteriorated to the point that she became bedridden. She lost control of her bodily functions and suffered from delirium and bouts of dementia. In 1914, eight days after her fiftieth birthday, she died.

Businessmen, bankers and other respectable members of society attended her funeral at the Metairie Cemetery. Her mausoleum of brown marble cost four thousand dollars, according to newspaper accounts.

Young Jack, who died in an automobile accident in 1937, was buried in his family's ostentatious mausoleum in St. Louis Cemetery No. 1.

Whenever Ant returned to New Orleans to visit Buddy's grave, he'd sit with MayAnn, too. Her grave was easy to find because he paid for her to be above ground. An angel served as her tombstone inscribed, "She danced."

Ant had not had a relationship worth mentioning in the fifty odd years after MayAnn's death. He was, by his own admission, a lonely man who carried a profound emptiness within—even stubbornly clung to it. In his most rueful moments, he'd lash himself with the cat'o'nine tails of loathing for his self-serving disregard of MayAnn and her heart's desire. But he rarely went to that place. What was the point?

Instead, he took the philosophical high road, a shunt around the heart, by telling himself that a person with nothing to lose has nothing to fear. His deepest shame, he acknowledged, was not trying to care about something worth losing. The not caring sapped him until he gradually lost his vitality. He gave up playing music because, in his later years, smoking robbed his lungs of their capacity. In truth, he gave up on love. Weeks went by without shaving or even bathing; he was often taken for a derelict, a ragged bum on the street. In 1940, he was discovered dead in his New Orleans boarding house room after the landlord noticed the stink. Everything he owned fit in a small cardboard box.

END

ACKNOWLEDGMENTS

My profound gratitude goes to my long-time heart friend Shaw McCutcheon for his spontaneous generosity over the years that allowed me to stay on course. Thanks to Katherine and Eliza Livingston for their generous offer of the Square House in the Oregon woods as a refuge while I wrote. Connie Buchanan guided me, with compassion and knowledge of an excellent editor, to kill my darlings so the narrative could emerge. The sharp eye and keen intelligence of Annie Gottlieb helped to sort the flowers from the weeds. And to Mary Horrocks, my partner, who supported with encouragement whenever I faltered.